THE
LOTUS
FLOWER
CHAMPION

THE
LOTUS
FLOWER
CHAMPION

NEW YORK TIMES BESTSELLING AUTHOR
PINTIP DUNN
AND LOVE DUNN

Entangled Publishing, LLC
644 Shrewsbury Commons Ave., STE 181
Shrewsbury, PA 17361
rights@entangledpublishing.com

Entangled Teen is an imprint of Entangled Publishing, LLC.

Visit our website at www.entangledpublishing.com.

Edited by Molly Majumder & Stacy Abrams
Cover illustration and design by Elizabeth Turner Stokes
Interior design by Toni Kerr

ISBN 978-1-64937-4-332
Ebook ISBN 978-1-64937-4-356

Manufactured in the United States of America

First Edition October 2023

10 9 8 7 6 5 4 3 2 1

entangled teen
an imprint of Entangled Publishing LLC

ALSO BY PINTIP DUNN

To Mama, aka Khun Yai Pacharee,
you may no longer walk this realm, but we feel your love
every day, every hour.

The Lotus Flower Champion is a breathtaking adventure, rooted in Thai mythology, awash with curses and powers from folklore. However, the story includes elements that might not be suitable for all readers. Obsessive-compulsive disorder, cancer, body horror, injuries, and death are mentioned and discussed in the novel. Readers who may be sensitive to these elements, please take note.

PROLOGUE

You never realize how valuable time is until you don't have it. When I was eight years old, I used to lie on the hardwood floor and stare at the clock on top of our fireplace.

Tick.

Tock.

Tick.

Tock.

Tick.

Tock.

I'd count the seconds for an entire minute, from the first tick until the long needle hit the twelve. And if I didn't look away quickly enough and I saw the hand pass to the next beat, I'd have to count the seconds all over again.

And again.

And again.

I'd be stuck there for minutes, maybe even an hour, before someone — usually Mama — rescued me.

But I'm not a kid anymore. I don't get to lie there and stare at the clock. Every moment I waste could be a moment

I spend with Mama.

1, 2, 3, 4, 5, 6, 7, 8, 9, 10, 11.

These are the numbers that run through my head every day, every hour, every minute. The set of digits might change — my magic number used to be four. And then seven. And now eleven. The compulsions ebb and flow. But they're forever present, a part of me, like a beast whose talons have wrapped around and buried themselves in my soul.

My life is far from easy. Every day, I go to school, or sit in my room, or simply exist, and a war wages within my mind.

Voices whisper inside me, forcing everything I touch, everything I do, to be symmetrical.

I check my tests over and over again, certain that I missed something.

A powerful urge makes me complete every sentence I read — and then reread it again, just in case. A paragraph could take me an hour to get through, a school assignment half the night.

Every moment of my life is a battle. I thought that my perpetual struggle with obsessive-compulsive disorder would prepare me to face any fight that loomed in the future.

Holy moly was I wrong.

CHAPTER ONE

T he penny arcs out, out, out…and then vanishes into the inky black waves that crash and unfurl against the coarse strip of beach. The Gulf of Thailand might be bigger, more dramatic, than any wishing well. But it swallows my desperate hope just as thoroughly. Just as uselessly.

I march across the wet sand, in my white canvas sneakers, trying to convince myself not to count my steps. Taking my shoes off is out of the question. My bare feet haven't touched any kind of ground in four years.

It's okay. It will be okay. It has to be okay.

If I tell myself enough times, maybe I'll actually believe it. Even though my long-time therapist has failed to convince me otherwise. Even if the hollow in my chest proves that there are some things that will never be okay, no matter how much effort we pour into "living for the moment" or "creating lasting memories."

I leave the beach and trudge up the steps to our private villa, pausing to wash my feet in a basin of water. I laboriously dry every inch of my feet and then trade in my sneakers for a pair of satiny house slippers. When I walk inside, Mama's sitting on the white-and-green striped couch.

"Ah, so Alaia lives!" she sings out. "I was beginning to think you were trying to steal my thunder, young lady. Not fair, when I had to suffer three rounds of chemo to get this close to dying."

"That's not funny, Mama." And it's not. But I'm just as guilty as Papa, just as guilty as the grief counselors, because I force my lips up anyway.

This is Mama's last trip. Her final wish. A vacation with her family in Koh Samui, where she was born, while she's still healthy enough to enjoy it.

And damn it, she *will* enjoy it. If it's the last thing I do, I will make Mama smile 121 times on this trip.

Her face catches the glow of the recessed lights. Her skin is still smooth, with only a few lines around her tapered eyes to reveal her age. With only a pallor to her light brown skin that betrays her illness. A Thai silk scarf is tied around her head. After her surgery, Papa bought a dozen scarves from her favorite silk house, each one brighter and more cheerful than the last.

It's as though he can keep Mama alive by the brilliance of those colors alone.

Mama flicks the peacock-feather ends out of her face as I sit down on the other end of the couch. "Maybe I don't want to be wise and appropriate all the time. Did you ever think of that?"

My heart twinges. Already, our family, neighbors, and friends talk about Mama in the hallowed tones of the dead. Celebrating every award she's ever won, tallying the patients she's saved. Putting her on a pedestal on which only the deceased can balance.

"I'm no saint," Mama continues. "No matter how much it

comforts A-ma to think of me that way."

"Maybe you really are that good," I venture. "Maybe you truly are that kind."

Her face softens, and she presses her hand against mine. I don't like touch, as a general rule—it makes me feel like I have bugs crawling under my skin. But Mama's touch is warm, comforting. Safe. Much like Mama herself. I don't know what I'll do when I no longer have access to it.

Blinking rapidly, I look away and scan the room. Whoever decorated this villa did not have an eye for symmetry. The painting of an ocean liner is askew, the potted plants are a few inches off-center, and white shells are scattered haphazardly on the glass coffee table. I am itching with all my might to fix the disorder.

Don't, Alaia. If you fix one thing, it will tempt you to fix more. Do not squander this moment with Mama. You don't know how many you have left.

Despite my pep talk, I reach out my hand automatically. I move one seashell so that it's perfectly aligned with another—and I would've moved a second and a third and a fourth—but Mama clears her throat.

Guiltily, I pull my hands away, my cheeks flushing hot at being caught. "I know. I know."

Mama just looks at me, her eyes gentle with understanding.

Lining up the seashells will not make me safer. I know that. And yet, logic can't stop the *feeling* that rises in me. It's like the universe is out of balance, the seashells a cosmic event that distorts my reality, and nothing can be right until I return the chaos to order.

I grit my teeth. With incredible effort, I walk to the end table and pick up Mama's medicine box. Shaking the assortment of orange, white, and light blue pills into my palm, I offer them to Mama.

It's my job to prepare Mama's medication. She used to do it for me when I was a little girl, giving me my pills every night, without fail. Now, it's my turn to return the favor.

Just then, the doorknob rattles and Papa walks in with a guy who looks slightly older than my seventeen years.

Mama perks up, and I try to figure out what to do with my hands. The guy is cute, no doubt about it.

He's incredibly tall, with black, close-cropped hair and a muscular body. Strong jaw, sharp cheekbones. A nose that flares slightly at the bottom, and golden brown eyes framed by thick lashes.

What strikes me most about him, however, is that he looks biracial, like me. Maybe he, too, has an Asian mom and a white dad, or vice versa.

"Alaia. Sweetheart. I'd like you to meet Bodin," Papa says. We've only been here a couple of days, and Papa's cheeks already radiate *sun-kissed.* "He's the boatswain on our yacht tour tomorrow, and he stopped by to introduce himself."

"How lovely," Mama says, eyes bright.

Bodin crosses the tile in a few long strides and bends his head over prayer-clasped hands in a wai, the Thai greeting of respect. "It's wonderful to meet you, Pa Moh," he says smoothly to Mama. "I will take good care of you and your family tomorrow."

Pa Moh, Auntie doctor. Two honorifics in one phrase, befitting the respect the Thai people have for both elders and physicians.

This guy knows *exactly* what he's doing.

I guess Mama falls for it because she pats his shoulder, each light tap broadcasting to me a message that's as clear as the chlorinated pool water. *See here? See how nice this boy is? How polite. How handsome.*

"I'm looking forward to it," she responds. "And since we're

leaving so early, I should turn in. Would you mind walking Bodin out, Alaia? I'd like Papa to help me up the stairs."

My eyes widen. By her second statement, my heart's pounding furiously against my chest. Seriously? She's picking *now* to play matchmaker? This trip is about her, about *us*, spending meaningful time together. Not about me awkwardly flirting with a boy who will ultimately have no significance in my life.

But there's only one response, and that's the polite one. "I'd be happy to."

Mama beams. "Wonderful. That way, you young people can get to know each other."

I bend down to hug her good night. "Do not play the death card," I mutter in her ear. "It's painfully unattractive."

"I'm not playing *anything*." Her eyes flash. "It's all true. I do want you settled. And I really am…dying."

Her voice cracks on the last word, along with my heart. Annoyance forgotten, I kneel in front of her, dropping my head on her lap. She threads her fingers through my hair like she wants to keep the strands forever.

"I love you, Mama," I say, and she smiles.

Six, I think. I've made her smile six times this trip. I wish I could magic away her cancer this easily.

She and Papa leave, and I beckon Bodin toward the front door. We walk outside into the balmy night. The palm trees sway gently in the breeze, and a million stars stud the black blanket of sky, making the short lamps that light the way redundant. Thailand even *smells* different than America— hot and sultry and somehow safe, even though I only visit A-ma and the rest of my extended family once a year.

"I'm sorry about your mom," Bodin says, his voice low and scratchy, as we stop at the edge of the curving driveway. "I know how it feels to lose someone, too."

Our gazes meet, and my chest gives a swift, hard bump—the ache of one lonely person recognizing another.

"Who did you lose?" I ask, although it's none of my business. But I can't help it. The pain in his eyes wipes out every nicety Mama's ever taught me.

His jaw tightens. "It was a long time ago."

A minute passes, maybe two, as I try to figure out how to smooth over the awkward moment.

I'm just about to blurt out a goodbye and run back inside when he looks up, his smile easygoing once more. The transition is so smooth, so seamless, that I have to blink.

"See those seven stars shining in the sky?" He points, neatly changing the subject. The warmth of his tone makes my stomach fall to the rocky beach. Because I've seen his real face now. Glimpsed his actual emotions. And so, I recognize the tone for what it is: the fake one he uses to win over tourists.

"You may know them as the Pleiades or the Seven Sisters," he continues. "But here in Thailand, we call those stars the mother hen and her six chicks."

The light from the lamps flickers over his face, highlighting some of his features and shadowing others, as he starts to tell me the legend.

An elderly couple wanted to make merit by providing a meal for a monk. Their pet, a mother hen, was happy to give her life for the good duty of feeding the monk, but her six chicks cried and pleaded with her to stay with them. The next day, the hen was boiled…and out of love for their mother, the baby chicks jumped into the pot after her. Because of their deep, abiding love for one another, the mother hen and her chicks were reincarnated as stars in the sky.

It is a lovely story, a poignant one. I'm sure I'll never look at this constellation the same way again. And he's a wonderful storyteller, his voice weaving magic, encouraging me to succumb to the wonder of it all. That must be the one he uses when he gives tours.

"That's super tragic and super touching, all at the same time," I say.

"As folktales often are," he agrees, an indentation appearing on his cheek. *Of course* he would have a dimple.

For a moment, I yearn for a different life. One where my mother isn't dying. One where I'm free to have a meaningless holiday fling. One where I'm actually confident enough to pursue it. But there's no point in wishing for the impossible.

He returns his attention to the sky. "Tomorrow we'll see the wildest things," he muses. "Homes nestled high on the rocky islands. The people who live there have to bring even their drinking water over by boat. Other islands are a little bigger, with a restaurant, maybe a few stores. Still others are so remote that they have yet to be discovered."

"Then how do we know they're there?" I ask.

"Rumors. Speculation." He slides a glance at me. "Do you believe in legends, Alaia?"

"I don't know." I've never really thought about it. "But the best lies have an element of truth. These stories are so old, they're probably based on *something*. Right?"

He nods, as though pleased by my answer. "Thailand runs through your blood. A country of folktales and legends, of myths and superstition. Some people dismiss the old beliefs as simply that: old. But not me. Not you. We know better."

I shiver. My logical side blames the sudden gust of wind, but my deeper gut acknowledges the true source: the piercing timbre of his voice, the raw candor in his eyes. An old soul, this one. I'm not used to guys my age being this deep, but I kinda like it.

A screech pulls me from my thoughts, followed by a

cacophony of barks, chirps, and clicks.

"What is *that*?"

He flinches. "That's the sound of two chingchok lizards fighting on the wall."

"So?" I ask, not understanding the reluctance in his tone. "Why does it make you look like you want to hide behind the palm tree?"

He shakes his head, as though he doesn't want to answer, but the noise crescendos. The lizards must be nearing the climax of their duel.

"The fighting is an omen of evil," he says haltingly. "It foretells that your family will suffer illness, maybe even death, in the near future."

I shrug with a nonchalance I don't feel. Have never felt. "Mama has cancer. It's terminal. I don't need a pair of chingchoks to tell me that she's going to die."

"No, not just Pah Moh." He chews on his lip, as though debating whether to continue. "You shouldn't take this to heart. Ultimately, it's just a couple of reptiles in their natural habitat. But the omen...well, it's meant to apply to your entire family."

CHAPTER TWO

Twelve hours later, and I still can't get Bodin's words out of my head. My entire family falling ill? Maybe even dying? What kind of tour guide tells his clients *that*?

Silly. I should be relishing this vacation, not obsessing over a passing comment. This superstitious mumbo jumbo is probably just part of the tourist adventure. Experience firsthand the mysticism of Thailand! Turn any natural animal behavior into an omen!

Well, no thank you. I have way better uses of my time.

It's late afternoon now, and we've been sailing on the yacht for hours. Although…"yacht" might be too glamorous a word. Rather than sleek and modern, the massive boat is wooden, chipped, and weathered. Still, there are thick foam cushions for lounging, and even a hot tub that fills with seawater…and the *views*…

The water stretches as far as the eye can see. *Heartbreak blue*, I think. Because it's the kind of bright, vivid color that makes your chest tight. That hurts the heart, that burns the skin, because we're not meant to brush up against so much beauty.

Craggy islands rise out of the water—mostly rock, with little vegetation. They sure don't look habitable, but here and there, I glimpse a crudely built shelter at the island's peak. These must be the homes to which Bodin was referring. Beyond rustic, but alluring in their own way.

The sky is expansive. It's the same one that touches down on my home in Washington, D.C.—and yet, here, the air feels fresher. More free. Devoid of the smoke and noise of the city.

"Think I'm too old to reenact the Kate-and-Leo scene?" Mama asks as she comes up behind me.

I turn. Her head is wrapped in a sunset-orange scarf that exactly matches her flowy sundress.

"Never. Didn't the captain say we looked like sisters?"

She smiles. *Eight.* Mama's wrinkle-free skin throws people off, and before chemo, she was constantly mistaken for my older sister. Since she got sick, though, the bald head—and a certain resignation in her eyes—add an age-appropriate wisdom to her face.

"Get up here." I make room for Mama, and she squeezes between me and the bow.

"I've spent enough of my life being practical," Mama muses. "It's about time I live a little."

"You're the queen of the world!" I exclaim.

We both fling out our arms. This moment, with the wind in my hair and the blue of the ocean before me—I'll remember it forever.

And then, the loudspeaker blares out "Party in the U.S.A.," and Mama and I start jamming to the music, just like we used to when I was a kid at our pajama dance parties. I giggle as we throw our arms and hips every which way. Some of my uneasiness recedes.

When the song ends, I jump down to the deck. "I'm parched. Want me to get you something to drink?"

"A ginger beer, if they have it," Mama says. The soda's been her favorite since she started chemo 'cause the strong ginger taste stems her nausea.

"Are you sure I don't need ID for that?" I tease. For the longest time, I thought ginger beer was alcoholic—because, you know, *beer*. Mama set me straight when I accused her of drinking too much alcohol during her recovery.

"Maybe just your school ID." Mama's lips twitch. "I'm going to find Papa on the sun deck. Don't forget to put on a second coat of sunscreen."

"I won't," I promise and ascend the stairs toward the indoor lounge. Mama herself never burns, but she quickly learned that her daughter's fairer skin is much more susceptible to the sun's UV rays. Even a few minutes in the sun can redden my cheeks.

Icy cool air engulfs me as I step inside. Only a few other passengers mill around the shaded lounge, with its rickety chairs and wooden tables. To my surprise, Bodin himself is manning the bar.

He's taller than I remember, a pair of sunglasses on his head, his arms muscular and tanned in a form-fitting T-shirt bearing the yacht's insignia.

I've been sneaking glances at him all day, while he was pulling up the line, fetching extra towels, gamely playing photographer…and flirting with the passengers. Can't forget that. Every time I looked, he was charming another person, making them laugh or blush or peek at him through their eyelashes. All the more reason why I should keep my distance.

"Alaia. I've been thinking about you." He flashes what I'm now learning is his trademark grin. "How are you?"

My heart bumps, even though I know it's a line. I know I'm probably the tenth person he's said this to.

"I'm good," I say as casually as possible. "You bartend? I

thought you were in charge of the equipment."

"With a crew this small, I guess I'm boatswain and first stew," he says. "Now, what can I get you?"

I give him our drink order, and as he retrieves them, I look out the floor-to-ceiling window at the sea.

Something glints in the water. A golden fin, smooth and slippery, like it might be attached to an eel. But that can't be right. Eels don't have fins. And the appendage is way too big to belong to any sea creature I've ever seen.

A trick of the light. Nothing more. The consequence of a sleepless night obsessing over a meaningless omen.

Except...the fin flashes again, fifty feet away. And then once more, fifty feet farther. Whatever this thing is, it sure travels fast.

"Do you see that?" I ask. "What is that thing?"

Bodin glances out the window and then back at me again. "The only thing I see is a vision of exquisite beauty," he says jokingly.

I roll my eyes, although my stomach flips. I've never been called *exquisite* before, even as a joke. "Good one. Does your company give you a book of pickup lines to memorize?"

His smile spreads wider. "Nah. I bought the book myself."

I giggle. He's just so ridiculous. "Do the lines ever work?"

"Not yet," he says, winking. "But I'm a guy with a lot of faith."

The warmth begins in my core and radiates outward. He's funny. I'll give him that. But judging by those gleaming brown eyes, the dimple waving at me from the side of his mouth? The lines *do* work. Entirely too well. Although I'll never admit it.

Bodin hands me the coconut water and ginger beer, his fingers grazing the back of my hand.

I recoil from his touch. I know it makes absolutely no

sense, but I just don't like it when people touch me—even if they're as cute as Bodin.

He withdraws his hand. "Sorry, I…" He struggles to come up with an appropriate apology.

But there's no need to say sorry because he did nothing wrong. It's *me*.

I don't know what to say. I rarely tell people about this part of myself. My aversion to touch feels deeply personal, and I sure as hell am not about to explain it to some stranger I just met.

That's when I notice exactly how close he is to me. Twelve inches. The current of electricity that hums in that space feels almost tangible.

For a moment, I stare into his eyes, and the look he gives me, intense yet gentle, is one that I could swim in for hours.

I take a small step back.

I don't know why. Actually, that's a lie. I know *exactly* why. He was getting too close. Too close for comfort. But part of me wanted him even closer. And now all I can do is beat myself up for ruining the moment.

"I need to find my parents," I say regretfully. This vacation is about spending time with Mama, not crushing on a guy I'll never see again. Maybe Mama should've thought about *that* before she threw us together last night. "See you later?" Or not.

No doubt, he will be the same as every other cute guy I encounter: someone whom I avoid so that I don't get hurt.

He clutches at his heart. "I'm counting down the minutes."

I smile—because how can I *not* smile?—and descend the rickety stairs to the first level of the yacht. It's a different route than the way that I came, but hopefully, it will take me closer to the sun deck, where my parents wait.

The yacht is larger—or at least more confusing—than I

remember. I must make a wrong turn, because I end up not in the open-air sun deck but in a dark corridor that dead-ends in a small, dimly lit storage area.

Hesitantly, I walk toward the light.

The smell hits me first—seawater ripened with fish guts. That alone should've made me turn around. For some reason, I don't.

The room is piled high with coolers and life vests, and a dozen slimy fish are laid out on a table in the center.

A white man stands at the table. He's got a scruffy beard and a long, salt-and-pepper ponytail—the captain of the yacht, I suddenly realize. Xander.

But Captain Xander's not just standing there. He's holding one of the fish, and—oh dear lord, he's inserting a hook straight through the eye.

My breath gets caught in my lungs, and I dart my gaze to the rest of the table. Sure enough, every fish has a hook through its eye.

"What are you doing?" I blurt. "Those poor fish."

Xander looks up. The instant he sees me, his lips curve— but not in a smile. No, his expression is too bone-chilling, too *evil* to ever be called that.

"On the contrary, little girl," he says. "The fish are already dead. I'm simply prepping them to be reincarnated as my twelve blind princesses."

I have no idea what he's talking about, but that doesn't matter. Because Xander flips the fish over, plucks out an eye with his fingers, and—in the creepiest moment of my life— *pops it straight into his mouth.*

I can't think. Instead, I just run. From the dimly lit room, down the darkened corridor. Pumping my arms, taxing my lungs. Up, up, up the stairs, so quickly that my foot slips on a step. So panicked that I grab the railing too hard and splinters shoot into my skin. Doesn't matter. Anything to get away from Xander and the bloated bodies of the fish.

I smash into Bodin, right where I left him a few minutes ago.

"Alaia!" His eyes widen. "What's wrong? Did you find your parents?"

I force myself to take a ragged breath, and then another. What did I just see?

BOOM.

An explosion rocks the boat, and I pitch forward. Bodin's arms shoot forward to steady me. Just as quickly, they retreat.

The moment is so chaotic that I barely register the touch. My heart's beating too hard. My breaths come too quickly.

What is happening?

A horn blares. Loud. Insistent. Repeating.

One, two, three, four, five, six, seven…eight.

Nine, ten, eleven, my mind automatically fills in.

But in reality, only seven short blasts sounded, followed by one long one.

Crap. My panic has nothing to do with the fact that the numbers stopped too early. Because that's not just a random horn sequence. It's the yacht's general alarm for an emergency, the one the captain told us about during the safety presentation this morning.

Oh, dear god, we're sinking.

CHAPTER THREE

My lungs contract. My heart knocks against my ribs. Adrenaline fills my veins, and my thoughts go haywire. I've never mixed well with loud noises...nor immense panic... nor chaos.

I force myself to think of only one thing—the most important thing.

"My parents," I blurt. "I have to find them. They were supposed to be on the sun deck."

"Let's go." Bodin grabs my hand. Even in this mess, I can't help but squirm my fingers out of his grasp.

We clatter down the stairs, and he leads me in the *opposite* direction from where I turned. Good thing I'm not navigating this yacht, or we'd end up in the Koh Samui Triangle.

Within seconds, we come upon a deck lined with loungers. Strewn across the bar tables are discarded coconuts and empty banana leaves that used to hold sticky rice cakes. But there's no flash of a brightly colored scarf. No Mama. No Papa.

Where are they? *Where?*

People surge across the deck like high tide over sand, breaking us apart. They're in all manners of beachwear. Wet suits, swim trunks, traditional sarongs that have been fashioned into cover-ups.

A little kid clutches his mother's skirt while she frantically shoves beige, purple, and pink Thai baht into her purse.

"Is this like at school?" the boy asks shrilly. "When we have drills and I have to hide under my desk. Is that what this is?"

"Something like that," the mom mutters, urging him forward.

I push into the crowd but get stymied by person after person heading in the other direction. I want to cry. In fact, I do scream, long and loud and frustrated.

Without a word, Bodin maneuvers in front of me, plowing a path through the throng with his broad shoulders. I fall into step behind him, too shell-shocked to do anything but follow.

And then I see Mama, pinned into a corner, her orange scarf askew, revealing a few inches of her bristled head.

"There!" I shout, grabbing at Bodin's shoulder as relief courses through me. "I don't see Papa, though."

"I've got her," Bodin calls over his shoulder. "Go find your dad and meet us on the aft deck, next to the lifeboats."

Implicitly trusting him to take care of Mama, I turn and let the crowd carry me forward, the way a current might sweep you across slimy, river-coated rocks. Elbows and chests jostle me, but I maintain my footing—just barely.

Thick, black curls of smoke rise from the center of the yacht. And then, another explosion sends shattered glass flying through the air, skimming the heads of my fellow passengers and grazing my cheek.

OOOUCH. I yelp at the sharp sting of pain, but my voice is drowned out by countless other panicked screams.

I bring my fingers to my cheek and pull away blood. The deep red color and the sticky feel turn my panic into a full-blown freak-out.

Beads of sweat break out on my forehead. I can't feel my hands; my feet don't exist. All I can do is pant, in and out. In and out. In and out. Too fast, too shallow. I've got to stop this, or I'll hyperventilate. Already, my vision's blurring around the edges. *Stop this. Stop this. STOP THIS.*

With incredible effort, I drop into a squat and hang my head between my knees. Papa. I have to think of Papa. He's somewhere on this yacht, and I need to find him.

I take deep breaths, the way my therapist taught me. Four beats in and four beats out. I can't give in to my fear now. My family will only suffer as a result.

You have to fight, Alaia. Fight.

After eleven breaths, I'm able to convince myself to move again. The panic's not gone, but I've erected large, solid walls in my mind to keep it at bay. When I emerge on the foredeck, however, to find it similarly crowded, the anxiety pounds its thousands of hands against my walls, demanding to be let in.

That's when I hear Captain Xander's voice over the loudspeaker. "Attention, all passengers. This is not a drill. I repeat, this is not a drill." His voice is smooth and melodic, as though this were a normal afternoon of splashing in turquoise waters. As though he wasn't just popping raw fish eyes into his mouth like Skittles. "There's been an explosion in the engine room. We must abandon this vessel."

My pulse roars ahead of me, not knowing or caring if I follow. Abandon vessel? That means we have to exit the relative comfort of this yacht to go…down there? Into the depths of the ever-increasing swells?

No way. There's a reason I declined the snorkel tour today, and that's because I can't see the seafloor—which means I can't trust it. Any number of creatures could be lurking down there, especially that enormous monster with the golden fins. Uh-uh, nope, and mai ao.

"Please report to your assigned lifeboat," Xander continues. "If you cannot remember if you've been assigned to starboard or port, a crew member will assist you."

I steel my jaw and climb onto a raised platform, more determined than ever to find Papa. I scan the crowd, but my vision is blurry. I didn't even realize that I was crying. A steady trickle of tears runs down my cheeks. I swipe at my eyes—one, two, three, four, five, six, seven, eight, nine, ten, eleven times. And then, I finally spot Papa.

He's boxed into the corner of the deck, too, but unlike Mama, he's kneeling next to a woman lying on a lounger with a very swollen belly. She's got her knees pulled up on either side of her, sweat plastering down her hair and shiny on her face.

You have *got* to be kidding. She's having a baby in the middle of this chaos? And chaining Papa to her side? What fresh hell is this?

I leap from the platform and shove my way toward Papa and the pregnant woman. When I reach them, they're counting breaths together.

"Contractions are three minutes apart," he tells me. A flush tinges his cheeks, and his eyes are bright, focused. Too focused.

Damn it. I know that look. It's his Doctor Face. And I don't need him to be a hero saving lives right now. He needs to be in that lifeboat with Mama and me. Where he'll be safe.

"The captain says we have to go," I say unnecessarily. "We're supposed to meet Mama by the lifeboats."

"There are complications," Papa responds. "I need to stay here, with Suzie and the baby, for as long as possible. We'll escape on a lifeboat at the last possible moment."

I want to howl. Of course there are complications. There always are. When you're the only child of two physicians, *complication* is a daily occurrence.

But not now. Not when our yacht is sinking in the middle of the Gulf of Thailand.

"Papa," I say, hating myself for the selfishness. "We need you."

"I'm the only obstetrician here." His words cut through the din like glass. "I took an oath. First, do no harm. There's no corollary to that vow."

He's right. Even before he opened his mouth, even before Suzie clutches her stomach and moans, I know the morally correct choice. It's been drilled into me since birth. Suzie needs him more than I do.

"Go find Mama. Stay with her."

I throw myself at Papa, wrapping my arms tightly around his back. He's a good six inches taller than Mama; his coloring is fair, while hers is dark. And yet, I always thought they looked a perfect match. It baffles me that strangers are often surprised to learn that they are a couple. The goodness in their faces binds them together more than any race, any religion.

"Hurry after us, okay?"

"I'll be there before you know it." His eyes are a deep, hazel promise that he doesn't have the authority to make.

"Hey, Alaia?" he adds as though it is an afterthought. "How come ants never get sick?"

My father, the comedian. He never met a punch line he didn't like. "I don't know, Papa. How?"

"Because of their little ant-y bodies." He grins, and it transforms his somber face into something youthful and vibrant.

I laugh a little, since that's what he wants. But the humor is largely swallowed by the lump in my throat.

"Now, go make sure your mother's safe."

I nod. With a "good luck" to Suzie and a final good-bye to Papa, I plunge into the crowd once more, trying not to wonder if those will be the last words I ever hear from him.

The next few minutes pass in a blur of automatic movements. I find Mama by the lifeboats, just like Bodin promised, even if the boatswain himself has disappeared. She puts orange life vests on me and herself, as I'm too overcome to function, and crew members lower us into a long, oval-shaped lifeboat.

A couple more hours, I think as I perch on the hard bench. A hundred and twenty minutes, and this will surely be over. We'll be back on a dry, safe vessel. My family will be reunited once more.

The lifeboat fills with about a dozen people—including Bodin—and Xander himself settles at the stern to steer. Ew. I can't help but remember those poor fish. I'll forgive him for whatever that was—as long as he gets us to shore safely. But right now I can't look at him. I stare out at the water instead, and for an instant, I glimpse a large, golden fin. Again? It's less than ten feet from our raft. One blink later, it is gone once more.

We speed away from the yacht, and a stiff breeze buffets us. Mama wraps her scarf around both our shoulders. She has both of our duffel bags, too, so at least I don't have to worry about my possessions. I lean my head against her shoulder and feel a tiny bit better. As always, Mama can make even the worst things feel manageable, just by her presence alone. I don't know how she does it. *Magic*, she always says with a wink. Even though I know better, I'm always tempted to believe it.

Behind us, the yacht looms, no longer weathered but proud, like it had been on the loading dock. No longer fast and efficient, now that it's idling in the middle of the sea. It becomes smaller and farther away, and I catch Bodin's eye as he passes out bottles of water.

He nods once.

It's okay. It will be okay. It has to be okay, his gesture seems to tell me.

I want to believe it so desperately that I'm willing to take this assurance from a guy I barely know. So much bad stuff has happened to our family this last year—Mama's cancer, the resulting flare-up of my OCD. I'm not sure if I can handle any more.

If only Papa was safe. If only he could be with us once more. Maybe, then, I'll be able to relax and know that I'll be able to survive whatever life throws at me.

I gulp down some water. All around me, people are slouching over, eyes closed. I place my elbows on my knees. Now that the adrenaline is fleeing, my limbs, my muscles, my very bones are tired.

The yacht is little more than a glow in the distance. To the left, I see dots of light—another marine vessel?—but those, too, seem to be getting smaller.

I drink some more water. The liquid is nice and cool on my parched throat. There's a slight aftertaste to it. Something… almost sweet? Is water sweeter in this part of the world?

The legend goes that seawater is salty because a merchant wished upon a magical mill for all the salt he could sell. His boat filled with so much salt that it sank. Is there a similar legend about spring water and sugar?

Bodin swims in my vision. Floating by on his back, legs scissoring up and out in the air. Bumping into the other passengers. No, that's not right. They're not swimming.

They're *sleeping*, every last one of them. A woman in the middle of unwrapping her beef jerky and sticky rice. A boy conked out over his iPad. Even Mama, who has to take ten milligrams of melatonin to get some much-needed rest.

"Why is everyone asleep?" I try to say, but the words sound funny on my lips. Maybe because they're the consistency of coconut and pandan woon. So are my vision, my limbs, my brain. Everything sags in the middle and droops on the sides, as though the layers of my body are melting into one another.

Xander appears in front of me and takes the bottle from my hands.

"You drank all of it," he says, pleased.

The truth comes to me slowly, reluctantly. Something's not right. We're moving away from the lights. Away from... help.

The chingchoks tried to warn me.

They tried to prepare me for death and destruction.

That's my last conscious thought before I black out.

CHAPTER FOUR

My hip bone presses against soft, yielding ground, and my head is heavy. Groggy. As though my brain's been dipped in a puddle and mud has lodged in the crevices. I roll over, tucking my left hand under my chin, trying to get comfortable. Except…my hand slides right through the ground, showering fine grains across my face.

My eyes pop open. A piercing blue sky floods my vision, just as blue, just as cloudless as it had been earlier. A palm tree with enormous fronds shades me from the harmful UV rays of a sun that's high in the sky. And beneath me…grit. On my face. In my hair. *Sand.* Doesn't matter that it's the whitest, finest sand I've ever encountered. It's all over me.

I leap to my feet, frantically brushing the grains off my arms, my legs. My neck, my face. In all the crevices that most people don't bother to care about or notice. At least my canvas sneakers are still on my feet, which means my bare soles have yet to touch the offending ground. Small comfort, this. My heart's still trying to bust my chest cavity wide open.

Something is majorly *wrong*. I would never willingly lie

down on the sand. I would never relax enough to drift off
to sleep.

The pristine beach stretches to the horizon of the
world, clean and untouched. It is flanked on the left by lush
vegetation, heavy with ruby red fruits. A majestic mountain
rises in the distance, behind the woods. To the right of the
beach, crystal-clear waters crash onto the sand. It's all I can
do not to plunge straight into the sea, to wash every last grain
off my body.

But who knows if the deceptive water is any cleaner?
Plus, memories tug at the edge of my mind. The smoky heat
of the explosion. Leaving Papa on the deck with the pregnant
woman. Passing out in the lifeboat.

This place *looks* like the epitome of paradise. No, it's even
better than what I could cook up in my wildest dreams. But
if that's true…if I'm *actually* in paradise…does that mean…

"Am I dead?" I ask out loud.

My only answer is the surf rushing up and retreating
along the wet sand.

I can't be dead. Surely, I would feel it, in my heart, in
my soul. If I were in heaven, my compulsions wouldn't be
shouting for my attention, distracting me even as I try to
unravel my circumstances. Besides, this…this *feels* real: the
hot sun baking my shoulders, the damp, humid air enveloping
me like a sauna. Heaven wouldn't contain such physical
discomfort. Right?

"Alaia?" a soft voice calls. "Sweet girl, is that you?"

I shade my eyes. A frail silhouette is making its way
toward me. I'd know that elegant gait, those angular shoulders
anywhere. And if my cognitive abilities have been impaired,
the sunset scarf is a dead giveaway.

"Mama!" I take off toward her, kicking up sand behind
me. My sneakers sink into the beach, making the run harder

than I expect.

Or maybe that's just my dehydration and fatigue. My stomach bounces around, emptied out. That, more than anything, tells me that hours have passed since my time on the lifeboat.

I reach Mama, and she wraps her arms around me tightly.

Tears spring to my eyes, hot and burning. She's here. She's safe. Even though she must've just wandered up the beach, part of me was panicking at her absence.

Which isn't healthy. Because Mama's not always going to be here. Someday soon, I'm going to have to face the world without her presence, her support. And I need to start learning how.

I pull back a few inches. "Where are we?"

"Not sure," she says, patting her eyes. She's always been a crier when it comes to me. "I've been looking for the other passengers."

"Yo! People!" a voice calls, as if on cue.

We turn. A group of three teens with their backpacks emerges from the palms, and they make their way toward us, led by a preppy guy with pale skin in khaki shorts and a designer polo.

"Hey—I'm Preston. Valedictorian of my high school class, attending Harvard in the fall." He smiles at us expectantly, showing us his toothpaste-commercial teeth, as though waiting for our hearty congratulations. His heavily gelled blond hair *might* have been perfectly styled at one point. Now it's just a puffy mess on his head.

"Oh my god, don't mind him. I'm Lola and this is my sister Rae," one of the girls says, grinning at us. She's about my age, with golden-flecked eyes and hundreds of shoulder-length braids. Her sister looks to be older, sharing Lola's warm brown skin tone, but *her* hair is cut short and bleached blond. "And unlike *some* people, we don't walk around with our resumés tattooed to our foreheads."

"Hey. You two latched onto *me*," Preston protests. "People can't help but flock to greatness." Overcompensating, maybe? Not because of his socioeconomic status, judging by his clothes. But maybe his height. It's hard to tell in the sand, but he's probably shorter than my five feet, five inches.

Me, personally? I *like* short guys. I find them less intimidating. But I know some people gravitate toward taller people. "More like Rae had to hold your hand and guide you onto the lifeboat, when you were cowering in the corner, trying not to pee your pants," Lola responds archly.

"Children!" Rae says, even though she's probably only a couple of years older than Lola and me. Mama introduces us, and then Rae demands, "Do you have cell service? The signal here is crap."

She sounds just like her sister, but harder. Harsher. Like she's been through a tragedy or two. While Lola's wearing a cute fuchsia spaghetti-strapped dress, Rae has on a pair of ripped black jeans and a sleeveless black top. Tattoos of twisted vines (or is that barbed wire?) cover her right shoulder and upper arm.

"None," I say, sliding my phone from my pocket and squinting at the zero bars and the low battery.

"What's the last thing you remember?" Rae demands.

I look at Mama, as though she can somehow jog my memory. "Drinking the water," I say slowly. "It was a little sweeter than it is back home. Halfway through the bottle, I started feeling woozy. And then I passed out."

Lola gasps. "I drank the water, too. Do you think we were poisoned?"

"Loss of consciousness, headache, stomach pain. Don't know how you all are feeling, but those are *my* symptoms,"

Mama says in a measured tone. "Classic signs of poisoning. And then there's the circumstantial evidence. We wake up here. No captain. No Bodin. No *lifeboat*. This is no accident."

"I'm here! I'm here!" The cluster of palms near us rustles, and a moment later, Bodin jumps nimbly onto the beach, his arms full of red fruit.

"What—were you *spying* on us?" Preston bunches his hands into fists.

"No." Bodin's face screws up in defense. "I was picking some fruit for us to eat. Why would I spy on you?"

Rae puts her hand on her hip, her blunt, black-polished nails curling against her black jeans. "I mean, you *did* pass out the bottles of water."

Bodin blinks as though not understanding. "Yes?"

"That water that was spiked with *drugs*," Lola clarifies, as though it is a foregone conclusion, rather than a suspicion that's feeling more and more likely.

"It was you. *You* drugged us!" Preston lurches forward, fists already swinging, even though Bodin towers over him by several inches.

Bodin ducks the blows easily and dances out of reach. "Woah. I'm here, too. If someone tampered with the water, it wasn't me."

"Why should we believe anything you say?" Preston snaps, his broad shoulders hunched around his neck.

"Look around." Agitated, Bodin crushes the fruit against his abdomen, and red drops spurt onto his shirt. "There's no sign of civilization for miles. No means of transportation. Not even a freaking radio I can use to call for help. If I plotted to strand you here, why would I strand *myself*?"

Mama puts a hand on his shoulder, and Bodin takes a shuddering breath, visibly trying to calm down.

"Where's the captain?" she asks.

"I don't know," he says miserably. "I woke up on the sand a while ago. The captain and the lifeboat are gone. My best guess is that he went to get help. We just have to sit tight until he comes back."

"What *is* this place?" I ask.

"I wish I knew." Bodin squints up at the sun. "The sun's high in the sky, so at least half a day has passed. I'm guessing we're still in the Gulf of Thailand, on one of the countless uninhabited islands."

"I don't care if we're on Mars!" Rae screeches at him. "How do we get out of here?"

He moves his shoulders, as helpless as the rest of us.

We look at each other for a moment. The sun beats down on us—I can *feel* my skin turning red—and a breeze blows against the droplets of sweat gathering at my neck.

"Someone will rescue us, right?" Lola asks hesitantly, tucking one of her braids behind her ear. "They wouldn't leave us here like this."

A beat passes. No one answers because, well…no one knows.

"Look on the bright side," I try as I gesture at the fruit in Bodin's arms. They look like big, red oranges. Grapefruit, perhaps? "We've got plenty to eat, and there are worse places to be than in paradise."

"Aren't you Little Miss Sunshine," Preston grumbles, ripping one of the fruits from Bodin's arms and tossing it to me. "As an award for being the most optimistic person here, you get to go first."

Mama reaches out her hand, alarmed. "Alaia, wait—" she and Bodin say at the same time.

I pay no attention. I realize, for the first time, that I'm parched, and I'm positive I had a grapefruit just like this for breakfast. Som oh, our waiter called it. My therapist is always harping about proper self-care, and if I'm going to survive this ordeal, I need hydration. Wrenching open the skin with my fingernails, I take a huge bite of the glistening flesh.

A sweet, tangy taste fills my mouth as satisfying rivulets of juice run down my throat.

"Is it som oh?" asks Mama, her eyes wide. In fact, all of them—with the exception of Preston—look on with varying degrees of concern.

"It's delicious." I grin, and their shoulders droop in relief.

That's when I feel it.

A small, nearly imperceptible itch scratches my throat. And then, it grows and intensifies.

I cough, trying to clear the irritation, but then my throat constricts more, and I cough again.

"Alaia." Mama grips my forearm. "Are you having a reaction?"

Bodin is next to me in an instant. "Can you breathe?" he asks, hitting the mark on his first try.

I cough once more as my airway tightens like a vise. And then I'm choking. Try as I might, I cannot get a single. Lick. Of. Air.

In my ninth-grade biology class, we learned the body can be deprived of oxygen for two minutes before death. Has that timer already begun?

"Alaia!" I hear Bodin yell as I sink to my knees.

Both my hands scrabble around my throat, but the air will not come. And with no cell service and no hospital in sight, there will be no help, either.

No. *No.* This can't be the way I go. Before Mama. In these grubby clothes. I haven't washed my hair—I haven't even had my first kiss.

My vision blurs, and my hands fall from my throat. No, no, no, no, no, no, no—

"It's the fruit," Mama says grimly. "She's in anaphylactic shock."

Every cell in my body screams in protest. Come on. Just a reprieve. That's all I want. A tiny sip of air. That's all...that's all...that's all...

"Use this!" a distant voice yells.

Someone hovers over me. I wrench open my eyelids and look into the most beautiful, fathomless eyes I've ever seen.

"This might hurt," Bodin says.

And then, without further warning, he stabs an object into my thigh. Owwww. The pain flares, adding to my torture.

But the next moment, the tightness in my throat decreases, and the grip on my lungs loosens. *I can actually breathe.*

Who knew something so simple could bring me so much joy? That shuddering breath, although achy and shallow, is the best one of my life.

"What...what happened?" I rasp.

Mama takes my hand firmly. Never have I been so glad to feel her warm, smooth touch. "You had an allergic reaction to the fruit. Thank goodness Preston had an EpiPen." She looks around the group. "No one eats any fruit, you hear? It is very likely poisonous."

"Just because she had an allergic reaction doesn't mean the rest of us will," Lola protests.

"And risk a reaction like that?" Rae picks up the auto-injector and brushes off the sand. "EpiPens only contain a single dose of medication."

"And you've wasted my only dose," Preston whines. "I'm deathly allergic to peanuts. What am I going to do if I need my pen?"

"Don't eat peanuts," Rae says, exasperated. "How hard can that be?"

"Easy for *you* to say," he retorts. "Many fine-dining

restaurants earn their stars from their sauce work. You wouldn't believe how many ingredients go into a sophisticated sauce, and if they miss even one ingredient…"

"I think you'll be fine," Mama says in her gentle way. "No fine-dining restaurants on this island."

"What are we going to *do*?" Lola's voice pitches wildly. "We're stuck on an island with poisonous fruit and no internet. If I don't post to my socials every few hours, I'll lose followers."

Rae snorts, but she drapes an arm around her sister's shoulder. "You'll survive if you lost a thousand or two."

Lola moans, and we all snicker, just a little.

Except Bodin. He lingers on the edge of the group, looking down at the sand, although there's nothing to see. No creatures move among its grains, and so, the sand remains in its mounds, still. Untouched.

He jerks up his head, as though feeling the weight of my gaze. His lips press together in a straight line. "Still think we're in paradise?"

CHAPTER FIVE

"Maybe we've been abducted by aliens and this is another planet!"

"What if we're all dead?"

"This is clearly the work of an evil government. They stranded us in the middle of nowhere so they could experiment on us."

Wild theories spin around me, and I press my hands over my ears before the voices of the other castaways suck me into their whirling vortex. I have to find an oasis in this chaos. I have to think.

There are twelve of us—the eleven passengers in our lifeboat, plus Bodin.

The other six had woken up a quarter mile away, and we ran into them when we wandered up the beach.

Twelve castaways, old and young, a mix of ages and personalities, with a heavy concentration of young adults. There's fourteen-year-old Kit—just a child, really, even though he already towers over all of us at six foot three—and his grandma, Khun Anita, an elegant South Asian woman wearing a bright yellow sari. She introduces herself as simply "Anita," of course—but we're in Thailand. I can't possibly address an elder without a term of respect.

Brothers Mateo (about my age and height and very cute, in a nerdy kind of way, with playful brown eyes and wire-rimmed glasses) and Eduardo (a few years older and built like a former football player who let his muscles melt into fat).

Finally, a dating couple, college students Elizabeth and Sylvie, who are celebrating their two-year anniversary. Elizabeth is short, curvy, and blond, while Sylvie is tall, striking, and Filipina.

Twelve. That's all I can think. One more than my magic number.

That's the number of fish that Captain Xander was prepping. The amount of hooks that he pierced through their eyes. And—what did he say? The number of blind princesses reincarnated as the fish.

Princesses, we are not. A more accurate description would be a diverse group of bedraggled castaways desperate to survive.

But twelve. It can't be a coincidence—can it? I don't know. Maybe I'm overreacting. Maybe there's nothing significant about this number. Maybe that's just my OCD, reading patterns into something that's not there.

It's a whole lot trickier to trust my gut when my gut is so populated with thoughts masquerading as truth. Nonetheless, twelve just doesn't *feel* right. There's one too many.

"The correct explanation is usually the most obvious one," Bodin says, his voice firm. He's not the oldest one of us. Not the smartest nor the strongest. Still, he knows these waters better than anyone else, so he's stepped into the role of de facto leader. "We probably passed out from smoke inhalation, and Captain Xander took the lifeboat to get help. See, he's left these coolers for us." Bodin gestures to a pair of large red coolers filled with water bottles, towels, and other gear. We found them near where the other six woke up. Between the coolers and our own individual bags, which about half of us brought to the lifeboat, we aren't entirely without resources. "This means he'll be back to rescue us at any moment."

Bodin could be right. Damn it, I want with every cell of my being for him to be right. But my lungs still hurt, even though they've been sucking down air for a good hour.

It can't be that easy. This island is no paradise. Something is desperately, painfully off here.

Rae slaps her hands onto her hips. "So, what are we supposed to do in the meantime? Work on our suntans?" Sarcasm drips from her voice, probably because she's never "worked" on her creamy brown skin a day in her life.

"No," Bodin says grimly. "We survive."

A few minutes later, Bodin produces a fluffy beach towel from one of the coolers and spreads it out on the sand, on a shady part of the beach. The palm trees grow in clusters here, giving us a much-needed reprieve from the sun.

"Everyone, please place your food supplies here," he says. "We should take inventory."

The towel *looks* clean. The purple- and green-colored stripes are bright and vivid, the white background unnaturally pure. White never stays *this* white unless it's been freshly laundered.

And yet, I hesitate. I've got Thai beef jerky and sticky rice—our family's typical travel snack—in my duffel bag.

Mama always prepares this duo for me because she knows how picky I can be. In particular, I prefer my food to be: a) not dirty and b) not touching anything dirty.

The jerky and rice are currently encased in a plastic bag and a small bamboo basket, respectively. But if they touch the towel, will they continue to be safe—or at least, *my* version of safe, which is hard to define but something I know implicitly at the core of my being? I truly don't know.

Mama nudges me as she adds her provisions of two curry puffs—pastry filled with curried potatoes—to the towel.

Be flexible, her eyebrows tell me. It's a lesson I need to learn, for the future as well as for this deserted island.

Too bad flexibility is the exact opposite of the rigidity that is my OCD. Still, my food is protected by plastic and bamboo. It makes no difference if these containers also touch a towel. Right? *Right?!*

Gritting my teeth, I slowly deposit my jerky and rice on the towel before I change my mind.

One by one, the other castaways relinquish their food items. The pile grows with granola bars, nam wah bananas, a squashed-up blueberry muffin, and a box of gluten-free crackers. Each item is an adequate snack for the person who brought it. But as a whole, this pile won't go far in feeding twelve shipwrecked people who need to survive an unknown amount of days.

"Hey." Lola nudges Preston lightly on the shoulder. "Weren't you telling us you had a whole green curry pizza?"

"Oh, um." He clutches his sleek, black-leather backpack closer to his body. "I ate it."

Rae narrows her eyes. "You've been with us since we woke up in the sand, and you were bragging about it. I haven't seen you eat *anything*."

"Pretty sure you just offered me a slice a few minutes ago,"

Elizabeth says evenly. "Just as you were ogling my breasts."

Several people dart glances at her ample chest, displayed by a low-cut T-shirt, even as Eduardo turns his broad back to the group, his spine stiff and unyielding. His brother, Mateo, shoots him a concerned look.

What's up with Eduardo? He's older than most of us—I'd guess twenty-two or twenty-three. Is he just annoyed with this teenage banter?

Before I can decide, Mateo grabs Preston's backpack and unzips it, pulling out a flat pizza box.

Khun Anita gasps and then gives her grandson a stern look, as though warning him never to be so selfish as to hide food.

In response, Kit pantomimes shooting a basketball into the sky, flicking his right hand at the wrist, likely bored with our conversation.

"That's mine!" Preston grabs wildly for the pizza box. "I paid a lot of money for this gourmet pizza, and I don't have to share."

He flips open the lid, picks up a slice, and then *licks* it. As we all watch in open-mouthed horror, he proceeds to do the same with the rest of the slices, his tongue long, pink, and thorough.

Mama slaps a hand over her mouth, probably nauseated from her medication, and the rest of the castaways explode.

"Ew! That's disgusting!" Lola shrieks.

"You should be ashamed of yourself, young man," Khun Anita scolds. "We are stranded on this island together. Now is not the time to think about yourself."

"The pizza will be rationed, just like everything else." Taking control of the situation, Bodin strides over, sweeps up the pizza box, and adds it to the pile on the towel. "A little saliva won't stop me from eating my share."

"Me, either," Mateo agrees, adjusting his glasses.

"And me." Sylvie stretches her long arms overhead.

"Same." Rae nods defiantly.

Well, no thank you. I don't care if I'm starving. I will not put that germ-infested, saliva-soaked pizza in my mouth. I take an involuntary step back, away from the group. Interestingly, Eduardo, who has turned back to face the group, does the same.

"Speaking of rations..." Sylvie says as she transitions from stretching to jogging in place. "Some of us have higher caloric needs than others. We should get more food."

Mama, mostly recovered but still looking wan, places a gentle hand on Sylvie's shoulder. "Should you be using up your energy stores, dear? We don't know how long we'll be out here."

Sylvie stares at her. "I have a big climbing competition in two weeks. I have to stay in shape."

"If we're out of here in two weeks," Bodin mutters from my right, so softly that I doubt anyone else has heard.

I turn to him. "What was that?" I ask in a low voice. "I thought you said the captain would be back any minute."

"I don't know when—or if—the captain will return," he admits.

I shiver, partly from the breeze that sweeps over the island but mostly from this cold truth. Deliberately, I step out of the shade of the palm tree and back into the sunshine. We can pretend all we want, but none of us—not even Mama, not even Khun Anita, both well-versed in adulting—have the first clue what's happening. We're all just guessing.

The other castaways are still arguing.

"I'm the biggest one here," Eduardo says, his first words to the group. "I should get the most rations."

Kit leaps forward, spins around, and shoots an invisible

ball. "I'm the tallest." I guess he was paying attention after all.

"And I'm the best-looking.," Mateo smirks, to let us know that he's just joking. "What difference does it make? We should *all* get the same amount."

"I'm gluten-free and vegan," Rae protests. "Which means I can't eat most of the food. I should get a bigger serving of my crackers."

"You *could* eat gluten and meat," Lola says. "You just choose not to."

"Enough," Bodin says. He strides to the center of our group, looking at each of us in turn. "We can't waste our time and energy arguing. It's got to be midafternoon by now, and we still have to build a rudimentary shelter by nightfall. For now, let's just pack the food away in the coolers and agree to divide it equally. Okay?"

We all nod—not because we're a particularly agreeable group but because we're all achy and tired and just grateful for someone else to take control.

Except, of course, for Preston. "Who died and put you in charge?" He scowls. "One of the old people should be our leader."

"Hey!" I interject. "My mama's not old. She's just sick." *And you know, dying*, I think but don't say.

"*My* grandmother, on the other hand? Old as dirt," Kit jokes, and Khun Anita slaps him playfully on the shoulder.

"Ow!" he screeches. "It's not my fault you two are oldies."

"It's lovely of you to defend my honor, dear," Mama says to me. "But it's really not necessary. I don't know the first thing about surviving on a deserted island."

"Me, neither," Khun Anita agrees. "In fact, I'd be grateful if it wasn't my responsibility."

"What does the oh-so-mighty Bodin know?" Preston mutters, not letting his objection go.

Our former boatswain shrugs. "Not claiming to be an expert here, but our tour company leads camping expeditions on islands similar to these. So I'm not completely unfamiliar with surviving in the wild."

"Bodin it is, then," Sylvie declares. "Anyone who disagrees can take it up with me." She raises her brows at Preston, the six-inch difference in their height more than apparent, and he backs down.

One crisis, at least, averted. A million more to get through.

CHAPTER SIX

The twelve of us divide into four groups: shelter, roof, sustenance, and fire.

Mama and I volunteer to construct the roof, since the least strenuous way for her to contribute is to sit under the shade and weave together palm fronds. We're working alongside Bodin and Preston, who will attempt to build a frame for our shelter out of bamboo trees. Kit, Eduardo, and Sylvie are keen to swim in the waters with rudimentary fishing gear (Bodin discovered a few hooks in the coolers). Rae and Lola press deeper into the woods to search for fruit that's actually edible. Khun Anita and Elizabeth are in charge of gathering kindling and firewood, while Mateo's certain that he can start a fire with the flint and one of the machetes also included in the gear. He read a book on fire-making once.

"Little weird for the machetes, flint, and hooks to be in the coolers," I mutter to no one in particular.

Bodin looks up from the bamboo he's currently hacking with the other machete. "Captain Xander's lifeboats are always packed with these supplies. In case of an emergency."

"Okay." Still seems a little suspicious to me, but I let it go. I should probably just be grateful that we have this equipment.

Bodin returns to his work, while Preston stands over his shoulder, regaling him with instructions. "Hit the bamboo precisely at a forty-five-degree angle. No, not like that. Swing from your shoulder, outward—"

"Done this before, have you?" Bodin asks blandly, wiping the sweat from his forehead.

"Not exactly," Preston says. "But I've watched every season of *Survivor*. *Studied* the game, like a true student would. *Just plop me in the wilderness with nothing but a blade and the clothes on my back*, I said in my application video. *I'd not only survive. I would thrive.*"

"Impressive." Bodin bites his cheeks as though holding back a smile. "Did the producers call you back for a second round of auditions?"

"No," Preston says shortly. "They don't know what they're missing." He grabs the machete from Bodin, swings wildly, and nearly falls over.

"Careful!" Mama calls from her spot under the palm trees. "I could stitch you up, but I'd have to use one of the hooks and the fishing line. It wouldn't be a pleasant experience without any antiseptic."

"Don't worry, Pah Moh. I'll take care of him." Bodin shoots her a winning smile, one that kinda makes *me* melt, even though it wasn't aimed at me.

Preston tosses the machete on the ground and stalks off. So much for Bodin having help with the shelter frame.

Which means I should probably also get to work. I scan the foliage, searching for the most accessible palm fronds.

"Let me help you gather the fronds," Mama says.

"No. You rest," I say quickly. "It will only take me a few minutes to gather the first batch of materials, and then, you can start weaving. Easy-peasy…"

"Lemon-squeezy," Mama finishes, just like I knew she would.

Suitably cheered, I grasp a green stalk and yank. I've got this. I can get my part of the job done in ten minutes, tops…but an hour later, I'm still working. The palm fronds are bulkier than I imagined. The leaves slice open my skin as I haul them onto my back. They sure look pretty waving in the wind…but I can't appreciate their beauty when I'm transporting dozens of them in one-hundred-degree heat.

When I've built a small mountain next to Mama, I drop down next to her, swiping an arm across my forehead. Thank goodness I opted for jean shorts and a cute white T-shirt on the yacht. "You've gotten so much done," I say, surveying the thatched roof that's beginning to take shape. "Should you take a break?"

"I'm fine." Mama attempts a smile. It's so pathetic that I can't even count it toward my tally. Sweat beads along her forehead, and her cheeks are rosy red. She's withering, fast. But even though she leans back against the palm tree, supporting her weight, her fingers continue to move.

I pick up a finished section of the roof. It's a bit of a jumbled mess. Holes here and there. And even though I'll have to lie under this roof at night, I grin. Typical Mama.

I line up my eye with one of the holes. Sure enough, I can see straight through to the other side. "Just look at this craftsmanship," I exclaim. "Now, this is what they call watertight. No way any rain is getting through this sucker."

Mama bursts out laughing. "Give me that." She takes the roof section from me so that she can patch over the hole. "I don't want you cursing my name when the rain comes."

I squint at the sky, which has gotten noticeably darker. Either the night is approaching quickly…or the weather's about to change. "We won't be here long enough to need a sturdy shelter. Right? I'm thinking we'll get rescued by the morning, at the latest."

"We have to prepare for the worst," Mama says simply and resumes her weaving. Except it's Mama, not me, and so her fingers move quickly, nimbly. She'll always be an 80/20 kind of gal, where she puts in 20 percent of the effort and receives 80 percent of the outcome.

I'm pretty much the opposite. I can never let go of those small details that will make a task whole.

I watch Mama work, fascinated by the flash of her fingers. And now that I'm finally still, the thought I've been suppressing since I woke up on the sand bubbles to the surface.

"I hoped Papa would be here," I blurt out.

Mama doesn't respond right away, her fingers moving in and out of the fronds. "It's better that he's not," she says finally, lifting her head and meeting my eyes.

Worry lurks under her expression, but she covers it up with the steadiness that's kept me anchored all my life. "You know Papa. He's not one to sit around. We have to hope that he made it onto one of the other lifeboats. That they made it to safety and that he's working with the authorities this very minute, trying to rescue us."

"Do you really think so?" I beg, wanting reassurance that I know she can't give.

Mama doesn't speak for a long time.

"It doesn't do us any good to believe otherwise," she finally says.

"Hey, Alaia!" Bodin calls out a while later. "Can you help me tie off this frame?" He's kneeling at the base of the shelter frame that he and Preston have constructed. Although a sulky Preston eventually returned to do some work, he's disappeared once more.

I relinquish my spot in the shade and crouch next to him. He motions for me to hold the bamboo steady so that he can tie a knot with a sturdy vine. "How is she?" he whispers.

Ah. So, he didn't need my help after all. He just wanted to check on Mama. Unnecessary—but sweet.

"I'm not sure," I say. "She's in good spirits. At least, that's what she's projecting. But she's not the healthy and fit woman she used to be. If I'm exhausted, then she's likely hanging on by a thread."

He glances over his shoulder. Mama's head is resting against the smooth tree trunk, her eyes closed.

"Does she take any medication?" he asks.

"Yeah." I surreptitiously wipe my sweaty palms against my shorts. "She keeps a stash with her at all times, so she's good for three days. But once those pills run out…" I chew on my lip, not wanting to entertain the possibility. "The doctors have given her three months to live. Without the pills, she'll deteriorate fast. And the end…won't be comfortable."

It's the first time I've said these words out loud. The first time I've discussed Mama's illness with anyone other than family. Normally, I'm a private person, even with my closest friends. But with Bodin, the words just slip out.

His eyes soften. "Three days. That's our deadline, then. I'll do everything in my power to get us out of here before then."

Warmth rushes through me. Suddenly I feel the urge to make contact with him, to be connected in some way. So, I carefully wedge the hem of my shirt over my skin, and I press both of my hands against his arm. His biceps are reassuringly solid under my symmetrical touch. If I were to touch him with one hand, it would be uneven, out of balance. But with both hands, the touch feels complete.

"Thank you," I say gratefully.

The moment lengthens. Our eyes lock together, and he leans closer, as though to confess something intimate or...I don't know, kiss me.

My mind scrambles. We just met. And yet...I *want* to explore this unfamiliar feeling. Is this it? Am I about to have my first kiss, right here, right now, on this godforsaken island, with the sun beating down on me and Mama twenty feet away, the other castaways liable to pop up at any minute?

I pull back. Two feelings battle inside me. One wants to explore this newfound desire; the other cowers at his touch.

I'm scared. I'm scared of him, of this, of my feelings. I can't deny there's something between us, but my OCD tells me to push him away. HE'S NOT SAFE, it blares in huge, capital letters. STAY AWAY.

Bodin eases back, confusion marring his features. "I'm sorry. I—"

"Don't apologize," I blurt out. "You don't have to be sorry around me. This is just the way I am..." I trail off, not sure how to be more specific but desperate to erase the awkwardness from the air.

"Bodin! Alaia!" Sylvie calls from the crystal-clear waters. "Could you come here, please? You need to see something."

Saved by a girl who is calf-deep in the waves, her limbs long and tanned and toned. With the endless blue expanse behind her and the white sands in front of her, the image could be an ad for any athletic brand.

"Race you to the water," I blurt out and then take off in a sprint.

My legs stretch; my muscles burn. I pound my anxiety out on the sand and then dive into the sea, submerging myself. The water is cool and refreshing against my overheated skin. More importantly, it's stunningly clear. I can see for what feels like miles. The soft white sands extend under the waves.

No sharp shells or rocks to slice open my feet. No seaweed or debris to tangle in my hair. Just the cleanest, most vibrant turquoise I've ever encountered.

When I finally surface, Bodin is standing with Sylvie, Eduardo, and Kit. All four of them frown at me.

"What is it?" I self-consciously wipe my cheeks, my nose. "Is there something on my face?"

"No," Eduardo says with a sigh, averting his eyes. "That's the problem. There's nothing there."

I look from Eduardo to Kit to Sylvie and then back down at the water. Clear, blue.

No debris. No shells. No sign of life.

I suck in my breath. Holy crap. "There are no fish in the water," I manage to say.

"That's right," Sylvie says grimly. "We've been searching for over an hour. And there's no sign of life anywhere."

CHAPTER SEVEN

Something wet drops onto my leg. I swat at my thigh and roll over to find a more comfortable position on the bed.

Okay, so "bed" is stretching it. Uneven slats of bamboo hastily flung together might even be too generous a description. The bamboo juts out at odd places, making me feel like I'm sleeping on a scratchy, metal grill. At least the platform keeps us off the sand—I have yet to see any evidence of bugs, but I'm not willing to risk it.

I shift, and my head plunks into a crevice between the slats. Ow. Maybe the sand is a better option after all.

Careful not to wake Mama, I ease myself into a sitting position. Seven prone silhouettes are stretched out on the sand. Bodin, Sylvie, Rae, Eduardo, Preston, Mateo, and Kit volunteered to forego the shelter, as there wasn't enough room for all of us. Well—*volunteer* is a strong word. Mateo had relented with a lot of good-natured grumbling; Preston had thrown himself on the sand with a lot of *bad*-natured complaining. Kit, on the other hand, had only acquiesced after a pointed look from his grandmother. There's talk of building another shelter tomorrow, should we still be here.

I had been trying to convince myself to brave the sand—but then Sylvie had said cheerfully, "Maybe an ant will crawl into my mouth while I sleep. Extra protein."

And that was it. Game over.

Not my proudest moment, but whatcha gonna do?

The white sand stretches uninterrupted to the horizon, illuminated by the moon. A sense of peace falls over me. The clouds seem to still; the waves cease to splash. For an instant, there is pure silence.

When I was young, I used to stare up at the night sky for hours, drawing the constellations in my mind. Back then, I felt so at peace with the world. So calm. Like all is as it should be.

And I want to cling onto the quiet, getting lost in those heavens, but then I feel another drop. Awake now, I scan the roof over me, searching for glowing rat eyes and creepy rat whiskers. But the only thing that greets me are the holes that Mama failed to patch. As I watch, another drop falls through a hole and lands on Mama's nose.

Which means…

It's raining. How perfect. Out of all the nights, it has to be this one?

And then, hard sheets of torrential rain pour down on us, leaking through the roof and soaking the sleeping people on the sand. It's uncanny how fast the rain comes, not slowly or gradually, but a full escalation in a matter of seconds.

"What. The. Frick?" Preston sits straight up and shouts at the gloomy sky. "Come on. How can it be raining?"

"Um, 'cause it's monsoon season?" Rae snarks as she runs into the shelter, wiping the water off her face. "Do some research, Harvard boy. Nobody comes to Thailand in July and is surprised by the rain."

For the next few minutes, we shuffle around, sitting up and squeezing together to make room for everyone. There's no more talking. First, because we're out of breath. And second, the wind howls in the air, picking up the water and drenching us, rendering the shelter nearly useless.

If possible, the raindrops have found a way to get rounder and fatter, stinging and lashing at my skin. The sky lights up. Long, blue beams of light stretch across the expanse, and then, loud booms crush my ear drums.

"Move over!" Lola shrieks. "I can't breathe. You all are squishing me like a pancake."

"It's fat boy over here." Preston jerks a thumb at Eduardo. "He's taking more than his fair share of space."

"Don't call him fat," Elizabeth says. "Unless that's the adjective he prefers. But that's *his* decision. Not yours."

Mateo simply glares at Preston, whose legs are flung out while the rest of us sit much more compactly. "He takes as much room as he takes. I don't know what you want him to do about it."

"*He* can go sit with the girls," Preston says darkly, "instead of crowding me with his fat ass."

Elizabeth clucks her tongue in annoyance. "Don't say—"

"Not. Happening," Eduardo says in a tone that leaves no room for argument. "I'm sitting right here."

"Preston. Pull in those legs!" Khun Anita barks.

"If we all rearrange ourselves, I'm sure we can find additional space for Lola," Mama interjects soothingly.

Preston heaves a big sigh, but then, amazingly enough, he crisscrosses his legs.

The bamboo creaks and groans as we shift around. Rae wraps her arm around her sister's shoulder, and Bodin sets out the empty water bottles in the sand, so that they'll refill with the rainwater. I'd kinda sorta hoped that he would sit next to me, as much as I don't want to be touched—but it's good that he's thinking of our survival. Sylvie challenges Kit to an arm-wrestling match, and the two venture out into the rain, where they'll have room.

Just then, a bolt of thunder splits open the sky, and I jump.

"It's okay. It's just Mekla and Ramasura, the goddess of lightning and the god of thunder," Mama says to me as we huddle together. Despite her current warmth, I know that every moment in this weather drains her health a little more. "Would you like to hear the story?"

I nod. I could be five years old again, begging Mama for just one more bedtime tale. Except for the chattering teeth. And pruned fingers. And sopping wet clothes.

"Ramasura was entranced by Mekla's beauty, as well as her magic crystal, and so he chased Mekla across the sky," Mama begins in a soft and melodic voice. Her Mama Bear voice, as I like to call it. When I was a kid, she used to read me hundreds of Berenstain Bears books. And so, forever more, her storytelling voice will always sound like Mama Bear to me.

Elizabeth, Khun Anita, and Mateo turn toward us, also listening.

"Try as he might, Ramasura could never catch Mekla," Mama continues. "So, frustrated and angry, he would throw his magical ax across the sky. However, Mekla never got hit, because she would flash her magic crystal, blinding Ramasura temporarily. And that is the story of why thunder chases lightning across the sky."

She lifts up my chin and looks into my eyes. And then, she smiles, in spite of our misery.

Eighteen, I think dazedly. I know that she's dying. I know as cold and tired and hungry as I feel, Mama must feel it worse. And yet, she's making the effort to reassure me. To protect me, with the few tools she has left.

And that means only one thing: I have to fight, too.

I can't feel my toes. They're not numb or throbbing. I don't feel any pain or stinging. They're simply not there.

It's a few hours later, still in the deep of night. I pull my feet out of my white canvas sneakers, setting them carefully on top of my shoes. My toes are there, albeit wrinkled, swollen, and pale. Carefully, I stretch out my legs, making sure that my feet don't touch the ground—and OW. The pain comes roaring in, a billion needles in my toes, my arches, my heels. My eyes widen, and I suck in the air, too fast, too often—

"Alaia!" Elizabeth breaks off her description of the anniversary meal she cooked for Sylvie last week. "Are you all right?"

"My feet went to sleep," I manage to say, putting my canvas sneakers back on and slamming first one foot—and then the other—against the bamboo slats. When that doesn't work, I pound on my foot, over and over again, until the pain finally, mercifully subsides. "No, *worse*. They died and went to heaven."

"Lucky feet," Sylvie whines. "I'd die, too, if I was guaranteed that I wouldn't go straight into another hell."

Elizabeth snorts, and I shake my head, smiling a little. The four of us—Elizabeth, Sylvie, Mama, and me—have bonded over the endless, sleepless night. As the hours wore on with no relief from the rain, Khun Anita had dozed off with Kit curled by her side. Despite his height, despite his obvious athletic prowess, he's just an overgrown kid. He still has that baby face, devoid of any facial hair. Eduardo stares out at the stormy sea, his back to the rest of us. The other five— Rae, Lola, Preston, Mateo, and Bodin—had been engaged in an animated game of Never Have I Ever, but they've since fallen quiet, lost in their own thoughts.

Part of me had wanted to join the game, to get to know the others—especially Bodin. But I avoid such games like the ants that may or may not be crawling in the sand. Too personal, way too revealing. Much safer to reside in my cozy cocoon with Mama.

When Elizabeth started to sob uncontrollably because of the torrential, relentless downpour, Sylvie gave her a change of her own clothes. They're not the right size—the long-sleeved tee hangs down to her fingertips—but at least the clothes are dry. Sylvie also suggested that we tell one another stories to pass the time. Mama's been regaling us with the Thai folktales she learned in her childhood. My favorite is the one about the good queen who was able to walk across hot coals because lotus flowers bloomed under her feet.

On the other hand, Elizabeth, a would-be chef about to attend culinary school, tells us about the most memorable meals of her life, from the sumptuous seven-course dinners she's had with her parents to the homestyle Filipino food she's learned to cook in order to give Sylvie a taste from her home.

"Could you go on?" Sylvie asks wistfully, reaching out to intertwine her brown fingers with Elizabeth's paler ones. She's softer now, the badass athlete left behind. "As hungry as I am, hearing you describe the food makes me feel warm."

"Sure." Elizabeth closes her eyes, getting back into the rhythm of her storytelling. "Adobo chicken is prepared by marinating the meat in a mixture of white vinegar, soy sauce, garlic, peppercorn, and bay leaves…"

I close my eyes, too, and lean my head on Mama's shoulder. I'm tired, so tired, but it's hard to sleep when you're as cold and soaked as we are. I don't know how Khun Anita does it. Still, Elizabeth's voice lulls me.

I've never eaten this dish before, and now, all I want is to get off this island so that I can try it. My mind conjures up a fragrant pot of chicken thighs, the skin a rich, mouthwatering brown, with the bright pops of green scallions sprinkled throughout.

I can almost taste it. I can *actually* smell it. No, really. The savory scent of garlic and soy sauce wafts around me, tingling my nose...

I sit straight up. "Can anyone else smell the chicken adobo?" I ask in a strangled voice.

"Elizabeth, you are some storyteller," Mama says, awed. "You describe this dish so vividly, it's come alive."

"Literally." Sylvie meets my eyes across the darkened shelter. "I'm with Alaia. I can physically smell the damn thing. It's like my mama's in the kitchen, about to serve me dinner."

She looks not awed like Mama, not tough like her usual self, but...scared. Before we can make sense of the situation, a scream wrenches the air.

My heart leaps into my throat, panic instantly rising as I swing my gaze around. We're so packed under our makeshift roof that it could've come from anyone. But only one person leaps up and runs out from under the shelter.

"I can't take this anymore," Lola cries, tilting her face to the sky. She lifts her arms, and her braids stream down her back, dripping rain. She'd look like a goddess if she weren't so miserable. "I didn't even want to come on this trip. I wanted to stay home and binge reality TV with my friends. Instead, I'm here, in the middle of nowhere, soaked to the bone. I am freezing, hungry, thirsty, and we don't even have a proper roof. Go on, God of Tropical Storms. I have nothing left to live for. Kill me now."

"*Lola!*" Rae says sharply. "This isn't helping. Come back under the roof. Now."

When Lola doesn't move, Rae strides out in the rain, wraps an arm around her sister, and guides her back to their spots on the platform. Her wild-animal keening fills the air, leaving no room for anything else.

I shiver. That could've been me. That *would've* been me, if I didn't have Mama, as well as Elizabeth, entertaining me with stories and eerily realistic smells.

My heart breaks for Lola, for all of us. We can pretend that rescue is coming soon, but the truth is, we're stranded on this island, with no way out and no way to communicate with the outside world. The conditions are terrible, heading swiftly toward unbearable. The odds of someone finding us during this storm are, well, next to nonexistent.

This SUCKS. And if my brain thinks I'm yelling, it's because I AM.

The worst part? The scent of the chicken adobo has disappeared.

The thing about storms is that they always end.

After a very, very, *very* long while, the sun materializes over the horizon as the raindrops slow to a drizzle and a bit of sky peers out from behind the clouds.

Finally. I thought this moment would never come.

We detach ourselves from the huddled mass underneath the roof and stretch our legs (and arms and necks and oh, just about every part of our bodies). There are exclamations about the rain we collected in our water bottles, and Bodin suggests that we gather dry wood to attempt to start a fire. Mateo never did get one going last night. I guess there are some things you can't learn from books.

Bodin and I barely interacted last night, although our

eyes did meet a few times over the crowd of bodies separating us under the shelter. Each time, I flushed and looked away. I don't know how to interpret these glances. Is he simply being a good boatswain, making sure each of us is holding up? Or does his attention mean something more? Do I want it to?

I don't have space in my brain to think about it. Especially because Lola remains under the shelter, unmoving, while the rest of us are scurrying around, searching for dry wood.

"Lola." I approach the curled-up ball of human. "Are you okay?"

She gives no indication that she's heard me.

Sometime during the night, she turned from loud and hysterical to silent and still. It worries me more than if she were still screaming. Usually when people go silent like that, it means that something truly awful has occurred inside them. Something broken and beyond repair.

"Lola," I say, a little louder this time.

She lifts her head as the final drops of rain fall and the sun ascends the sky, casting an orange-and-pink glow. The wind dies down, and the sea, once troubled, goes calm.

"I'm so happy I could cry," Lola says, wiping a tear from her cheek.

I blink. Here, I thought she was in a state beyond terror, and yet she seems relatively stable...

That's when she chokes. Oh no. We'd passed around a portion of beef jerky, and then pieces of a couple granola bars last night. Is there still a piece in her mouth? Will one of us have to perform the Heimlich maneuver? Was she so desperate for food that she ate the ruby red fruit? Is she going into anaphylactic shock, like me?

But even as I'm leaping to my feet, about to yell for help, a single golden flower floats from her mouth and drifts lazily onto the bamboo slats.

CHAPTER EIGHT

My mouth opens and then closes. And then opens and closes once again. What on earth? Did I see what I think I just saw?

"I'm sorry." I shake my head, hoping to clear it. "But did a flower *just fall out of your mouth*?"

Cautiously, I reach out and touch one of the golden petals. The flower is about the size of my thumbnail, with spiky petals surrounding a raised conical center.

Yep, that's a real flower, all right. A bulletwood, if I'm correct. It's one of the flowers my parents and I used to worship the Buddha in the various wats we visited last week.

"I think so?" Lola says, just as dazed. "It's beautiful, isn't it? Like a piece of the sun, after all this rain."

Another flower—the exact shape, size, and color as the first—tumbles out of her mouth.

My eyes widen. *Again.* Not a fluke, nor a figment of my imagination. This is real. This is happening.

Rae drops an armful of damp sticks in our makeshift firepit, where Bodin and Mateo are working on the fire, and approaches us. She plucks up the new flower, her brow furrowed with concern. "Have you been eating something strange?"

"No. I only had a bit of the granola bar. The beef jerky made me feel nauseated, so I gave it to Mateo." Lola shoots me a hesitant glance. "I wouldn't eat anything from this island, not after Alaia almost died yesterday."

"What's going on?" Mateo asks from the firepit, aka a circle of rocks, as Bodin strikes the machete against flint once more.

"Every time I talk, a flower falls out of my mouth," Lola says.

A spark comes to life, but Bodin is so startled, he drops the flint and the fire goes out. He doesn't seem too concerned, though, and he and Mateo abandon the project and edge closer to us.

There's an expectant pause as all four of us stare at Lola's mouth.

"A flower didn't drop out just now," I venture.

Rae shows Mateo the two flowers that have already fallen out. "Weird," he mutters, turning the flowers over in her hand.

"Maybe it won't happen again," Bodin offers. "Can you say something else? What's the first thing you're going to do when we get rescued?"

"Hug my dog, Blueberry," Lola answers immediately. "I'll pepper her with so many kisses, she'll think she's getting a shower. She's the best dog in the world."

Not one but *three* bulletwood flowers drift from her mouth in quick succession.

"There goes that theory." Mateo settles on Lola's side, a little closer than necessary.

Lola pounds each foot against the platform, a seated,

teenage version of throwing a tantrum. "As if I didn't have enough problems already. I hate my life and everything in it."

"Even me?" Mateo asks impishly, picking up her hand.

"Watch it," Rae says. "You just insulted your dear older sister."

"Not to mention my poor, rickety shelter," Bodin adds.

I don't pay any attention to their banter. Because something glints inside Lola's mouth. Similar in color to the flowers...but different. "Look!" I point.

We fall silent. As if in slow motion, a pink, segmented worm crawls its way from Lola's lips, snaking down her chin, its slimy body curving and twisting.

I scream. Loud enough to reverberate to the other side of the island. Long enough to make every head on the beach turn in my direction.

Hell, I'm even more freaked out than Lola. Maybe she's in shock, or my reaction stunned her, but she simply spits out the worm and frowns while I backward crab-crawl as fast as I can.

Next thing I know, I'm toppling over the edge of the platform, and my body goes rigid as I slam into the soft (but not *that* soft) ground.

When I manage to scrabble to my feet, the worm—or whatever that slimy segmented creature is—wriggles away on the sand, and I want to throw up on Lola's behalf.

"Did that... Is that... You..." I begin several sentences, but they all get lost in the acid surging up my throat.

Lola wrinkles her nose, her first hint of distaste. "That's so gross."

"Gross?" I echo.

Gross? Just GROSS?! I can think of a million adjectives to describe this situation, the kindest of which is *gross*.

I want to run to every scientist in the world and beg them

to eradicate the worms from the Earth. Yes, I understand their necessity to the balance of nature, blah, blah, blah. But the thought of that thing in my body…inside my *mouth*… just no.

If it ever happened to me, the world would stop spinning on its axis. That's it. The end. Dead, dead, dead.

Sounds dramatic, I know. But that's how it *feels* to me: that worms are—unironically—crawling under my skin, that I would never, ever recover from this state of shock.

Four deep breaths, I instruct myself. *This is not about you. This super strange phenomenon is happening to Lola.*

Mama, Khun Anita, and Kit run over, no doubt because of my scream. The others must still be deep in the woods, out of earshot. Mama comes immediately to my side, while Rae succinctly explains what's happening.

"Maybe she ate a rapidly multiplying flower and it's regenerating in her stomach," Khun Anita suggests. Her perfectly black hair, long and loose yesterday, is now gathered neatly in a low bun.

"*And* she swallowed worm cocoons along with the flower," Kit exclaims, the most excited I've ever seen him. He places his chin on his much shorter grandmother's head, and Khun Anita shoos him off and sits down.

"It's not a terrible explanation," I say slowly, "except Lola's already denied eating anything."

"Besides, it's doubtful that the flowers and worms would survive the acids in her stomach," Mama says.

"I know!" Kit crows. "A worm crawled into her mouth while she was sleeping, bro. It's been chilling there, tangled with her tonsils, waiting for its chance to emerge."

My stomach flips. Good thing it's been empty for the better part of the last twenty-four hours, or else its contents would *definitely* be splattered across the sand.

"Not likely." Lola tilts her head as though considering the idea. "Like the rest of you, I haven't slept all night."

Am I seriously the only one who is put out by this worm? What is *wrong* with them?

"You are missing the point." Rae shoves her hands into her short, bleached hair, like she might pull out the strands. "You're all trying to approach this problem rationally, when there is nothing logical about this situation."

"You might be right," Mama says in a voice designed to calm us all down. "Which makes it more important than ever to hold on to our wits. Please explain what you mean."

The soothing tone works, at least on Rae and me. My stomach unclenches, just a little, and Rae sinks down in the sand in front of Khun Anita, who places her hand on Rae's shoulder. I'm not sure if they, too, bonded overnight, or if Khun Anita is just being maternal.

"Think about what we've been through," Rae says tiredly. "The yacht of our dreams blows up, and we're whisked away to this mysterious remote island. This place looks like paradise, but the fruit is poisonous, no fish swim in the waters, and there's no trace of Captain Xander or the lifeboat. We're hit with a storm nothing short of a typhoon, although last time I checked, the skies in the vicinity of Koh Samui were clear."

"And believe me, she checked," Lola chirps. "Every hour, on the hour, because she was paranoid about a yacht tour during the rainy season."

Rae ignores her. "Now, my sister is coughing up flowers and worms. Does any of this sound logical? Or *probable*? Something else is at play here." She looks at each of us in turn. "Something we have yet to deem possible. Something… paranormal."

Bodin scoffs. "What are you saying? That we're about to turn into werewolves and vampires?"

"No. Nothing as Western as that." Rae turns to her sister. "Give us a list of facts. Your name, your age, your favorite color. Keep emotion out of it."

"Why?" Lola asks.

"Just do it," Rae says with the annoyed exasperation reserved for older siblings.

Mateo pats her hand encouragingly, and she begins, "Um, okay. My name is Lola. I'm sixteen years old, and my favorite color is pink. Good enough?"

Rae nods. "There! Do you see what I'm talking about?"

I exchange a confused look with Bodin. Kit sprints a few yards and leaps into the air. I don't know if that's supposed to relate to our conversation or if he's just practicing his vertical.

"Er... I don't see anything," Mateo says.

"Precisely," Rae says. "She didn't cough up a flower *or* a worm."

She's right. I scan Lola, the platform around her, and the sand in front of her. No new flower. Definitely no second worm, thank goodness.

"What does that prove?" Bodin asks. "No object came from her mouth earlier."

"I'm trying to establish a pattern," Rae says impatiently. "When Lola speaks words of sympathy or kindness, the golden flowers of bulletwood fall from her mouth. When she speaks out of anger, worms crawl from her mouth. When her words are neutral, nothing happens. Here, watch. Say something sympathetic," she commands Lola.

Lola blinks, as though not understanding.

Rae sighs. "Something kind, something generous. Honestly, it's a pretty broad category. Anything positive will do."

"Uh, I bet you're really good at basketball," Lola tells Kit, who's moved on to under-the-leg, reverse layups with his imaginary ball. "Your grandmother must be so proud."

"He's already on an AAU team that competes up and down the East Coast of the United States," Khun Anita says. "You should hear me in the stands. The ref threatened to give Kit's team a tech if I didn't quiet down."

"I thought techs were just for players and their coaches," Bodin remarks.

Khun Anita beams. "They made an exception, just for me."

One...two...three... Flowers spill from Lola's mouth, joining the ever-growing pile on the platform.

I gasp, but Rae holds out her hand. "We're not done yet. Say something angry," she instructs Lola. "Again, the worms aren't picky, so long as you're negative."

"I was *really* pissed at you for making me come on this trip," Lola blurts out. "So mad that I took all of your ripped jeans and sewed them up."

"I did that, too!" Khun Anita chortles. "For my granddaughters. I never understood why they weren't more grateful."

Rae takes a deep breath, closing her eyes. If she's anything like me, she's counting to eleven.

The rest of us stare at Lola. Sure enough, a tiny pink head pokes out of her mouth, followed by the slimy white body.

I gag. I can't help it. It's the most revolting thing I've ever seen. I'll have nightmares about the worms for years, if not the rest of my life. But this time, with Mama's presence keeping me steady, I hold it together—barely.

"How did you know that?" Bodin gapes. Even Kit pauses his pump-fake, spin-around, fade-back moves.

Energized, Rae paces in front of us, her sneakered feet adding footprints to the churned-up sand. "I study Southeast Asian folktale and literature in college. That's why we're in Thailand—so that I could take a summer course at Chulalongkorn University."

"Let me guess." Lola sighs. "Another boring folktale? She's talked about nothing else this entire trip."

Another worm crawls out. Revulsion courses through me, but a magnitude less than before. Exposure therapy at work. Show me another million worms, and maybe I can react as nonchalantly as Lola.

"Pah Moh probably knows this one," Rae says. I'm touched that she's picked up on the name that Bodin uses for Mama, rather than calling her by her given name, Pacharee. "And you, Alaia. You've probably heard this folktale as a bedtime story." I nod, although I can't imagine which folktale she means. If I'd heard any story about worms, I would've immediately blocked it out.

"Hey, I never got any bedtime stories," Kit says, nudging his grandma's shoulder.

"That's because you fell asleep as soon as your head hit the pillow," she retorts. "Now, hush."

Rae clears her throat. "Phikul Tong was a kind maiden who gave water to an old woman she encountered, so that the woman could drink and wash up. The old woman, who was really an angel in disguise, rewarded Phikul Tong by granting her wish that the golden flowers of bulletwood would fall from her lips whenever she spoke words of sympathy."

"*That's* what she wished for?" Kit interrupts. "*I'd* wish for the ability to fly. Can you imagine me dunking the ball from half-court?"

"Shhh!" Khun Anita, Lola, and I say at the same time.

Bodin leans against a towering palm tree, arms crossed, face impassive.

"Unfortunately for Phikul Tong, she had a stepmother who abused her by making her speak all day, so that the stepmother could sell the flowers that fell from her mouth at the market," Rae continues.

"As a result, Phikul Tong lost her voice and could no longer speak. The stepmother, consumed with greed, sent out her own daughter, Mali, to give water to the old woman. However, Mali encountered not an old woman but a beautiful girl in an elaborate dress. Jealousy led Mali to refuse to give the girl any water—and speak to her rudely, to boot. The girl, who—you guessed it—was an angel, put a curse on Mali so that worms would drop from her mouth when she spoke out of anger."

Rae takes a breath. "And that is the story of Phikul Tong—the relevant portions, at least."

Lola stands, the most perturbed I've seen her since objects started dropping from her lips. "What are you saying? That I'm both Phikul Tong *and* Mali?"

She backs away, as though getting away from us will also mean escaping the truth.

"No, Lola," Rae says gently. "Obviously, your situation is not a replica of the folktale. I'm just pointing out the similarities…"

"That's the same thing as saying I'm cursed." Lola looks around wildly. "I can't… I can't be here anymore." She takes off into the woods, hopping over gnarled tree roots and disappearing into the brush.

"She shouldn't be alone," I say.

"No kidding," Bodin agrees.

By unspoken agreement, Bodin, Rae, Mateo, and I run after her, leaving Kit shuffling across the sand, hunched in a defensive position, as he boxes out his grandmother. Mama, on the other hand, remains sitting on the platform, content to let us healthy young people handle the situation.

Bodin leads the way, protecting us from most of the

bramble with his muscular shoulders. However, thin branches whip into my face, and my side scrapes against the brush when the path narrows. Thankfully, we don't have to run for long.

At the first break in the trees, we find Lola crouched in the middle of a puddle, rocking back and forth.

Rae sucks in a sharp breath. "The puddle. Tell me you see what I see."

There, made prominent by last night's heavy rainfall, lays a pool of water. The only thing weird about it is that Lola's plopped in the center of it.

Oh, wait. The pond does possess some strange curves. Smaller pools fan across the top of it, almost in the shape of a…

"Footprint," Mateo breathes.

"Buddha's footprint, to be exact." Rae presses the palms of her hands into her eyes. "Just like the puddle in the shape of an oversize footprint that a hunter found in the seventeenth century. A temple, Wat Phra Phutthabut, was built around it, and thousands of people visit every year."

"What's happening to me?" Lola cries. "What is this place?"

Rae kneels by her sister, soaking her jeans from the knee down. "Hate to say it, little sister," she says grimly. "But it looks like we've stumbled onto an island where the old folktales come to life."

CHAPTER NINE

Clap…clap…clap…

The sound of one palm slapping another. Applause. But that doesn't make sense. We're not actors in a theater production. We're just *us*, on a deserted island, listening to Rae's preposterous explanation.

Clap…clap…clap…

A hallucination. That must be it. I'm just imagining the clapping sound—kinda like a ringing in the ears, but much more sinister.

Clap…clap…clap…

The others are looking around, too. Which means either this is a group hallucination, or the clapping is all too real.

The leaves rustle. Twigs break. The clapping continues. I tense, all of my muscles activated by the fight-or-flight response. Although, who am I kidding? I've always been a flight kinda gal. At the first sign of conflict, I run. Or hide. Both, if I can manage it.

And then, Captain Xander breaks through the brush and strides into the clearing.

My knees go weak. Finally. We're saved. Help has arrived, and this torture vacation is over.

I could cry from happiness. If I wasn't so uncomfortable with touch, I would run to Xander and embrace him for rescuing us.

Except…no one else looks relieved. Bodin's face has gone rigid, Mateo looks like he's about to throw up, and Rae shifts in front of her sister, as though protecting her.

What? Why? The captain's back. Shouldn't that be a good thing?

Xander's exchanged his crisp, white uniform for a pair of ripped jeans and a worn Yale sweatshirt. A belt is slung around his waist, holding all sorts of equipment—an oversized phone, a taser, a set of keys. The beard's gone, and his hair is loose and wild around his shoulders.

Those pale, pale eyes glitter, as cold and hard as jade. But not nearly as pretty…and a whole lot more evil.

Instinctively, I shrink away. That cannot be the face of our rescuer. Something is majorly wrong here. Mateo and I should be jumping for joy, Bodin should be shaking the captain's hand, and Rae and Lola should be sobbing happy tears.

Instead, we watch in silence as Xander reaches the middle of the clearing and plunks his hands on his hips.

"Congratulations," he says. "I counted on you figuring this out sooner or later. And you did, a whole day earlier than expected."

Rae rises from the puddle, the water dripping down her black jeans. "Figure *what* out?"

"This." Xander gestures around us, taking in the clearing, the trees, the entire island. "That the Thai folktales are—and have always been—rooted in reality. That the abilities featured in those old stories lay dormant within us, and it only takes some prodding to draw them out."

"She was joking," I manage to say. "Or maybe it was hyperbole. But she wasn't *serious*."

Xander turns those pale eyes on me. "Her college studies notwithstanding, Rae isn't the only person who could've reached this conclusion. Others of you have grown up hearing the stories. However, it takes a certain amount of independent spirit to connect the dots. You have to be willing to step out from behind your mother's shadow."

He's talking about me. I should take offense—and I probably will, later—but my mind's spinning too wildly at the moment.

Is he telling the truth? Impossible. I grew up in the age of *Twilight*, but the reason that sparkly vampires captured the preteen consciousness was because they *weren't* real. They were make-believe, a figment of the author's imagination. Werewolves are just as fictional as Mae Nak, the Thai ghost who died in childbirth but continued to live with her soldier husband, performing daily chores. Stories to entertain, to enchant. Not the truth.

And yet…and yet…there's no denying the golden flowers that dripped from Lola's lips.

"What are you saying?" Lola lurches to her feet to stand next to her sister. "What do worms falling from my mouth have to do with us being stranded here?"

Rae is still gaping. "How did you get here at the same moment that I had my realization? That is, unless…"

She looks around wildly. Because she's just figured out what I have. He *couldn't* have known that we were getting close to reaching this conclusion…unless he's been watching this entire time.

When I nearly died from anaphylactic shock. When the tropical storm soaked us to our bones. When Lola reached her breaking point during our sleepless night.

He watched. Probably laughed. Maybe even ate popcorn. And didn't do a damn thing to alleviate our suffering.

But how? Was he hidden in the trees with a telescope? Are there hidden cameras in our camp? I haven't seen any, even though we've been breaking down trees and tearing apart palm fronds. But I wasn't exactly looking for one, either. Hell, maybe he has an entire army of spies, hiding in plain sight.

Xander half turns to me. "I have to say, I'm a little disappointed that you and your mother didn't make more of Elizabeth's ability to recreate smells. I thought for sure Khun Moh, the revered doctor, would have connected it to the tale of the woman who could steal the scent of curry."

So, the smell of the chicken adobo was also real, I think dully. Given the rest of Xander's outlandish claims, the statement is not as shocking as it should be.

"You mean this was all a setup?" Mateo asks, outraged. "You were just sitting there while we suffered?"

Rae balls her hands into fists. "You monster. Look at my sister. Look at what you and this godforsaken island have done to her."

"No, I'm not a monster," Xander says quietly, his eyes going soft and blurry. "I'm just a modern-day scientist, exploring a phenomenon that the ancestors already accepted and embraced. I'm a lonely man on the precipice of a dream, on the verge of unlocking what *should* be impossible."

I have no idea what he's saying. I can't even begin to imagine to what he's referring. But goose bumps pop up on my skin nonetheless.

"Of course, I don't expect you to understand that," Xander continues. "You're emotional. I get that. I would be, too, if I hadn't eaten anything but some paltry rations."

His gaze shifts to Bodin, eyes focused once more. "My boy, how have you been treating our guests? Rainwater and stale granola bars?" The captain shakes his head, as though vastly disappointed. "Come now. I've taught you better than that."

A series of emotions fires across Bodin's face. Rage, betrayal. A multitude more that I can't read.

He's been strangely quiet this entire conversation. In a way, he has so much more to be angry about than the rest of us. We're just guests, meeting Captain Xander for the first time. But the captain is Bodin's employer, maybe even his friend. It's clear the history between them runs deep.

And yet, Xander left him here on this island to suffer, maybe even to die…just like the rest of us.

"You jerk," Bodin spits out, his limbs vibrating with rage. "I worked my butt off for you, day in and day out. Charter after charter. Year after year. And *this* is how you repay me?"

Xander slaps him on the shoulder, oblivious to—or more likely ignoring—his boatswain's anger. "Not to worry, my boy. You're tired and hungry. A grand banquet is being set up at camp as we speak. Why don't we eat, and then we'll talk? You know what they say: a shipwreck always looks better on a fuller stomach."

I frown. What kind of wretched people actually say that? And what is up with Xander and Bodin's interaction? The captain seems to be *taunting* his former employee. Is there bad blood between them? Is *that* why we're here, as casualties of their conflict?

Lola sniffs the air. "I smell peanut butter."

My thoughts come to a screeching halt. Peanut butter? Did she say *peanut butter*?

I inhale sharply. Oh my goodness, yes. Underneath the salty breeze, I catch a whiff of something sweet, nutty. Unmistakable. That might not interest Preston and his peanut allergy, but it certainly excites *me*.

I catch Lola's eyes. An instant later, we break into a run toward the shelter.

My heart bumps against my chest, and as we round the corner and burst out of the woods, it bumps even harder.

The rest of the castaways are gathered around a long table, excited chatter wrenching the air. I first see Mama's narrow shoulders, Eduardo's bulky physique. Elizabeth's eyes are closed, her chin tilted to the sky, as though to give thanks.

They are flanked by what must be Xander's employees. People in silver jumpsuits, with oversize, misshapen hooded masks.

And then, the crowd parts, and the entire glorious feast comes into view.

Glistening clusters of grapes snuggle with spiky red rambutans, while purple mangosteen reside inside a bowl alongside three—no, four!—varieties of bananas. Stacks of club sandwiches, bits of bacon and avocado peeking out from behind the multigrain bread, vie with a taco bar, complete with tropical salsa and queso fundido. Fried chicken crowds against mac-n-cheese and baked beans. Lamb vindaloo pairs with steaming hot naan, while moo dang tops fragrant jasmine rice.

There seems to be something here for everyone—not to mention, in the midst of all those sumptuous dishes, *my* favorite food in the entire universe: crispy red apples and gobs of peanut butter.

I'm done surveying. I hope my senses have absorbed their fill, because from now until the rest of eternity (or at least ten minutes from now, when I've stuffed my belly), I will be consumed with one thing alone—my beloved apple-and-peanut-butter snack.

Before I know it, I've walked to the table and crunched into my first bite, and my taste buds explode. That crisp, tart apple. The creamy, nutty flavor. I could just cry. In fact, I do—big, fat, happy tears sloshing down my cheeks. After the horrors of the last day and a half, who would've thought that it would be this pedestrian dish that would level me?

I open my eyes, and Mama's in a similar state of rapture over her congee and soft-boiled egg, sprinkled with bits of scallion and fresh ginger. This traditional breakfast hasn't always been her favorite, but ever since cancer infiltrated her body, she's preferred it more and more, as the dish is both tasty and easy on the stomach.

All around us, my fellow castaways fall ravenously onto the food, rapture in their eyes. Sylvie crams perfectly fried lumpia into her mouth, and Kit gobbles up spinach rice and salmon drenched with béarnaise sauce.

Carefully, I put down my plate of apples and take a step back. Something...is off here. Yes, we're hungry, and sure, *all* of the food looks delicious. But these people aren't just fulfilling a bodily need. No—they've been transported, just like I was, because this food has a special meaning.

Is it possible that Xander filled this banquet with each of our favorite foods?

"Bodin?" I ask in a strained voice, as he's standing on my other side.

"Hmmm?" he replies, his mouth full. He's just bitten into a stalk of scallion, which had been marinating in a jar of vinegar. So, the khao moo dang must be meant for him.

Sure enough, he's carrying a plate of rice covered with roasted red pork and a reddish-brown gravy garnished with a boiled egg and cucumber slices.

"Is this your favorite meal?" I ask, gesturing at his plate.

Bodin blinks. "Well...yeah. How did you know?"

"Not my fav, but pretty darn close," Lola says, her mouth full of club sandwich.

"Same." Eduardo looks up from his plate of Nicaraguan

carne asada and plantains.

Elizabeth places a lychee in the center of the elaborate fruit salad she's assembling. "Guilty."

The chill that's been forming at the base of my spine begins to climb. All of our favorite foods. But how? We didn't list them on the forms we filled out for the yacht tour. Does that mean that the captain somehow…*researched* us? Exactly how long has he been watching us?

My gaze collides with the only person who hasn't been stuffing their face. The captain, standing at the edge of our group but by no means the outsider. Oh no. If he's controlling our group, then he's about as interior as he can get.

"But *we* picked you," Rae whispers. "The other day, Lola asked if we could go on a snorkel tour. On a whim, I called the number that was on the brochure at our villa. This trip wasn't planned. It was never a part of our itinerary. How could you possibly know what I like to eat?"

The captain grins, as though pleased by his own ingenuity. "Who do you think put the brochures in your villa?"

Rae trembles. "You preselected us to be your playthings?"

He shrugs. "Maybe."

My veins turn to ice. This…this…was premeditated? The entire time we were in the villa, when I struggled not to count my steps on the beach, when I shook out Mama's colorful collection of pills, when I tilted my face to the stars, caught under Bodin's spell, the plan had already been put into place for us to end up here. The details are so meticulous, the intention so evil, that my mind is blown.

"Stop toying with us." Khun Anita stalks to the front of the group, the bright yellow sari flowing behind her. She wags a finger in Xander's face. "Why have you brought us here? What is your purpose?"

He chuckles. "I thought you would never ask."

CHAPTER TEN

Xander sweeps up one of Lola's bulletwood flowers from the pile on the ground and tucks it behind his ear. The delicate flower should render his appearance harmless, defenseless. But it achieves quite the opposite.

We stare at him, transfixed. Only Preston continues to yank off hunks of moo ping from the skewers with his teeth.

"For those of you who have yet to figure it out, this isn't just your average remote island in the Gulf of Thailand," Xander begins in a gravelly voice. "You are all the new test subjects in a very special experiment. In my years of research, I have found that people can do incredible things while under pressure. When the human spirit is shoved against a boulder, when it's locked up and starved, that's when our abilities flourish. That's how a grandmother is able to lift a truck off a baby. That's why dear Lola started shedding flowers when she had enough of the storm."

His voice grows, amplifies. "You see, when the human body reaches its emotional limit, it unlocks supernatural powers—the very same abilities that have been long featured in Thai folktales."

Mama's knuckles bump against mine. Automatically, she reaches out and brushes my *other* hand, knowing that I would need the other touch for balance.

"By isolating you from civilization and allowing you scant resources, I am testing your human spirit," Xander confides. "I am manufacturing a set of conditions that will break your abilities free." He turns in a slow circle, his hands outstretched. "In return, all I ask is that you push yourself to your very limits. I want creativity. I want drama. I want inspiration."

He stops. I'm not sure what he's expecting. Some stunning display of human virtuosity? An elaborate scheme of self-sacrifice?

But we're not some upper echelon of the human species here. We're just passengers on a yacht that got hijacked.

And we've just been told that we're trapped on a magical island.

My vision widens, as if I'm a spectator and this is happening to someone very far away. Numbly, I watch the cast of characters and their reactions as my hearing flattens to a thin, high keening.

Sylvie turns on Xander but is rebuffed by a pair of his guards. She walks away instead and punches a palm tree with her fists, over and over again. I can't tell if she's angry or if she thinks she can unlock an ability with bloody knuckles.

Elizabeth drifts over to stand with Lola and Rae, seeking comfort, showing solidarity. The two girls form a special group now, one in which the rest of us may soon become members.

Lola's crying, on the verge of another freak-out. I can't hear what she's saying, but worms drop with alarming frequency from her lips. Bodin and Rae collect the worms, shoving them into the bamboo baskets that once contained my sticky rice. For what? To use as bait? To *study* the slimy creatures? I really don't want to know.

Meanwhile, Eduardo has plopped onto the sand, his shoulders moving up and down as he tries to suck in enough air. His brother kneels by his side, helplessly patting him on the back.

For once, Kit is still. No sudden movements, no leaps or fake-outs. He's wiping at his eyes, again and again, with one hand, while clinging with his other to Khun Anita's fingers. In any other situation, I might think it was sweet. Here, I can't feel anything beyond shock.

Preston continues to chow down on moo ping.

And that leaves me — and Mama.

She turns me with both shoulders, cupping me on either side of my face. The keening cuts out, letting in the roar of everyone's voices yelling over one another.

"I don't understand what's happening," I say in a small voice. "I don't know how we ended up here."

"This wasn't the vacation we were expecting," she says, her tone ever calm, ever soothing, "but we are together. We will get through this."

I nod because that's what she wants. Not because I actually believe anything she's saying.

Xander surveys us, his foot tapping impatiently, as though we're taking too long with our emotions.

"Pathetic. Every last one of you." He sniffs. "Let me break down the rules. For every person who unlocks a psychic ability, you will receive a reward, something that you desperately need. It could be food, or it could be something else that will make camp life easier. Two of you have achieved this feat so far — Elizabeth and Lola. Elizabeth's ability to manufacture scent bought the lot of you this great feast. It will be cleared away in a few minutes by my trusted employees. Your second reward, as a result of Lola's flowers and worms, will arrive tonight. Not food, unfortunately. The lot of you will not eat again until another one of you unlocks another psychic ability.

"If all twelve of you manage to unlock your abilities, then I will send you home, intact and whole," he continues. "Your time on this island will be nothing but a nightmare, a memory that will fade, slowly but surely, over time."

"And what if we don't?" Preston calls out, his jaw still working away at the moo ping. He's laid the empty bamboo skewers into piles of ten, and by my count, he's devoured thirty skewers—and still going strong. "It's not fair if I'm being held back by the ordinaries."

Xander examines Preston with barely restrained delight. "I'll tell you if you can eat a skewer of moo ping in a single bite," he dares.

The captain raises his brows. Without another word, Preston shoves a skewer into his mouth—and then pulls it out clean.

"Very good," Xander says. "My chef prepared the moo ping just the way you like it. Extra fatty, skip the toast squares. Did he do a satisfactory job?"

Preston nods reluctantly.

"Now, what if I told you to eat the skewer as well?" Xander taunts. "A little extra bamboo can't hurt anyone."

"I'd tell you which body parts you can shove these skewers up," Preston growls.

The captain nods, satisfied. "I like it." He turns to our group at large. "Now, to answer Preston's question, if for three days in a row you fail to unlock the abilities of a new person, then all of you, sadly, will die."

Die? Did he say *die*?

My heart plummets to the sand as a wail goes through

the crowd. I'm not sure I can breathe. The world closes in on me, my vision blackening around the edges, my lungs in a vise, tightening, tightening.

I can't die. Not like this. I'm supposed to be saying goodbye to Mama. Preparing her for a peaceful death. Not exiting this world *with* her. No. Just no. This cannot be real.

It cannot, cannot, cannot, cannot, cannot, cannot—

"Alaia!" Mama says, alarmed, as I sag into her. "Help me. Someone, help me."

Strong arms wrap around me and lower me carefully to the ground. Bodin, I can tell. But it's Mama who guides my head down between my legs. Mama who whispers, "Breathe. Just breathe," into my ear.

Khun Anita pushes her way to the front. "We all die, huh? Now *that's* a bummer. What if we decide we don't want to play your sick game?"

Xander grins, as though expecting—and deriving triumph from—the question. "There's no way off the island. You are well and truly cut off from civilization. As you have discovered, there is no other source of food." He moves his shoulders carelessly. "If you don't play my game, then you're done. It makes no difference to me, really. I'll just try again with a new group of subjects. And you'll die knowing that you've achieved nothing but to doom more people to this fate." He smiles nastily, spins on his heel, and starts to saunter off.

"You won't get away with this." I rasp, finding my voice, "The staff at the villa will look for us. When the authorities investigate the boat wreck, they won't find our bodies. And they'll wonder where we are."

"On the contrary." Xander turns, his melodic tone resurfacing. I hate it even more than his gravel voice. "The yacht disappeared off every radar fifty miles before the first bomb exploded, powered by the same abilities that made Malaysia Airlines Flight 370 disappear. We're now tucked away on a remote, uninhabited island." His smile spreads. "All you can see of our compound is a tiny shack, perched at the top of this rocky island. The authorities won't even know where to start searching."

He opens his mouth extra wide, showing me his discolored teeth. "You can rest assured. No one is coming for you."

CHAPTER ELEVEN

Only when Xander leaves us, the dense mass of trees swallowing him whole, do I notice that the food's gone. The buffet table, along with its bounty, has disappeared, leaving only an indentation in the sand. Not a grain of rice. Not a crumb of naan. No lingering skewer or fruit pit. Even the *tablecloth*—which we could have used as a tarp—is no longer here.

I was so distracted by Xander's revelations that I didn't even see the employees with the weird, misshapen hoods packing up the buffet.

"I should've eaten more," Lola mutters. "I only had half of a club sandwich."

Elizabeth shakes her head, as though disgusted with herself. "*I* should've scavenged the buffet for ingredients. I could've put together several nice meals for us."

At least I wasn't the only oblivious one. But my heart still sinks at the missed opportunity to pack away some food. Who knows when we'll eat next?

"Looks like I was the only one with the right idea of stuffing myself silly." Preston grins broadly, showing us his teeth, which have a glistening bit of pork stuck in them.

I shade my eyes, scanning the shadowy forests and the stretch of beach for a glint of silver. "There!" I point down a well-trodden path that disappears into the broad-leafed canopy. "That's one of Xander's employees."

"Well, what are we waiting for?" Sylvie shouts. "Come on, Kit. Let's find out where they're going."

The two athletes sprint after the employee, their long legs quickly eating up the distance.

I'm not a runner—never have been—but I'm not about to sit at camp, doing nothing, when escape could be within our reach. So, I dash after them, too. Bodin, Lola, Rae, and Mateo apparently have the same idea, and the group of us barrel down the path, forced to run single file.

Quiet, we are not. The lone employee must've heard us the moment we started the chase. Certainly, any wildlife that lives in these woods would be on high alert. But no birds squawk in the bushes. No small creature rustles in the trees. No *bigger* animal lunges out to attack us, thank goodness for that.

Looks like both sea and forest animals are conspicuously absent from Xander's island.

The trees grow denser as we run, the bushes thicker. Pretty soon, the leaves flirt and even touch over our heads, filtering the sun so that it dapples our skin with blotches and streaks. The ground grows more moist as well. Instead of the dry and cracked dirt that met the sand, the earth here has had plenty to drink. It pulls down on my sneakers so that each of my steps is accompanied by a wet *plop*.

We've only run about a mile, judging from the same amount of huffing and puffing I do as when I'm in gym class, when we catch up with Sylvie and Kit, neither of whom has broken a sweat.

They stand in a flat clearing, devoid of any trees. Stranger still, they're staring up at a wall. A *literal* wall in the mountain, rising at a ninety-degree angle. The rock facade is so smooth it has no hand or foot holes whatsoever, and it runs as far as I can see in either direction.

One thing's clear: we're not going to be able to scale this wall—not even Sylvie, our rock-climbing champion.

"I don't get it," she says, frustration saturating each syllable. "Where did they *go*?"

"We were only a few yards behind them, bro," Kit adds. His deep voice is always a shock, in the few times he chooses to speak. "I *saw* the guard's back, bro. And then, an instant later, poof! They just disappeared."

"Bro." Sylvie can't quite muster up a smile, even though it's clear she's teasing Kit.

Lola screeches to a halt, the last one of us to arrive. "This is the worst." She bends over, grasping her knees. "I'm so out of shape."

She coughs up two worms, which she spits to the side. Mateo rubs small, comforting circles on her back.

I can't resist a peek at Bodin, to see if *he* notices that I'm also exhausted. I, too, could use some comforting—sans the touch.

But he's too busy running his hands across the burnished red stone. "It's like someone sanded down and polished this portion of the mountain," he muses. "It can't be natural."

"What are you suggesting?" Sylvie demands. "That some evil scientist plunked us down on this island, demanded that we play his game, and then spent gazillions of dollars sanding down a mountain in order to trap us on our little beach?"

"It's possible." Bodin pushes against the vertical wall. "Rock solid," he says, shaking his head. "Rae? Any folktales that might explain this?"

Rae, too, is huffing at the air. Her tight black jeans have to be hotter and more constricting than my jean shorts or

Lola's sundress. But she's no stranger to pain, as evidenced by her tattooed arm sleeves. And so, she gamely scans the ground, searching for *something*.

"A-ha," she mutters, approaching a haphazard pile of rocks. Shifting the rocks aside, she picks up a leaf, long, thin, and green. "I found it."

"That's the leaf of a palm," I say, not understanding. "Arranged together, they form a fan around the stalk. I should know." I hold up my sliced-up hands. "I only gathered a million of them to build our roof yesterday."

Rae shakes her head impatiently. "This leaf's different. You see, there's a folktale about Muang Laplae, which is a legendary hidden city that can be found only by chance. The only way to access the cave on the other side of the solid mountain wall is to use a magic leaf as a key." She twirls the leaf in her fingers. "Just like this one."

She strides to the wall and begins to poke the tip of the leaf into various crevices.

We wait, with pent-up breaths and utter silence…

…and nothing happens.

Rae frowns. "It's not working."

"Well, of course it's not working," Lola bursts out. "Muang Laplae is a freaking fantasy, not a user manual."

Mateo adjusts his glasses. "Even if Xander is telling the truth, which seems unlikely, the special abilities apply to *us*, right? Not our physical surroundings?"

"I don't know," Rae admits. "The folktales concern both."

"I'm pretty sure Xander said *magical island*," Bodin says.

"Me, too," Sylvie chimes in.

Kit, the boy of few words other than *bro*, merely nods.

I, however, am still hung up on Mateo's phrasing. "What do you mean, *unlikely*? You think this whole island is what— some sort of simulation?"

"Not exactly." Mateo rubs his neck. "I mean, the scent of curry, the Buddha's footprint that Lola told me about. *They* could be manufactured. Even this ridiculous barrier." He nods toward the rock wall. "Like Sylvie said, it would cost a ton of money. And yet, it could be made."

His tone is even and measured, his thought process logical. Finally. Someone I can relate to in the whirlwind of chaos of my other fellow castaways.

"But how would Xander manufacture Lola's flowers and worms?" Mateo asks. "I've, uh, examined her mouth." His cheeks redden, and Lola, all of a sudden, appears fascinated by the clumps of dirt on the ground.

I blink. Could they have actually *kissed*? Already? My mind goes straight to hygiene. *I* have a small tube of toothpaste in my backpack. But do *they*?

"There's nothing inside her mouth," he continues. "That is, until she says something positive or negative. So, yeah, I believe Xander about some of it. Just not all of it."

Rae gives him the side-eye. "You and I need to have a talk. Later."

"Oh my god, Rae," Lola groans. "Could you please stop being yourself for two seconds?"

Rae ignores her sister. "So, you're saying this wall isn't actually the entrance to Muang Laplae, and I can't open it by sticking this leaf into various cracks?"

"It's unlikely," Mateo repeats. Gotta give the guy credit. Although his cheeks are still flushed, he's standing his ground. "My brain just isn't computing that scenario."

Rae looks at each of us. "Does everyone agree?"

Slowly, we all raise our hands, even Kit—although that might've just been a one-handed shot.

"It's settled, then," Rae says grimly. "We *are* trapped on this island by an eccentric gazillionaire."

CHAPTER TWELVE

"No. I don't accept that," Preston spits out after we get back to camp and inform the others about the insurmountable barrier. It's got to be early evening by now, judging by my stomach's rumbling and the deepening sky, which cradles the sun in the west with a few fluffy clouds.

A fire burns in the circle of rocks, where Sylvie reunites with Elizabeth with a flurry of kisses. Apparently, Eduardo and the oldies—what we've been affectionately calling Mama and Khun Anita, after Kit's playful lead—were able to do what the young guys couldn't: build a fire.

Mama smiled proudly when I congratulated her—a smile that I'm totally counting in my tally—and Kit tackle-hugged his grandmother so exuberantly that she almost fell over.

"I refuse to be anyone's lab rat," Preston continues. "I am getting off this island. Now."

"Um, hate to damper your enthusiasm," Eduardo says wryly. He seems to have no problem looking at Preston, the other guys, and the oldies. But I have yet to see him make direct eye contact with any of the girls. "But how?"

Preston blinks rapidly for a moment. And then, he turns to the ocean.

"I'll swim," he says.

I nearly laugh. Swim? He does realize, doesn't he, that there's not a glimpse of any land or vessel on the horizon? Nothing but blue, blue waters. Considering that the human eye can see up to three miles uninterrupted, the likelihood that he'll find another island before he gives in to fatigue is slim to nonexistent. Not to mention the current, whatever creatures lie in the deep, and the myriad other horrible things that could happen if he ventures into the sea.

"There's nothing out there," Bodin says harshly. "Face it. We're stuck."

His resolute tone hits me hard. This...this nightmare is real. There's no hope of escape.

"I don't care," Preston insists. "I'm the best swimmer my high school has ever seen. I have to try."

"It's too dangerous," Mama says. "If your parents were here, they wouldn't be happy."

He snorts. "That's what *you* think, because you've got this oh-so-precious relationship with your oh-so-precious princess."

I take an involuntary step backward, stung. Preston can be a jerk, sure. But this is the first time he's been openly hostile toward me.

"Not all parents are like that, okay?" he bites out. "They don't always love their kids. Sometimes, they're tortured by our very existence."

Before we can react, he rips off his polo shirt and runs toward the water. I start after him, but Bodin stops me with his hand.

"If he wants to drown, don't go with him," he murmurs.

I frown. I wasn't about to follow Preston across the sea, but shouldn't we try to stop our Harvard-bound friend from this rash decision, no matter how exasperating he is?

Preston splashes into the water, the salty spray of the waves wetting his shorts. Without hesitation, he dives right in.

Khun Anita mutters under her breath, and Kit pantomimes shooting a basketball—*again*. (Seriously? Read the beach. But the boy's only fourteen, so maybe he gets a pass.) Elizabeth clutches Sylvie's hand, fear plain on her face, while the Ruiz brothers argue about whether they should go after Preston. Rae and Lola are nowhere to be seen.

I exchange a worried look with Mama as Preston's strong, confident strokes slice into the waves. He's traveled a good several yards, but he still appears to be in the shallow depths, judging from the brilliant turquoise color—

CLANG!

My heart jumps along with my feet.

Like a rock hitting a wall—a very strong and sturdy wall— Preston seems to have smashed into…something? Jarred by the hit, his body reels back, and he lurches to his feet in waist-deep water, a hand clasped against his head.

"What is it?" Khun Anita walks into the water, not caring that her long sari is getting wet.

"There's something here. A wall of some sort." Preston slowly reaches out with his hands, testing. Just like Bodin did an hour earlier, he presses his palms against a barrier that does not give. Only, this time, the wall is invisible.

I stare at it and him and the clear horizon that unfurls for miles. The view looks exactly as it should: an idyllic scene of a tropical paradise. But as Preston moves along the "wall," establishing the boundary with his hands, it quickly becomes clear that *something* is preventing us from leaving the immediate vicinity of the beach.

"What *is* it?" I mutter. "Magnets? A force field? Hardened air?"

Bodin shakes his head slowly. "Does it matter, if it turns this island into a prison?"

The last word hits me right in the center of my chest and sinks slowly through my stomach and down to my shoes. A prison. Not heaven. Not only a magical island. But Xander's very own penitentiary from hell.

Not paralyzed by similar thoughts, Khun Anita wades farther into the water until she's by Preston's side. She puts her hand on his arm and gestures back toward the shore.

"Come back, Preston!" Eduardo calls. "You'd have to be the Hulk to smash through that wall. We might be marooned on this magical island, but an Avenger, you are not."

"The captain wants emotional extremes?" Preston asks mockingly. "I'll give him the outlier of human behavior."

He punches the wall with his fist, hard. Once. Twice. Three times. Blood pools at his knuckles, dripping into the water.

"Stop it!" I shriek as Bodin and I run to the water's edge. "It's not going to break."

"Get something sharp, then," Preston snaps. "We're shattering this wall, if I have to die doing it."

I sigh. I'm sorry that he's had a rough life. I'm sorry— more than he'll ever know—that his parents don't love him. I wouldn't be the person I am without Mama believing in me at every turn. But he's not doing himself any favors by being this self-destructive.

Sylvie, apparently, doesn't agree. She grabs what looks like a tree trunk and runs with it into the water. When she nears the barrier, she throws it with all her might, looking like a fierce javelin warrior.

CLANG.

The wood splinters, peeling back in five sections, so that it resembles an overgrown flower. It bounces back, narrowly missing Khun Anita and Preston. Sylvie dives under the water just in time.

They'll give up now. They have to. Whatever objects are strong enough to pierce that magical barrier, we certainly don't have access to them on this beach.

"We have to *dig* underneath the sand," Sylvie suggests. "We can tunnel right below the barrier."

"Great idea!" Preston barks. Maybe he means to be enthusiastic, but he's so frustrated that every word that leaves his mouth sounds angry.

Mateo and Eduardo wade into the water. They even rope Kit into joining them. All five of them—minus Khun Anita, who makes her way back to the beach, her shoulders slumped—disappear under the waves, and clumps of sand begin to arc out of the water and through the air.

Bodin stands on the beach, his hands on his hips, frowning. I can tell he thinks their efforts are pointless—join the club—but he doesn't make a move to stop them.

Which means I shouldn't try, either. We can all think for ourselves out here, and who's to say that my opinion is correct? Besides, the sand is clouding the water, and my stance on things I can't see through is *very* well-defined.

Instead, I walk away, catching up to Mama and Khun Anita. Elizabeth is gone; I wouldn't be surprised if she left in search of Lola.

As the only two people who have unlocked their abilities, they're experiencing this ordeal differently. They're probably more anxious. They've *got* to be more freaked out. I'll have to check on them both later.

The three of us make our way to the shade. I settle down next to the two older women, making sure I crouch down as I walk past so I don't tower over their heads—a simple gesture of respect that I learned as a child.

"Mama?" I say, my throat dry, once Khun Anita lies on

the sand and appears to doze off. Her wet lower body juts out of the shadows and bakes in the sun.

"Yes, my love?" Dark circles tug down her eyes, and her skin looks as fragile, as *rippable*, as tissue paper. And yet, the same steadiness gleams from her pupils. I cling to that. It's the only life preserver I have left on this sandy beach.

"Do you think Papa's on an island like this one?" I ask in a small voice. Now that we know that Xander's engineered this entire nightmare, it seems unlikely that Papa's safe in civilization, working frantically to reach us. Still, I have to ask. "Or do you think he somehow escaped?"

Mama reaches out and smooths a piece of hair behind my ear. My locks are beyond saving—when I touched them this morning, all I felt was a tangled nest—so I know that her aim is to comfort me, rather than groom me.

"Mama, the other side," I whisper.

She smiles kindly, tucking another piece behind my other ear, thereby restoring order in the universe.

"Alaia, I love you with all my heart," she says, "and your eyes are begging me to lie to you, to protect you. I *want* to do that, more than anything." She stops, chews on lips that are beyond chapped. She's had dry lips all of her life, and this deserted-island living isn't helping. "But I won't be on this earth much longer, so I can't coddle you. You have to find a way to be strong without my help. Without my presence."

I wince. I've known this from the moment that Mama's doctors declared her cancer terminal, but I haven't been able to face it.

"I don't know how," I whisper.

"Everything you have to thrive is within you," she says. "All you have to do is find it."

"Kinda like my latent psychic ability?" I manage to joke.

Mama smiles. Twenty-three. About a fifth of the way. I

pray that we live long enough to get to 121. "Exactly like that."

But as lovely as her smile is, in spite of the way it tears me up just to put me back together again, I can tell that she's struggling, too, as she reaches for her next words.

"Papa stayed behind on that yacht," she says quietly, "and Xander had complete control of that vessel, just like he has over this island. If Papa didn't go up in flames when that boat exploded...well, there's a high possibility that he's trapped on an island somewhere, just like us."

"So, he's *not* working with the authorities?" I plead. "He's not going to show up any minute to rescue us?"

I'm not sure what I'm looking for. Mama's already established, long ago, that she won't lie to me. And yet, old habits die hard, and I can't help seeking that one sliver of comfort, that last shred of safety, that comes from Mama's reassurance.

"No, nam phung, he's not."

I close my eyes, the finality of her answer sinking in. It's even more poignant because of the nickname she uses — nam phung, the Thai word for "honey." It's not an actual endearment in Thai, nor is it the American word — but a special blend of two cultures. Just like me.

A growing cacophony of voices drags my eyes open. The digging gang, plus Bodin, are back.

"That was a ridiculous waste of energy," Mateo says, taking his glasses out of a pocket of his cargo shorts and putting them back on.

"It was worth a try," Sylvie argues. Her tanned, toned legs are streaked with mud. "How were we supposed to know that the barrier extended below the sand?"

Turning his back to Sylvie, Eduardo wipes water droplets from his eyes. "We tried. We failed. What's next?"

"A boat," Kit offers. What do you know? He can talk about something other than basketball. "A really fast one that will zip around the island, faster than the wind can follow. We'll race the wall, gaining speed and momentum, until BAM." He pounds a fist into an open palm. "We find an opening and crash right through."

Bodin snorts. "Please. Where are you going to find a motorboat? That's precisely why we're stranded here. Because *there is no boat.*"

Preston advances, getting right up in Bodin's face, so that they're nose to nose. "What the hell's wrong with you? At least the kid's suggesting something. All you do is shoot down our ideas without offering anything in return. It's like you want us to be trapped here."

Bodin shoves Preston in the chest. "Get away from me."

"Try me." Preston pulls back his fist, gearing up for a fight.

I rise to my feet, hands up as though that can ward off the violence. I'd hoped that the physical exercise would wear down Preston's rage. Guess I was wrong.

"That is enough," Khun Anita's authoritative voice thunders. "Stand down, both of you."

"Fighting amongst ourselves will not help," Mama says. "Let's just all take a minute and calm down."

But Preston pays no attention to the oldies. Like a beast has been unleashed, he charges at Bodin, knocking him to the ground. Bodin bucks once, twice, with an almost supernatural strength, dislodging Preston from his body. Once free, Bodin leaps to his feet in one smooth motion, but Preston is too fast for him, throwing a punch that connects with Bodin's lip.

Blood sprays into the air.

My heart drops, and I cry out. "Help him, please!"

The Ruiz brothers spring forward and drag Preston back by his shoulders. That gives Bodin enough time to flip onto his stomach and curl into a ball.

But Preston will not be stopped. He pulls away and continues to pummel Bodin's back, over and over, without thought, without reason. It's as though he's possessed, and the brothers are helpless to shut down the onslaught.

A high-pitched squeak erupts from the group. Startled, Eduardo stops short halfway to Preston, and Mateo looks around wildly. The squeak sounds again, louder and more pained. Preston is thrashing, no longer landing blows on Bodin's back. He stands up and flails like a mouse caught in a trap. The squeak pierces the air, anguished. Desperate. Is the noise…coming from *him*?

The brothers crawl backward, terrified, so that when Preston finally topples to the ground, landing on his butt, there's a circle of space around him, giving us a clear view of his mouth, which has shrunk to the size of a pinhole.

"Well," Bodin says wryly, rolling into a seated position. "I guess that takes care of rations for another day."

CHAPTER THIRTEEN

Squeak. *Squeak.* SQUEAK.

A series of noises erupts from Preston, differing in volume and intensity but nonetheless sounding remarkably similar. He presses his hands over his mouth, then lets go, as though the pressure might somehow turn his mouth back to normal.

Sadly, it doesn't.

I bring my hand to my own mouth in sympathy as we all stare, fascinated.

"Even I know this one," I say, looking at Mama. "Remember? You used to tell this tale to me when I was a kid."

But the lore is nothing like seeing the images come to life before me.

"Morality tales to make young children behave," Mama explains to the others. "If you slapped people around on Earth, you might be reincarnated with hands the size of pancakes. And if you spoke disrespectfully to your parents, you would be reshaped with a pinhole mouth."

"Will it…go away?" Khun Anita's hands flutter up and down. "How will he eat?" She darts a glance at her own grandson, as though to check that *his* mouth has not reformed. But Kit continues pacing around, all six feet of him in motion, as usual.

"I don't know," Mama admits. "In the stories, the transformations are permanent, but this is different. This is real life."

"He can suck up food through a straw," Sylvie suggests. "We can fashion one out of bamboo leaves."

Eduardo wrinkles his forehead. "*If* our next rations include any liquid food items. Whatcha think, buddy?" He nudges Preston's foot gingerly. "Want to slurp up vindaloo through a straw?"

Preston lets loose a string of indignant squeaks. Have to give it to the guy, he's communicating quite well, using only a single sound.

"Maybe they'll bring us nutritious smoothies next time," Sylvie says soothingly.

Preston's squeaks grow louder and more incensed. Guess he's not a fan of smoothies, either.

Khun Anita straightens her yellow sari and pats the black bun of her hair (surprisingly neat, given our island living). After only a day in her presence, I recognize the gesture: she grooms herself when she's about to take charge.

Sure enough, she holds out her hand to Preston, as though he were a child. "Come along. Let's find you a place to relax. If you let the anger flow out of you, you may get your mouth back yet."

Who knows if she's right, but it's as good a theory as any. Preston must think so, too, because he takes Khun Anita's hand and plods away dutifully, leaving the rest of us staring after him.

• • •

By nightfall, Preston's mouth has returned to normal. He sits at the edge of our camp, quiet, withdrawn. *Completely* out of character, but I guess he's afraid to say anything lest his mouth shrinks once more.

The story spreads rapidly among the castaways, and for the most part, we leave him alone, with the more maternal types—Mama, Khun Anita, Elizabeth—swooping down to check on him once in a while. Bodin, on the other hand, steers completely clear of Preston's path.

In the past thirty-six hours, we've made major progress in establishing a livable space. We have two shelters now: the original one, with the palm-frond thatched roof and bamboo floor, and a smaller lean-to, consisting of a frame covered with large fronds. A fire blazes between the two shelters, surrounded by a ring of smooth rocks. It's not exactly professional, but it's not half bad.

Mother Nature herself reigns supreme, injecting beauty into our primitive surroundings. It's a cloudless night—no rain, thank goodness. The long, orange flames of our fire reach into the deep navy sky pierced with stars. With no ambient light, the stars glow like the purest, most brilliant diamonds. They command attention like actors on a stage, with the sky relegated to nothing more than a backdrop.

Why does such exquisite beauty cause a lump to grow in my throat? The sight makes me feel so small, so humble. It makes me think of Papa.

I hug myself. No one's coming for us, now that Xander's revealed our shipwreck to be nothing but a sham. Papa's lost, maybe forever, and Mama has only two days' worth of pills remaining.

"Alaia, check it out." Lola comes up next to me, gesturing down the beach. Three figures approach our camp, carrying dark bundles in their arms, their silver uniforms reflecting in the moonlight.

"Looks like Xander's been watching too much *Squid Game*," she comments.

When Xander's employees come closer, I scrutinize their outfits more carefully. Sure enough, I see the resemblance to the guards on the popular show. Xander's employees wear long-sleeved silver jumpsuits, rather than red, but their black shoes and gloves hide every square inch of skin. Their masks stretch over their heads like a hood, but while the white cloth is fitted along the skull, it is loose and long in front of the face, protruding outward.

"Are they wearing oxygen masks?" I ask Lola, trying to make sense of the bizarre shape.

"That, or they're hiding some facial disfigurement."

I frown. "*All* of them?"

Lola shrugs. "The ones this afternoon were also wearing the same mask."

The sight of the strangers draws the rest of the castaways forward. We all watch in silence as they dump their lumpy packages a safe ten feet from the firepit—presumably our reward from Lola's ability surfacing, as Xander promised—and then, the three of them depart without saying a word.

Sylvie and Kit exchange a look, and then they take off after the guards. This time, however, the guards have less of a head start, so they start running, too. Or rather, they leap into the bushes...and disappear once more.

"What. The. Hell?" Sylvie halts in her tracks. "Everyone, fan out. Search the area. They have to be here, somewhere."

Um. The last thing I want to do is to wander into the dark, creepy woods, with no light and no weapon, where who knows *what* might be lurking. Although—let's be honest, if I had a weapon, I wouldn't have the first idea how to use it.

"Partner up!" Bodin announces. "Pah Moh and Khun

Anita will stay here and tend the fire."

I shoot him an appreciative glance. He's always looking out for Mama, even in the midst of chaos, and for that, I'm grateful.

He must misinterpret my look as an invitation, however, because he comes immediately to my side.

"Wanna be my buddy?" he asks.

All I can do is nod.

We begin to comb the woods to the left of where we lost sight of the guards, since Sylvie and Kit have that area covered. Bodin searches five feet to the right of me, close enough to hear me yell but not so close that we're duplicating our efforts.

I squint into the dark, trying my hardest not to freak out. A few yards into the woods, the night envelops us completely as we leave the warm, *safe* glow of the fire behind.

There are black shapes everywhere. *Branches, tree trunks, and shrubbery*, I tell myself. *Nature's clothes. Nothing scary.* And yet, my imagination shapes them into sharpened claws about to unfurl, vicious teeth snapping at the air, glow-in-the-dark eyes watching, watching…

Wait a minute. That's not my imagination. It's an actual swath of silver fabric.

"Bodin. I found something," I hiss.

He hurries to my side. My shoulder, ever so slightly, brushes against his chest. But this time, it's okay. Both of our bodies are encased in clothing, so it's just fabric pressing up against fabric. No skin-to-skin contact. In this context, under these circumstances, his touch doesn't repulse me. In fact, it comforts me. His solid presence is a reassurance, coaxing my nerves to stay inside my skin.

"It's one of the guard uniforms," he says, holding up the jumpsuit so that it catches a sliver of moonlight. "See the elongated mask by the hood?"

I blink. "Are you saying one of the guards is *naked* out here? How does that help them disappear?"

He shakes his head slowly. He doesn't have any more answers than I do.

And then, I see it. Scaly, reptilian skin. Enormous swishing tail. A definite pair of eyeballs on its flat head.

I scream, jumping into Bodin's arms. That *thing*— whatever it is—retreats into the bush and wriggles away. Still, I continue jamming my face into Bodin's chest, plastering my body against his ribs, his hip, as though I can somehow crawl inside *his* skin, where I'll be safe.

"Shhhh," he says into my hair, his arms cradling me. "It's gone now. It can't hurt you."

I cling to his words. *It can't hurt me, it can't hurt me, it can't hurt me...*

Although his touch can.

Regaining my wits, I wrench myself out of his embrace. What am I doing? Why am I breaking my internal rules, the ones that have protected me and allowed me to survive all of these years?

"I'm so sorry—" I gasp.

"Hey. You once told me I had nothing to be sorry for," he says, his steady eyes holding my gaze. "The same holds true now."

I nod, even as my cheeks flush. I *threw* myself at him. I couldn't have gotten any closer if I'd tried.

We search some more, although this time, I can't bring myself to stand five feet away. However, I'm careful not to touch him again.

We don't find anything else, nor do we encounter any more monsters who might eat us alive, and half an hour later, we've regrouped with the others back at our camp, all of us standing around the fire.

Lola and Mateo found a second silver jumpsuit, but no one else had a close call with a living creature.

Kit suddenly steps to the side and picks up a bundle. In all of the excitement, I had completely forgotten about the packages that Xander's employees dropped off for us. "Sleeping bags!" he whoops. "Water-purification tablets. Toothpaste. Now, that's a reward."

Enthusiastic chatter breaks out as others move forward to claim a sleeping bag. Even Mama smiles—twenty-six. The flames highlight the wrinkles in her paper-thin skin, and she looks like she would benefit from sleeping for a week straight.

"These old bones aren't getting any younger," Khun Anita says, stretching. "This is my cue to turn in."

She waddles forward and picks up the navy nylon material—

"Wait!" Rae shrieks. "We have a problem."

"What is it?" Bodin asks. He hangs back with me, Mama, and a few others.

"Our kind and benevolent captor bequeathed us with only ten sleeping bags," Rae says sourly.

Lola blinks, not understanding. "But there's twelve of us."

"There's no way it was a mistake." I look first at Mama, then at Bodin, for confirmation. "He knows each of our favorite foods. He wouldn't have accidentally sent the wrong number of sleeping bags."

"Precisely," Rae says, but her eyes hold no bitterness. Only defeat.

"He did this on purpose." The realization hits me, and my knees go weak. "This is his way of creating conflict. He *wants* us to fight over the sleeping bags, so that another one of us will manifest our ability."

"Well, screw him," Rae says. "I'm not one to be patient.

You can ask my sister"—Lola nods extra vigorously, at which Rae rolls her eyes—"but I'm about to keep this anger buttoned up. I refuse to give him the satisfaction. So, I don't want *anyone* bickering over the sleeping bags, you hear?"

Bodin steps forward, into the ring of firelight. The bruises on his face are turning purple, both of his eyes rimmed with black. "Look, we're all mature enough not to devolve into brawling," he says unironically, even though his bruises must still hurt. I can't even look at him without wincing.

"But have you thought about just playing Xander's game?" Bodin continues. "Three of our abilities have surfaced. Maybe the rest of us should focus on pushing ourselves emotionally so that we can bring our abilities forward, and then we can get outta here."

"Um, sorry, dude." Rae crosses her arms, not sorry at all. "I think you mean well, but I, for one, don't understand your relationship with our captor—"

"We don't *have* a relationship," Bodin interjects. "He betrayed and tricked me, just like the rest of you."

His words hang in the air, igniting a current of suspicion. Even though it feels like a million years have passed since I first set foot on the yacht yesterday morning, we haven't known each other for a full two days. Trust has yet to be established.

"No offense," Elizabeth says, "but are we supposed to just believe you?" She might be soft-spoken and kind, but strength underlines her voice just the same.

"How are we supposed to believe *anybody*?" Bodin rakes a hand through his overlong hair. "All of us here could have some kind of connection with him. I mean, Lola's into fashion, right? Maybe she's working as Xander's stylist."

Lola's mouth drops comically. "You think *I* came up with those hideous silver jumpsuits? And Xander's wrinkled, hasn't-showered-for-a-week attire?" She shudders. "Please tell me you have more respect for me than *that*."

"That's my point," Bodin says. "It's preposterous."

"It's not Bodin's fault he worked for the worst employer on the planet," Mama says. "He's been nothing but helpful since we woke up on this island."

Rae waves away her words. "Look. It really doesn't matter. There's still oh, about a zero chance in hell that I'm going to let myself be manipulated by our so-called captain. And that means I'm not playing his game."

"Even if that's our only way out?" Bodin protests. "Xander promised—if all twelve of us manifest our abilities, he'll let us go."

"Where have you been? Hiding under a rock? Have you watched a single movie in the last two decades?" Preston bursts out and then slaps a hand over his mouth, his eyes bulging. He lowers his hand cautiously. "How's my mouth? Am I actually saying these words, or are they in my head?"

"You're good, man." Eduardo pats his shoulder.

Mateo speaks up. "Preston's right. We have no guarantee that the captain will do what he says."

"He'll never let us go," Elizabeth chimes in as she clutches Sylvie's hand. "It's too dangerous for him. Any one of us could go to the authorities. He could be hunted down. Sure, it's a fantastical story, and maybe no one would believe us. But what if someone did? It's much safer for him to lock us away in a dungeon for the rest of our lives, or even worse—"

"Kill us," Sylvie finishes grimly.

"No, thank you." Rae shakes her head. "I'm not about to give up the only leverage I have. I say we get some rest, and we figure out a way off this island in the morning." She sighs. "If only one of you had developed an ability that could actually help us, like flying. These passive talents are next to useless." She stops, her mouth still open as though she's realized what she's just said.

"No offense," she offers weakly, but the damage has already been done.

"Well, I guess if I'm so useless, then I might as well go to sleep," Lola says, snatching up a sleeping bag. "As my sister so nicely implied, I'm contributing next to nothing with my presence."

Worms drop out of her mouth in twos and threes, falling to the sand and burrowing in it.

I should scream. I recognize that in myself. But I've seen the worms so many times, I'm actually getting numb to the sight. Amazing.

"I didn't mean—" Rae holds up her hand, but Lola ignores her sister.

She grabs two more rolls from the pile and tosses them at Elizabeth and Preston. "You two also get a sleeping bag, since our useless talents are what provided these rations to begin with. And you." She throws a sleeping bag at Sylvie. "You get one because you said the flowers I wove into my braids are cute, when everyone else was just focusing on my worms."

Lola marches off, with Elizabeth meekly following her, Preston aggressively stomping, and Sylvie bringing up the rear.

The pile of sleeping bags is limited—and quickly dwindling. Six bags remain, to be divvied up among the eight of us.

"I volunteer to sleep on the sand," Mama says quickly, "so long as Alaia gets a sleeping bag."

"Oh, sweetie, you don't have to do that," Khun Anita interjects. "I'm sure one of these men…"

"Will what?" Eduardo scowls. "Volunteer to trade in our

comfort just because we have a Y chromosome?"

"Well, yes," Khun Anita says, taken aback.

"No thanks, Grandma." Eduardo stuffs a roll under his arm. "I spent most of last night on the edge of the shelter, getting soaked by the rain. I'm due some comfort as well." He stalks off.

Khun Anita turns to her grandson. "Kit—"

But it's too late. The fourteen-year-old seizes not one but *two* sleeping bags and hightails it to the shelter. "It's every person for themselves, Nani. I'll save you a spot."

Three bags left. Rae, Mateo, Bodin, Mama, and I remain.

"Pah Moh gets a sleeping bag *and* a spot under the shelter," Rae says. Mama starts to argue, and Rae holds up her hand. "That's nonnegotiable. We might be young, but we're not completely without respect." She looks at Mateo and Bodin, who nod quickly.

"I'll be bold and take one, as well," Rae adds with a saucy grin. "I'll leave it among the three of you to fight over the last one."

"Alaia needs—" Mama starts to say.

"I'm fine," I cut her off, even though I don't mean it, humiliation blazing my cheeks. "You go ahead."

Mama hesitates, as though torn between protecting me and accommodating my OCD, but then she joins the others under the shelter.

I can't look at the boys. I have been coddled all of my life, being a neurodivergent only child. I live in a certain bubble, protected by Mama and Papa from a disordered world. As I grew older, I realized the kind of burden my dependence was putting on my parents, especially Mama. It's strange: most kids crave independence from their parents, but to me, they're safety. When I'm with them, it feels like things can't go wrong. And that's all I ever crave, really. For things to feel *right*.

But, well... I'm ashamed of hiding behind Mama's protective shield. I'm ashamed that I'm not my own person. I'm ashamed that I haven't tried harder to be independent. I'm ashamed that I can't even speak up to claim a bedroll, even though sleeping without one is unfathomable.

The truth is, sometimes my OCD has its claws so twisted up with my soul that I can't tell where it ends and I begin. I can't tell what parts are really me—and what parts are my mental disorder. I rely on my parents so much because I don't know if I can trust myself. And that is the biggest shame of all: because if I can't trust myself, then what will become of me when Mama's gone?

"Don't worry about it, Alaia," Bodin says, misinterpreting my expression. "You can have the sleeping bag. I don't mind sleeping on the ground. Whatcha think, Mateo?"

"I agree one hundred," Mateo says, a dimple flashing in his cheek. "It's the least I can do to make up for my brother being a boor."

Relief floods through me, even if a different shame cuts through that feeling. I got the sleeping bag without having to beg for it—but only because I took advantage of the generosity of these two guys. I can't dwell on that part, however. Because procuring a sleeping bag is only the first hurdle. All of the spots underneath the main shelter *and* the lean-to are now full. I feel bad enough that I didn't volunteer to give up the sleeping bag. I can hardly insist that someone, probably Mama, sacrifice, so that I can sleep elevated off the sand. And thus, the second, and more important, hurdle remains. How on earth am I going to sleep on the ground with just the thin barrier of a nylon bedroll?

CHAPTER FOURTEEN

The sand rolls out to the water, most of it shrouded by the black night, with who knows what lurking beneath its surface. Crabs? Baby turtles? Countless species of insects?

I swallow hard. What was I thinking? I could probably handle crabs or turtles. And other than Lola's worms, I haven't seen any bugs on this island. Whatever magic is keeping the fish away must apply to insect life as well. And yet, it's not like me to willingly lay my body—my face!—on the ground, even if they are protected by a sleeping bag.

I can't… I can't do this. I wanted to be brave. I wanted to sacrifice for Mama, like she's done for me all of her life. But it's dirty down in the sand. It *doesn't feel right* down in that sand. The sand will knock me off the delicate, precarious balance that I spend my life building.

An overwhelming sense of paralysis floods me. *I can't, I can't, I can't.* My two favorite words of the English language. At least, that's what Mama told me once in a moment of frustration, during one of my meltdowns.

It might've been when I refused to get on the airplane,

right before my cousin's wedding, because my OCD told me it wasn't safe. Or maybe it was when I wouldn't lay down on a hotel bed because I was certain the sheets were dirty.

Mama tries to be patient. I know that. She tries as much as humanly possible, but she has her limits, too. Her face swims in my vision: the kind, tapered eyes; her strong, flared nose. And a rush of love tries to push out the intrusive, meddling thoughts.

Do this for her. Get a handle on yourself, take charge of these obsessions, for Mama.

No. I can practically hear Mama shouting. *Don't do it for me. I won't be here much longer. Do it for yourself.*

If only I knew how.

"Alaia?"

I open my eyes, unclench my teeth. Bodin hovers near me, his cheeks pinched with concern. His head blocks most of the midnight sky, and the glow of the fire warms his face. Mateo plopped himself on the sand next to the shelter, where Lola was sleeping, and Bodin and I decided that the spot next to the fire was the best place to sleep. Me, because the flame would warm my cold extremities. Bodin, so that he can also keep the fire going throughout the night.

"Are you okay?" he asks.

I give him a shaky smile. "I, um, don't like sleeping on the ground." Understatement of the century. "But it should be okay, since I have the sleeping bag. That should protect me from all the, uh, *sandiness*. It's almost like sleeping in a bed. Really." The false reassurance is more for my benefit than his.

"But you did it before," Bodin points out. "The first day we were here. We all woke up in the sand."

Ah, that's the crux of the problem. My OCD doesn't respond to reason or logic. It's a feeling, a compulsion, an urgent need inside me. It's a black hole of emotion sucking me down its vortex, and I can't control it until I claw and scratch my way out—

"If you're that worried, you can always use my stomach as a pillow," Bodin says.

The words are so outrageous that my swirling, repetitive, run-on thoughts screech to a halt.

"Wh—what?" I stutter.

"My abs. You can lay your head on them." To demonstrate, Bodin stretches out his long frame directly onto the sand. No sleeping bag whatsoever. I don't know how he can stand it.

He then lifts up his shirt and pats his stomach. Even in the moonlight, I can see the distinct lines of his six-pack.

"Um." I try to string together a coherent thought. "No, thank you."

"You're right." Bodin sits up, and his shirt slides back into place, thank goodness. Being this close to his bare skin is scrambling my brain. "I wouldn't want to put my head on this slab of rock, either. It would be like trying to sleep on granite."

He grins, and I can't stop myself from mirroring his lips. That smile is infectious, even if I feel awkward standing here while he's sitting.

Bodin furrows his brows, thinking hard. "I know. Maybe my chest can serve as your pillow." As soon as the words leave his mouth, though, he's shaking his head. "Nah, that would never work. Have you *seen* the size of these pecs?" Cartoonishly, he makes his pecs bounce. "I would never subject you to such torture."

I giggle. Bodin's got a lean, ropy frame with plenty of muscle—but a body builder, he is not.

He shakes his head mournfully. "I didn't want it to come to this, but a guy's gotta do what a guy's gotta do. Because I am a gentleman, and because it might be the only soft part of this well-honed body…" He pauses dramatically. "I will offer my butt as a pillow."

I burst out laughing. If Bodin was trying to distract me from my emotions, mission accomplished. He pulled me out of myself and grounded me in the physical world. I carefully lay out my sleeping bag and sit down on it, making sure not a single grain of sand touches me.

"Gee, let me think." I tilt my head, pretending to give his offer deep thought. "I'll take my chances with my sleeping bag, thank you very much."

"You wound me." Bodin clutches at his heart. "What's the problem? Is my butt not big enough? I demand a critique."

This is the most ridiculous conversation I've ever had. "Your butt's fine."

He grins slyly. "Why, Alaia. Is this your way of telling me that you've been checking out my backside?"

This sends me into another fit of giggles. "No. Of course not." I barely get out, and he just sits in the sand, beaming at me.

"You feeling better?" he asks when I finally stop laughing.

Now that I'm more relaxed, I can actually follow the three-step process for dismantling an OCD thought: identify it, label the thought distortion, and disprove the thought with counterarguments.

This is just sand. It can't hurt me. I slept on it yesterday morning, and nothing happened. More importantly: my sleeping bag acts as a protective barrier.

Tentatively, I lay back, making sure there's a few inches of sleeping bag above my head, and it's not bad. I curl up on my side, safety established.

"Yes, I do feel better. Thank you," I say.

"Anytime." He turns toward me, mimicking my form—curled up, with a hand tucked under my chin. Intentionally or not, he remains a good five or six feet away, for which I'm grateful. I don't think I could handle his proximity if he were any closer.

I should be nervous right now. I should not know what to do with my hands. I should be worrying about my breath, even though I used some of my toothpaste earlier, since Xander had bequeathed us with more.

And I *am* all of those things—but more than anything, I feel comfortable.

The faint murmur of conversation drifting from the shelter has died down. The only things we can hear are the wind rustling the leaves and the occasional grunt of someone shifting.

"Can I ask you something?" Bodin's voice is hardly more than a whisper. "Do you feel the same way as Rae?"

"Doubtful," I say wryly, "since she and I are pretty much opposites. She's brave, I'm meek. And so on and so on."

"I mean, do you agree with her about not playing Xander's game?"

"It doesn't bother me too much to be a pawn," I say slowly. "If it gets Mama and me home safely, I'll happily be manipulated by him. But I can't play Xander's game for another reason."

My throat thickens, my eyes sting—the classic signs that I'm about to cry. But I've already freaked out once during this conversation. If I'm striving to be strong and independent, I need to get my easily triggered tears under control.

"Mama's pills," I blurt out. "She only has two days left. Even if Xander is telling the truth, I doubt we're getting out of here before they run out." I rise up on my elbow and twist around. The shadowed bodies under the shelter remain still. I can't tell which one is Mama, but no movement is a good thing. No movement hopefully means that she's resting.

"She's already fading fast," I continue in a low voice. "Without her medication, she'll get even sicker." I squeeze my hands into fists, my nails digging into my palms. "All Mama wants is to die in peace. That's why we're in Koh Samui. She didn't want to waste away in some hospice. She wants to pass with beauty all around her, surrounded by the people she loves best—Papa and me." I take a deep breath. "If three of us come into our abilities every two days, then it will be another six days before we can expect to go home. We've got to get off this island sooner."

Bodin nods, and then it's his turn to roll onto his back. He laces his fingers behind his head and stares up at the stars.

"It's possible that I've been to this island before, on another charter with the captain," he says and then stops. "Some of the foliage, the vegetation, seems familiar. So does the view: miles of water in every direction, with no land in sight." He stops again. I want to reach into his throat and drag out the words, but Bodin is relaying this revelation on his own time.

"If I *have* been here, we must have visited the *other* side of the island, because that's where the people were. Pop-up stands serving smoothies and fresh coconuts. Vendors selling meat on skewers and bamboo baskets of sticky rice."

"Civilization," I say in an awed voice. "Wifi. *Help*."

Bodin gestures toward the mountain range that rises majestically behind the forest of trees. "I think our way off the island is on the other side of that mountain range."

My pulse leaps. "Let's go wake the others, gather up our supplies. We *have* to try to get around that wall again—"

A loud snort cuts me off. A bear? That reptile-like animal I saw earlier? But no. It's just Preston rolling onto his other side. The bamboo poles rattle as though they might break, but a few seconds later, he starts snoring—loud, guttural growls that sound like a broken engine.

At least his pinhole mouth hasn't returned.

"It's too late to set out now," Bodin says gently, and my shoulders droop. He's right, of course. "If we head west, we might be able to find a section of the mountain that's not walled off. But we're not doing that in the dark, and we'll need our rest. We'll head out first thing tomorrow."

"Tomorrow," I echo. It's the most promising thing I've heard since I woke up on this hellish paradise a day and a half ago.

CHAPTER FIFTEEN

The smells wake me up. Fried, eggy bread, maple syrup—the good stuff, not the kind that's more sugar than syrup. At first, I think I'm dreaming of my favorite breakfast, so I snuggle deeper into the nylon bedroll. But then, my eyes pop open.

Those scents aren't the hazy, fleeting senses of a dream. My nose tingles; my mouth waters. This is vivid, present, *real.* So, either Elizabeth's been creating smells again—or Xander's restocked our food rations overnight.

I jump up, brushing off my skin in case of any sand. Luckily, the sleeping bag seems to have done its job, and I don't find a single grain. No Bodin across from me. All that's left of him is a big, comma-like indentation in the sand.

The other castaways begin rousing. Lola shrieks and runs to the banquet table. "Shrimp and grits. My absolute fav. Thank you, thank you, Preston, for being a complete jerk."

A waterfall of flowers drifts from her mouth, along with an errant worm, as though her ability doesn't know what to make of the backhanded compliment.

I walk toward the table, too, at a much slower pace. Sure enough, the banquet table has been refreshed. I dish up a bowl of jok, or congee, and bring it over to Mama.

"Oh, nam phung, you shouldn't have," Mama says tiredly. She's the only castaway yet to get up, although she is wide awake. I help her to a seated position, rolling up her sleeping bag and tucking it behind her to prop her up.

She's…weaker than yesterday. Her eyes shine out at me, but her lips don't curve. Is she still exhausted? Too sickly? Will she ever reach 121 smiles?

Shakily, I count out her morning pills from the fanny pack that's always at her side. All of a sudden, the scents of the banquet make me want to throw up. Mama only has one more day of pills left.

"How was your night?" Mama asks. "I meant to stay awake in case you needed me, but I must've drifted off." She shakes her head, disgusted. "I don't know what's wrong with me."

"You're sick," I say, my heart cracking. I want to dig a hole, right in this sand, so that I can stick my head in it and hide forever from the obvious. But I lick my lips and push forward. "You need to rest as much as you can. Don't waste energy worrying about me. I'm fine, Mama. I promise. My OCD has barely bothered me since we woke up on this island. I guess I've been too preoccupied with surviving."

Not true. While OCD is a strange disorder—and it tends to abate when my mind is preoccupied with another ailment, such as a sprained ankle or the flu—it has clearly continued to infiltrate my mind. Last night was a case in point. But I don't need to tell Mama that.

"Thank you, Alaia. You're my baby. You know that?" She spoons some jok into her mouth, just two or three broken grains of rice, really. It hardly counts as sustenance, but at least she's trying, even if it's only for my benefit.

"And you're my Mama," I respond.

I join the others at the buffet. Bodin has reappeared, his hair tousled and his eyelids heavy. He gives me a sleepy, what-up head nod, and my insides sizzle, although I don't know *why*. Mateo and I both reach for the strawberries, and gentleman that he is, he lets me go first. And Preston, whose mouth remains normal, is carefully cutting up his eggs Benedict and eating them daintily.

I take my first bite of French toast. It's rich and syrupy and perfect, but I can't savor it. Because something's wrong, and it's been wrong ever since I woke up this morning.

And I'm just now realizing it.

I march over to Bodin and beckon him to follow me to the center of the beach, away from the others.

"Why, Alaia, I can't wait to get my hands on you, too, but everyone's watching, including your mom," he jokes.

"Cameras," I say, ignoring him. "They're watching our every move."

Bodin blinks. "Huh?"

"Xander's watching us, right? It could be cameras. It could be his employees. It could be a favorite perch in a tree. How on earth are we going to attempt to cross the mountain range without them noticing?"

"I've already thought of that." He straightens, probably because of the crick in his neck from talking to me. "I haven't seen any cameras, have you? And we've pretty much tossed this area upside-down in building our shelters."

I nod in agreement.

"There's no way he's got enough people to monitor this entire island," Bodin continues. "And I really don't think he expects us to venture far from camp. That's why he plies us with our favorite foods, because he thinks it'll keep us trapped here, like a bunch of stray dogs. A small group of us just needs to slip away. It'll be hours before they notice us missing, and maybe by then, we'll have reached the other side."

I frown. "I don't like it. We're counting on a whole lot of assumptions here."

"That's all we've got," he says grimly. His eyes glint, no longer sleepy but focused and determined. "It's not the most foolproof plan ever, but it's our only plan. They'll either apprehend us—or they won't. In the worst-case scenario, we'll be right back where we started."

I nod reluctantly. A small chance is better than none, and if a glimmer of hope exists that Mama can find peace before she dies, I'll take the risk, every time.

"A *small group* is not five people out of twelve!" Eduardo exclaims a short while later. "It's just math, people. That's nearly half. You don't think Xander will notice that half of us are missing?"

"It's just the way it works out," Rae says, her hands on her hips once more. The vibrant greens, pinks, and teals of her tattoos shimmer in the sunlight. Upon closer examination, a naga snakes down one arm, while vines holding lotus flowers climb up the other. Stunning artwork, really. "Bodin is our best choice to navigate this environment. Sylvie's our best climber. I need to keep an eye on things, and there's no way in *hell* I'm leaving Mateo here with my sister—"

"You act like I've never kissed anyone before," Lola grumbles.

Mateo reddens. "Listen, I would never treat your sister with disrespect—"

"If we're about to perish at Xander's hands?" Lola interjects. "Hell, yes, we'd be making the most of our last moments on Earth." Several flowers drift out of her mouth. "See, even my talent agrees."

Khun Anita pretends to cover Kit's ears. *He* flushes and knocks away her hands while Elizabeth doubles up in laughter.

"And I haven't even mentioned our resident princess," Rae continues as if no one else has spoken, "who *insists* on coming, even though no one is sure why."

She's talking about me, of course. I'm not the most obvious choice to traverse the mountain—I know that. I'm not particularly athletic, and I've never been the outdoorsy type. I'm deathly afraid of bugs, so I may very well be more of a hindrance than a help. But none of that matters. Mama's *my* responsibility. I will not sit around while others do the hard work of saving her.

As embarrassing as it is to admit, that's what I've been doing all of my life. I may not be the helpless princess that Rae believes I am...but her accusation holds a glimmer of truth. Which means it's time to change. I just hope my newfound strength isn't too late.

"It will take all five of us to figure out a way around that vertical wall," Bodin says firmly, shutting down any further arguments. "The rest of you will just have to be *extra* active so they don't notice for a few hours."

Kit nods solemnly. "Not a problem, bro. Nani says I have the energy of three teenage boys—"

"Bro," Sylvie interjects, but I know it's just her way of saying goodbye to him.

I give Mama a final tearful hug, and then we set off, our backpacks stuffed with the supplies we think we'll need. Bodin leads the way, heading west, swatting the bushes ahead with a long stick to scare any wild animals away. There isn't any wildlife near our beach—other than the creature I saw—but that doesn't mean they won't pop up as we get farther from camp. Bodin remembers the other side of the island teeming with life—birds, monkeys, tons of fish.

I strain my ears, but I don't detect any squeaks or chirps. Just the heavy plodding of our feet as we move deeper into the woods. "Who's been rock climbing before?" Sylvie asks, breaking the group's silence.

Rae whips her head around, her bleached hair subdued by the shadows. "Shhh!"

"Oh, please. We're already making so much noise. A little conversation can't hurt." Sylvie dismisses Rae's admonition with a confidence that I can't help but envy.

"I've climbed all the big ones," she continues. Her toned calves flash in front of me, as though confirming her statement. "Yosemite National Park; Kalymnos, Greece; Dolomites, Italy."

"Is there anything you don't do?" I ask admiringly.

"The more extreme the sport, the more likely it is that I've tried it," Sylvie answers cheerfully.

"I go to the climbing gym. I even have my belay license," Mateo says, coming to stand next to me. He pushes a hand through his dark hair, making it stand up in spikes. It's stiff with what I assume to be salt water, rather than the hair products we are sadly without. "So if you need a helping hand—literally—I'm here."

I smile at him gratefully. No wonder Lola is so taken with him. He's genuinely a good guy.

We push deeper into the woods, and soon enough, we're doing more clambering than walking, as the terrain becomes steeper and more slippery. It rises at a forty-five-degree angle and is covered in undergrowth or exposed tree roots. One wrong step, and you could sprain an ankle, or worse, tumble down the incline.

"I've got lead," Sylvie announces. She practically scampers up the slope, as though she were a mountain goat in a previous life.

I bite my lip and move, oh, about ten times slower, as I pick and choose my next step. I've travelled through these woods before, when we first ran after the guards, but we're taking an entirely different trail in an entirely different direction today—one that is *way* more treacherous. I'm just contemplating whether a smoothish rock or a mess of roots is sturdier when Sylvie yelps. Her arms flail wildly, and she slides down several feet and crashes into Bodin.

He catches her, stopping her fall before she knocks down the rest of us. His arms are wrapped all the way around her waist, and they hold their position, panting and leaning against each other for support.

A twinge of *something* goes through me. I'm not jealous—I don't think. Sylvie has a girlfriend, and the purpose of Bodin's embrace is clearly to prevent an accident. And yet, seeing him making close contact with another somehow makes *me* want to experience that same contact. Which is beyond weird. After a minute, they untangle their limbs and straighten up.

"This terrain isn't the same as what I expected." Bodin frowns, his words shadowed with doubt. "Maybe...I made a mistake."

"You were wrong about the terrain, or you were wrong about this island?" Rae snaps. You would think she'd have learned from Preston that taking a nasty tone isn't wise. "Maybe you've never been here at all. Maybe that was just wishful thinking, or I don't know, just a *really* bad sense of geography."

Yikes—now she's getting personal.

"How would you know if it's the same island, anyhow?" Rae continues, hip jutted out. "Don't they all look the same? Same sand, same vegetation, same freaking view, since all we can see is water for miles on end."

"It's the same island," Bodin insists, as though her skepticism is shoring up his confidence. "I think."

"Look—we're here now," Mateo says. "Whether or not this is the same island, it doesn't hurt to keep going."

"Fine," Rae says shortly. "But we'd better ask Alaia if she wants to call it quits. I'm sure one of you boys would fall all over yourselves to escort the princess home."

I suck in air sharply. Why does she have to bring *me* into this conversation? I haven't said a single word.

"I haven't complained once," I point out. "Besides, for someone who doesn't want to play Xander's game, you sure are getting emotional."

Where this bravado comes from, I have no idea, but I decide to revel in it, because it has wiped the smirk right off Rae's face.

"Are you sure, Alaia?" Bodin asks. "This isn't the terrain that I expected. It could get ugly up there."

Him, too? Now *that* hits directly, in a way that Rae's put-down never could. I'd hoped he had more belief in me than that.

"I said I'm staying," I repeat, annoyed.

"She's got this," Mateo says encouragingly.

Sylvie nods. "Alaia's a tough one."

I shoot her a grateful look and give Mateo an even bigger smile.

He extends his hand, offering me help up the incline. I hesitate, but my OCD doesn't surge to the surface. It doesn't tell me that his hand is dirty. It doesn't predict that touching him will lead to bad things.

Maybe it's because the contact is functional, rather than incidental, or maybe it's just because Mateo radiates warmth.

"Let's get going, then," Bodin says gruffly. His eyes are focused directly on Mateo—or more specifically on the hand that pulled me up the terrain.

And in his gaze I see a hint of sadness that I don't understand. If he were jealous, I'd get it. That's what I kinda, sorta felt when his arms were around Sylvie. But sadness? Why?

I shake my head, pushing the thoughts away. The lack of nutrition is probably making me overthink and overanalyze, even more than usual.

Bodin turns and nods at Sylvie to take the lead. My face heats as we continue up the mountainside. I'm so silly. Bodin and I didn't kiss last night. We didn't spend the night in each other's arms.

All we did was lie next to each other, five feet apart, as the fire burned behind us—or rather, behind *me*. It didn't escape my notice that he gave me the spot closer to the flame.

But that was just…polite. The manners of a good guy. It didn't mean that we had any kind of special connection, and so he *wouldn't* be looking at me in any sort of way.

I'm so confused. I've never understood boys, and I'm not about to try now when I should be focused on surviving.

And then another thought creeps into my mind. Mateo offered me his hand, and I accepted it with my right hand, leaving my left one lonely.

A cold river fills my veins as once again the universe shifts and I have to rebalance it.

I drop back to where Mateo is climbing. I've become good at this. It's quite awkward to simply just touch someone for no reason, so you need a good excuse. Something believable and innocent enough that the person will forget it the next moment.

"Thanks for helping me out back there," I say casually.

"No problem," he responds.

"Yeah, I've never really climbed before," I admit with a small smile.

"These aren't the best of circumstances, but climbing can be quite fun when you're not doing it to save your life," he says.

I pretend to giggle to keep the mood light, and that's when I go in for the kill.

"Oh, you have something on your shoulder," I say. Gently, I swat his shoulder with my *left* hand, thereby restoring the order inside of me.

"Thanks," is all he says. We start climbing again, and pretty soon, he outpaces me.

When I next glance up, the mountain rises…higher…and higher…and higher. The height spooks me beyond belief. The never-ending expanse of jagged gray stone intimidates me to my very core, but it's even worse when I climb up the rest of the slope to join my fellow castaways.

We've hit another wall.

CHAPTER SIXTEEN

The wall has the same burnished red stone, the same smooth facade without a single crack. What's worse, we've climbed so far west that we can see that it extends all the way to the edge of the island.

"Damn it." Sylvie kicks the wall with her sneakered foot and immediately starts hopping up and down. "Ow, ow, ow!"

"Serves you right," Mateo says blandly. "What did the wall ever do to you?"

They start bickering, but I block out the noise because something glints at the top of a tree next to the wall. I squint. If I'm not mistaken, it's a palm frond…encased in gold.

"Look." I point up. "A golden palm frond. In the folktale, a palm leaf opened up the cave behind the wall, right? Well, what if *that* is our key to crossing this wall?"

"That would make sense," Rae muses. "If Xander manufactured this wall, then it certainly is *not* the legendary hidden city. But he could be so obsessed with the mythology that he fashioned a key out of a palm leaf."

"It's so high up, though," Bodin says. "How are we going

to reach it?"

"Pffft." Rae shakes her head. "Count me out. I'm terrified of heights."

"You are?" I crease my brow. "Then why did you volunteer for this expedition?"

She examines her black nail polish, which is beyond chipped. "To prove to myself that *I* control my life. Not fear."

Um, wow. Rae and I have more in common than I thought. Who would've guessed?

"I could probably make it up this tree," Sylvie muses, eyeing the tree trunk with its protruding knobs and branches. "I climbed more difficult obstacles than this during my *Ninja Warrior* years."

"Not happening," Bodin says flatly. "I don't care if you were the Last Ninja Standing. You're not climbing that tree."

"I was competitive," Sylvie protests. "I made it to the semifinals two years in a row."

"I'm impressed," Bodin says. "Truly. But we have no equipment here. No safety pads, no harnesses, no medics. We can't guarantee your safety, and you aren't breaking your neck on my watch. Or even if you only break your leg, how are we supposed to carry you down?"

"It's just like bouldering," Sylvie counters, bending down and tightening her shoelaces. "It's my life and my choice, and I've decided."

Before any of us can react, she takes a running leap toward the tree and begins to shimmy up.

"Sylvie, wait," I say, alarmed. "Please. I didn't think it through. It might be too dangerous. I don't want you to get hurt."

She grunts to acknowledge that she's heard me. But she doesn't stop.

I want to physically drag Sylvie off the tree and shake

out her misguided bravery. I admire her nobleness, but if she really wants to help the group, she needs to stay alive. But short of leaping on top of her, so that we *both* tumble to the ground, I'm not sure what I can do.

We all watch, the atmosphere stiff with tension, as Sylvie disappears into the leaves. A few seconds later, she reappears, perched on a wobbly branch. Her muscles tight with concentration, she edges out onto the branch, farther and farther.

Please don't fall. Please don't fall. Please don't fall.

All of a sudden, she turns and looks down at us. "This branch is shaking under my feet," she calls. "And the ones higher up are even thinner. I don't think it will support my weight. But I have to try."

"No, Sylvie, don't!" Mateo yells. "It's not worth your life."

Apparently, she disagrees. She reaches up her hand...

...and a loud crack splinters the air.

No, no, no.

My heart screams as the four of us charge forward in a pathetic attempt to break Sylvie's fall. But she's still above us, hanging onto a branch. The crack sounds again, and an enormous dark mass descends upon her.

The black mass stops by Sylvie's head, kinda, sorta... hovering? What?

Are those...birds? Impossible. I've never seen a bird that large. But then my eyes focus, and that mass is a flock of black birds, all right. The loud cracks must be their wings beating against the air. They flutter around Sylvie's body, their feet outstretched to grab onto her. Their wings beat wildly, and they lift into the air.

My heart thunders. Are they kidnapping her? Suffocating her inside their wings?

But just as I'm about to hyperventilate with the panic,

the birds slowly, gently, and surely lower Sylvie to the ground.

I fall to my knees, confused but weak with relief. She's alive—and seemingly unhurt.

As Sylvie straightens, the birds circle over our heads, the wings sending down a draft that stirs up the dirt. A sweet, musty smell also drifts down—an avian scent, a scent of wildlife, one that I haven't detected since I woke up on this island.

"Thank you, friends," Sylvie says, her cheeks red. "I owe you one."

I frown. She's thanking us? But we didn't do anything.

The birds bob up and down, almost as though they're bowing. With one last circle in the air, they lift into the sky and disperse, leaving us humans gaping after them.

"Holy crap! Were you talking to the birds?" I ask.

Mateo crushes Sylvie in a hug. "You're okay," he gasps in between sobs. "You're okay. Thank goodness."

She hugs him back tightly.

Guilt rushes through me. Mateo and Sylvie aren't particularly close. They know each other about as well as anyone else. Not like me. I bonded with Sylvie our first night. She and Elizabeth and Mama and I traded stories for hours. *I* should've been the first person to hug her.

But I've never been good at making the first move. If I wait, if I let *them* act first, then I can't be rejected. Right?

Sylvie catches my eye over Mateo's shoulder and reaches out her hand. That's all the encouragement I need. I push aside the intrusive thoughts and react from pure emotion, encasing Sylvie, and parts of Mateo, in a hug. Rae runs up and throws her arms around us, and then Bodin comes forward, too.

All of a sudden, I'm experiencing my very first group hug. My back molds against Bodin's chest, and my cheek nestles on Sylvie's shoulder. My hands grip Mateo's arms, and Rae's nails rake along my skin.

I'd always assumed that I would hate group hugs, given my aversion to touch. But it's actually kinda nice. We're all smushed together, so there's no judgment, only joy. More importantly, it renders my need for symmetry moot. With all of our limbs tangled together, I don't have to worry if my left and right sides are balanced.

And then, everyone begins speaking at once.

"I'm so glad you're safe," Bodin says.

Rae lifts her brows. "Did you snag the golden key?"

"How did you get the birds to come help you?" Mateo asks.

"Talking to animals like a Disney princess? We should call you Sylvie-ella," I say jokingly.

Sylvie half laughs and half cries. "I might be able to answer some of your questions if you let me breathe."

Slowly, we break apart. I know why *I'm* hesitating. This might be the first time that I've truly felt like I belonged in a group. I hugged these people—and I didn't even freak out. I don't know when—if ever—I'll feel this way again.

Sylvie's white sports shirt is streaked with dust. There are leaves in her hair and tear tracks through the dirt on her cheeks. But she's still standing, tall and strong. Most importantly, she's holding a single long, thin golden leaf.

"It was the strangest thing," she says wonderingly. "I heard a noise when I was out on the branch. I turned and locked eyes with this sleek, black bird perched in the tree." She shakes her head. "I don't know why I did what I did next. It felt like instinct. I couldn't reach the golden frond. And so, I pleaded with the bird to help me."

"What's more amazing is that it actually listened—and recruited its friends," Mateo marvels. "There *is* wildlife on this island. Just not around our beach."

"You can talk to animals!" I exclaim. "That must be your latent ability. There's nothing more stressful than being an inch away from your goal—and not being able to reach it."

"She's right," Rae says, her eyes widening. "That power is all over the folktales."

Sylvie blinks, as though processing the last few minutes. "I've always loved animals. And I *knew* I had a special kinship with my dog, Waffles."

"You have a dog named Waffles?" Mateo scrunches his eyebrows.

Sylvie nods. "She's a big, bad German Shepherd with scary teeth but a sweet disposition. I love the juxtaposition."

"The point is, we now have one more day of rations. Or another reward." Bodin taps his hiking stick on the ground, as though trying to steer the conversation back on track.

"Do we, though?" I ask. "Unless someone's watching us this very moment, Xander will have no way of knowing."

"True. I guess it only matters if our mission fails and we *need* those rations." Bodin steps aside with a flourish, making way for Sylvie. "Would you like to do the honors?"

She hesitates, holding the long, thin leaf like it might shatter. "Um. What, exactly, am I supposed to do with this key? If that's what it even is."

"There's no obvious keyhole." Rae taps her fingers against her chin. "No chinks or cracks. I'd suggest just touching the tip of the leaf to the wall. Any point will do."

Sylvie steps forward. We all brace ourselves because there's no telling *what* might happen. She gingerly touches the golden key against the burnished, polished mountain…

…and to our utter astonishment, the wall parts, revealing an enormous, yawning cave.

CHAPTER SEVENTEEN

The mouth of the cave is narrow but tall, stretching fifteen feet above our heads. I can only see a few feet inside before the dark shadows devour the bright rays of sun. The ground is made up of pebbles, stones, and larger rocks scattered at random intervals, while thick, wet moss coats the cave walls and ceiling.

"Are we actually going in there?" Rae shudders in spite of the line of sweat that's gathering at her hairline. "We have no idea what's inside. We could encounter another obstacle, like this wall. Or worse, we could run into a multi-armed creature who will rip us apart."

"Why, Rae. You don't seem the type to believe in monsters," Bodin says.

"That was before I landed on an island where the old legends come to life," she retorts.

I swallow hard. Rae knows her Thai folktales inside and out. No wonder she's hesitant. She understands, more clearly than any of us, what horrors we might face.

"Can't you ask the birds what's on the other side of this

mountain?" I ask Sylvie.

She shakes her head. "I did. They didn't answer."

"Well, call them back and demand one," Rae says.

"I don't think it works that way. But okay, I'll try." Sylvie takes a deep breath, releasing it slowly from her body. And then, her eyes flutter closed and her hands form into fists. Concentrating, concentrating.

I scan the skies, hoping to glimpse a black wing or two. But there's nothing but the cloudless blue sky.

Sylvie opens her eyes once more. "It's not working. They're not answering my call."

We fall silent, even though no amount of quietness can help us process the unknown.

"Maybe…your ability comes and goes?" Rae ventures.

"Or maybe I haven't come into any powers at all." Disappointment saturates Sylvie's words. "Maybe the thing with the birds was just one big fluke."

"Forget the birds. I vote we keep going," Mateo says with a glance at me. "If we go back, *we'll* be the sitting avian creatures, pun intended. We'll have food but no medicine. We'll play Xander's game, but we have no guarantee that he'll ever let us off this island."

"Seconded," Sylvie says immediately. Her cheeks have cooled to their normal tan shade, and some of her calm, steady demeanor has returned.

"Thirded," I say in a small voice. If this expedition is largely for my mother, I can't be the one who backs down.

"Rae?" Bodin inquires. "This is strictly voluntary. None of us would judge you if you decided to go back to the beach."

She crosses her arms and sighs. "Fine. I'll keep going. Just don't come crying to me when a three-headed elephant charges into you."

We spend a few minutes gathering sticks and twigs, in

case we need to build a fire, as well as some leaves, in order to mark our trail. Stones or gravel wouldn't show up against the cave floor, and the cave walls should shield the wind. We just have to hope they don't blow away. Sylvie fishes out a flashlight from the backpack that she brought from the yacht. (Shoulda known that our extreme-sports-loving champion would come prepared with what we need to go caving.) We've got plenty of rainwater in the plastic bottles, as well as a supply of water-purification tablets, courtesy of Xander's reward. And yet, I've never felt less prepared.

"Welp. It's now or never," Rae quips.

I gulp and say goodbye to the sun.

Bodin strides into the cave first. Sylvie and I follow, with Mateo on our heels and Rae bringing up the rear.

What has become of my life? I never would've guessed, in a million, billion years, that I would voluntarily enter a deep, dark cave, possibly filled with insects and wild animals and deadly mythological creatures.

Desperately, I run through the little survival theory that I know. I'm already in the center of the group, Bodin and Sylvie in front of me, Rae and Mateo behind me. Theoretically, I am the safest here, shielded on all sides. Not that this position would protect me for long if we *are* attacked by a vicious creature. Nor would I expect Rae to give herself up in an epic sacrifice to save me. But it's better than nothing.

As we walk deeper and deeper into the cave, the natural light filtering through the entrance disappears. We are surrounded by black shadows on all sides. From the bouncing beam of the flashlight, I can see the same mismatched rocks padding the ground, the same moss-covered walls falling in sheets around us. The only difference is that the tunnel is slowly closing in, making our path smaller and tighter.

I'm not claustrophobic. Never have been, but something

about this cave is giving me the creeps on top of my creeps.

"Do you hear that?" Bodin asks, halting in his tracks.

Which causes Sylvie to stop, which causes me to run into her. I tumble backward, and then, as if in slow motion, my foot catches on a pesky pebble, and I am falling straight onto a particularly large and jagged rock when a pair of competent arms grabs me, inches from disaster.

"Careful!" Mateo says, a hint of annoyance in his voice. At first, I think the displeasure is directed at me, but his steely eyes, illuminated by the flashlight, glare at Bodin. "There's a line of us following you. You can't just stop without warning—"

"Don't fight, please," I say, pulling away from Mateo and trying not to feel icky from his touch. I participated in the group hug, true. But this is a different time and a different context. One moment of exposure doesn't erase years and years of aversion. I turn to Bodin. "What did you hear?"

Bodin's gaze flickers to Mateo, and then he shakes his head, letting go of the tension. "Listen."

We all strain our ears. There's the gentle inhale-exhale of the people breathing around me. The constant thrumming coming from my own chest. Pebbles rattling as someone shifts their weight.

And then—I hear it. A soft and mellow whooshing sound. It's calm yet melodic, reminding me of soothing times, like when Mama and I used to bump into each other in the kitchen at midnight, both kept up by twin bouts of insomnia. It's the sound of running water.

"A stream," I say.

"More like a small river, from the sounds of it. If we can find it, I bet it'll lead us out of this cave to the other side of the island," Bodin says, grinning.

Yes. Thank you, pra Buddha cho. I needed something—

anything—to go right, with all the horrors that we've encountered. I needed one break, and this is it.

"Let's go," I say, bouncing on my feet.

When nobody moves, I stride to the front of the group without a thought of my safety or the scary creatures lurking in the dark. We're getting out of here. We'll find help and procure Mama's pills. We'll reunite with Papa and be together once again—

The ground is yanked out underneath me, and I scream as I plunge down into nothingness.

CHAPTER EIGHTEEN

I fall.

A high-pitched scream—mine?—slices through me as the air whips up around me. I have no time to prepare, to analyze. I am pure adrenaline, pure instinct, as I point my toes, because some random show I watched years ago said that when falling into water from a great height, you should point your toes to minimize impact.

And then, I hit.

The water is cold and stark. It feels more like concrete than liquid as I crash into it. Pointed toes or not, the pain slaps my every nerve.

I open my mouth, gasping for breath, but my head is underwater, and my lungs fill with liquid. Frantically, I claw above my head...but I don't know which way is up.

I twist and turn, my lungs burning, my eyes popping. *Just pick,* my mind blares. *Pick a direction and go.*

I do. But I must've chosen wrong, because a few precious seconds later, my fingers dig into mud.

I'm drowning. The thought slams into me, more jarring

than the impact of the water, more searing than the pressure in my chest. I'm drowning, and there's not a damn thing I can do about it.

My limbs go weak. I no longer have the strength to push the water away from my body, and I open my eyes to deep, black murkiness. The lull of unconsciousness pulls at me — and I can't bring myself to care.

Stop fighting, it croons to me. *Come into the quiet, where you can rest.*

If this is death, it doesn't seem so bad. I no longer hurt. The pain in my lungs, in my heart, washes away with the river. Perhaps, I'm better off this way. Maybe one day, soon, I'll be with Mama again.

But just as I close my eyes and sink toward the muddy bed of forever sleep, blinding light licks my face.

"Breathe!" a distant voice shouts.

The pain comes roaring back as a fist smashes into my stomach. I choke, and water pours out of my mouth. The fist comes down again, forceful, full of life.

"Breathe, Alaia. Breathe!" the same voice yells, but it still comes from miles away. All I can do is cough as my throat screams its objection and my eyes blur with tears.

"You've got this, Alaia." The voice softens. The fist opens into a palm and rubs soothing circles on my back. "Breathe for me. Please."

I splutter one more time, and then I try a shallow breath.

My throat is scratchy and raw, and my lungs object the moment that little bit of air hits. This is ridiculous. How can breathing, the most natural building block of life, hurt this badly? But with every sip of air, I feel my body absorbing the oxygen, thanking me like it never has before.

"That's it. You've got this. Keep doing what you're doing."

My ears pop, and the voice comes into focus. Bodin.

All of a sudden, I become aware of the pebbled ground under my body, the chilly air against wet skin. The smell of cave clobbers me once more—mossy rock and dank, moist earth. But instead of a ceiling twenty feet above our heads, the cave opens up to a glimmer of blue sky.

I blink. The natural light wasn't visible before. I would've noticed. I must've floated farther down the river than I thought before Bodin dragged me to shore. Mateo, Sylvie, and Rae hover above me. Their clothes and hair are dry, so there must've been an alternative way down other than jumping—er, falling—into the river.

"You scared the crap out of me." Sylvie presses a hand to her chest.

"Long way to fall," Mateo remarks. "That will knock the breath out of anyone."

"You okay, princess?" Rae asks, real worry in her eyes.

Too much to process. Too soon. I pull my knees to my chest, forming a ball with my body.

"Alaia, you're safe now," Bodin says gently. "You're okay."

I look up. Wet hair drips around his face. His shirt clings to his chest, revealing solid muscles, and his eyes glimmer with concern.

He looks just like an ethereal being sent from the heavens to protect me.

Silly. My perspective is clearly clouded by the fact that he just saved my life. He could've gotten hurt or even died, but he did it anyway. For that, I will be forever indebted to him. That's the only reason I find him so mesmerizing.

I know this. And yet, I long to touch his furrowed brows and smooth away the worry with my fingers. The desire is compelling, almost irresistible, and so I reach out my hand to do exactly that.

And that's when I notice it: the back of my hand is

smeared with mud.

I freeze. The splotch is so evident, so *palpable*. It mars my skin, disrupts the orderliness I try to maintain at all times, even out here on a deserted island.

"Alaia? What's wrong?" Bodin asks.

I hear the words, but I also don't. Because I'm too busy staring.

My nails are grimy. Dirt is caked underneath them from when I tore at the ground, desperate for escape. I know without looking that my other hand is the same.

The clothes that I wear—stone-washed jean shorts and a ruffled white top with a bow tied at the center—were already dusty from two days on the island. But now, they are sullied with mud, sweat, and what looks a whole lot like blood...

I gasp. No way. I pat my arms, my chest, my torso, looking for the source and finding none. That's when I realize that my face is wetter and stickier than the rest of my body. I reach up and then pull away red fingers.

"You must've given her a bloody nose when you smashed into her," Mateo says with a disapproving frown at Bodin. "You need to be more careful."

"Oh, yeah?" Bodin retorts. "What did *you* do when she fell into the river? Stand there and watch."

I don't pay attention to their bickering because my own thoughts race faster and faster as I examine my arms and legs, finding more and more grime. My panic grows with each passing moment.

I don't like germs. Who does? But I *really* don't like them. Being covered in blood, dirt, and god knows what bacteria, with no way to clean or disinfect myself, is my worst nightmare—literally. At least once a month, I wake up drenched in sweat because of this exact scenario.

My body is *coated*, every square inch tainted by the river.

I whip my head around, frantically searching for something that can fix this mess.

But there's nothing, damn it. Just more dirt, more bacteria, more germs...

My breath comes faster. I can't fill my lungs, even though the oxygen is *right there*. I'm no longer underwater, but I'm in just as much danger of drowning.

I can't *do* this. I can't exist with this much dirt on me. I can't. I can't. I CAN'T.

I don't want to break down in front of the others. But a tear makes its way down my cheek, and I can't stop it. Another one comes, and I can't stop *that*. And then another. And another.

A loud noise shatters the silence. It's awful. A scream that shreds the heart, rips the soul. A wailing so wretched that it must originate in the depths of hell itself. Pure terror personified.

Every head swivels toward me. Aw, crap. One guess who's making the sound.

Bodin's eyes widen. "Are you hurt?"

He crouches beside me and tries to wrap his arm around me, which is the absolute worst move he could make. I am not in the space to be touched, and I shriek so loudly that my ear drums tremble. Bodin stumbles back as though I slapped him.

Mateo, too, lowers himself, so that we are eye to eye, but unlike Bodin, he keeps a respectful distance away.

"Tell me how I can help," he says softly.

"I-I n-n-eed w-at-ter," I say through sobs.

"Water?" Sylvie raises her eyebrows. "But she just got out of the river. Why does she need more water?"

"Shhhh," Mateo says without taking his eyes off me. He moves to his backpack and takes out his water bottle, offering it to me. "Take this."

"But that's your drinking water," I protest weakly.

"You need it more than I do."

Emotions swirl through me. The world *still* feels like it's going to collapse. It's not rational. There's no logic behind the feeling that the grime on my skin is going to kill me.

But my OCD isn't reasonable. It defies judgment; it betrays common sense. It jeers at me that no matter what I do, I will never truly be clean again. It's a ghost that haunts me, driving me mad with its circular, repetitive thoughts.

"Here you go," Mateo says, handing me a clean piece of fabric. An extra T-shirt that he must've packed for a day on a yacht.

Careful not to waste a single drop of water, I douse the T-shirt and get to work.

Dab and scrub. Scrub and dab.

I don't know how Mateo guessed that I wanted to clean myself, but I'm too preoccupied to question it.

I start with my arms. The slight sting that comes with each scrub also comes with a certain satisfaction and relief. I try to be conservative with the water—but the resolve evaporates as a little voice whispers inside my mind. *Are you sure it's clean? Did you miss a spot? There's a speck of dirt there. You should go over that area one more time.*

I empty the bottle on just one arm, which is now red and raw, but Mateo swoops down before I can start to freak.

"I have more water," he says, handing me another bottle.

I go through bottle after bottle. Both of his and both of mine.

Bodin paces along the river, Sylvie closes her eyes and tries to sleep, and Rae? She stares but doesn't say a single word, not even a snide comment or two.

Mateo, on the other hand, keeps handing me bottles like it is the most normal thing in the world.

But as my arms, legs, face, and even hair become clean(er), I look at my clothes in dismay. They are filthy, and given my extreme need for privacy, there's a negative chance in hell that I'm willing to strip down so that I can wash them.

"You can borrow my shirt," Mateo says, once again guessing correctly at my distress. "I'm tall enough that it would be long on you. You could wash the clothes and then put them back on."

"Seriously, dude?" Bodin says, his first words since he tried to touch me. "Lola's not even here, but you're dying to show off your abs, aren't you?"

"Hardly. Scrawny guys like me don't have a six-pack," Mateo says patiently. "Alaia wants clean clothes. It's not a ridiculous need. I'm sure you wouldn't like it if yours were covered in blood and grime."

Bodin arches an eyebrow. "And you know this because...?"

"Because he's right," I fire back, my voice cracking, my throat raw from the water I swallowed and regurgitated. "I can't stand that my clothes are dirty."

Bodin blinks, surprised at my passion. Mateo ignores him and turns back to me. "Would you like my shirt, Alaia?"

I nod silently.

In one fluid motion, Mateo pulls his turquoise polo up and over his head and hands it to me.

I take it gratefully. When I slip it over my head, it falls to mid-thigh, just like he predicted. The next logical step would be to remove my shoes so that I can more easily slide out of my shorts. What's more, my toes are squishy and wet inside the canvas sneakers. I'd like nothing better than to air them out. But for years now, I've protected my bare feet with some sort of sole, be it flip-flops or slippers or sneakers. It's too uncomfortable to even *think* about taking them off.

And so, I leave on my canvas sneakers and wiggle out

of my disgusting shirt and shorts underneath Mateo's polo. When he tries to take my clothes, however, I yank them out of his grasp.

Something about his fingers touching my clothes sets me off. Besides, I have to be the one to wash my clothes because I'm the only person who will do it right.

He lets go immediately, as though he is reading my mind.

Another bottle of water is found, and I work the blood and dirt out of my white shirt and jean shorts, washing away the visible *and* invisible impurities.

Once I am satisfied that they are clean, I carefully put on my sopping clothes and then remove and return Mateo's shirt.

Finally, I can take a full breath once more. My skin is red and raw, but I am relatively clean.

The feeling of relief lasts one minute, maybe two. The sun has set outside the cave, and shadows slither down from the opening above.

I begin to feel nervous again. I see one, two, *three* specks of dirt. I'm not clean after all. I pick up the bottle and shake it to see if there's any water left.

"Not again!" Rae explodes. "We've been here for hours."

"Calm yourself, Rae," Sylvie says in a warning tone.

Mateo steps forward. "I know it's hard, Alaia. Believe me, I understand. But you're as clean as you're going to get. If you scrub anymore, you'll draw blood. You can fight this. You are strong, and you are brave. You are in complete control of your life. Nobody else."

My mouth parts. How *dare* he look at me with pity in his eyes? I can't stand it when people treat me like a sick puppy who needs to be helped. But then it dawns on me. He knows. Somehow, someway, Mateo has figured out my secret.

CHAPTER NINETEEN

I stare at Mateo. "How-how did you know I have…"

"Obsessive-compulsive disorder, right?" Mateo asks plainly.

My heart sinks to the crumbly ground. There are no maybes or ifs about it. He's definitely guessed the reason for my strange behavior.

I thought it wouldn't bother me to hear the words said out loud, but I was wrong.

Outside of the mistake I made in middle school, I haven't confided in anyone other than my family about my OCD. I learned my lesson in a single instance. Never again—or so I thought. My secret was on a strictly need-to-know basis, which means: doctors, teachers, guidance counselors. Not friends. Certainly not acquaintances.

I step away from Mateo, from the others, my cheeks flaming with shame. How? How did he know? Okay, so my behavior just now wasn't *exactly* normal, and people casually throw the term in conversation as though it is an adjective, as in "I'm so OCD about my hair today!" It irks me to no end. But *true* OCD, the severe kind that interferes with daily functioning, isn't very common. *These* symptoms of OCD aren't well-known. Are they?

"My brother has OCD, too," Mateo says in a low voice.

I blink. Ex-football player Eduardo, of the burly shoulders, has the same disorder as me?

"His rituals fall more within the scrupulosity subtype, but he has compulsions about contamination, too," Mateo continues. "As hard as this Island of Hell has been on the rest of us, I know it's been doubly hard for you and Eduardo. You've come so far. You've survived a shipwreck, poisoned water, anaphylactic shock, a raging storm, *and* a near drowning. And you didn't even come close to giving up. Don't let OCD beat you now."

"I can't. I don't know how." Tears fill my eyes, and I teeter on the edge of a breakdown once more.

But before I can fall into the abyss, Mateo steps closer to me and looks directly into my eyes. "Yes, you do. You fight your compulsions every day of your life. Tell it *no*. Tell it you don't care what it thinks. You are clean and you don't want to scrub your skin any longer. And if it tries to talk back at you? You have my full permission to throat-punch it."

I sob and laugh, burying my face in my hands for I don't know how long.

"It's late," Bodin says finally. "We're exhausted. Our senses are dulled, and it's not safe to stumble around these caves without a clear head. I'll build us a fire, and we'll stop here for the night. Alaia—all of us, really—need to rest."

One by one, we settle onto the ground—me last, sitting on my backpack so I don't have to touch any more dirt. Sylvie and Mateo empty the sticks and kindling out of their backpacks while Rae takes out the remaining leaves. Bodin makes quick work of building a fire, and we all gather around the flames, fighting the nighttime chill that has descended in the caves.

"I'm sorry." I pull my knees to my chest, focusing my eyes on the orange core of the fire. "I'm sorry I fell in the damn river. I'm sorry I delayed all of us here. I'm sorry I used up so much drinking water. I'm sorry I felt like I couldn't get clean." My voice cracks on the last word, and I lay my cheek on my knees and just breathe.

"You don't have to apologize for who you are." Sylvie's eyes shine at me, reflecting the flame. "It's no more your fault than my fibromyalgia is mine." She wets her lips as though debating whether to continue. "That's why I'm such a risk junkie, you know. There are days when I'm flat on my back, hurting so intensely that I can't even sit up or walk around. I feel so helpless, then. Trapped by the pain. A prisoner in my own body. So, on my good days, when my trigger points *don't* flare, I push myself to the extreme."

Rae opens her mouth as though to speak. She closes it and then tries once more. "I don't understand you, Alaia, and I won't pretend to," she says haltingly. "But unlike you, I *do* have to apologize. I...shouldn't have spoken to you like that. It was rude and insensitive. You're obviously haunted by your demons, and I didn't help the situation. For what it's worth, I'm not mad at you. And I hope you're not *too* mad at me." She offers me a half smile.

"No, I'm not mad," I say. "Actually...I'm grateful to you both. For understanding."

Never in a million years did I expect such support from Sylvie, much less Rae. There's a reason why I've kept my disorder a secret. I've always assumed that other people's reactions would be negative. That they would despise me, or worse, pity me. I never dreamed that they would simply accept me.

Only Bodin, who has retired to a shadowed corner of the

cave, hasn't spoken.

I shouldn't care. I only met the guy a few days ago. After this ordeal is over—and it *will* be over—I won't see him again. He should have no impact on my life. And yet…I do care.

Deep inside, I feel a twinge of pain at the thought of Bodin rejecting me because of this. Hating me for my mental condition. I don't want him to be angry with me. And yet, if he complains about how much time we wasted or how silly and ridiculous my fears are, I will never be able to forgive him. Because my worries *aren't* silly or ridiculous—not to me. Still, I don't want to cut him out of my life, because whether or not I want to admit it, I *like* being around him.

The group of us, with the exception of Bodin, say good night and settle around the fire, too exhausted to talk any longer. I carefully spread my sleeping bag on the ground— I'm the only one who thought it was necessary to bring one— and lay with my back to the flames, the same position as the previous night.

Instead of closing my eyes, though, I look toward Bodin's corner. He sits on the cave floor, his long legs stretched before him. The moonlight has shifted so that it now bathes him in a silvery glow. His body and posture give off an air of relaxation, and his expression is almost but not quite blank, nearly disguising his worry…and pain?

What? Why is Bodin hurting at this moment? Stress is to be expected. We're desperately searching for a way off this island, to avoid the evil clutches of our captor. Exhaustion, sure. We've walked for miles today, to not get very far. But pain? Over what?

Too late, I realize that I'm staring. I'm about to avert my gaze when he catches my eyes.

His spine goes rigid, and for a moment, I think he's going to turn away. Instead, he creeps to where I'm lying and sits on the ground a good five feet away. "Do you mind if we talk?"

"Why would I mind?" I ask.

"I..." He swallows as words fail him and his internal struggle rages full force. I can almost see the claws of the two monsters inside him tearing at each other. The wreckage seems disastrous. Just as quickly, however, the battle fades away. His eyes go placid, and resolve snaps into his features.

"I thought maybe you didn't like me anymore," he says.

"Me?" I blink. "What reason do *I* have to be mad at *you*?"

Bodin dips his head, his eyes trained on the ground, although I'm pretty sure he can't see anything, since my body is blocking the fire. "You jerked away from me," he mumbles, "like you were repulsed by my touch. And yet, you let *him* comfort you. You wore his T-shirt. Your fingers brushed his as he handed you bottle after bottle, so many times that I lost count."

"Oh, Bodin." I raise my hand but then let it dangle in midair. "It wasn't about you or Mateo," I say, withdrawing my hand. "If Mama tried to hug me in that moment, I'd push her away, too. My OCD..." I stop and wet my lips. My secret might be out in the open, but that doesn't mean that I'm used to talking about it. Doesn't mean I have any practice explaining myself. "It flares and recedes, depending on the context. Depending on my stress levels. I was panicking when you tried to put your arms around me. Less so when Mateo comforted me."

He nods as though accepting the answer. But he still can't look at me, and he draws with his index finger on the ground.

"I'm so sorry that you almost drowned." His voice turns scratchy. "And I'm sorry that the stress of it sent you spiraling. I'm sorry that you have to live with your OCD."

Finally, he looks up, and even though his expression is shadowed, it is so soft, so tender, that it ignites a fire inside me, one whose flames rival the heat licking at my back.

"I don't understand the disorder," he continues. "Like Rae, I don't know anyone afflicted by it. I don't have a chronic condition that can compare to it. But if you ever need help, please know that I'm here. Maybe I could help you count or clean things." He gives me a small smile.

I can only gape. While his speech started off in the right direction, it certainly did not end well.

"That's not necessary," I say, my voice unintentionally frosty.

His eyebrows crease, confusion settling in once more.

Aw, crap. I take a slow, steadying breath. He means well. He can't possibly know that his offer was the absolute wrong thing to say.

"The only way to treat OCD is to stop doing compulsions," I say haltingly. Awkwardly. Again, I blame my miserable lack of practice explaining myself. "Other people *helping* me with my rituals is an accommodation, which only makes the disorder worse."

He sucks in a breath. "Oh, gosh. I had no idea—"

"I know," I interrupt gently. "And I'll keep reminding myself of that."

"I *want* to learn," he says forcefully. "Just…be patient with me?"

"Deal," I say softly as he lays down next to me, closer than he did the previous night.

"Is this okay?" he asks.

I nod. Whether or not I would ever admit it, a sense of peace falls over me. Bodin's presence is…comforting. Even as it is exciting. How I can feel both at the same time, I'm not sure.

But my eyes flutter closed, the physical exhaustion taking over despite the turmoil in my mind. The last few days have been…too much. One revelation after another. So much shock and trauma that my poor brain can barely process it. And now, people outside my need-to-know circle are learning about my OCD. They're not acting like my former friend in middle school, whom I confided in during a sleepover. And who avoided me *after* she learned my secret, as though my mental disorder was somehow contagious. Instead, my fellow castaways are *accepting* both my compulsions and me.

I can't decide what's more unbelievable. An island where folktales literally come to life? Or me choosing to confide my secret to others—and not regretting it?

CHAPTER TWENTY

Mateo pulls back his arm with the grace of a baseball pitcher and launches a small, flat stone into the river. It skips two, three, *four* times before it eventually sinks into the water.

The early morning rays drift through the overhead aperture, bathing our skin in a hazy glow. The others are still sleeping. On the other side of the embers, Rae lies on her back with her bag over her feet, while Sylvie emits light, even snores. Bodin faces me, his body relaxed but his hand gripping the flashlight, as though ready to spring into battle at the first signal.

I watch Mateo, my knees pulled into my chest. The pile of stones next to him dwindles, and when he gets down to five, maybe six, rocks, I take a deep breath and approach.

"I never thanked you for helping me with the water," I say, as I lay down my backpack and plop down next to him. "You didn't have to, and I—I appreciate it."

"It was no problem, Alaia," he says solemnly.

He holds up one of the rocks between his thumb and

index finger. I take it and launch it across the river, just like he did.

Except, it plunks, heavy and awkwardly, straight into the water, just like *I* did yesterday afternoon.

"You're a natural," Mateo observes, laughter in his voice.

"I offer lessons," I say. "But you'll have to book quickly. My schedule fills up fast, since I'm *very* popular."

"I bet you are." His humor fades away, his eyes turning serious once more. "That's something I've never been."

"What, popular?" I pick up another stone and launch it across the water. This time, it bounces *once* before sinking to the bottom. "Me neither. But I never really wanted to be, you know? Then, people are watching you all the time. Idolizing you or tearing you apart. I'd much rather slink along the shadows, unnoticed."

"But you're so pretty." I start to protest, but he rushes on. "Whether or not you know it, people *do* notice you. Me, on the other hand?" He shakes his head self-deprecatingly. "I've never been under the illusion that I look like Bodin. Lola's the only girl who's ever showed any interest in me, you know."

"Well, it was *their* loss," I say fiercely. "Anyone would be lucky to have you as their boyfriend."

He smiles sadly. "I appreciate the vote of confidence. But I do wonder, if circumstances weren't what they are, would Lola even be willing to talk to me, much less kiss me?"

"Yes." If I say it emphatically enough, will he believe me? "You have to give her some credit. Lola's a smart girl, and she no doubt sees how good you are. How kind. How caring."

"I *hope* so," he says.

The silence swells, so for a moment there's nothing else in the cave, no danger lurking in the darkness, no evil scientist controlling our lives. Just the two of us by the river, our pile of rocks sunken to the muddy bottom.

Someone clears their throat.

I startle, leaping away from Mateo, even though we've done nothing that I would hide.

The others are awake. Sylvie and Rae rub the sleep out of their eyes, while Bodin is putting materials in his backpack.

"We should get going." Bodin addresses the group of us, his eyes dark and unreadable. "We've got a long day ahead of us."

The natural light disappears as we descend into the cave's depths. The river ends abruptly in a pool of water, so we pick a tunnel and move into it, farther and farther from the natural skylight. I swallow hard. The sunlight is like an old friend, and saying goodbye to it once again feels neither safe nor comforting. We have the flashlight, sure. But the beam throws odd shapes onto the cave walls, highlighting a patch of slippery moss here and a protruding stalagmite there. It reminds me of all the dangers that we cannot see: the monsters and booby traps hidden by the darkness.

My sneakered feet slide across the ground, the loose pebbles rolling against one another in a staccato rhythm. Behind me, Sylvie is depositing leaves at regular intervals. The air smells and tastes stale, and I inhale dust with each breath.

The heavy atmosphere isn't helped by the fact that Bodin appears to be ignoring me. He hasn't said a word to me since he saw me with Mateo this morning.

I want to make things right between us. I want to recreate the trust that enveloped us last night by the fire. But how do I explain to him that Mateo and I have nothing but a warm friendship…when Bodin hasn't really asked? It's all I can do to place one foot in front of the other.

"Hey, you," Rae calls out. We've changed our hiking formation today, and I'm second in line, behind Bodin and in front of Mateo. Sylvie and Rae bring up the rear.

At first, I think Rae's talking to me, but then Mateo yelps, and I realize that she's poked him in the shoulder. "You're breathing too loudly. I can't hear a darn thing."

"What's there to hear?" Mateo asks.

"I don't know," Rae says grumpily. "Maybe the slithering of a monster like Krasue? She's got the head of a young female attached to a bunch of exposed entrails—"

"Entrails?" Sylvie's voice pitches higher. "You mean like stomach and intestines?"

"Exactly," Rae says. "As folklore has it, she's always hungry and her snack of choice is blood and raw flesh."

"Yummy," Bodin comments.

"If Krasue is lurking around these tunnels, we're goners, anyway," Mateo says reasonably.

"Not if I push you down and run in the opposite direction." Rae smirks.

"Now, now," Sylvie says. "Not much of a morning person, are you?"

"Caffeine withdrawal is a real, documented condition," Rae agrees.

I let out a small giggle—better that than a yelp of terror. But as I do, a clawing pain reverberates through the empty walls inside me.

Hunger. It's been twenty-four hours since we last ate, and I am ravenous, especially with the energy I exerted yesterday. But as badly as I'm suffering, Mama must be even worse off, without her pills and cancer eating away at her health. So, I grit my teeth and try to ignore the pangs in my stomach.

"I haven't even told you about Phi Kong Koi," Rae

continues conversationally. "He's a one-legged vampire that likes to haunt wooded areas. They say he enjoys sucking blood from intruders with his tubular mouth. That's why you should always cover your extremities while you sleep."

I stumble, remembering the backpack over Rae's feet last night. My sneakers offer *some* protection—but not enough. "And you couldn't have told us this earlier?"

"You didn't ask," she says smugly.

We continue walking—although that's a generous way of describing it. More accurately, we push farther into a darkness so deep it is nearly solid, not knowing what dangers wait to devour us.

Clatter, clatter, clatter.

Clatter, clatter, clatter.

Clatter, clatter, clatter, *crunch.*

Wait a minute. What was that? Just my imagination gone awry, or a subtle change in our path?

Clatter, clatter, clatter, *crunch.*

There it is again. Bodin's swinging the flashlight, so I squint at the ground when the beam points down. Ah. A dried and crumbly leaf, like the ones we gathered outside the cave. That's what made the noise.

Except...Sylvie, who volunteered to scatter the leaves, is last in our hiking formation. Which means: any leaf that she has dropped to mark our trail should be *behind* me.

"Um, guys?" My wobbly voice echoes against the cave walls. "I hate to say this, but I think we might be walking in circles."

Oof. I plow right into Bodin's back.

"Seriously, dude?" Mateo says, annoyed. "Again?"

Ow. I rub my nose. Thankfully, it's not bleeding once more.

"Are you okay?" Bodin asks, peering at me, which might

be the first words he's said to me this morning.

I nod wordlessly.

Sylvie grabs her flashlight back from Bodin and kneels down. "Alaia's right. Look!" She holds up a yellow-veined leaf that's crunchy along the edges. "This is exactly like the leaves that I've been dropping. We've been here before."

"Some leader," Rae mutters. "Next thing you know, Bodin will lead us right back out the cave the way that we came in."

Not helping. "Maybe you could try calling out to an animal again," I say to Sylvie. "One of your birds, maybe an owl. Something that can guide us out of this mess."

Sylvie straightens, uselessly brushing the dirt from her mud-stained shorts. "It's worth a try. Maybe my ability has decided to show up once more." She hands her flashlight to Mateo and closes her eyes, her chest rising and falling.

Nothing happens.

"Maybe you have to *really* want it," Rae says, "like when you wanted the key that was just out of reach."

"Think about Elizabeth," I suggest. "All of our loved ones back at camp, counting on us to make it through this cave. To get help."

"AAARGHHH!" Mateo grabs Sylvie by the shoulders, and she leaps up, nearly smacking her head against the cave wall.

She glares at Mateo. "What. Was. That?"

He shrugs. "I was scaring you. To get you in the right frame of mind."

"That's not how I felt when I wanted the key!" Sylvie yelps. "I have to be desperate. Stressed. Adrenaline has to be pumping through my body, my mind has to be whirling with a thousand thoughts a minute—"

Mateo counts off each item on his fingers. "Sounds about right to me. And check it out: it worked."

He tilts the flashlight to the cave ceiling.

There, flapping around in the beam, is a small, furry, black bat, zooming dizzily in a zigzag direction, as though to say, "Follow me."

We follow the bat.

Bits of conversation drift up from the back of our group, but Bodin and I don't talk. He does check over his shoulder every couple of minutes, though, to give me an encouraging nod or wink. The air between us has thawed somewhat, with the arrival of the bat, and with each gesture of acknowledgment, I float a little higher.

Which won't do. I *need* to pay attention to my surroundings, so that I don't trip and break my neck.

As we troop after our winged leader, anticipation builds. I'm certain that we're approaching *something* in our journey. I just don't know what it is.

The opaque blackness becomes more transparent, and shadows begin to fade. And then—up ahead. A ray of sunlight, shining through scattered pinpoint holes in the rocky ceiling. The pinholes turn into quarters and then plates and then spare tires. The blue sky shimmers down on us once more from another aperture in the cavern's roof.

"We've got to be approaching the exit," I say.

"Maybe," Bodin says doubtfully, his eyes on our friendly neighborhood bat.

"The walls are shorter now," Mateo says behind me. "They've got to be only about ten feet."

"We're rising!" I exclaim. "That has to be a good sign."

"Alaia, please take two steps to your right," Bodin commands.

"Why?"

"Because I'm about to stop walking, and considering that you've smashed into me twice now, I'd like to save your cute little nose."

Cute? Did he just call me—or at least my nose—cute?

I halt my stride, and so does he, half-turning to me.

"Do you hear that?" he asks.

I listen—and there it is: the steady hum of a current.

"Another river?" Mateo asks, joining us.

Bodin nods curtly. "Hopefully, this one will actually lead us out of the cave." He points a finger at me. "You, no running. We can't have you falling over any more cliffs."

I give him a salute. "Yes, sir!"

He actually smiles.

We inch forward carefully. A dozen feet later, still inside the cave, the rocky ground ends abruptly, and we come upon another cliff.

My pulse pounding in my ears, I peek over the edge. And then, my heart plummets right down into the abyss.

Below me lies a stream of liquid, all right. But instead of the murky water we encountered before, the brook here runs thick and red...

CHAPTER TWENTY-ONE

Blood.
As in the deep, red rivulets that run down my forearms when I scrub too hard. As in the gush of red that spurts from a bullet-ridden Mama in my nightmares.

Blood. That's all I can think. That's all I can *feel*, racing, circulating in the veins under my skin.

In spite of Bodin's warning, every cell in my body screams at me to run. Away from this stream, away from the blood. But the others are already starting to examine the water. I have no choice but to stay with them, especially since Sylvie's bat, no doubt spooked by the red river, takes off down one of the many tunnels, flying too quickly for me to follow.

And so, I trail after the others down a slope so that we're level with the water. Gritting my teeth, I peer back at the stream. And—oh—oh, it's not blood, after all. The liquid is too translucent, too watery for that. The water rushes by, brilliant and red, gleaming a bit brighter where the sun from the overhead gaps hits.

"What is it?" I ask.

"No clue." Bodin prods the water with a stick.

I'm not sure what to expect—for the water to sizzle, or the stick to burst into flames? Neither happens. When he pulls out the stick, it is simply wet and tinged slightly red.

"Rae?" I turn to our resident folktale expert. "Can you explain this?"

Rae juts out a hip and places her hand on it. "*Now* you want my opinion?"

I nod as nicely as possible, and she lets her arm drop.

"There *is* a legend about red waters that swirl in the wrong direction and crocodiles who can change into human form," she says. "These croc-people feel no hunger and can easily survive without eating. But I don't see any crocodiles. Do you?"

I bend down to get closer to the water—and then I jump backward, screaming.

A massive…*thing*…snaps its jaws in the air, missing my face by mere centimeters. If I had leaned in any farther, I would no longer have a head. I scream again, rolling away from the stream's edge as quickly as possible. And then I scream once more as the creature slides back into the water and disappears under the red surface.

Sylvie croons words that I can't quite decipher but sure sound comforting.

"What was that thing?" I gasp when my vocabulary returns. "Can you communicate with it?"

"No," Sylvie says. "I tried to tell it that we mean no harm, but my thoughts are…blocked? Kinda like the way I'm obstructed when I try to communicate mind-to-mind with a human."

Bodin frowns. "How would you know that? Unless you've tried to send one of us a telepathic message."

"What's the problem, Bodin?" Sylvie asks archly. "Don't

want any of us sharing secrets that don't involve you?"

Maybe they continue the conversation. Maybe they don't. I can't pay attention because a pair of eyeballs rests just above the water's surface. The rest of the creature's body is concealed under the red water. As soon as I see these eyeballs, I begin to notice other pairs. No less than ten sets of eyeballs stare at me from the stream, each belonging to…

"The aforementioned crocodiles," Rae says triumphantly.

I round on her. "How can you use a word like *aforementioned* when I just about lost my head?"

"Oh, excuse me," she retorts. "I'll be sure to use itty-bitty words in the future, for your itty-bitty brain."

"Use this!" I shriek, throwing a fist in front of me. Sylvie grabs me, holding me back, so that I end up swinging at the air.

"Easy, princess," Rae says evenly. "You don't want to start a fight you can't win."

After a few cartoonlike flails, I go limp. Holy crap, what was I thinking? If Sylvie hadn't stopped me, would I actually have…*hit*…Rae? I've never been violent toward anyone or anything in my entire life.

This island is changing me. Not necessarily for the better. Perhaps that's what Xander intended, but the realization makes me more determined than ever not to play his games. To hang on to *my* identity—whoever that is—no matter the cost.

"What are the crocodiles doing in the water?" Mateo tosses a smooth rock back and forth, as though he's considering skipping it across the surface.

"Swimming," Rae says. "Waiting to chow down on people silly enough to stick their heads in the water." She glances at me, but I refuse to rise to her bait.

"It doesn't matter," Bodin cuts in.

"Alaia was almost eaten alive!" Mateo exclaims. "How does that not matter?"

"Of course *Alaia* matters." Bodin lowers his voice and speaks directly to me. "More than you'll ever know." He locks his eyes on mine. His words should fill me with warmth, but his gaze is soaked with apprehension, and it halts any happiness I might feel.

"I just meant, it doesn't matter if crocodiles live in these red waters or not," he continues, raising his voice again. "We're not going swimming. I doubt they'll bother us if we leave them alone. The fact remains: following this stream is probably our best bet out of here."

"Why can't Sylvie just summon another bat?" I ask, which seems like the logical solution.

"He doesn't trust me," Sylvie says, her eyes fixed on Bodin's face. "He's afraid of what I might be telepathically communicating to you guys without his knowledge."

The tension flares between them, becoming a live, palpable thing. Bodin stares at her for a long moment, and then he relaxes the hands, which he had fisted.

"Of course I trust you," he says to Sylvie. "But the first bat didn't lead us out of this cave. It only took us to these red waters. Don't let the sun above mislead you. We're no closer to the exit than we were before. I'd like to try something else."

She nods but doesn't speak. Even Rae and Mateo are bizarrely quiet.

"I don't care what we do," I finally say, "so long as we can go five minutes without me almost dying."

Sylvie barks out a laugh, and one by one, the others follow suit. Honestly, my comment wasn't even *that* funny. But I suppose so much stress pulses through the air that we'd do anything to cut through it.

I'd much rather laugh than cry, especially since I know that once my waterworks start, there's no stopping them. Because today is Mama's last day of medicine.

CHAPTER TWENTY-TWO

We follow the stream for what seems like hours. Although I walk as far from its edge as possible, practically hugging the cave walls, my muscles remain tight, ready to flee at the first sign of crocodile. The openings in the cave over our heads disappear once more, and we plunge back into darkness.

I start counting my steps, and once I start, I can't seem to stop. Multiples of eleven. It doesn't matter how many sets, so long as my steps fall into neat, precise groups of eleven.

This was my very first ritual, when I was eight years old. The first indication that something was off about me. Since then, my OCD has graduated to different, more complex compulsions. But the numbers remain, like a basic foundation, surfacing in times of stress.

1, 2, 3, 4, 5, 6, 7, 8, 9, 10, 11.
1, 2, 3, 4, 5, 6, 7, 8, 9, 10, 11.
1, 2, 3, 4 —

Uh oh. Bodin has halted in front of me, giving me plenty of room to stop. Steps five through eight take me right up to his body. There's nowhere else to go, so I continue stepping in place.

9, 10, 11.

Only when my steps are complete do I look up. Holy crap—Bodin is encased in a brilliant glow. When did *that* happen?

Cautiously, I step around him, and my mouth drops open.

The ground gives way to a sheer cliff that falls two stories to a pit of crocodiles. More reptiles than I can count swarm over one another. In the center of the pit, a particularly tall stalagmite holds a golden glass orb. The orb emits a warm radiance that brightens the cave like daylight. Even from where I stand, the glass ball seems to beckon me, to pull me into its powerful and mysterious aura.

I blink. And then blink again. Even after all the impossible phenomena that I've witnessed, I still can't believe my eyes.

"It's part of the legend," Rae says, awed. "This sacred crystal, guarded at all times by a pit of crocodiles, is the source of all magic. Or at least magic on this island."

"Holy crap!" Mateo exclaims. "You mean all we have to do is get our hands on that orb, and we'd bring Xander to his knees?"

"Unlikely," Rae retorts. "First, you'd have to get past a pit of crocodiles. And second, if the folktales are correct, that crystal is damn near indestructible."

Sylvie sighs dreamily. "Still, it's a thing of beauty. Can you imagine having *that* on your nightstand?"

"Crocodiles," Bodin reminds her. "They'd rip you to shreds before you get within a foot of their treasure."

I give the crystal one last longing look. As awe-inspiring as its very presence is, the orb's not helping us with our mission, at least at the moment. "We still have to find a way across the chasm," I say, redirecting my friends' attention.

Forty feet across the pit, the trail picks up again. Too far to jump across, and unlike the previous drop-offs we've encountered, there are no gradual slopes leading to the bottom. There's nothing but sheer rock walls to my left and right, curving around until they meet again on the opposite side of the pit.

"Should we turn back?" I ask reluctantly.

"And go where?" Bodin inquires. "We're not getting your mother her medicine by giving up. Our only hope is getting to the other side."

He has a point. But that doesn't make a pathway across the pit materialize.

"So, what do we do? Walk on the invisible bridge to the other side?" Mateo takes off his glasses and cleans them ferociously on his not-so-clean shirt.

Before Bodin can respond, Sylvie points across the chasm. "Everyone, look."

I squint. The trail disappears into a tunnel, but that's not what's caught Sylvie's attention. She's pointing at…could it be?…a ray of natural light. And not just any ray of light. Judging from the angle, it originates not from a skylight in the ceiling but from an opening that leads to the outside world.

I suck in a breath. "We made it. On the other side of this monstrous pit is our ticket to freedom."

"*If* we can get there," Sylvie says.

"Your birds," I say. "They managed to deliver you safely to the ground. Do you think they'll transport us?"

Sylvie chews on her lip. "I'll ask." She shoots a look at Mateo. "No scaring me this time. It's possible I'll jump so far that I'll fall into the crocodile pit—and take you with me."

Mateo nods sheepishly.

Sylvie closes her eyes and breathes deeply. She's barely into her second breath when winged creatures begin to appear on the other side of the chasm. The big black birds from before, along with their smaller cousins: birds with iridescent blue feathers. Pigeon-like creatures with white feathers and a black underbelly. Large-billed crows whose ombré feathers start at midnight blue and fade to violet purple.

Rae's eyes widen. "Wow. You're getting really good at this summoning business."

"I don't feel like I'm any better," Sylvie mutters. But the proof is right there across the pit, staring at us with their beady eyes.

The birds hop around, jostling for dominance. One of the black ones spreads its wings, showing off its enormous wingspan. Others just peck at the ground and look at us, as though awaiting further instruction.

"Um, Sylvie?" Bodin says. "You might want to tell the birds to come over to us."

"I'm trying." She squeezes her eyes shut. "They're not listening."

"They're not listening...or they *can't* cross the chasm?" I ask.

We study the birds once more. They aren't knocking into an invisible wall, but they seem to be afraid of something... or someone.

"Smart birds," Mateo comments. "I wouldn't want to fly over a pit of snarling crocodiles, either." He pantomimes rolling up his nonexistent sleeves. "All right, all right. You don't need to keep begging. I'll climb across the rock wall."

"Are you kidding?" I burst out. The cave wall isn't entirely smooth. There are more indentations and protrusions than the polished vertical wall we encountered outside the cave. But still, the course looks treacherous at best. I wouldn't send my worst enemy across that obstacle. "Even if you survive the twenty-foot drop, you'll get eaten alive by crocs."

"Simple solution: don't fall," Mateo replies calmly. Finished with his sleeves, he now moves to straighten his nonexistent bowtie.

"You just said you wouldn't want to fly over the pit," Sylvie protests.

"I don't want to. Doesn't mean I won't." Mateo drops his hands, finished with his pantomime, looking at each of us in turn. "Look, if I can get to the other side, I'll build a ladder so that the rest of you can cross. We don't have another choice. We either fall in line with Xander's demands, or we forge our escape. Besides, I'm *good* at this. Maybe not a champion like Sylvie, but I'm at the climbing gym every week. Gotta maintain the few wee muscles I do have." He flexes jokingly — but he's right. His arms may be thin, but they're hard with strength.

Sylvie straightens to her full six-foot height. "You said it yourself. I'm a better climber than you. So if anyone's climbing across, it's *me*."

"Do you see how precarious those holds are?" Even as Mateo speaks, one of the pigeons pecks at the edge of the opposite cliff, and chunks of rock break off and fall into the pit. "I'm four, five inches shorter than you. And no offense, but these scrawny limbs probably weigh a whole lot less."

Sylvie stares as the blue bird joins his friend and more rocks tumble into the pit. "None taken."

"It's still too big a risk," Bodin interjects.

"Nah, it's a *calculated* risk," Mateo says. "One that we're going to have to take."

"You," I correct, tears building behind my eyes. "It's a risk that you and you alone will take."

"Someone has to do it." Mateo sets his shoulders. "And I'd rather it be me than any of you."

Still thinking of others, until the very last minute.

I nod, although I don't want to because the gesture means that I'm okay with this course of action. And I most certainly am not. I'm not okay with allowing Mateo to endanger himself. I'm not okay with being held hostage on this prison of an island. I'm not okay with Mama dying.

But this is my life, damn it. And I have to live it, even while others are risking theirs.

Bodin claps his hand on Mateo's shoulder. Whatever tension had existed between them has evaporated. "Climb steady, my friend."

First Sylvie, and then Rae, rush forward to hug him.

"Give my love to Lola?" he asks, his eyes misting.

"If you make it to the other side, you have my full blessing to pursue my sister," Rae responds in a rare display of softness.

And then, it's my turn. "Hold on really, really tight," I say.

He smiles, the worry gone from his clear brown eyes. "If there was ever a time for me to be confident, it's right about now."

And then, it happens so fast, I barely have time to process. Mateo grabs ahold of a rock protrusion and swings to the first ledge. His hands are steady; his feet are firmly lodged. He looks over his shoulder and winks at us. "Told ya I'm good."

The knot in my throat eases just the tiniest bit. Of course he's good. He's Mateo. He's going to be all right. He has to be.

With practiced ease, his fingers find the next handhold, and his feet move onto the next grooves. Just like that, he's a couple feet farther along.

It's actually a joy to watch him as he moves expertly across the wall. His movements are economical but effective, his hold steady and unwavering. When he reaches the halfway point, my chest starts to lose the feeling that it's being squeezed by a metal band.

He's gonna make it. He's gonna be all right. He'll build a

ladder, and we'll climb to the other side. We'll get help. We'll save Mama.

He's three-quarters of the way across now.

"You can do it, you can do it," I chant under my breath, so as not to distract him. "You can do it, you can—"

Mateo yelps as his hand falls from the wall, clutching a crumbling piece of rock.

I go numb. Oh dear god, the handhold broke. It *broke*. And then, the ledge Mateo stands on also disintegrates, and he's scrabbling up the wall, trying to find purchase with his feet.

"Mateo!" I or maybe someone else screams. I can no longer tell the difference between the panic inside and outside my brain.

"Hold on, brother." Bodin frantically dumps his backpack. "I'm coming. I'm *coming*."

Whatever qualms he had about climbing earlier have disappeared. But as Bodin reaches out to grab the first handhold, to my surprise, it's my hand that grabs his arm and stops him.

"You can't," I say, my tears brimming over. "It's too dangerous. If that rock broke, another one might—and probably will under your weight. We can't lose you both."

He looks at me with a mixture of emotions I don't have time to decipher.

"Help!" Mateo yells. "I'm losing my grip."

He's hanging from the wall with a single hand now, both feet dangling. Even from here, I can tell his muscles are shaking. He won't be able to hold on for much longer.

I look around wildly. Rock, rock, more rock...and birds.

"Sylvie!" I screech.

"On it," Sylvie says, hands slapped over her ears.

But if the birds were curious about us before, they're

plain indifferent now, pecking at nothing on the ground.

I scan the wall. There's got to be another handhold, another groove. Something for his feet to rest on, to give his hand a break.

There! A small but promising notch in the rock.

"Mateo! On your right, about thirty degrees, there's a handhold," I say. "If you can reach it, you can pull yourself up."

He instinctively looks at exactly the right spot. He swings once, misses. He swings again—and manages to grab onto the notch.

As he does, the original protrusion breaks away, leaving him with the much smaller, much more difficult hold.

"Help!" Mateo hollers. "I don't want to die. I don't want to die!"

We are out of options. There is nothing left to be done. No holds left to be held, no lifelines to be thrown. Any moment now, Mateo will lose his grip. The hold will break, or he will let go, and he will die. And there's not a damn thing we can do about it.

It's funny how time slows during the most crucial moments in your life. I could be reading a book or playing the piano, and the hours pass in an instant. But now, as I stare at Mateo, waiting for his imminent death, every heartbeat feels like an eternity.

His hand flexes in the notch, and his body rises a few inches. But it's not because he's pulled himself up. No, his arms seem…shorter than before. What?

My mind must be playing tricks on me, because a moment later, Mateo plummets into the pit of crocodiles.

CHAPTER TWENTY-THREE

N o.
My mind rebels, refuses to compute. Mateo can't be dead. He cannot be gone. Just this morning, he was talking to me about Lola. Rae just gave him permission to date her. He has to go back to camp. They have to pursue their relationship, see where it leads. He simply can't be gone.

But nothing stops his fall into the pit. The birds don't form a flock and shepherd him to the ground, like they did with Sylvie. He doesn't suddenly sprout wings and fly to safety. Even the shorter arms, which I might or might not have imagined, don't do a damn thing to help him.

He just falls and falls and falls.

I close my eyes, unable to witness his impact with the ground.

"Mateo," I whisper, the anguish strangling my voice. I want to yell until my throat is raw. I want to beat my fists against the rocky ground until they bleed. But the shock robs me of any energy, so all I can do is sink listlessly to the ground.

Not so with the others. They scream, babble, and cry so loudly that I can't make out a single word.

And then, a loud rumbling fills the cave, as though a piece of machinery is coming to life. Right before our very eyes, a metal beam shoots out from the top of the opposite cliff and extends all the way to our side, where it snaps into place.

My mouth parts. Bodin, Sylvie, and Rae fall silent. A bridge across the pit. But only if we're willing to walk a very narrow beam across a crocodile pit, twenty feet in the air. It might as well be a tightrope.

"Cross the beam if you want answers," a voice intones, its volume magnified so that it fills every vein and capillary in my body.

A message from God? Surely not. But the voice has the same omniscient vibe, as though it can peer into our brains and see our every thought.

"It's a loudspeaker," Bodin says.

The four of us look at each other as the implications sink in.

"What?" Rae explodes. "That's *Xander*?"

"If there's a loudspeaker, there must also be cameras," Sylvie deduces.

"They've been watching us this entire time." I moan. "We never had a chance of getting away."

And here I thought I couldn't feel any worse. Despair washes over me, mixing with the grief and creating an unbearable cocktail of emotions.

I can't do this. I can't stand this much pain. I can't exist any longer—

Clap…clap…clap…

The slow clap disrupts my pattern of thoughts. Across the pit, Xander emerges from the shadows. He appears freshly showered, unlike the rest of us, although he's wearing the same clothes as before: raggedy jeans and an old Yale sweatshirt. Either our resident evil scientist is extra thrifty, or he's got multiple versions of the same outfit.

"Really, Xander?" Rae shouts across the cavern, all bravado. "Get a new act. This slow clap and popping out of nowhere is getting boring. You take down the sinister vibe a notch every time you repeat it."

Um, she can speak for herself. Frankly, the very sight of Xander still terrifies me, no matter *what* he's doing.

"Xander." Bodin gasps. "What are you doing here?"

The fakety-fake captain shrugs, unconcerned. "If you want answers, you know what to do."

Sylvie snorts. "Um, no thanks. I already survived one near-death experience yesterday. I'm not about to undertake another at the whim of a so-called scientist."

I look up at her and Rae. They couldn't be more different in appearance. Rae is a five-foot-two Black woman with bleach-blond hair, tattoos, and multiple piercings. Sylvie is a muscular, long-legged Filipina woman pushing six feet. But they might as well be twins in their strength. They don't get pushed around by anyone. I kinda want to be either of them when I grow up.

"The beam is solid metal. It won't break, I promise," Xander cajoles. "I just want you to come closer, so that I don't have to yell while we talk."

"Never," Rae and Sylvie say as one.

Xander raises an eyebrow, as though amused by their defiance. "What if I offered you and your friends five more days of rations, without any other abilities having to surface? You'll be heroes. That's what this little expedition was about, yes? Finding a way to help your families and friends?"

The others shake their heads, even as I consider how a steady supply of food will bolster Mama's deteriorating health.

"If you want me, you'll have to drag me kicking and screaming across that beam," Rae says. "I am not voluntarily endangering myself *or* returning to your control."

The amusement falls from the captain's face, so that his normal, resting expression returns: cold, hard cheeks and empty eyes. "That's where you're wrong. You've been under my control this entire time."

A chill runs up my spine, down my arms, along my legs. It's like my body is doing the freaking wave. But the fear finally triggers my fight-or-flight response, and I get shakily to my feet, my muscles bunching.

Before our very eyes, the facade of the friendly captain descends over Xander's face again. "You."

"M-me?" I stutter. Shoulda stayed on the ground, out of his notice.

"You want medication for your mother. Pain-relieving pills, so that she doesn't suffer for the last days of her life. Am I correct?"

All I can do is nod.

Xander bends and sweeps out his arm in a courtly gesture. "Done. Cross the beam and convince your friends to do so, and she'll have access to any medication she needs."

"But you need twelve of us, right?" I ask, my mind spinning. "Like the folktale of the twelve blind princesses. So, you *have* to give us those pills, or Mama will be so hurt that she can't participate in your challenges and your experiment will be one big failure."

He gives an amused snort. "You're a clever one, aren't you? But alas, you're wrong here. Whether or not your mother is in pain is of little consequence to me. She's *here*, and so that's enough to fulfill my quota of twelve subjects. Which, by the way, is *not* necessary. You could say that twelve is simply my lucky number. That's something you'd be familiar with, wouldn't you?"

He knows about my OCD.

The thought numbs me, even if it shouldn't be surprising. No doubt his research on his potential subjects is as thorough as it is in-depth. And yet, the idea that this evil stranger knows such a personal detail about me makes me shake so hard that I want to puke.

"So, what will it be, little girl? Leave your mother in pain — or play my game?"

Pushing aside my nausea, I turn to the others. The beam's not *that* narrow. Even Bodin should be able to plant his foot directly onto it. If it were an obstacle at a playground, six inches from the ground, we'd all race across it, no problem. We just need to ignore the twenty-foot drop and the pit of crocodiles waiting underneath. No biggie.

Before I can speak, Sylvie holds up her hand.

"I lost a parent to cancer, too," she says, "and I've never been scared of heights. It's a yes for me."

Bodin chimes in, "I hope my vote goes without saying."

My confidence grows a notch, but I always knew Rae would be the difficult one. I drop to my knees, prepared to beg. "Please, Rae. I'll do anything — "

She noisily expels air. "Oh, get up. You're embarrassing yourself."

Our eyes meet, and something passes between us — the first moment of connection since we met.

"It's a trick," Rae mutters. "You know that, right? We can't trust that man or anything he says. His word is meaningless."

"Please," I say. "I know we can all cross the beam safely. Even if there's a small chance that he'll give Mama her pills, that's better than nothing."

Rae sighs. "You don't have to convince me. I'll even go first."

She strips off her shoes and socks, squares her shoulders, and strides to the beam.

Not my enemy, anymore—if she ever was. Rae is my hero through and through.

CHAPTER TWENTY-FOUR

Rae places one bare foot on the slim surface, and her entire body trembles. I remember too late that she said she was terrified of heights.

She might not be as tough as she likes to pretend—but she's badass brave, all the way down to her toes.

I take a deep breath. If Rae can take the lead, then I can certainly follow.

Except…I don't remove my shoes, the way Rae did, so my grip might not be as good as hers. And the beam is much narrower than I thought. There's hardly an inch on either side of my sneaker, so there's little margin for error.

But I can't think about failure or death. I just focus on putting one foot in front of the other. Extend both arms to keep the balance in my core. Make sure I don't sway too much to either side, or I'll meet the same fate as Mateo.

The tears surge up my throat—but no. Thoughts of Mateo are off-limits. I have to put all of my attention on surviving.

Look straight ahead. Hone my concentration. And then—I can't help myself—my gaze flickers down. The crocodiles have their snouts tilted up, jaws open wide, waiting for one of us to fall. A clod of dirt shakes loose from my shoe. One of the crocodiles snaps it out of the air and swallows it whole.

Not. Reassuring. That could be me. But it's not. No matter how deep I have to dig, it will not be me.

Halfway across the beam, a stiff breeze buffets me. But how…? The whole time we've been in the caves, I haven't felt a semblance of wind, even underneath the gaping skylights. And now, the air blows at me *not* from across the pit, where there might be an exit, but from my side, where there's nothing but solid rock wall.

I look up. Xander's watching us, arms crossed, expression smug. That's when I get it. The breeze is not natural—it's as manufactured as this steel beam. Designed to make our already difficult task more challenging.

Ahead of me, Rae stops walking. Her calves tremble, and her breath comes in long, shuddering exhales. It doesn't take any special ability to sense that she's freaked out.

"It's only wind," I say in a low voice. "Not strong enough to knock us over. He doesn't want us to die. He only wants to mess with our minds."

Rae nods, acknowledging my words, even if she doesn't dare turn around. A moment later, she takes a step. And then another. Behind me, I hear the shuffle of Bodin's bigger feet. He's at my back again—no surprise. For some reason, he's taken it upon himself to be my protector.

I don't *need* protection, from him or anyone else. Or at least that's what Mama tells me. That's the hard lesson I'm trying to learn before she leaves my life forever. But my bravery is still a work in progress, and I can't help but feel reassured by Bodin's presence.

Rae takes her final steps and crosses onto solid ground. I'm next. Just eleven more steps, I'm guessing, now ten…

For no reason at all, I look down again. A flash of…blue? Is that right? I'd know that color anywhere, considering I wore it some time ago. Mateo's shirt. It's got to be.

My foot slips. Silly. The last thing I should be doing on a skinny ledge is letting my mind wander. I squint and I don't see any blue anywhere, so it must have been my imagination. I regain my footing, but on my very next step, my sneaker skids *again*…

Bodin catches me around the waist. "Careful," he says into my ear. "It would be a shame to lose you to crocodiles who don't even need to eat."

I quickly go on edge, pushing his hands away.

"There's something…slick on this beam." I frown at the oily black liquid coating the metal in front of me. "We need to move carefully."

Inch by infinitesimal inch, I make my way along the metal bridge. My muscles are so tight that they start to cramp, and I'm one tremor away from being knocked off balance. But I do it. I cross the pit safely, with Bodin and Sylvie close behind. It only takes nine steps to reach the end, so I step twice on the solid ground.

Bodin and Sylvie join Rae on the dirt, sweat pouring down their faces, but I stand, even as I pant with exhaustion. Xander simply waits, his hands tucked behind his back.

"What was the point of that?" Rae—who's had a little bit more respite than the rest of us—bursts out. "Do you just like torturing us? At the end of three long days, after witnessing our friend go down, that challenge—or whatever the heck you want to call it—was just cruel."

Xander rocks back and forth on his heels. "That wasn't my intention. As I've told you from the beginning, my purpose here is to push you to your emotional extremes. I thought one of you might be fatigued enough to be pushed over the brink—

but I was wrong." He shrugs. "You win some, you lose some."

His casualness is like a kick to my stomach when I'm already down. Inside my sneakers, I curl my toes inward, tensing my entire feet. "Where's Mateo?"

"He's never been safer." Xander pulls a handful of breadcrumbs from his pocket and scatters them on the ground. The birds swarm him as though they haven't eaten in a week—and maybe they haven't.

"That's a lie," I retort. "We saw him fall into the pit. We have no proof that he's not dead and dismembered, split up in the tummies of each of the crocodiles."

"Thanks for that visual," Bodin mutters.

"What about a third option?" Xander raises an eyebrow. "The one you already know but refuse to admit to yourself?"

Sylvie lifts her face from the ground, and her entire left cheek is caked with dirt. "You mean when his arms got shorter?"

She saw that, too?

"That's right." Xander nods, as though this is a classroom and Sylvie is his top student. "His powers are starting to surface."

Bodin's mouth drops. "Mateo turned into a crocodile?"

"A crocodile *person*," Xander clarifies. "He can resume partial or full human form, but he will transform into a crocodile with the moon every night. And in spite of your oh-so-shocked faces, it's not such a remarkable occurrence. In fact, it's a very pedestrian talent, for a very pedestrian boy." He gestures toward the pit. "As you can see, that's the ability that most of my subjects manifest."

My head jerks up, even as my heart rejoices that Mateo is not dead. "What are you saying? Does that mean... you've done this before? We aren't the first people you've kidnapped?"

Xander laughs, long and loud. It echoes through the

cavern, and the crocodiles grow more agitated, climbing over each other as though they're trying to escape from the pit.

"You can't possibly think I did all of this for you?" He stands and walks over to the pit, sticking his hand into the empty space. A moment later, a crocodile shoots into the air, no doubt propelled by his friends, and taps his snout against Xander's palm. "I have a very complex operation here, all designed for one purpose alone: to find my Lotus Flower Champion, the person whose one rare talent has been eluding me my entire life."

The cold begins in my core, frosting its way up my spine, vertebra by vertebra.

"Most people would call me a dreamer. Or less generously: a fool. To continue to persist, after I've failed again and again." His voice strengthens in volume and tone. "But I will not give up hope—not when salvation is within my reach. By my best estimate, there are hundreds of people with this latent ability scattered across the world. I just need one of them to fall within my control."

"But the Thai authorities must be suspicious about all the missing people, after all of this time," Bodin says.

Xander whirls toward his former employee. "Do you not think that I've thought this through? Do you not assume that I've planned every last detail, in order to make this operation a success? You've known me for a long time, Bodin. You should know by now that I leave nothing to chance."

He shakes his head sadly. "That kind of question only comes from a mind that accepts what it sees. That cannot imagine a world outside of the box. What makes you think all of my *disappearances* occur in the vicinity of Koh Samui or even Thailand? Why do you assume that's where we are now? Ever heard of Malaysia Airlines Flight 370? There are ways to make people vanish. And now, perhaps, you can answer the question that's been plaguing decades of journalists: where all of those people went."

I blink. No *way*. Did Xander just take credit for the disappearance of MH370? Sure, he mentioned it before, but I thought he was just grandstanding. Is he actually *responsible* for that flight vanishing?

Xander claps his hands together, not slowly this time, but briskly and impatiently. "Okay. Let's get you lot back to camp so that we can continue our game."

"Continue?" I echo. "But we never started."

Our captor breaks into a smile, so wide that I can see his chipped cuspid. "Don't you get it yet? You've been playing the entire time. This whole island is a game. The polished wall with a golden key hidden just out of reach. The extra sticky mud in the river that made it incredibly difficult for you to wash off. Even Mateo's rock wall, whose handholds were designed to crumble after he reached the halfway point."

He sneers at me. "How you didn't reach your emotional breaking point, I'll never know."

I return his stare, not giving anything away—even though I am shaking, trembling, vibrating on the inside. He's procured a lot of information about me. He might even know that I have OCD, but he has no idea how it feels to live with this disorder.

He doesn't know that I am tested every second of every day, from wake to sleep—and often during the night, as well, in the form of stress dreams. He doesn't know that meltdowns like that are a regular occurrence in my everyday life. So, the mud might have pushed me to the brink…but I've been there many, many times.

I don't say anything, though. Because, in this game, knowledge is power. And although my advantage may not seem like much, it's the only one I've got.

CHAPTER TWENTY-FIVE

Once we exit the cave, we step into an environment very similar to the one we left behind: the *other* side of the mountain, several stories above sea level, miles of green trees, the sparkling turquoise waters beyond.

No fruit vendors waiting to offer us cut-up pieces of pineapple. No robust forest teeming with wildlife. No civilization. Bodin couldn't have been any more wrong. It's hard to fault him, though, when he's being escorted under armed guard like all of us.

But there is one major difference to the scenery. We've stopped near a makeshift helipad, a large rectangle of flat dirt ground that's been cleared of any vegetation. There's a helicopter waiting. My heart leaps. A way off this island. *Could any of the other castaways have any flying skills? Can we overpower Xander and his guards and escape? How heavily is the helicopter guarded?*

As if he can read my thoughts, Xander snaps handcuffs on my wrists—or at least, they *feel* like metal bracelets. Except they're invisible. Nothing concrete appears to bind my wrists, but I can't move them, just the same. Hardened wind? A weird magnetic force? No clue. But the cuffs bite into my skin as sharply as any crocodile teeth.

"It's always the quiet ones," he snarls right in my face. The scent of garlic intermingles with his natural bad breath, making me want to puke. If my vomit splatters all over him, so much the better. "Take your pills." He hands me a couple of packets of brightly colored tablets. I accept them with my fingers and raise my cuffed wrists to check them. They're the medicine that Mama needs, all right. But there's only a two-day supply.

"But you said we could have all the medication she needs—"

"I never said for how long," Xander interrupts, showing me his teeth once more. "Did you really think I was going to give you an infinite supply?"

I open my mouth but snap it closed. Disappointment swirls in my stomach. Rae was right. We can't trust anything our captor says, and thus, there's no use arguing with him. We are completely at his mercy.

"I have my eye on you," he continues. "When you break, it won't be anything *I* did, but your inherent weakness getting the best of you. I cannot wait to watch your epic defeat…at your own hands. In fact, I'm having popcorn flown in, just for the occasion."

Right *again*. Witnessing our torture is pure entertainment for him.

The temptation to spit on him is strong. It's not vomit, but at least I can generate that bodily fluid at will. But I don't spit, and I don't say anything. I'm stronger than my OCD. (Mama's been telling me this for years, and I'm finally getting around to believing it.) This whole damn island is an exposure for me, so I'm building more and more resistance every day.

Xander walks down the line, cuffing the others, and then struts off, leaving us behind with his uniformed guards.

They flank us on either side, with traditional Thai krabongs—or blunt sticks used as weapons—on their shoulders and shields in front of their chests. With a few curt gestures, they usher us toward the waiting helicopter.

We clamber on, one by one—Sylvie and Rae in the middle row, and Bodin and I shoved in the back.

That's when one of the guards standing on the helipad removes their oversize, misshapen hood and reveals a distinctly reptilian head, complete with a crocodile snout.

I gasp. "A croc-person!" The guard is human from the neck down. Human arms, human legs, human torso. It is one thing to listen to Rae and Xander refer to one, an awe-inspiring experience to witness one myself.

"Unbelievable, isn't it?" Sylvie says, twisting in her seat to speak to me, the headset squashing down her hair. "One of them brushed my forearm with a hand. It had calluses and rough skin, just like the rest of us."

"Because they *are* one of us," Bodin says. "Weren't you listening? They were probably kidnapped by Xander, just like us, and then forced to serve him once they came into their shapeshifting ability."

"It could be Mateo," Rae says. She continues to face forward, not looking at any of us, but the regret comes through her voice loud and clear. "I should've been…nicer to him."

Sylvie picks up her hand. "Hey. You're doing the very best that you can. And that's all any of us can ask for."

The pilot climbs into his seat—another crocodile person. He doesn't even bother with his hood. I guess their identity is no longer a secret. I sincerely hope he's retained enough of his human brain to fly this aircraft.

"Where's Mateo?" I call over the whirring of the helicopter blades.

"Don't worry about him," the pilot yells back. But while I can hear Rae over the headset, back to her badass self and grumbling about the lack of seat belts, I don't hear the pilot's voice in my ear, which means he must be on a different channel.

Before I can respond, the helicopter lifts into the air, leaving my stomach behind. I'm not a good flier even in the best of conditions. A choppy helicopter, piloted by a crocodile? My heart rate's skyrocketing before we've cleared the mountains.

Bodin peers at me. "Your knuckles are white."

I try to relax my interlaced fingers. "These cuffs make it hard to grip anything else."

He holds my gaze for a full minute before he nods toward the large square windows. We're high in the sky, as impossibly blue as the sea below, with only a few wisps of clouds to mar the expanse.

"Every bit of knowledge gives us more power," Bodin says. "For example, now we know there's a helicopter on the island. Which means we've got a potential getaway vehicle."

"He's right," Rae says, pressing her face against the window. "And here, we've got the advantage of a bird's-eye view. Quick, people, tell me what you see."

I twist toward the window, imitating her position, though I don't press my face against the glass. Although smudged and most certainly dirty, it allows us a view of the entire island.

Just as Bodin predicted, the island is bisected by a mountain. The green vegetation of the undulating slopes sparkles like emeralds, lined on either side by white sand beaches.

"I see a waterfall. Looks romantic," Sylvie says wryly. "Maybe I'll bring Elizabeth back some day."

"Look!" I point at the peak of the mountain, where a hut with a thatched roof is perched. A ribbon of smoke floats out of the chimney. "That must be where Xander lives. More importantly, it looks just like the huts that Bodin pointed out to me—"

"Which means we're definitely still in Thailand," Bodin concludes. "Even if Xander wants us to believe otherwise."

"And there!" Rae says. "See underneath the hut, where there's glimpses of concrete? There's a whole damn compound there. This operation is more complex than we know. We never stood a chance."

Bodin presses his lips together. That's when I remember: it was his idea to attempt to traverse the mountain in the west. But he shouldn't feel badly. We pushed him into a leadership role and forced him to make a decision.

"It's okay," I whisper, taking the initiative. Being brave. "There's no way you—or any of us, really—could've known."

He smiles at me gratefully.

A feeling inside me surges up, all bubbly and effervescent. This, I realize, is how it feels to be courageous—and to reap its rewards.

The helicopter touches down on the beach, and our fellow castaways emerge from the palm trees, shading their eyes from the sand that the blades have kicked up. I automatically count them. Lola and Preston. Khun Anita and Kit. Elizabeth. Eduardo. But where is Mama?

I scan the tree line—and there she is. Bringing up the rear, 'cause she's not as fast as the others. In fact, she's hobbling, using a spindly, twisted branch as a walking stick. Her frail body is nearly bent in two.

Hot tears stab at my chest, my throat, my eyes. She's deteriorated so much in the short time we've been gone. Although the blades are still rotating, I fling open the hatch door and hop onto the sand.

"Alaia, wait!" Bodin calls, but I don't listen. Because Mama is right there, within my reach. And with Mama, everything will be okay again.

I sprint in her direction, kicking up even more sand than the helicopter, but at least I have the wherewithal to slow down as I approach, so that I don't knock her over.

As soon as I reach her, I throw my arms around her. Or at least I fling my cuffed wrists up and over her head. It makes for a cumbersome hug, since I'm basically squeezing her between the vise of my arms, but she's been so skinny since she started chemo, it hardly matters.

"I'm back. I've missed you so much. How are you?" The words tumble out of my mouth, one after the other, giving her no chance to respond. "I have your pills. Here. Take them now. Do you have water?" I remove my arms from around her body and try to reach into my backpack, where I'd stuffed the precious packets of pills, but the cuffs make my hands clumsy. Instead, I turn my back so that Mama can get them out herself. "Take them, Mama. You'll feel better as soon as you do."

She digs out the pills and swallows them dry. "Better save some of your words," she says, her voice low and brittle, as though it—along with her body—is in danger of breaking in two. "Someone's waiting to see you. He just got back half an hour before you."

I look past Mama to the main shelter, where a figure sits on the bamboo platform. Mateo! My heart leaps. His clothes are a little stretched out—no doubt because a crocodile had been wearing them—but he's fully human from his legs to his torso, from his fingers to his head.

I let out a whoop and run to him. "Mateo. You're un-harmed. Uninjured." I stand there awkwardly for a moment. This feels like a situation where I *should* hug him, but I can't bring myself to do it. Instead, I sit next to him on the platform.

"For now." He scans my face. "Did Xander explain to you...the nature of my ability?"

"You turn..,into...a crocodile?" I say haltingly.

He nods. "With the moon every night and in times of stress. I've already made the transformation once. It's creepy in there, in the mind of a crocodile." His eyes are glued to my face, as though searching for a sign of revulsion. "I'm still *me*, but I'm overwhelmed by the instincts of a reptile. It's like trying to think in the middle of an ear-splitting concert."

He licks his lips, which are humanly pink. "The other crocs tell me that with practice, I'll learn how to delay the transformation and even partially shift, so that I'm less susceptible to the moon and other forces. Of course, they also tell me that with every transformation, I'll lose more and more of my humanity. Sooner or later, I'll cease to be Mateo at all. I'll be just another one of Xander's employees, with only enough humanity to execute his will."

"How long do you have?" I ask in a small voice.

"A few weeks. Maybe a month or two, if I'm lucky." He pauses, uncertainty warring in his eyes. "Lola says it doesn't matter. That my situation doesn't change her feelings. But how is that possible? Why would she want to start a relationship with a crocodile?"

"Give it a chance," I say sympathetically. "It's early days yet. We've been on this island for—what? Four days. And we've been away half of that time. Just let…nature take its course."

The words seem wrong, somehow. They're the ones that I would give a friend back home. But we're not home. We're on a twisted island, trying to survive, where one day feels like a lifetime and four days is an eternity. Given the uncertainty of our futures, I don't blame Mateo for wanting to lock down his relationship status.

"Thanks, Alaia." He ducks his head. "Do *you* think I'm a freak?"

"Of course not!" I exclaim. "We're going through some weird stuff. Like, you-couldn't-make-this-up kind of bizarre. But you'll always be my friend."

The others start trooping back into camp. Sylvie and Elizabeth's arms are linked together. Rae and Lola chatter nonstop, copious amounts of flowers falling out of Lola's mouth and drifting away in the breeze. Preston lopes behind them, silent because his mouth is once more a pinhole. Sylvie and Rae's hands are free, so the pilot must've dismantled their cuffs.

I twist my own wrists. Better go see the pilot, too, to get mine off.

As I stand to go search for the pilot, Rae punches Preston playfully in the arm. And—I kid you not—his cheeks flame fire red. Has he learned humility since we've been away? Or has Rae's distance made his heart grow fonder? Talk about bizarre. They'd make an interesting couple, but stranger things have happened on this island.

I trudge toward the beach as Eduardo and Kit resume their places on a court marked with lines of ash. The hoop has been constructed out of twisted-up bamboo, and a coconut stands in for the ball.

They begin to play. Eduardo is probably a decade older

than Kit, bigger and more muscular, and yet Kit seems to have the edge on him. The kid's got bounce. With his soaring height, he makes dunking the coconut look easy.

But there's more. I stop short and gape.

Kit seems to be working with the nature around him. He'll toss the ball to a pile of sticks, which passes the ball back to him. He shoots the coconut into a tree branch, which knocks it through the hoop.

"What on earth?" I ask.

"Kit manifested his ability while we were away," Mateo says, his eyes lighting up. He's so full of life, brimming with wonder. It's almost unthinkable that all of that will be lost in a few short weeks. "He can transport his soul from vessel to vessel. According to your mom, he should be able to transfer it to both sentient and non-sentient objects—a monkey, a naga, a pile of gold. Anything goes. But no animals or gold here, so he hasn't been able to try."

"Are you saying that's Kit passing the ball to himself? And not, say, a pile of sticks?"

"Yep." He bobs his head up and down.

"Amazing." I look back at the game, where Kit has just scored his fourth bucket on Eduardo. The ability suits him to a T...but not everyone's ability does. Take Mateo, for example. What reason does he have to shapeshift into a reptile? It doesn't make any sense.

A thunderous whirring fills the air, and the helicopter rises above the tree line, whipping the hair out of our faces.

The chopper's leaving? But...but...

I run as fast as I can, through the trees and onto the beach. The leaves slap my face, my shoes sink into sand, but I don't notice. My full attention is on the helicopter getting smaller and farther away with every second.

Presumably with the pilot driving it.

Bodin's the only person left on the beach.

"I tried to stop him," he says wryly. "But he said that Xander expected him back. And he took the tool to dismantle the 'windcuffs' with him. That's what he called them, anyway."

So, they *are* made out of wind. But that's not the biggest reveal at this moment. I look down at my wrists, held unnaturally close together.

"Oops," I say sheepishly. "I guess I was a little too excited to see my mom."

Bodin arches an eyebrow. "Were those extra few seconds really worth it?"

"I guess we'll find out," I say, even as I know I'll be regretting my actions in a couple of short hours.

CHAPTER TWENTY-SIX

Scratch the two hours. Make that two *minutes* before regret takes over my brain.

It's awful not having your hands free. These annoying wind bracelets make everything more difficult. It's hard to perform camp chores like gathering firewood. It's hard to pull the sweaty strands of my hair out of my face. It's even hard to eat from the buffet that Xander's employees are refilling—our reward, I'm assuming, from Sylvie or Mateo or Kit manifesting their ability.

I eat a little bit and then give up the attempt when I keep dropping food in my lap. While my fellow castaways chow down, I hang back and observe the team of six croc-people that's doing Xander's bidding. Are they the same guards as before? Hard to tell. Now that some of us have seen the crocodiles, they no longer wear their funny-shaped masks (which, in retrospect, is the perfect shape to accommodate their crocodile snouts.) From the neck down, their very human bodies wear silver jumpsuits. From the neck up…well, their crocodile heads are also very similar.

Although that's not quite true. Now that I've been studying them, I can detect subtle variations in their crocodile forms. Rounder snouts, slightly thicker scaling. Eyes set lower or higher, as well as jawlines with more or less of an overbite.

They deposit the final dishes on the buffet table—stir-fried basil chicken and Thai omelets—and I jump to my feet.

I already let the pilot—and his key—slip through my fingers. I'm not about to miss another opportunity to get these cuffs off.

"Excuse me," I say as politely as possible, although I can't prevent the stress from leaking into my voice. "Your, um, friend left on the helicopter before he set my wrists free. Could you help?"

They must understand me. They took orders from Xander. They executed his demands perfectly, and the pilot croc actually *spoke* to me. I don't expect them to become my best friends. But they don't even acknowledge me.

Pretty sure that I *haven't* developed the psychic ability of invisibility, so I jump right in front of another croc-person's path. "Excuse me," I say, less politely and more authoritatively.

To my surprise, he actually stops, but I can't tell if it's because of my words or because he doesn't want to plow me over.

I hold out my cuffed hands. "Please. Do you have a key to take them off?"

The croc-person looks at me with his beady black eyes and shakes his head…sadly? Not sure. I've had no practice reading the facial expressions of reptiles—or any nonhuman creature, for that matter.

Before I can plead my case, he neatly steps around me and continues on his way. I try the same approach with three more croc-people and get even less results. Either they aren't allowed to talk to me—or they choose not to.

Dang it. I throw myself on the ground behind a copse of bushes (on top of my trusty sleeping bag, of course). Let the others chase down the departing guards in another dead end. I need to begin the miserable act of feeling sorry for myself.

I jiggle my hands back and forth. The wind remains hard and unyielding. What's more, the leaves with their spindly stems cling to my hair, almost like insects.

I swallow hard. I'm locked down by these wind bracelets. Will I ever get free? The thought pound against the periphery of my mind. I grit my teeth. No, don't do this. Please.

Of course, my OCD has never done anything just because I asked. I visualize a smooth, polished wall holding off the intrusive thoughts. But that just reminds me of the burnished wall caging us in, and my resolve crumbles.

I have to get these cuffs off. I am trapped. The world shrinks around me, getting smaller by the moment. Squeezing my body, flattening my lungs. I can't *breathe* with my hands restrained. I can't live. I can't exist. I need them off me, now. This very second. I can't go on any longer. I can't, I can't, I can't—

"Alaia." Khun Anita's melodic voice drifts over me. "What are you doing down there?"

I curl more tightly into a ball.

"I may be short, but even I can see over these bushes." The voice—the smile in it—is genuine. About half as comforting as Mama's, which is the best compliment I can give someone. "Can you come out of there, please? I need your help."

I reluctantly climb out of the bushes, which brings me fully into Khun Anita's view. The copse, however, continues to shield us from the rest of the camp.

The older woman hands me a sharp shell, as well as a large handful of her waist-length hair. "Could you cut my hair?"

The request slices through me like the gleaming cream-colored shell. "But your hair," I protest. "It's so long, so lustrous—"

"Still black, too, with the help of a bottle of dye or three." She winks.

"Why do you want to cut your beautiful hair?" It would be akin to butchering off a limb for me. "And why do you want *me* to do it?" I hold up my cuffed wrists. "As you can see, my hands are indisposed."

"I want to do an experiment." She beckons me closer, not answering my last question. Her kind eyes tell me, however, that she chose me for a very precise reason: she wants to distract me from my panic. "These have been hard days. Some of the most difficult of my life, at least physically. But not emotionally. You see, Alaia, I'm an old lady—"

"You can't be older than sixty," I interject. There's wisdom in her face, sure. But although her skin is soft, her face is relatively wrinkle free, just like Mama's.

"You're very sweet." She smiles, and the *one* line in her forehead pops into existence. "And I have a lot of life left in me. But what I mean is: I've already had the best days of my life. And I've already experienced the worst pain imaginable."

She glances over her shoulder, toward the makeshift coconut-ball court. For a moment, Kit's head comes into view as he launches himself into the air. He must've already finished his enormous plate of spaghetti and meatballs. Kinda surprised that he's playing sports so soon after a full meal. Mama would say, *he's young*, in a tone of voice that suggests that youth itself is a superpower.

"I worry about Kit," she continues. "That child is destined for greatness, and I don't want his life cut short because of this sojourn into hell. I don't want him to suffer. But this worry pales in comparison to what I've already experienced:

my daughter's death."

Her eyes trace the planes of my face, my cheeks, my nose, as though she is superimposing her daughter's features over mine. "I held her hand. I watched her die. *That* was the worst moment of my life. The most exquisite torture that I've ever endured, a test of my will that I didn't believe I could survive."

"Oh, Khun Anita. I'm so sorry—"

She moves her finger to her lips, shushing me. "It was a decade ago. But oh, how I cried. It's unnatural, you see. Children are supposed to bury their parents, not the other way around. The biggest tragedy of any parent is having to survive their children." Her voice cracks.

"I bet she was an amazing woman," I say.

Khun Anita's lips twitch. "She had her moments. But I won't put her on a pedestal, the way your mom says has been done to her. For good or for bad, she will always be my baby, as Kit is now."

Over her shoulder, Kit bounces into the air again, his arm swinging wide as he dunks the coconut through the hoop. Noticing my gaze, Khun Anita turns, too. The sheen of sadness in her eyes turns to pride.

Soon enough, however, she faces me once more and taps the shell that I'm still holding. "Cut."

That's right. Khun Anita didn't tell me about her daughter's death to pass the time. This story is why Khun Anita wants to perform an experiment.

"So, that's when you manifested your ability," I guess.

She nods. "It's a subtle ability, not as showy as the others. But it's a power, nonetheless. Your mom confirmed: it's straight out of the folktales. I can embed messages into a fragrant lock of my hair, just like in the stories." She picks up her waterfall of locks and lets it fall through her fingers, scrutinizing it as though she might read its DNA between the strands.

"My Aruna—modern, independent woman that she was—she refused to tell me the name of Kit's father. What's more, her dying wish was for Kit to grow up in the United States." She shrugs, but there is nothing careless about the gesture. "What could I do but pick up and move to the States, leaving behind my husband of forty years? My late husband, oh, he was a stubborn man, set in his ways. Refused to leave India. It wasn't an easy decision for us to live apart, but it was important to my daughter. And so, every summer, Kit and I visited him in India for three months. The rest of the time, we lived in the United States, and my husband and I communicated primarily through letters."

She dabs her eyes, but her spine remains straight; her shoulders stay square. It must be this strength that's allowed her to sacrifice so much for her daughter, for Kit.

"One day, on a whim, I put a lock of my hair in the envelope," she continues. "And wouldn't you know it? My husband could sense everything I had to say in my letter, just by holding that piece of hair. More than that, he could conjure my presence, my skin, my touch, my smell. All of his senses were activated, as though I was actually present, in person.

"From that moment until his death, I simply sent him a lock of hair every day, and he knew exactly what I wanted to convey." She pulls the long strands around her fingers. "That's why I grew my hair so long. Because I never wanted to run out."

"And you never questioned this ability?" I ask.

"I didn't have the framework or the vocabulary to explain it," she replies. "But the supernatural occurs every day, if you know where to look."

I run the pad of my finger over the shell—and come away

with a cut. "You want to recreate the experiment here." It's a statement, rather than a question.

"The only person I ever attempted to communicate with was my late husband." She wets her lips. "I need to confirm that it *is* an ability that I manifested. Maybe…my husband and I imagined the whole thing. It's possible that we missed each other so dearly that it was simply wishful thinking."

I give the shell back to her and hold up my cuffed wrists once more. "Anyone else would be better qualified for the job."

"No," she says firmly. "I want it to be you. You and I may be from different generations, but we're the same. And I'm not just talking about our lustrous locks." She smiles sadly. "I lost a daughter. You're losing your mother. That connects us." She swallows. "Xander believes our abilities manifest when we're pushed to our emotional extremes. But I think it's more than that. I think it also depends on the forming and severing of connections, in a deep, complex way. My ability wouldn't have come to the surface if it wasn't for my daughter; Preston wouldn't have manifested a pinhole mouth if he didn't carry his father's abuse so close to his heart."

She presses the shell back into my palm. "You're the only one who can do it, Alaia."

I nod, not daring to speak lest the enormity of my emotions betray me. Khun Anita holds up a thick section of her hair. Although my cuffs hinder me, the shell is so honed that it slices through the hair in an instant.

Khun Anita holds the lock between her palms and whispers a message into its strands. She then ties the hair around a young palm tree, making sure it shows clearly against the green trunk and doesn't blow away.

"There," she says, stroking the literal hair bow that she's formed. "And now, we wait."

CHAPTER TWENTY-SEVEN

And we wait. And wait. And wait.

Apparently, I picked such a good hiding place that none of the other castaways even think to wander in this direction, not even Mama. Of course, it's possible — and even likely — that Khun Anita had informed Mama that she would distract me.

After an hour, Khun Anita pushes herself off the flat boulder on which she's been sitting. "My bones are creaking. And your mother will be wondering where you are. The hair will be here tomorrow. If no one finds the hair and follows the message embedded within it by then, we can always lead somewhere here and ask them to touch it."

She pats me on the cheek and then trudges back toward camp.

I stand slowly, first shaking out one foot and then the other. They're both tingling due to me sitting in the same position for so long. But that's not why I'm lingering.

The sun has sunk into the sea, leaving behind orange and purple streaks, as though the sky itself mourns its departure. The water splashes onto the beach in a lulling pattern, a gentle meeting of the elements rather than an angry give-and-take. It's been peaceful here, sitting next to Khun Anita, listening to the waves, watching Mother Nature paint the sky.

My mind is calm. No intrusive thoughts jostle for dominance. In fact, I'm not thinking at all, and I'm not quite ready to lose this peace.

I walk along the beach, right at the water's edge. The waves kiss my sneakers, soaking them bit by bit. I wish I could take them off—no doubt, barefoot in the sand is a more romantic aesthetic—but such an action is inconceivable.

A few yards later, I realize I'm not alone. A figure sits on a large rock, its snout tilted toward the sky. Not a fellow castaway, then, but a croc-person.

I walk toward the rock, making plenty of noise so as not to startle them. They turn as I approach, and in the dim light, I recognize him, still in his silver uniform—the one croc-person who bothered to acknowledge me, the one who seemed to smile sadly at my troubles.

"Lovely night, isn't it?" I say as I perch on the rock next to him. And it is. The stars are beginning to peek out. I can identify the cluster of the mother hen and her six chicks, which Bodin pointed out to me only a few days ago. So much has happened. Everything has changed. And yet, the same sky continues to blanket us. The same stars sparkle proudly, indifferent to what happens below.

There's comfort in that. No matter what I do—live or die, survive or fail—the stars will continue to shine. The world will continue to spin. Life will go on.

The croc-person grunts, which is more than I was hoping for.

"I have a favor to ask," I say slowly, holding up my wrists. "These cuffs—"

"I know." His voice is low, gravelly, and very guttural, as though he's swallowed a bunch of rocks and they're grinding against one another.

"So you *can* speak," I say wryly.

"For the time being," he says. "Words get more difficult to retrieve with each transformation."

I bite my lip. Inside this croc-person is a human, just like Mateo, imprisoned in a cage that gets more permanent with each passing day. It seems shallow to bother him with my cuffs, and yet, I only have a short reprieve before I spiral once more.

Before I can figure out how to phrase my request, he holds up something small and shiny. I suck in a breath. Is that what I think it is?

"I didn't have the tool when you asked me earlier. Now, I do." Each word is slow and guttural, but I understand him easily. So, the croc-people *are* allowed to interact with us. The others, earlier, just couldn't be bothered. I'm touched and honored that this croc-person would go to so much trouble for me.

Without speaking, he fits the tool into my invisible cuffs and turns until I hear a *whoosh*. Just like that, the wind dissipates, and I'm free.

Joy bubbles up inside me, and I look at him, gratitude in my eyes.

"My name is Three," the croc-person says.

"Three? Like the number?" I ask.

"Yep."

"I'm Alaia," I say, even as I wonder if all the croc-people are stripped of their original names when they become Xander's employees. An impersonal number, versus a unique identifier, keeps them in line. It reminds them, even if they sometimes walk on two feet, that they are always something separate from humanity. Always under Xander's control.

Which, frankly, makes two of us.

"The windcuffs were a test, to push you to your limits,"

Three says. "The helicopter pilot didn't leave by accident. Xander instructed him to take off without uncuffing you. It wasn't your fault."

My mouth parts. The voice inside me has been berating me all afternoon. I was careless. I wasn't thinking. I was too impulsive. And with a single speech, Three has laid my self-recriminations to rest.

"Thank you," I say. "That means a lot to me."

He stands, and I swear that he winks. If my memories from visiting the crocodile farms are correct, crocodiles have extra eyelids, the third one being a transparent membrane that covers their eyeballs so that they can see under water.

"Wait—" I say, as something occurs to me. "If the windcuffs were a test, will you get in trouble for helping me?"

"Not important." There's no tone in a croc-person's voice, no nuance. I can't tell if Three means that he won't get in very *much* trouble—or if he will but he doesn't want me to worry about it.

I'm more touched than ever. This croc-person, whom I don't even know, sacrificed to alleviate my pain and suffering, just because he is a decent creature.

With this much goodness in the world, we *have* to be able to escape this hell of a paradise. Good triumphs over evil. That's what happens in every fable, in every folktale, right? And it has to apply here, in Xander's world, because this is the island where those tales come to life.

"I have to go," Three says abruptly. "But if you or your mother or any of the other castaways need anything, just ask for me. Three. The others will know who you're talking about." He points up at the night sky. "The moon's coming."

"What happens when the moon comes?" I call.

But he has no response for me. With one last tip of the head, which I'm beginning to equate to a smile, he hurries away.

CHAPTER TWENTY-EIGHT

The footprints that Three leaves in the sand with his bulky black boots are heavy and distinctive. What *does* happen with the moon? Three is clearly a trained employee. He can partially transform into a crocodile from the neck up, which means he shouldn't be susceptible to the moon, not like Mateo—

I freeze. Mateo. I completely forgot. I should be with him when he transforms with the moon for the very first time.

My heart in my throat, I scan the night sky. No moon yet, but there, a spot on the horizon glows, as though about to give birth to our natural satellite.

I still have time.

Turning, I run in the opposite direction from Three's footsteps, toward camp. The long flames of the fire reach into the sky, beckoning me back. When I arrive, however, sweaty and out of breath, all ten of my fellow castaways, minus Mateo, are clustered around the smaller lean-to.

I head toward the sunset orange scarf wrapped around Mama's head. The fabric is stained with dirt and who knows what else, but it still functions effectively as a beacon.

"Mama! What's happening?"

She picks up my wrist, rubbing at the tender skin the cuffs left behind. That's Mama for you. She notices every detail of my body. A new hairstyle, a different shade of eyeshadow. I used to joke that it was her superpower. Now, I wonder how true my statement was.

"Mateo's inside." Mama gestures at the lean-to constructed out of enormous palm leaves and a bamboo frame. "He wanted to transform in privacy, but he asked us to stay close by."

I catch Bodin's eye, on the edge of the crowd, and he nods once. I want to go to his side, to show him my newly freed wrists. But there's so much hushed anticipation in the group that it's almost a tangible wall holding me back.

"Something's moving." Lola appears on my other side, her hair grazing against my left arm. Casually, so she doesn't notice, I touch my right finger to her other arm.

Equilibrium restored, I squint at the elongated black triangle that is the opening to the lean-to. There! A ripple of something, a bit of moving shadow...

A scaly snout pokes out of the lean-to, turned iridescent green by the firelight, followed by a crocodile head. A ridged back. Stubby fore and hind legs. A swishing tail.

"This is the best magic trick!" Preston shouts gleefully, making full use of his temporary human mouth. "In goes Mateo, and out comes a crocodile."

"Shush." Elizabeth gives him a stern look, which he blithely ignores. He's deriving so much joy out of Mateo's suffering that his mouth will likely transform at any moment.

The crocodile stops in the middle of the cleared circle, as though unsure how to proceed.

No, not the crocodile, I correct myself. Mateo. The

crocodile is Mateo.

"Hey, brother, you're going to be okay." Eduardo approaches Mateo and extends his hand. "I know it's creepy inside the mind of a reptile, but we're here for you."

The crocodile snaps its jaws at Eduardo, almost taking off his hand.

Eduardo pales and snatches his hand out of the air, hiding it behind his back. He shakes his head back and forth, as though questioning if the crocodile is truly his brother.

I don't blame him. I'm also having a hard time reconciling the crocodile with the boy I sat next to this afternoon, especially since I didn't witness the transformation.

But then, the crocodile curls in on himself. Unlike Three, he doesn't seem to be able to talk, at least in this form.

Sylvie steps forward, and I remember all of a sudden that she can communicate mind-to-mind with birds and bats. Does her mental telepathy extend to crocodiles, too? It didn't while we were in the caves, but maybe the recipient has to be open to her entreaty.

"He's sorry, Eduardo," Sylvie says. I guess that's a resounding yes. "He loves you, but his mind's all jumbled up. He didn't mean to scare you. He understands if you don't feel comfortable coming closer. He wouldn't be comfortable, either."

"Th-thanks, brother," Eduardo says in a shaky voice. Instead of approaching, however, he takes one large step back, so that he's within range of the heat emanating from the firepit. "I love you, too. I just need a moment."

I swallow. I know what I *should* do—but I don't want to. My feet yearn to stay rooted to the spot. I cannot approach a crocodile. I just can't.

And yet…it's also Mateo. My friend. Which means I have to show him that I'm not afraid of his new body. And perhaps, if I say something, Lola will, too.

I compromise. Standing where I am in the circle, I say, "It's okay, Mateo. We know it's you. And you're perfectly safe here."

I nudge Lola, making sure that I don't touch her bare shoulder with anything other than my own covered one.

"I… Mateo, you're still as cute as ever," she manages to say, her voice husky with tears. "Even though you could probably use a good dose of my Jo Malone lotion."

Mateo pads closer to me—or, more accurately, closer to Lola. His muscles are tight, his movements deliberate. It's like he's holding himself in check, so he doesn't do something he'll regret.

Every cell inside of me shouts at me to run, but I force myself to stay perfectly, utterly still, in support of Mateo, in support of Lola. In different ways, they both have propped me up on this island. The least I can do is *not* run screaming into the woods.

Ever so slowly, Mateo reaches out his foreleg to Lola, who has crouched down to be closer to him, but he doesn't touch her. He's got five fingers, without any webbing between them, like his human form. The difference is: his fingers are thicker now, almost bloated, and covered in scales. A few seconds later, he retreats.

"He wants to say *thank you*, Lola," Sylvie narrates. "For not being repulsed by him. It means the world to him. But he can't trust himself, or rather, his crocodile instincts, and he would never forgive himself if he accidentally hurts you. That's why he's backing away."

"I understand," Lola says, sniffling. "But Mateo, please know that I care about you, whether you're a crocodile, a human, or something in between. That won't change."

Sylvie opens her mouth, as though to translate more of

Mateo's thoughts. But at that moment, Bodin whirls around. "Who's there? What do you want?"

The words are barely out of his mouth before we're swarmed by croc-people. They come at us from every direction, with shields and krabongs. I throw up my hands in a weak attempt to protect myself. But they're not interested in me.

They surround Mateo, throwing a net over him. Fury ignites in my stomach, and I scream, although it just gets lost in the chaos. Mateo struggles, his powerful tail thrashing wildly, but cannot throw the net off his back. If there's one thing these croc-people know, it's how to restrain one of their own.

"Where are you taking him? What do you want?" Lola shrieks. "Mateo belongs with us. He's not part of you, not part of Xander's army."

The croc-people ignore her. But once Mateo is secured, five of them turn and make a beeline for a different target each. Elizabeth. Lola. Preston. Sylvie. Kit.

"You're coming with us," one of the croc-people says. Deep, guttural. Maybe all of them sound the same, but I still recognize that scratchy voice.

"What? Why?" Rae scrabbles forward, desperate to reach her sister. "Why them?"

Three scans our faces, not to find me but to *avoid* me. "The five of you, plus Mateo, have manifested your abilities — and they are not the one for which Xander is searching. None of you are the Lotus Flower Champion. And thus, you are no longer useful to him. At the same time, your new powers are a threat. So, you must be…neutralized."

CHAPTER TWENTY-NINE

"**N**eutralized?" Rae explodes. "What does that mean?" She wraps her arms around her sister's waist, trying to wrestle her away from the guard. The croc-person calmly snaps a pair of windcuffs on Lola, as though Rae isn't there.

"I think it means Xander's going to kill them," Eduardo says, looking warily at the krabong that a guard points at his face.

"Not. Helpful," Rae snaps as Lola twists around to face her older sister, tears streaming down her face.

"I don't want to die, Rae!" she screams. "Don't let me die!"

With a gentleness I've never seen, Rae wipes away her tears. "I know, sissy. I know."

"You're not dying," I say, setting my jaw, my teeth. I'm as determined as I've ever been. "Not if we have anything to do about it."

Although I didn't intend them to be, my words serve as a battle cry. Those of us that are free begin to attack, all at once. I launch myself at the croc-person restraining Sylvie and sink my teeth into their shoulder. The guard yelps as my teeth cut through the uniform, and satisfaction rushes through me, even though I know I'll have to brush my teeth and rinse out my mouth a thousand times later.

Khun Anita shoves her frail body in between the guard and her grandson, Rae kicks out furiously at any and all employees, and Eduardo starts picking up croc-people and tossing them aside. He can't get to his brother inside the net, though. For every guard he disposes of, two more get in his face. Bodin attempts his own rescue and jumps into the group of three guards who surround Preston, and even Mama gets in on the action, wrapping her scarf around a crocodile snout and pulling with all of her might.

The battle lasts two, maybe three minutes. We are simply outnumbered and outmatched. The guards try to hold back; I can tell. But I still receive blows over my eye and in my stomach. Pain ricochets through me, and I ride the wave until it abates. The remaining tingles tell me it's going to bruise, but I've always been able to bear physical hurt more than emotional discomfort.

All twelve castaways are now restrained, some by cuffs, some by arms bent behind backs. Blood drips down Bodin's face, and Rae snarls as a guard yanks her arm a little too hard. Khun Anita and Mama, too, are similarly subdued, but at least I can't see any obvious injuries. Eduardo's on the ground, surrounded by three guards. No one touches me, though.

A guard stands over me, his muscles tense. "No sudden moves, little girl. I won't touch you unless I have to. Three's orders."

Too stunned to question his words, I pull my knees to my chest, keeping as still as possible.

Three shakes his head and sighs. "No one said anything about death," he says. "Please don't struggle."

"Why else are you taking us, if not to kill us?" Preston bellows, yanking his hands uselessly in their cuffs.

"You will not be harmed," Three says in his slow, gravelly way. "But you will be held in such a way that you pose no harm to yourselves—or anyone else."

Rae breaks free of the croc-person holding her arm and advances on Three, coming up to his snout. Each of the croc-people takes a step closer to their apparent leader, krabongs at the ready. Three waves them off, although the muscles in his neck are tight with tension.

"You mean *imprisoned*," Rae spits out. "You're going to lock them up in a cage like an animal. Don't tiptoe around the truth. We already know that you're monsters. You don't even have a human face that you can hide behind."

"Rae—" I struggle to my feet, but she's not finished.

"You're pathetic," she screeches in Three's face. "You have no power of your own. You only do what Xander tells you to do. What a waste of a human life. Oh wait—you're not human anymore, are you? Hell, you don't even have to wait for your next life. Your crocodile face tells us everything we need to know about your soul: it's ugly and wretched and reptilian."

"Leave him alone," I say to Rae. She stumbles a couple steps away from Three, whose fingers have begun to tremble on the krabong. "It's not his fault. He's just following directions."

Rae whirls on me. "Oh, so you're defending monsters now?" She shakes her head bitterly. "Color me not surprised. You're not losing anyone. Your mother's standing right next to you."

"I'm not defending him." And I'm not. Because of Three, Mateo is thrashing in a net, his tail getting more and more tangled in the rope. Sylvie and Elizabeth are holding each other, as though they're about to free-fall through the sky with no bungee cord. And Kit's sitting on the dirt ground, his face buried in his knees, while Khun Anita kneels by his side, a comforting hand on his back. A guard stands behind each of them.

All of my friends, threatened by the true monster behind this scenario: Xander.

But Rae's lost interest in my allegiances. She faces Three once more, her demeanor changing from harsh to conciliatory.

"My sister's got bulletwood flowers dropping from her mouth," Rae tells him. "She's as gentle as the morning dew. She's not a danger to *anyone*. Take me instead."

"I can't," Three says regretfully. "Your power hasn't surfaced."

"But mine has." A new voice enters the conversation.

We all turn to Khun Anita, who gets to her feet slowly, brushing the dirt off her wrinkled sari, her thick black hair cascading down her back.

"They won't negotiate with you," I say. "Any attempt to trade will fail."

With my eyes, I plead, *Don't tell them your secret. Stay here with us, where you'll be safe.*

"I'm not interested in a trade." Khun Anita's head is held high; her eyes are solid steel. "My grandson is fourteen years old. He cannot be without a guardian. He cannot be without me."

Kit lifts his head. "Nani, no. You don't need to sacrifice for me."

Khun Anita smiles beatifically. "What do you think I've been doing all of my life, boy?"

"But, Nani—"

She rumples the thick, black hair on her grandson's head. It's no mystery where he got that beautiful hair. "I promised your mother that I would protect you. And this is me protecting you."

"I'm sorry," Three says, his already thick voice thickened. He looks at Khun Anita with real sorrow in his eyes.

But I need to remember that Three is not my friend. He may have been kind to me, but he is fully and unequivocally on Xander's side, executing his orders and hurting my friends.

"My instructions are clear," Three continues. "We only take those who have manifested their abilities."

"Ah, but I have," Khun Anita replies calmly.

I try to catch her eye, but she stares straight ahead at Three, unflappable. I look around wildly, and like a homing pigeon, my gaze returns to where it always does: Mama.

She interprets the plea in my eyes and nods. "Nothing good will come out of this, friend," Mama says to Khun Anita, her frail voice matching her frail frame. Out of all of us, she alone is no longer within five feet of a guard. No doubt they judge her threat level to be minuscule.

"I understand your maternal instinct," Mama continues. "I feel it, too, with every breath that I take. But they'll put you in different cells. They won't let you anywhere near him."

"That may be true. But you, of all people, know that I have to try." Their eyes meet, and an unspoken understanding passes between them.

I want to shake them both. Forget motherly. Forget sacrificing yourself for other people. This is survival, damn it. And as much as I admire and respect their selflessness…I can't bear to lose Khun Anita, too.

"I can prove to you that my ability has surfaced," Khun Anita tells Three. "Send one of your guards into that copse. There, if they look at the young green palm, they'll find an object that's out of place."

Three stares at her, at Mama, for a long moment, as

though trying to peel back their brains. He then gestures to one of the croc-people, who disappears behind the dense grouping of trees.

In the silence that ensues, stress saturates the air. The guards all take fighting stances, one foot forward, the krabongs over their heads. One quick movement, and the tension could boil over.

"I'm going to hug my sister," Rae announces.

The guard pulls Lola closer by the cuffs. "No touching."

"She's my sister," Rae says, spreading her arms out wide, as though she's about to embrace them both. "You're taking her away. I'll hug you both if I have to."

The guard turns so that her back shields Lola from Rae.

"We can't have you slipping her any weapons," the guard says.

"What weapons?" Rae looks down at her tattooed arms and her ripped jeans. "We're at your mercy for food and water. Where are we going to find a weapon?"

"We don't take any chances," the guard with his knee in Preston's back says. His poor prisoner doesn't speak—although he aims pitiful eyes at Rae, as though asking for a goodbye hug as well. "Two groups ago, a prisoner managed to construct an impressive spear out of a sharpened stick and a fork."

"Is that why we have no forks on the buffet?" Kit asks weakly. "I've been eating my spaghetti with a spoon." The humor falls flat, but I gotta admire the kid for trying.

We fall silent once more, and I crouch next to Kit. "You were bouncing all over the basketball court," I say, trying not to move my lips. "Can't you transport your soul to a krabong or something?"

"I wish." Kit nods toward his hands. "These cuffs…"

I peer at the wind bracelets. I'd mistakenly assumed that

they were the same as the ones that bound my own wrists. But these cuffs aren't invisible. They're...*glowing*. Faint zigzags of energy skim the surface of each wrist. I can't tell if the light originates inside the cuffs or if—like the moon—the wind is reflecting another energy source. But one thing is clear: these cuffs do more than simply restrain their captive.

"I think my power's been drained," Kit murmurs.

I suck in a breath. He's right. Nothing drips from Lola's mouth. Preston's mouth is perfectly human, and neither birds nor scents flock around Elizabeth and Sylvie. Only Mateo's forelegs don't appear restrained.

My knees go weak. I stand up before I can topple to the ground. Unimaginable technology. Limitless resources. We are so horribly outmatched that it's becoming harder and harder to see a scenario where we best Xander.

"The cuffs neutralize their abilities, but they remain unharmed," Three says, noticing my horror. He doesn't miss much. "They will be safe, like I said," he says to all of us, although his eyes remain on me. Why?

I lick my lips. "You said to come to you if I or the other castaways ever needed anything." It's a long, desperate shot, but that's all I've got. "Well, I need your help now. Let my friends go."

"I'm sorry," Three says. "I can't."

"You lied to me?"

"No." He shakes his head. He might've meant the action to be subtle, but with his long snout swinging back and forth, it's anything but. "I meant what I said. I will do anything in my power to make your life easier. Unfortunately, very little is in my power."

I move one shoulder. "So, your offer is meaningless. It has the same effect as a lie."

Three opens his jaws, as though to dispute my conclusion,

but the guard who went into the copse reappears, holding the lock of Khun Anita's hair.

"Grandma's right," the croc-person says. "Her powers have surfaced. She's coming with us."

"What powers?" the employee holding Mateo's net asks.

"We'll discuss it later," Three says abruptly. "Let's go."

I reach for Khun Anita, but my fingers close around air. She strides forward, her head held high. I know that she'll continue to fight, imprisoned or not. Which means I need to be strong as well.

The croc-people lead our friends away, with three of them carrying Mateo's crocodile body.

The few of us remaining watch morosely. Rae, Eduardo, Bodin, Mama, and myself. Out of twelve original castaways, five of us remain.

The only thing I'm sure of is that tomorrow, our number will be fewer.

CHAPTER THIRTY

As soon as our friends are gone, Bodin approaches Mama and offers her his arm. "You must be exhausted," he says.

For the first time this evening, I scrutinize her face. For all of the notice she gives *me*, I can't believe that her fatigue hasn't registered before. The flame from the fire highlights fine lines in her face. Her eyes are glazed, as though she's been awake too long, and her breathing seems…labored.

My heart pounding, I step forward. "Mama, are you okay?"

"I'm fine, sweetheart." She waves me off. "Just need to sleep. I'm going to let this young man walk me to the shelter. Maybe get me a bottle of water?"

"It would be my pleasure," Bodin says gravely.

I shoot him a grateful look, and they make their way through the sand, Mama leaning more heavily against his arm than I would like. He's practically carrying her.

I bite my lip. We've only been on this hell island for four days, and Mama's deteriorated so much. Too much. How much more time does she have? This close to the end of her life, she deserves cool, clean sheets and tall, frosty glasses of ginger beer. Not this.

"This is *awful*," Rae pronounces, dragging me from my thoughts. She crosses her arms and scowls at Eduardo and me in turn. The lengthened shadow that the fire tosses on the sand performs the same action, doubling the injury.

Eduardo sinks to the ground and kinda huddles into himself, his big linebacker body curled into…well, a big linebacker ball.

I raise my hands, palms out. Rae's just lost her little sister to the hands of an unfeeling scientist. We're stuck on this twisted paradise. And we have no control over what happens next. I give up.

"It can be my fault, if you want," I offer. "I don't mind."

Rae blinks, as though all sense and rationality has fled my brain. "But it's *not* your fault," she says slowly. "Obviously."

"I thought it might make you feel better," I say. "You know, to have someone to blame."

Rae grins, fast and ferocious. "I had that coming. And you're probably right. Lola usually bears the brunt of my bad temper, but I couldn't exactly lash out at her when worms and flowers were falling out of her mouth. I guess I directed it at you instead. Sorry."

"Apology accepted." I duck my head. "I, uh, have been known to take my emotions out on other people, too—namely, Mama."

She narrows her eyes. "I was also hard on you for another reason. You remind me of Lola. You're both so much stronger than you think. So, you should actually be flattered that I would consider you as a stand-in for my sister."

"Oh, I am. So flattered." I hold up three fingers, bending my thumb to touch my pinkie. "Girl Scout's promise."

"You. Lie." Rae shakes her head, but her lips are curved, too. Just the tiniest bit. "I bet you were never a Girl Scout."

"I certainly was." I bob my head. "For about two weeks. And then Mama got on my case about how a Girl Scout is helpful and considerate and does all of her chores. It got annoying...so I decided I wasn't a Girl Scout anymore."

"Brat." I swear there's a note of affection in her voice. "Told ya you were like my sister."

"The brattiest," I agree. "My poor mama. She has the patience of an angel."

"You're not half bad, Alaia," she says. For Rae, this counts as high praise. "But as much as I *don't* hate you, I need to be alone right now."

I give her my cheekiest salute. "Gee, thanks. I love you, too." And oddly enough, I kind of mean it.

Rae disappears into the woods, in the opposite direction from camp. I start to head off, too, so that I can check up on Mama, but as I turn—

Yep. The ball of Eduardo. Still there. Still unmoving.

I barely know the guy. Have exchanged only a few sentences with him. But I can't just leave him here. Not when Mama's in good hands. Not when he's Mateo's brother. And especially not when I have a pretty good idea why he's frozen.

I amble over and plop down next to him. He, too, has the foresight to spread out his sleeping roll, so I sit on the edge of it. He senses me, I can tell, because he shifts ever so slightly away, even as he maintains his impressive imitation of a beach ball.

I've never met anyone else with OCD before. Oh, sure, I've heard *stories* of people. Mama's many acquaintances never fail to tell her about this cousin or that aunt who suffers the same compulsions as me. But I certainly don't know them. And they're not remotely close to my age.

I want to bond with him. Ask about his particular brand of compulsions. Find out if the rituals fade as one enters their twenties and the brain more fully develops. But although we've been stranded on this hell island together, he has yet to make eye contact with me. Not a single time.

"I've been stuck, too," I say conversationally, wondering if he'll even bother to respond. "Usually at corners. The beveled edge of a table, or a banister with all of those decorative grooves?" I shake my head at the unnecessary evils. "I can never get the symmetry just right. I have to touch with my left hand, then my right, but then my finger accidentally rolls a millimeter or my nail clicks against the wood, and so I have to do it again. And again and again, until someone stops me. Usually Mama. But in the caves, it was Mateo who helped me when I thought my head was going to explode. When I believed that I would never get clean, ever again."

Eduardo lifts his head from his arms. "You have OCD?"

"Yeah," I say.

"And Mateo told you about mine?"

I nod, not sure if he'll be angry that his brother shared his disorder with me.

To my surprise, Eduardo's shoulders relax. "He must trust you, then. He and I have an understanding. I said it was okay for him to share my condition with a person he trusts, since it's his lived experience, as well as mine. Matty's been rescuing me since he was a little kid. And I..." He looks up at the stars, but I know he doesn't see any of the constellations. "I shied away from him like he was repulsive to the touch."

The poor guy. Not only was his brother carried away—in a net, no less—but he's been beating himself up for wronging the one person who's always been there for him. No wonder he's wrapped his arms around his legs. There's nothing else holding him together.

"You're a good person," I say. "Mateo believes that, and I believe *him*. He loves you through and through, and he understands that it was a natural reaction. He forgives you. He knows that anyone would've had that reaction, had they been in your position."

"So, you can communicate with animals now? Like Sylvie?" Eduardo asks doubtfully.

"Nah. I'd be handcuffed if I could." I stretch my arms up and in front of me, so I can narrow the sky into the triangle of my hands. Maybe that one patch of stars will help me find the right words to alleviate his pain. "I know because if I had a brother like you, and I adored and looked up to you the way Mateo does, that's how I would feel."

"You didn't back away from him," Eduardo points out. "You talked to him as though he were still in human form."

"Yeah, but that's only because *you* paved the way. You gave me time to reconcile my feelings, to unjumble my thoughts. I would've been too scared to talk to him, otherwise."

Eduardo stands, his movements quick but graceful. You can see the athlete he once was in the way he stretches to wake up his body once more.

"How old are you, kid?" he asks as he bends himself in half.

"I'm seventeen, just like your brother."

He straightens. "When I was your age, I still hadn't fully embraced the necessity of exposures. Oh, my therapists had tried to drill it into my head, that exposures were the only surefire way to noticeably decrease the severity of my compulsion. But I didn't *truly* get it. I still believed that the compulsions were a part of who I was." He snorts. "Like it was a *part* of me to stop whatever I was doing, plug my ears, and pray to God fifty times a day."

He shakes his head, disgusted. "You would not believe the number of hours I devoted to my rituals, day in and day out."

"Try me," I say wryly. I know enough about scrupulosity OCD to know that it makes an individual obsessed with being a good person, so much that they constantly question their morals, religion, and ethics. They fear that they may have inadvertently crossed a line — even though it's obvious that they have not.

He flashes me a grin. "Yes, I suppose only someone who's experienced it could understand. But take it from me, kid. Your OCD is *not* a part of you. Don't delay your exposures. It will only make your compulsions worse, not better."

I nod slowly. I, too, have received the lecture from therapists on countless occasions. But it's one thing to acknowledge a set of facts. Quite another to believe in their truth to the very core of my being.

I want to believe that the OCD is not a part of me. I do. I wish, more than anything, that I could let the anxiety recede, so that the true Alaia, the one that I am at my core, the one that isn't plagued by a million "what-ifs," can come to the surface.

"Your best is good enough," Eduardo continues, his voice barely audible above the whistling of the wind. "I promise."

I've heard those words before. But they mean something entirely different, coming from someone who's lived through a similar hell. "Thanks." I clear the gunk from my throat. "That's helpful."

"Can you please leave me now?" he asks gently. "I know you mean well, but I need to bear this pain by myself."

I nod and creep away, respecting his wishes. Did our interaction ease his suffering, if only slightly? Maybe. Maybe not. I don't have many answers in this complex, messed-up world, but I feel just the tiniest bit less lonely in this isolated island of my mind.

Sometimes, that's all we can ask for.

CHAPTER THIRTY-ONE

Mama is asleep, her eyelids closed, her breathing slow and even. Someone—Bodin?—has made a nest of the extra sleeping bags so that she is supported on all sides. The additional padding might make the bamboo slats bearable, if not downright soft. My heart unclenches, just a little. She'll have tough times ahead—that was never in doubt. But I'm grateful for every moment of peace left.

As I walk up, however, the figures chatting by the main shelter come into view. That's right—*figures*. As in two of them. Bodin, whom I expected, and the traitor of the worst kind: a croc-person.

I snarl. "What are you doing here?"

The croc-person holds up his hands—or rather, forelegs. The appendages are still human-shaped, but now they're scaly and tinged blackish green. "Relax. It's me. Three."

"I know who you are," I snap. "I had a whole conversation with you on the beach under the stars. Did you think that I wouldn't recognize you?"

He keeps his forelegs in the air, as though I might

attack. Smart reptile. "Most humans have difficulty telling us apart."

I wave my hand impatiently. "That's because they don't pay attention. Now, get away from Mama."

"Three brought more pills for your mother," Bodin says. "I thought you would be happy, since Xander only gave us two days' worth."

I relax my shoulders but keep up my guard. As Three's actions tonight have proven, he's more my enemy than my friend.

"Don't expect me to thank you for having a shred of decency," I say, my eyes narrowed.

Three takes a step back, as though to appear less threatening. But a step doesn't do much when you've got a jaw that can rip apart a human's limbs. "I'm not looking for thanks. That's not my motivation for being here."

He casts a look at Mama—and so I do, too. My gaze snags on a tray next to her, which holds a battery-operated fan, a copper basin filled with water and a lotus flower…and a tall, frosty glass of ginger beer.

I freeze. Mama's favorite drink. The one that she sips in order to stave off nausea.

"What, are you reading my mind now?" I bare my teeth at Three. I may not be a reptile, but I can be scary, too. "The way that Mateo communicated with Sylvie. Is that an ability you croc-people have?"

Three looks at me blankly. If I were better at reading crocodile expressions, I might even say it was genuine.

"The ginger beer," I clarify. "I was just thinking that Mama deserves cool sheets and a frosty glass of her favorite drink. How did you know to bring it?"

"Because her drink of choice was in Xander's files on each of you." Three hunches over. A row of thick ridges has formed along his spine, and each scale pokes out from the uniform, through what must be specially designed holes. "Communicating with animals was Sylvie's power. We all have one ability, the way we have one nose, one heart, one brain. Only one…unless…" He trails off.

"Unless what?" Bodin asks.

"Unless you're the Lotus Flower Champion. It's been rumored that the person with this rare talent will have multiple abilities."

"Well, don't look at me," I say. "I can't seem to manifest even one ability, much less two."

Not that I want to, especially after tonight. In fact, I need to stay calm and stave off my emotional turmoil for as long as possible, so that I can be here with Mama. So that I can spend every last moment with her.

"You need to leave now," I tell Three.

Harsh? Maybe. But I won't let my guard down again. Three has shown me that he can flip-flop from one side to the other before I can take my next breath. Tonight alone, he was my friend and then my enemy. And now he's here, trying on the friend persona once more. It's not going to work.

"Okay," he says, backing away. "But please don't worry about your friends. They will be safe in Xander's compound. They will be placed in individual cells until they agree to cooperate with him, but they will have enough to eat and drink."

I blink. So Rae was right. "Xander has a compound up in that mountain?" I ask, fishing for more information.

"Yes," Three says. "The tunnels that led you to the crocodile pit—that was the maze, put in place to test new islanders like you. The other half of the mountain has been outfitted with Xander's headquarters, the cells, and storage for the supplies. A boat only gets out here maybe twice a year, or so I've heard. So there has to be plenty of space to keep the resources we need to run the entire island."

His jaw opens as if to say more. But then, he gives a shake of the head. "Don't forget my offer. Anything you need, just ask."

I scoff. "You mean your *useless* offer?"

Three nods, the distinct air of sorrow surrounding his gesture. "Call it whatever you want. Just know I'm doing the best that I can."

He turns, and my mouth drops. *That's* why his movements are even more lumbering than before. He has a tail now, long and spiky. It emerges from the seat of his pants without ripping the fabric. There must be a built-in slit in the uniform.

"The longer they fight the change that comes with the moon, the more difficult it is to hold off," Bodin says. He and Three must've bonded longer than I thought for Bodin to have this information. "Nearly all of the croc-people would have transformed by now. It's through sheer willpower that Three was able to maintain human form long enough to bring your mother her pills."

"I don't care," I say stubbornly. "He tricked me. And I don't forgive betrayal easily—if at all."

Bodin sighs. "You've got a hard heart, Alaia."

Maybe I do. But only because my circumstances have made me this way.

Three reaches the edge of the circle of light cast from the firepit. He almost makes it. He almost steps into the darkness and disappears from our sight.

But suddenly, he falls in one seamless motion. By the time he hits the ground, he's been fully transformed into a crocodile. He scuttles into the shadows, and I feel the air of sorrow, more tangible than ever.

For the first time, I realize: the cloud of sorrow isn't emanating from Three. It's coming from *me*, coloring my every thought and perspective.

And it's difficult to remember why, exactly, I have to keep my heart so hard.

CHAPTER THIRTY-TWO

B odin and I settle on the far side of the firepit, a fair
distance from the main shelter, where we can keep an
eye on both Mama and any potential intruders.

So much has changed since the last time I slept here. The
blanket of stars above us feels more vast. The wind whistling
in and out of the leaves sounds lonelier. No doubt it carries
the sobs that Rae has let out in a secluded spot in the woods.
It is tinged with the demons that wrestle in Eduardo's mind.
Our fellow castaways will not be shutting their eyes at camp
tonight, but they are with us nonetheless.

"It's so quiet," I say to Bodin in a low voice. Any louder,
and I might shatter the strange silence that has descended
with the night.

We're arranged like parallel bookends once more —
facing each other, with the fire at my back and the sea at his.
Only this time, less than a foot separates us. I find comfort
in routine, and three nights in a row forms a pattern. Does
Bodin know that? Or does he simply favor his right side?

"I kind of like it," he says, tucking his hand beneath his

cheek. "Not that I want our friends to be locked up. Far from it. But I'm not used to being around so many people. Other than the charter guests that I interact with, I'm usually alone."

"How come?" I ask, suddenly curious about his life. I already know who he is at his core. Trustworthy, brave, thoughtful. He's been my rock this entire journey. But what made him that way? "Don't you have family, friends? I want to hear it all, starting with your childhood."

"My life's history, in three sentences or less?" He grins. "I know I'm tall, but that's a soaring order."

"Oh, come on," I protest, coming up on one elbow. The nylon sleeping bag slides beneath me, reassuring me of its protection. "Let me guess. Tallest kid in your class, with soulful eyes and baby cheeks. Did all your classmates have a crush on you?"

"They did," he says solemnly.

"You're supposed to say no and act humble. Not agree with me."

He smirks. "Guess nobody ever taught me that lesson."

"Good thing I'm here," I say.

"Yes." An expression that I can't decipher passes over his eyes—or maybe that's just a shadow created by the dancing flames of the fire. "Good thing."

I think how little I actually know about this guy. He's trustworthy, yes—I'll bet my life on it. (Even if I wouldn't wager Mama's, because her life is sacred.)

"Can I ask you something? Does this bother you, us sleeping next to each other?"

It's an interesting question, and it deserves a thoughtful answer. "You mean, because of the asymmetry of me being on my side or the, uh, intimacy?"

Holy crap, I can't even say the word without flushing. All of a sudden, I'm very glad that the hot flames are at my back.

It might explain any telltale redness.

"Both, I guess?"

"Well, now that you've pointed out the imbalance to me, I won't be thinking about anything else," I say honestly and roll onto my back. That's just how my OCD works sometimes. I can be blissfully unaware of my uneven state, but once I notice it, I can't *unnotice* it.

"Oh, god," he says, horrified. "I wanted you to be comfortable. I didn't mean to single-handedly ruin our romantic moment by the fire."

I giggle. "Yep," I tease. "No kiss for you tonight."

"You mean a kiss was on the table?" He covers his face with his hands. "I hate myself."

My smile freezes. I was kidding. At least, I *thought* I was. But now that he's acting (maybe?) like I was serious, I'm vaguely mortified. And intrigued. And...warm. Is it warm out here? Between the fire and the tropical air, I feel like I'm about to burn up.

Of course, yanking my blouse over my head would probably send the wrong message.

I clear my throat, fervently hoping that the shadows cloak my embarrassment. "So, um. Your childhood?"

He rolls onto his back, too, and tucks his hands behind his head. Unlike Eduardo, I can tell that he's actually studying the constellations—and deriving comfort from them.

"My childhood was quiet. Sad," he says, his eyes on the sky. "I hate to be a cliché, but there it is. It was just me and my dad most of the time. My mom took off when I was young. Two pesky little boys didn't fit in with her life as a model and spokesperson. So, there my dad was, a single white farang in Bangkok, with twin boys to raise."

"Wait a minute," I interrupt. "Twins? Are you saying there's someone on this Earth who looks just like you?"

He doesn't grin. Doesn't make a joke about being double the fun. He merely lies there, his lips pressed into a straight line.

"There was," he says eventually. "He died in a motorcycle accident when we were nine years old."

"Oh. I'm so sorry."

"We were strolling the sidewalk, next to the street vendors. He walked on the outside, like always, because he knew I was afraid of the oncoming traffic."

I nod. Bangkok traffic isn't for the weak of heart. The lanes are ad hoc and congested. Motorcycles weave between cars like they're playing a video game with infinite lives.

"My dad hated that about me," Bodin continues. "Thought I was weak for being scared. Useless for hiding behind my brother's strength. It was never a secret which one of us he favored."

He swallows. "Out of nowhere, a motorcycle swerved onto the sidewalk. Mowed my brother over…and left me entirely untouched.

"It was…a double tragedy. Not only did my dad lose a son, but he lost the brave one. The one who was supposed to follow in his footsteps. The one who would make him proud. He grieved like his soul would shatter, and I think a piece of it did break off that day. A cold, sharp shard that he would preserve forever, to remind him of what could've been. Maybe that's why he turned so cold toward me. And maybe that's why I've spent the last ten years trying to be enough for him."

"You were a little boy," I protest. "All of us are afraid of something. Hell, I could list ten of my phobias right now."

"You know what I'm really afraid of?"

"What's that?"

He rolls back onto his side so that he can face me once

more. "Falling for someone who doesn't return my feelings."

I swallow, my throat suddenly dry. "Have you ever, uh, experienced that?"

"There *is* this one girl," he says, his tone contemplative. "Should I tell you about her?"

"Yes?" I say, when I really mean *maybe*.

"She's pretty. I noticed that in the first half second. But that's not why I'm drawn to her. Why I want to be around her all the time. She's the *opposite* of what I'm used to. You see, she has the biggest capability to love out of anyone I've ever met. She doesn't trust easily, but when she does open up, I can tell that she gives all of her heart."

My ears roar. It's like someone's put the ocean inside of them—and turned up the volume. "She sounds…nice."

I *think* he's talking about me. Why would he be discussing someone else, when we're lying here next to each other?

"She *is* nice. There's only one problem."

I sit up so that I can face him without being asymmetrical. "What's that?"

"I'm not sure if she's interested in another guy," he confesses in a rush. "I know, I know, sounds impossible, right? But this other guy's good-looking, too, although not as much as yours truly. More than that, he's just a really decent fellow.

"I thought I had my chance when this guy turned into a crocodile, but well." He sighs. "It only seemed to make my girl more attached to him. I felt like I was witnessing some tragic love story."

"You're jealous of Mateo?" I blurt out. "But he's with Lola."

"Well, yeah." His mouth turns serious, elongating into a straight line. "That's never stopped anyone's feelings before. You were so excited to see him, you couldn't even bother to take off your windcuffs."

"I was excited to see *Mama*, not him," I correct.

"I've got the advantage, because I have human hands," he continues. "But I don't want to be the default choice."

"He's a friend," I manage. "I care about him a lot." I take a deep breath. It's time to be brave now. As brave as I've ever been in my life. "But I don't have any romantic interest in him. Not the way I have in somebody else."

"Somebody else, huh?" Bodin says, his lips quirking. "That Preston, he's a lucky guy."

"He *does* have a certain charm," I agree.

Bodin sits up and lifts his hands to the middle of my neck, right at the most sensitive spot. "I'm going to tickle you," he warns, probably to give me time to stop him. But I'm in the right moment, the right frame of mind. His touch doesn't inspire discomfort anymore. In fact, I *want* him to touch me. I think it will feel...nice.

"Do your best," I dare him.

He does, and I squirm. "I'm kidding!" I yelp. "Who likes charm, anyway? Not me. I like 'em boring and rude."

He tickles even harder, and I retaliate. When we're both laughing and out of breath, we smile at each other, next to a roaring ocean, under a starlit sky. Our circumstances are less than ideal...but there are worse places to be.

"I don't know what tomorrow will bring," Bodin says, his expression sobering. "But there's one thing I want to do before it all goes to hell."

"What's that?" I ask.

"This."

And then he carefully, deliberately, and gently fits his lips to mine.

CHAPTER THIRTY-THREE

A loud horn blasts into the air. I jerk awake. What? Where? The dawn light filters through the tall, tall trees, and the sky is a pale version of its impossibly blue hue, so it's early yet. *Too* early, for someone who fell asleep well after the moon hit its peak.

Groggily, I push myself up on my elbows. Around me, on the patchy ground, Bodin, Rae, and Eduardo are slowly waking up.

Wait a minute—*ground*? As in, dirt and grass?

In an instant, I am up, brushing off any dirt or possible bugs that could be on me. The only thing clouding my mind from the panic is my confusion. I fell asleep on my sleeping bag next to the firepit, in the center of camp. After having a single, perfect kiss with Bodin. Most people say that first kisses are awkward…kind of gross…not particularly enjoyable. Mine was pretty much the opposite. Not too rough. Not too soft. It was delicious, not to mention addictive.

Here, there's no sand. No firepit. No shelter…which means no *Mama*.

"Um, guys?" I ask in a wobbly voice. "Where are we? And where's my mama?"

I take in my new surroundings. Thickets of trees grow at a slight incline around us, forming a clearing that's more egg-shaped than circular, but it's clearly manmade. Tufts of grass poke up through the dirt amongst flat stones, big and small. The pebbles that I dislodge with my movements roll downhill, and the air here smells crisper: less like the ocean and more like the earth.

"We're still on the island," Rae says, reaching the same conclusion as me. "On the mountainside. Remember that dense forest we saw from the helicopter? I'll bet you anything we're somewhere in there."

"What have we got here?" Eduardo lunges forward and retrieves a short dagger from the tall grass. Its hilt is black, banded by rings of gold, and it fits in his grasp like it was made for his hand.

Rae fishes out a double-edged sword, long and shiny, from the patch of grass in her corner, while Bodin uncovers a traditional krabong and shield like the ones the croc-people were using.

I look down—and my mouth falls open. I can't believe that I missed it before. There, only partially hidden in the grass, are a lethal-looking blowgun and a sheath of darts.

I pick them up gingerly. Each of these weapons was placed in a specific quadrant of the clearing—and probably not randomly, either. The sword, the dagger, and the krabong are meant for close-range battles. They require skill and a certain amount of athletic ability, which my three fellow castaways all have.

Me, on the other hand? I would never trust myself with a weapon that required much expertise. Here's hoping that you just kinda huff and shoot with a blowgun.

Feigning confidence, I swing the sheath over my shoulder and pick up the blowgun. Whatever we're about to face, I want to be ready.

Bodin drifts over to me. "Insert the pointed tip of the dart into the mouthpiece," he whispers. "You then put your dominant hand a quarter of the way down the barrel; your other hand will extend farther out to support the entire length. To aim, look down the sight…but if your target is moving, adjust your aim above and in front of the target."

I swallow hard. So a little bit more complex than blow and shoot. But at least our first interaction after the kiss isn't awkward. In fact, it's strangely comfortable. "My mama—"

"Could be anywhere," he interjects. "Let's not jump to conclusions. She's probably sleeping peacefully back at camp. There are a lot of reasons why she might not be here—the most obvious of which is that she's too sick to participate in whatever the hell challenge this is."

"Agreed," Rae says, coming up to us. "This is definitely one of Xander's challenges. You don't just wake up in the middle of nowhere, surrounded by weapons, on accident."

"But…what are we supposed to do?" I voice the obvious.

"Battle." Eduardo takes a practice lunge with the dagger. His back is straight, his form strong. I'm not sure if he's ever wielded a deadly weapon before—but he's a natural. The point of the dagger sparkles in the now rising sun, and I can imagine it cleaving a person in half.

I shiver. Maybe I should be practicing, too. At the very least, I should figure out how hard I need to blow into the mouthpiece.

"But there's no one here." Rae frowns at her reflection in the double-edged sword. The weapon droops awkwardly, as though it's too heavy for her hand. Maybe I'm not the only one out of my league.

Eduardo lunges again, deeper, harder. The dagger thrusts squarely into his invisible opponent's throat. "Exactly. There's no one here. So we battle each other."

Rae's sword thunks onto the ground. "Why?"

"To win the prize," Eduardo says, as though it's apparent. "To be free. Isn't it obvious? The last person standing gets to go home."

"Um, buddy?" Bodin says. "I think you've been watching too much TV."

Rae strides over to Eduardo, using her sword as a walking stick, and pokes a finger into his chest. Hard. "Of all the ridiculous things to say. You're willing to start slaughtering your friends, based on zero evidence?"

Eduardo swipes her finger away. If he's anything like me, he's not a fan of being touched. "You take one step closer to me, and I'll start with you," he snarls.

It's just a show. I think. They're taking their frustrations out on each other. I hope.

"Stop it," I say. "Don't you see? This is exactly what Xander wants. He wants to pit us against one another. Make us paranoid, so that we don't work together as a team. We'll never get out of here if we self-destruct."

"But we *aren't* a team," Bodin points out, swinging the krabong casually. Like Eduardo, the weapon seems like a natural extension of his arm. "The only thing we have in common is that we all woke up on this island together."

I shake my head. "I don't believe that. Not anymore. I don't trust easily, but I trust each of you. I know, at my core, that you're good people. Xander's strategy is to create chaos, to be divisive. To wake us up too early, in a strange place. Much easier to push us to our emotional limits if our brains are fatigued and our thoughts are all jumbled up. This is one big mind game, and we can't play into it."

To my surprise, Rae nods. "She's right. We can't turn on one another." But she can't resist poking Eduardo one more time. "But I've still got my eyes on you, buster."

"Keep your distance, if you know what's good for you," he growls.

"We found our weapons hidden in the grass." Bodin speaks up. "Maybe there's something else we need to find, something that will make the objective of this challenge clear."

He, Rae, and Eduardo begin to search, poking in the bushes and looking inside trees. But this isn't *Survivor*. We're not searching for a freaking immunity idol. This is Xander's Game, and his idea of fun is to twist our emotions into a pretzel—and then tighten the knot.

The weapons were stashed on the ground, so I scan the tree line, where emerald leaves meet sapphire sky and lonely trees stretch their bare branches into the empty expanse. Up, down, and around, my gaze flows, as it traces tall, short, and middling trees, and then—

"Mama," I say, my throat thick with tears.

"This again?" Rae says as she sticks her hand into a hollowed-out log. "We talked about this, Alaia. You need to let go—"

"She's not back at camp," I interrupt. "Look!"

I point at the highest tree, whose glowing leaves are, fittingly, closest to the red-hot sun. There, hanging horizontally from the uppermost branch, lies a human figure, wrapped up in a white sheet, with a sunset orange silk scarf tied around her head.

Eduardo squints. "What is that? Is she lying in some sort of hammock?"

"Does it matter?" I snap.

"Of course it matters. You want your mother to be

comfortable until we can rescue her, don't you?"

"Don't worry, Alaia," Bodin says, by my side once more. "We *will* rescue her."

I inhale slowly, filling my lungs with the smell of the earth, the vegetation, the growth. Of Mama. Of the scent of safety that is uniquely hers.

If there was ever a time to be brave, this is it. "Xander thinks this little trick of his will break me. He's wrong." I survey the smooth lower trunk of the tree that's holding Mama captive. The closest branch is about eight feet off the ground. Mama is twenty feet above that.

Interestingly, a bunch of leaves, which I thought appeared burnished gold because of the sun's rays, actually *is* gold. A cluster of leaves next to it shares the same strange sparkling phenomenon—but in silver. Strange, but not something I can dwell about at this moment.

"Bodin, can you give me a boost?"

"I should go first—"

"No," I say. "I'm lighter than you. I don't know if the branch will hold your weight—or Eduardo's. Besides, it's *my* mama. I'm going."

He nods, not arguing any further. He kneels by the trunk, and I climb up, dropping my blowgun and sheath of darts to the ground. In another time and another circumstance, I might have been embarrassed scaling his body. Now, I'm tunnel-focused on saving Mama, even as scenes from last night flash through my mind.

I straighten so that I'm standing on his bended knee. Even on my tiptoes, I can't...quite...reach...the branch.

"I'm going to have to jump," I say.

"Don't worry about me." Bodin's voice is only slightly strained. "I can handle the impact."

I let all of the air flow out of my body, with my arms still overhead. And then, I jump. Got it! Pieces of bark flake off the branch, and the wood digs into my palm, but my grasp is steady and strong.

Holy crap. The muscles in my arm are already burning. I wish I'd worked a little harder in gym class. I kick up my legs and swing my body, so that I can press my feet against the tree trunk. I walk up slowly…and then, I'm hanging from the branch like a koala. From there, I pull up with my arms, hug the branch, and, by some miracle, manage to wriggle on top of the thick cylinder.

"I did it," I gasp. "I don't know how. If *that* didn't bring my abilities to the surface, I don't know what will."

And that's when the monkey attacks.

CHAPTER THIRTY-FOUR

I scream and fall from the branch, hitting the ground with a force that rattles my entire body. The monkey leaps nimbly on top of my chest.

Its eyes. Deep red, unnatural. Mechanical in the way it clicks around, surveying the scene. Its body is made of metal on metal, the joints of its claws exposed. Not a real monkey, then, but a robotic one. A humanmade, killer one.

Whack.

The monkey's head rolls off, slapped by the force of Bodin's krabong.

"Are you okay?" he asks.

I barely have time to nod before, without warning or countdown, the sky goes dark. No, not the sky. Just my vision, as dozens and dozens of robot-monkeys rain down from the tree.

Bodin charges forward, dismantling the heads of two monkeys with one clean strike of his krabong. Eduardo is right behind him, stabbing the monkeys in their exposed joints.

I struggle to my feet and lunge for my blowgun. Moving with a speed I didn't think possible, I grab a dart, push it into place, and blow with all of my might.

The dart hits the monkey currently storming me straight between the eyes. The thing falls over and doesn't get back up.

I turn, sensing an oncoming attack, and shoot another in the heart. As I do, I spin again, this time catching a third monkey in its side.

Huh. I might actually be good at this. Who knew?

I shoot my way over to Bodin, who is clubbing monkeys left and right and up and down.

"Keep your back to me," I say, trying to save my breath. "That way none of them sneak up on us."

"Good idea!" he calls.

We turn our backs on each other and spin in a slow circle, sending robotic monkeys to their short-circuited demise.

But not all of us are doing so well. To my left, Rae is swinging her sword wildly but doing little damage. Two more robots jump into the mix—and all of a sudden, she's swarmed by a barrel of killer monkeys.

And then, a *real* monkey—at least one with natural brown fur—rushes up to the troop and begins to stab its robotic imitations with a familiar dagger—one with a black hilt banded by rings of gold.

I almost drop my blowgun. What on earth? That's *Eduardo's* weapon. Where did my friend go? And how did a real monkey—wearing clothes, no less—come into the mix?

Don't fail me now, lungs! I shoot two robotic monkeys on my right, and then another one that is just dropping from the tree. My dart has just barely struck the invader's foot when the brown monkey scampers back up the tree, snatches a gold leaf from one of the branches, and stuffs it into its mouth. Right before my eyes, the monkey transforms into a naga, its brown fur melting into silver scales. It has no arms, so the dagger falls to the ground, but it expertly wraps its newly serpentine body around the robotic heads, twisting them clean off.

My jaw drops, and I stop fighting altogether.

"Alaia!" Bodin yells. "A little help here."

In the few seconds that I zoned out, twenty, thirty killer monkeys have formed a circle around us, with an endless number of them continuing to drop from the tree.

I snap to the present and although my lungs whimper, I reach into my sheath for another a dart—when I discover a new problem.

"Um, Bodin? I don't have any darts left."

He sucks in a breath. "Can you yank some out of the dismantled monkeys?"

"Only if their friends wait patiently for me to perform the operation."

"Crap," Bodin curses. He doesn't voice the rest of his thought, but he doesn't need to. The fifty or so monkeys now staring at us project the message loud and clear: we are so dead.

The army of killer robots advances, eyes bloodred, their manufactured teeth as sharp as knives. I sag against Bodin's back and close my eyes.

I tried, Mama. I'm sorry I didn't save you. I only wanted a little peace for you before you passed. I'll see you in the afterlife.

I brace myself for the slaughter. Prime my limbs for being ripped off, prepare for my head to be separated from my body.

But nothing happens.

I open my eyes—and gasp. Every last monkey has collapsed onto the ground and is holding on to their heads, completely incapacitated.

"What happened?" I blurt, whirling around to face Bodin.

He crouches and waves his hand in front of a fallen monkey. No response—not a single snarl or snap of the jaw. "It wasn't me."

The naga lands next to us, its forked tongue licking off flecks of the strange silver leaves. A moment later, Eduardo stands in its place, his shirt ripped to shreds. "Me, neither."

Rae steps gingerly over a dismembered head and a gut of wires. Her sleeveless black top is ripped, clear indentations of teeth on her shoulder. But she's smiling as she holds her sword like a true warrior. "I think my ability surfaced," she says wonderingly. "Just in the nick of time."

Bodin arches an eyebrow. "Your power being…?"

"It's just like in the myths," she says, still stunned. "I swing a special double-edged sword. And my enemies collapse with a debilitating headache."

We look at the field of monkeys clutching their heads. The metal parts, sea of wires, and barely held-together bodies litter the entire clearing.

"Not headaches," I mutter. "Your double-edged sword short-circuited them."

"A modern update to an ancient folktale. Kinda like mine," Eduardo says wryly, looking down at the chest that was covered by monkey fur and scales not too long ago.

"And your ability is…what?" Bodin asks. "Transforming into other creatures, like your brother?"

"Only by munching on the leaves of a sacred tree." Eduardo jumps up and grabs the same branch that was so difficult for me to climb. The branch bends down with his body weight, nearly breaking, and he plucks a gold leaf from its stem.

"Here, watch. I have no idea what I'm going to transform into. But I take a different form every time." He pops the leaf into his mouth, munches on it like it's the most exquisite cuisine…and then promptly turns into a pile of gold coins.

"Huh." I tilt my head, as though viewing Eduardo from a different angle might yield a new result. Nope. Still an inanimate collection of gold coins. Dull at that. "How's he going to turn back into a human again, if he doesn't have a mouth?"

Rae sighs and sweeps the coins—er, Eduardo—into her jeans pocket. "The leaf's magic will likely wear off in a few hours."

"Better make sure he's not still in your pants when that happens," Bodin suggests.

Rae shoots him a glare that would wither the silver and gold leaves, sacred or not.

He lifts up his palms. "What? It's sound advice."

I'm no longer listening. Through all of this excitement, I haven't forgotten the true purpose of this challenge: Mama.

I squint up at the sunset orange scarf, waving in the wind like a flag. Still there, thank goodness. I'm about to ask Bodin for another boost when a black bird (real? mechanical?) swoops through the sky and gnaws on the bindings of the "hammock" with its beak.

My heart stops. *No. Don't do this, you silly bird. Go away. GO.*

The bird makes one final snip. The ropes break. And down, down, down tumbles the white sheet holding Mama.

I rush forward, time slowing to a crawl. Logically, I know that I can't break her fall. From that height, the only thing I'll succeed in breaking is my own head. But instinct has no logic; love, no reason.

I slide onto my knees, my arms outstretched to catch Mama and…ow.

The foam body breaks upon impact and scatters in disjointed pieces all around me.

Mama was never in danger after all.

Damn that Xander.

CHAPTER THIRTY-FIVE

"Almost there." Bodin points at the curl of smoke rising above the treetops. "That smoke is coming from our firepit. I'm guessing it's about a mile away."

I smile at him. He's been nothing but encouraging during our long hike down the mountainside, through the dense forest, and back toward camp. His steadfast optimism, the curve of his lips—these are the only things that keep me going.

I ran out of energy miles ago. My limbs are vermicelli noodles, my muscles have aches upon aches, and my lung capacity has shrunk to the size of a grain of rice. I don't know how long we've been walking. I just know that there's only two of us remaining.

After the foam body smashed into the ground, I stared numbly at the disparate pieces—a sphere for the head, a rectangle for the body, and cylinders for the limbs. I might still be there if the croc-people hadn't converged on us. Without explanation, they slapped windcuffs on Rae and scooped up the gold coins that are Eduardo, collected all four of our weapons, and escorted our friends away.

Rage filled me, all the stronger because it was so helpless. Ever since we woke up on this island, Xander has been toying with our emotions, taking pleasure from our pain. Enough. He's not a scientist. The experiment he's conducting on us isn't "research." He'd better be glad I haven't come into my ability, because the way I'm feeling right now, I wouldn't hesitate to rain havoc onto Xander's head.

Please, pra Buddha cho. If I do have an ability inside of me, let it not be passive. Let it be powerful enough to save us—and bring down Xander, to boot.

"Hey, Bodin?" I ask as the treetops hug over our heads, shielding us temporarily from the hot rays of the sun. The air here is cooler, the ground moist, but not muddy. "Can I ask you something?"

"Hmmm?" He grabs a gnarled stick, swinging it in front of us to move the worst of the brambles out of my path.

"Back at the clearing," I say slowly, gathering my thoughts, "I experienced the worst moment of my life. Seeing Mama— or who I thought was Mama—hurtling down to the ground. Knowing that I could do nothing to break her fall. My life flashed before my eyes, or at least—my life with *her*. The way she would roll me in my blankets like a burrito. The magic kisses she would give me to tuck in my pocket. All the moments of my childhood and beyond. And then the foam mannequin turned out *not* to be Mama. Which is miraculous. But my ability didn't surface. Why?"

"I was wondering that, too." Bodin holds back a bendy branch, gesturing for me to go first. He follows at my heels, and the branch whips back into place.

"Not just you, but for the both of us," he amends. "I didn't manifest, either. That endless outpouring of monkeys—it was intense."

"Both Eduardo and Rae, certified badasses, came into their abilities," I say, working through the facts. "That scenario was obviously designed to break *me*, as it was Mama's scarf tied on the mannequin. But here I am, same old me." I glance down at my less-than-athletic body. "Huffing and puffing, with no ability to speak of."

"I *like* the same old you," he says, reaching back and squeezing my hand. I don't mind his casual little touches anymore. In fact, I look forward to them. Crave them, even.

"Everything that's happened since we arrived on hell island has been designed to wear us down. Our bodies have been pushed to our physical limits; our minds have been jolted by surprise after surprise." I look up at Bodin. "What else? What else about my life will Xander twist and manipulate? I can't even tell what's real and what's fake anymore."

"*We're* real," Bodin says, true urgency in his eyes. "No matter what happens, to either of us, my feelings for you are genuine. Please believe that."

"I do," I say softly.

But suddenly, I'm too impatient to linger. Because I recognize our surroundings. The white sand, undulating gently to the water. That precise grouping of three palm trees. The flat rock that Lola liked to sit on, braiding bulletwood flowers into her hair. The structures that we painstakingly built: the firepit, the lean-to, the main shelter.

We're home—or at least the one place of comfort we've managed to carve out of this nightmare. I sprint across the sand. In the distance, I see a figure that appears to be Mama, under the shelter where she belongs. Where she'll be safe.

As I run, it occurs to me that I shouldn't be able to move this quickly. A short while ago, I couldn't even talk without panting at the air. Amazing how the sight of a loved one can rejuvenate you.

"Mama, you'll never believe—"

The words die in my throat. Mama's here under the shelter, all right, her head bare instead of covered by an orange scarf, sleeping bags cushioned around her. But she's lying on her side, curled into a fetal position. She's shivering in spite of the sultry island air.

A croc-person kneels by her. Not just any croc-person— Three. He dips a washcloth in a coconut shell filled with water and tenderly wipes her forehead, her neck, her ears.

He glances up, and I have to swallow twice before I can get the words out. "How...how is she?"

"She's burning up. I think she has some kind of infection." Even in that gravelly voice, Three sounds helpless, which makes my stomach plummet. "I'm trying to bring down her temperature. Keep her pulse points cool. But the fever just won't break." His voice cracks on the last word.

No. The dread fills me, so familiar, so cold. Creeping up my toes and radiating through my body. No. This can't be the end. I just got her back, when her crushed body was revealed to be a mannequin. This can't be the moment where I say goodbye.

"I tried giving her coconut water by squirting some in a syringe into her mouth, but she can't swallow anymore." Whatever desperation he can't convey with his voice shines clearly in his eyes. "The liquid just runs out of her mouth. She's dehydrated, Alaia. She needs an IV, as well as antibiotics. There are some in the infirmary, in the cave at the north end of the mountain. The other croc-people told me about it. But the cave is sealed with some kind of magic, to prevent anyone from entering."

"Will Xander...?" I can't even ask the question.

Three shakes his head, his snout moving back and forth.

"I asked him. I *begged*. He… He won't budge. He refuses to help her because she's no longer any use to him. He generally prefers younger subjects, but he brought along her and Khun Anita as leverage. In case you or Kit needed the extra push to come into your abilities. But you already endured the falling mannequin, and so, she's served her purpose."

I sink onto the platform next to Mama. She is my only focus. Her wan, tired face. The sheen of perspiration on her forehead. Her glassy, unfocused eyes.

"Mama, it's me," I say, licking my lips.

Her pupils flicker in my direction, and then they sharpen on my face.

"Alaia," she rasps, as though my name is glass coming out of her throat. She raises her hand, but she doesn't have the energy to move it farther. I duck my head underneath her palm so that she can rest it on my hair.

"Don't move," I beg her. "Don't try to talk. Conserve your energy. We'll get you help." Tears fill my eyes. Forget the 121 smiles. I will not let her die like this, if it's the last thing I do. "Just hold on."

"Are you…in danger?" she asks haltingly. Her hand falls off my head, and she points one feeble finger toward the lotus flower floating in the copper basin. The one that Three had brought her the previous night. But instead of the fresh pink blooms of before, so delicate and pretty like Mama, the petals are now shriveled up. Dying.

"The lotus flower…withered," Mama continues, one labored word at a time. "That's how I knew…you were in… danger."

"Not anymore, Mama." I settle her hand gently by her side. "I'm safe now."

She nods, tired out by the conversation, and her eyelids droop.

"Sleep," I whisper. "Rest. You're my mama."

"And you're my baby," she mumbles, her eyes closed.

I rise and join Bodin and Three, who are chatting a few feet away.

"The withering lotus flower is a Thai folktale, too," Bodin tells me. "Your mom has manifested her ability. She can sense danger to her loved ones with the health of a lotus flower."

"Don't tell Xander," I plead with Three. "He's already made it clear that he's not going to help her. If he takes her into his custody, there's no telling how he'll torture her."

"I won't," Three says. "You can count on me."

I nod. "Please watch over her."

I've hardly taken two steps, however, before Bodin lopes after me. "Alaia. Where are you going?"

In response, I stop and press my lips fully on his, doubling the kisses I've had in this lifetime. But...if this is the last kiss I ever have, I want it to be a good one.

After a few searing seconds, Bodin wrenches away. "Look, I'm never going to complain about kissing you. But you haven't answered my question."

I turn and start walking once more. I was never a good sleeper. As a baby, I used to wake every couple of hours, scratching at my skin because of an undiagnosed milk allergy. And then, in my childhood, I woke up screaming from OCD nightmares. Not the ones most people dream, but the ones that represent hell to me. An unfinished sentence written on a whiteboard so that I couldn't complete reading it. Various posters and street signs flying past at warp speed, too fast for me to name and catalogue the shapes. An errant touch, one half of a ballet exercise—a leap on my right side but not my left—so that I would remain unbalanced and incomplete forever.

Each and every one of those times, Mama woke from

a light sleep and came to my side. It didn't matter how physically exhausted she was or how emotionally draining the day had been. Always, she stroked my hair. On countless nights, she whispered soothing words of comfort. To me, she *is* peace, the only one that I've ever known.

And now, at the end of her life, I will give her the peaceful death that she deserves.

"Alaia—"

"Mama needs help," I say tightly. "She needs that IV. She needs antibiotics. I'm getting into that cave. I don't care what it takes."

"Yes, yes, and yes." We move down the beach, one of his long strides to every two of my shorter ones. "How?"

"I don't know," I admit. "But I'll figure out a way."

He maneuvers so that he's facing me, and I stop. "I'm coming with you."

"No." As terrified as I am about heading out on my own, this is the easiest decision I'll ever have to make. When it comes to Mama's safety, Mama's peace, I have no doubts. All the *what-if* scenarios fade away, and the only course remaining is the correct one. The right one. The only balanced path in the universe there is.

"I need you here. To keep an eye on Three, whom I don't fully trust. More importantly, to fight off the croc-people, should they try to take Mama away."

I take a deep breath. "I'm not strong enough to resist them, but you…you can take on a group of them. I saw you battle with the krabong. It's like you've been training with it your whole life. You can cause the very same damage with a stick. Please," I conclude. "Do this for me."

He nods. "You only have to ask."

I start to walk again, alone. But while my solitary state was a shackle around my neck before, I feel light now. Strong.

As though I could take off into the air.

"Alaia, wait."

I turn, and I know I'll never forget this image for the rest of my life.

Bodin stands so straight, so tall. The newly risen moon frosts his hair, and the tumultuous ocean crashes at his feet.

"You need a weapon," he says. "Let me make you a spear. It'll take me twenty minutes, tops."

"I don't need a spear."

I point to an object by his right shoulder, a few feet behind him. It sticks out proudly from the glistening white sand, drawing the moon's light as surely as the boy himself.

It's Rae's double-edged sword.

CHAPTER THIRTY-SIX

Bodin jumps so high that his head partially blocks the moon. "What is *that*?"

"A double-edged sword with black leather wrapped around the hilt." I approach the weapon cautiously. In the absence of the sun, the silver of the blade should dull. Instead, it catches so many of the moon's beams that it seems to sparkle with its own light source. "Is it Rae's? Looks just like it."

"Has to be," Bodin says distractedly, staring at the blade. "There's only one sword like this on the island."

I lift my head. "How do you know?"

"Something Three said. One blowgun. One dagger. One of every magical weapon. Only the krabongs are in common use." He tugs me a few inches away from the sword, closer to the noisy rush of the sea. "How long has it been there? And *how* did it get there?"

I look up the beach. There are my footprints in the wet sand, walking right past it, and Bodin's longer, bulkier prints, parallel to mine.

"Did we just not see it when we passed?" I asked.

"Dark out here," he mutters. "But the way that thing's gleaming, it's hard to believe we missed it."

"So, it just...appeared?"

He lifts his shoulders. "Maybe."

I reach for the hilt—

"Don't touch it." Bodin yanks my hand back. "They took our weapons," he says, his tone wobbly. "But if this is Rae's sword, then she has a special kinship with it. Her ability allowed her to bond with it, so to speak. So it's not just a weapon. It interacts with her energy. It may even follow her instructions."

"You're saying *Rae* sent the sword here? In order to aid me?"

"Possibly. But that doesn't mean you can touch—"

With one smooth motion, I grasp the hilt with both hands and pull it cleanly out of the sand.

Bodin blinks. "Scratch that thought."

I test the heft of the sword—and then take a practice swing, trying to imitate Eduardo's form.

"Hey!" I exclaim. "How come you haven't fallen over, clutching your head?"

He steps closer. "She lent you the sword. Doesn't mean you also inherit her ability. Besides..." He moves the sword, his hand over mine, showing me the proper way to swing it. "I'm not your enemy, am I?"

"Quite the opposite." I grin as we slice the blade through our invisible opponent, right in his chest.

Too soon, Bodin leaves me to head back to camp, and I abandon the beach to continue my journey through the woods.

The dark closes in. The moon casts shifting, elongated shadows. They could be anything. Robotic monkeys, hiding within a tree's branches. A naga who is *not* Eduardo, slithered in from the sea. A crocodile, waiting patiently for one wrong step so that it can swallow me whole.

And eyes. Eyes that live in the night, that feed on my fear. Eyes that rise with the moon, that are born from my nightmares. Hundreds, thousands of eyes watching my back, scouring my body...when there only needs to be two to put me in danger.

Two eyes, one mind, following my every move.

I run faster, hoping to escape the dread. Paranoid—that's all I am. Terrified to the tips of my toes. But I can't shake the sensation that someone's watching.

I wish the monsters would come out of the dark. Then I could, I don't know, *count* them. It wouldn't do much to dispel their power, but it would sure help me.

I count my steps instead.

1, 2, 3, 4, 5, 6, 7, 8, 9, 10, 11.

I nimbly leap through the night, my strides long, my pace fast. The moon reflects off the sword, lighting my way through the dense maze of these woods.

1, 2, 3, 4, 5, 6, 7, 8, 9, 10, 11.

A rush of energy fills me. I'm anticipating obstacles—exposed tree roots, a fallen log—long before they arrive. I shouldn't be able to do this. I just hiked down a mountain today. I shouldn't have this kind of energy.

1, 2, 3, 4, 5, 6, 7, 8, 9, 10, 11.

Either the moon shines more brightly, or my senses have gotten more precise. I can *feel* the dark, its contours and its edges, its energy and its pulse. And it is no longer scary to me.

Even if someone is watching.

I arrive at the mouth of the cave, at the northernmost

tip of the island.

Here, I hesitate, just for a moment. If Three is right, magic seals the cave closed. Magic that can perhaps be pierced by a sacred double-edged sword. I have no idea if this will work, but the certainty that it will grows inside me.

I've got no one to ask out here. No one to confirm my decision or poke holes in my conclusion. All I have to rely on is…me. And that, perhaps, is my biggest fear of all.

I always knew that I would have to grow up someday. That eventuality always felt in the far distant future. But the time has come, and it is now. I'll never forgive myself if I don't give my all to secure Mama the peace that she deserves.

I don't count. I don't even give myself time to think. Instead, I plunge the sword straight into the cave's entrance. Energy shoots into my arm, the sensation of an invisible wall crumbling. And then, I'm in.

Holy crap, I was *right*. I'm never right—or at least that's how it feels. But I'm also not usually the one making the decisions. It's always Mama or Papa or some other authority figure.

The blackness swallows me whole, but a rush of information washes over me. I am like a bat who emits sound pulses to determine its location. And yet, I'm not using my ears to conceptualize the dark. Nor my eyes, nor my mouth. I can simply sense the tunnel in front of me. I instinctively feel when to turn right to continue down a smaller path, and when to duck my head to avoid a low-hanging stalactite.

I don't know how long I walk, twisting and turning down this maze of tunnels. The feeling of eyes at my back never blinks, never wavers. At times, I swear that I can hear footsteps softly treading behind me.

But it's so dark that I wouldn't be able to see my stalker if they were a foot behind me, so I ignore the sound. In time,

I get used to the footsteps. I decide that they are nothing more than the echo of *my* own feet. A manifestation of my desperate wish for company.

Eventually, I glimpse a light in the distance. My heart quickens. The infirmary. Have I finally reached it? Or am I about to walk into another one of Xander's miserable traps?

I inhale, and to my surprise, the air is frosty as it hits my lungs. When I breathe out again, I can see water droplets in the air.

Wrapping my arms around myself, I creep toward the archway that's emitting the light. The urge to give up and run back into Mama's arms is strong. But I'm out of options here. If I *don't* press forward, there will be nothing left to which I can return.

I find myself in a small chamber so cold that icicles drip from the low rock ceiling and along the curved walls. It's the infirmary, all right. Cabinets line the cave wall, filled with meticulously organized medical supplies.

I dash inside the cave and rifle through the cabinets. Yes. An IV bag, lying neatly next to syringes and tubes. And over here—a selection of antibiotics for infections. I'm not sure which one Mama needs, so I grab them all. I shove everything into a blue plastic bag that looks like a vomit receptacle and turn to leave the room.

That's when I see a rectangular metal box, similar to a coffin, standing on a high pedestal in the center of the room. I was so laser-focused on Mama's supplies that I hadn't even noticed.

Run! every instinct in me shouts. *You have the supplies Mama needs. That's the priority. That's always been the priority.* But I can't help it. I creep toward the coffin—and gasp.

Through the glass window on top of the box, I can see a little boy. He can't be more than eight or nine years old. His eyes and mouth are closed, the long brush of eyelashes dark against forever young skin. His hands are clasped together on top of his chest. A peaceful sleep. Except—not so peaceful. Because an eight- or nine-year-old boy is meant to be active. Even in sleep, they should be spinning like a clock. This boy is dead, at a tragically young age.

I lay the double-edged sword on the metal box and bring my ice-cold hands to my mouth, where the puff of my breath does little to warm them. The boy looks...familiar, although I'm not sure why. There's something about his jaw, maybe, or the shape of his lips...

My ears prick. There it is again—the almost inaudible sound of a pair of feet as they try to sneak up on me. It's not my imagination this time. Not an echo. Eyes drill into the back of my head. I am not alone.

I casually lean both hands on the metal box, right next to the hilt of the sword. I have only one chance to do this. One attack with the element of surprise.

I slowly exhale, letting all of the breath deflate from my body. And then, I whirl around and thrust the sword up to their throat, coming eye to eye with the person behind me. Recognition floods through me.

My stalker is Bodin.

CHAPTER THIRTY-SEVEN

My heart thunders in my ears, and I can't seem to catch a breath. Those are *Bodin's* footsteps that I've been hearing? What? Why?

I shake my head to clear my jumbled thoughts, and as I do, the sword slips an inch below his Adam's apple.

He could've overtaken me, then. His reflexes are quick, his muscles strong. It would've been a cinch for him to disarm the sword, whirl me around, and hold the blade to *my* throat.

But he doesn't.

I lift the blade to his jugular and back him up until his spine hits the icy wall. I let down my guard once—but I won't do it again.

"Are you following me?" Part of me is still wondering if I've gotten this all wrong. All of me is wishing, desperately, that there's a perfectly reasonable explanation for this scenario.

"Kinda?" he says. It's more question than statement.

I bring the sword up a millimeter, touching skin. If I move it any closer, I'll draw blood. "It's a *yes* or *no* question."

His gaze, which has been bouncing around the cavern, meets my eyes. "Yes," he says, his pupils darker than the night. "I was following you."

"Why?"

"I wanted to make sure you were safe." His eyes drop. He studies the sword, and then my hand, as though assessing what I'm capable of. "I wanted to help you, in case you ran into any trouble."

"Lie," I say. "I asked you to stay. To protect Mama. You knew that would be more important to me."

He has no response. He simply closes his eyes, the dark, luscious lashes brushing against his skin.

Wait. His skin is darker—a smooth rich brown, while the other is pale, ethereal. But that could be because Bodin's been living in the outside world, under the hot, beating sun. But those eyelashes—thick, impossibly long. I knew I recognized them.

"Who is that boy inside the coffin?" I demand.

"Don't know. This is the first time I've seen him." He opens his eyes. Looks straight into mine. In anyone else, this might signify truthfulness. But I see it once again—that flicker of sadness.

"Don't lie to me, Bodin." My hand trembles; so does the sword. If I don't get ahold of myself, I might accidentally kill him before I find out if he deserves it. "If I ever meant anything to you—and I'm beginning to suspect that I *didn't*— tell me the truth."

He shakes his head, lowering his eyes.

"This whole time." Now even my voice is shaking. "You've been working with Xander *this entire time*. You pretended to be our friend. You flirted with me. You kissed me. How. Dare. You?" I blink. My eyes are wet, but I refuse to cry. Not for this guy. "At least Xander was upfront about torturing us. What kind of sick person are you, that you get off on *using* us—"

"Xander is my father," Bodin blurts out.

I lower the sword. "What?"

"You can put down the weapon. You're not going to hurt me." And then, with one quick movement, he easily disarms me. The sword goes clanking into the corner, where its tip lodges into a swell of ice.

"You were right," he says regretfully. "I have been training with these weapons all of my life. You're no match for me. You never were."

My shoulders droop. It all makes so much sense now. All those times he tried to dissuade us from fighting Xander. To submit and fall into line like good soldiers. It was his idea to go on our first expedition through the mountain. His misinformation that made us hope that there was civilization—and therefore help—on the other side.

He lied to us. He used me. He took my most vulnerable emotions and manipulated them for his own gain.

I should be angry. I should be raging and screaming. Instead, all I feel is numb. Maybe it's from the sub-freezing temperature in this room. Or maybe it's merely a side effect of being manipulated one too many times.

I look at him. At the mouth that I voluntarily kissed. At the chest where I would sneak glances. Who is this person? Did I ever know him at all?

I should never have trusted him. I should've suspected. Everything else about this godforsaken place was an illusion. A manipulation. Some contrivance that Xander set up as a means for one thing alone.

The captain told us from the very beginning. Everything on this island is designed to trick us. To manipulate our emotions until we're pushed past our limits. He warned us to believe at our own risk.

And I fell for Bodin anyway.

He's pacing before me, agitated. Back and forth, over the frozen floor. I think I see the beginning of a rut worn into the ice. But hell, maybe that's an illusion, too.

I wish I felt *something* as I watch him. An emotion beyond this deep, cold emptiness inside me. But there's just... an absence. So absolute that it takes up space, as a physical object would.

"Tell me," I say listlessly. "I'm not foolish enough to believe it will change anything. But I would like to know."

"You've already heard most of the story," he says in a low voice. "As much as I could, I tried to be honest—to be genuine—with you."

Ah. There's the first crack in my heart. The first piercing jolt of hurt. The sensation's not as desirable as I thought, so I quickly stuff it down the black hole of my soul.

"That boy...is my brother," Bodin continues. "My twin. A motorcycle accident killed him ten years ago. My father, Xander, couldn't accept the outcome. He wouldn't come to terms with the fact that his favored son, the one he was supposed to mold in his shape, was gone. So, we moved here, to this remote island in the Gulf of Thailand, and he had my brother cryogenically frozen.

"You see, he had already found the sacred crystal orb, the one that is the source of all magic. He'd been dabbling with his scientific experiments and had learned that people had latent abilities inside them. And when they were in close proximity to the crystal, their abilities could be brought to the surface in very specific ways, if you knew which buttons to push. If you knew which emotions to target. He came into his own powers when my twin died—the ability to turn turmeric root into gold.

"With his newfound unlimited wealth, he was able to turn

this island into his very own science lab. He believed that he could save his son yet—the favorite one, for all intents and purposes, his *only* one. All he had to do was find his Lotus Flower Champion. The one who possessed the rarest ability of all: the power to reverse death."

I inhale sharply. "That's the purpose behind his games. The reason he kidnapped us and brought us to this island."

"Yes," Bodin says simply. "My dad's obsession built this island. Imprisoned dozens upon dozens of people. Ruined lives. All for a chance to cheat life and the fates."

The emptiness inside me is filling again. Not with emotions. So long as I'm in a cryogenic chamber, I'm freezing my pesky heart—and its accompanying liabilities—for as long as possible.

But I'm filling with plans. With strategies. With thoughts of Mama and ways to get us out of here.

"And you just went along with it?" I have to keep him talking. As far as my heart is concerned, I'm done with this conversation. Done with *him*. But he doesn't have to know that.

"I was nine years old," Bodin says, his eyes black with sorrow, deep with anguish. "What was I supposed to do?"

I don't care. I don't! What does it matter if he feels guilt, when he's one of the reasons we're here?

"You haven't been nine years old for a very long time, Bodin."

The sword. That's my best bet. He hasn't made any attempt to restrain me. To secure the weapon. He's underestimating me, as usual, and that will be his downfall.

"Alaia, you have to believe me," he pleads. "I really tried—"

His efforts—whatever they were—will be lost in this chamber forever. I lunge forward and shove him as hard as I can. Because he wasn't ready, wasn't braced, his feet slide out from underneath him on the icy floor, and he falls backward, smacking his head on the cryogenic box.

I rush to the corner, wrap my hand around the hilt, and pull. The blade must not have been buried very deeply, because it dislodges immediately.

Bodin stumbles to his feet, his hand clutching the back of his skull, and I run from the room, back into the dark, twisty tunnels. My feet slide against the loose pebbles, shifting my center of balance, making too much noise.

Artificial lights flood the tunnels, and I realize that the caves are less natural, more technologically outfitted than I originally thought. These tunnels must be Xander's living spaces, his corridors, his rooms.

The incessant drumming of footsteps pounds behind me. Not just Bodin, this time, but a battalion of Xander's employees chasing me.

I risk a look over my shoulder. An army of croc-people is after me, in various states of transformation. Many are still fully reptiles, slithering on their bellies on the ground. Some are crawling, awkwardly pulling themselves along, with a human leg or arm. Only one is fully upright, his short forelegs gripping a blowgun.

My blowgun, if Bodin is to be believed that there's only one on the island. I try to summon the weapon with my mind—but alas, I have no more special kinship with it than I do the recessed lights above my head.

I hurry down the tunnel. I don't have much time. Any second now, the croc-person holding the blowgun will develop human arms. Then, he'll be able to point and shoot. It won't matter how much distance I put between us, then.

But if I can exit these tunnels, if I find my way back to the outside, there'll be trees to hide behind, shadows that

I can disappear into. I can get lost in the woods, and my back wouldn't present as one large, bobbing target. It's my only hope, so I pour all of the reserves of my energy—and the reserves of those reserves—into my burning legs, my pumping arms.

And then, I hear it. A *whoosh* in the air. I know exactly what it means, because each time I huffed into the blowgun, I heard that very same noise.

I turn, and the world slows to a crawl. The blowgun falls to the croc-person's side as he raises his free human arm in triumph. I launch myself to the ground, but the dart's coming too fast. At that velocity, it will strike me before I can take cover below its arc. I fall, my eyes wide open, as I watch the dart's flight.

That's how I see the moment that the dart breaks in midair. It snaps right in the middle…and the two halves tumble harmlessly to the ground.

I hit earth a moment later, with a thud that jars my brain enough that I wonder if I'm seeing things. Maybe the dart didn't fall to the ground. Maybe it's buried deep in my heart and I'm bleeding out on this dirt floor as the croc-people converge on me.

And if the dart *didn't* get me, well…then I'm about to be eaten alive by a bask of crocodiles. Either way, I'm done.

I lift my head experimentally, for one last look at the world, and a wave of dizziness admonishes me.

Every last croc-person has fallen to their knees, their heads bowed with respect. Bodin brings up the rear, his expression a mixture of shock and confusion.

"Congratulations, Alaia." Bodin shakes his head, as though he can't quite believe he's saying these words. "It looks like you're our Lotus Flower Champion."

CHAPTER THIRTY-EIGHT

What? I shake my head, but the words don't make any sense. All I know is: they're no longer attacking me, at least for the moment.

My sword. Where is it?

I look swiftly around. There, a few feet away on the dirt ground. I must've lost my grip on it when I fell. I scrabble forward and grab the hilt, twisting around and holding the double-edged blade in front of me.

But nobody has moved. The croc-people remain on their knees, their heads bowed. Bodin stares at me, his eyes blinking rapidly as though he's trying to work out what just happened.

Him and me both.

I replay the moment in my mind. The dart races toward me, and then it snaps by some invisible force and falls to the ground.

My thoughts whirl. So, it was a faulty dart, or maybe someone's playing a trick on me. If it's not either of those… well, there's also the possibility that my ability has manifested.

So what? We've seen much more impressive abilities. I

watched Mateo transform into a *crocodile*. Rae incapacitated an entire army of robot monkeys with a single sweep of her sword. Who cares if I can break darts in the air?

Xander, apparently, since he appears at the end of the long tunnel. He sweeps forward, stepping between the croc-people, cutting a path through the sea of their bodies.

He comes to a stop before me, wearing the same outfit as before, even though it's the middle of the night. Does he wear these clothes while he sleeps? Does he even sleep?

I crab-walk backward, dragging my sword along the ground.

"My dear," Xander begins. "You don't know how long I've been searching for you."

"Stay back!" I yell. "Don't get any closer."

"You're safe here." Xander turns his palms up, as though to show me he's harmless. "You are the most valuable person on this island. Believe me, nobody is going to lay a hand on you."

Don't contradict him, a voice inside me begs. If he mistakenly believes that I should be protected, then it's not my job to prove him wrong.

And yet...and yet...it will somehow be even scarier if he's right.

"You're mistaken." I continue to move backward. It's a long tunnel. I'll never be able to get away, not with an army at his disposal—but the more distance I put between us, the better I feel. "One measly dart broke in the air. I can't reverse death. I wouldn't even know how to begin."

"Ah, you can't reverse death *yet*," Xander corrects. "But I believe one day, soon, you'll be able to. You see, most of us have one ability and one ability alone. It is the few with the rarest of talents that can manifest multiple abilities, each one more impressive than the last."

I shake my head. No. I'm not the person he's describing. I can't be.

"You must trust yourself, my dear Alaia," he continues. "When you witnessed what you believed to be your mother falling to her death, you were right in believing that you had manifested an ability.

"We made you walk ten miles down the mountainside, with no food and little sleep. Not only did you survive, but you were able to revive your muscles during the process so that you ended the hike fresher and more energized than when you started."

He's right, I think, dazed. That happened. But there has to be an explanation. I just can't think of one right now.

"You then sailed through the woods, with its maze of tangled roots and confusing turns, in the pitch black, as though it were a child's playground. Each of your senses has been magnified by a factor of a hundred, and still you didn't notice.

"That was when I began to suspect." Xander clasps his hands together. "To hope. To pray. That you might be the one to bring my child back to life. But I've been disappointed—no, *devastated*—before. That's why I waited until you entered my innermost chamber, which held my innermost heart. My son, may he rest in temporary peace."

I dart a glance at Bodin. I can't help it. Like the others, he listens in grave silence, although a pulse beats steadily at his temple.

"And then, when the dart broke and fell inches before it struck you, I knew." His voice drops to a fervent whisper. "You're the best hope I've found, in my decade of searching. And if I'm right, in a few days' time, you will reunite me with my boy."

I have no clue if Xander is right. Probably not, because I'm not some savior. I'm not anybody's best hope for anything…

unless it's being most likely to be fooled by tall boys with long eyelashes.

But Xander's not trying to torture me or lock me up, so who am I to argue? Although he refused to let my friends go, he's given me permission to go back to the beach, back to Mama, to live — and wait — in relative peace, until the full extent of my abilities manifests.

The helicopter drops me off on our sandy beach, but this time, no one comes forward to greet me.

Please, pra Buddha cho, I pray as I climb down from the chopper and it lifts off once more. *Let Mama be here. Let Mama be safe. Let me not be too late.*

The camp has been completely transformed. I blink, twice, to make sure that I'm not hallucinating. To make sure this isn't a mirage that's appeared out of thin air.

Our rickety shelters have been removed, replaced by sleek open-air huts that are as nice as our villa in Koh Samui.

A spa area has been set up in one of the huts, complete with an outdoor shower, lounge chairs, and fluffy white towels. Another hut boasts a comfortable couch in front of a large-screen television.

But where is Mama?

I scan the rest of the setup, my heartbeat settling only when I spot her in a hospital bed in the main hut.

I quicken my pace and then break into a full-out sprint. Mama's hooked up to an IV, the bag hanging on a standing metal hook next to the bed. What's more, she's *sitting* against the headboard, propped up by some pillows.

It's what I always imagined. Clean, white sheets. Mama, freshly bathed and comfortable. A stack of paperback novels on her bedside, next to a tall glass of ginger beer.

There's only one difference from the picture in my head: Mama is nowhere close to dying.

"Mama!" I fly to her side. "You look so…well."

"Sweetheart!" She hugs me tight, and then pulls back to check my face, as though to make sure it's really me. "You're safe. I was so worried. Three brought me another lotus flower, and it wilted again."

"You probably should stop replacing them," I say wryly. "I get the feeling they'll all fade away."

"Not if I tuck you next to me and keep you here." She scoots over in the hospital bed, and I squeeze in next to her, even though there's only room for one. I lay my head on her chest, just like I used to as a little girl.

Back then, I thought that so long as I was listening to the steady thump-thump of her heart, I would be safe, I would be protected. Everything would be okay.

Well, I'm grown-up now, and so much has changed—especially my definition of "okay."

"How are you feeling, Mama?" I ask, looking into the face that I know as well as my own. Maybe even better, since I see it more often than my own reflection in the mirror. "You seem so…healthy…and a few hours ago, you were—"

"Dying?" She takes a sip from her ginger beer and shakes her head wonderingly. "I can actually *taste* this. The sweetness on my tongue, that bright hit of acid. I thought, for sure, I'd lost all of my senses. And I'd have been pretty pissed if my last taste of life was a bite of rice porridge filled with sand."

I hold her wrist, letting my thumb rest on her pulse. Steady. Strong. "What happened while I was gone?"

"I'm not sure." She sets her glass down, looking at the tray table as though it had just appeared. And from her perspective, it probably did.

"My eyelids were heavy. So heavy, like someone had strapped sandbags to them. I was trying to stay awake, because I knew you would come back to see me, one final

time. And I knew that moment would be important for you."
She looks into my eyes, more awake, more alert than she has
been in days. "And then, I must've drifted off, because the
next thing I knew, new life had been breathed into me."

"That's what it seems like." I scrutinize her face. Her skin
is still smooth, still soft, but there's new energy inside her.
A glow that starts deep in her core. "There's no way that
hydration did this alone. Was Three here? Did he give you
the antibiotics?"

"Yes, and I also administered something else," a voice as
tough and dry as old leather says.

I start as a figure sits up on a couch on the other side of
the hut. No wonder I hadn't noticed him. Lying down, his
crocodile skin blended with the dark wood. In my peripheral
vision, I must've mistaken his silver jumpsuit for the couch
cushions.

It's Three—but not like the Three of yesterday evening.
This one moves stiffly, as though every one of his joints hurts.
His reptile skin extends down his neck and disappears under
his jumpsuit. It also covers both hands. He can still walk
upright, like a human, but his movements are creaky and slow.

He approaches Mama and me on the bed, holding a
crystal orb the size of my hand. It glows as though it has
its own source of light. It's got to be the same as the one on
a pedestal in the crocodile pit, the one guarded by all the
reptiles. The one that's apparently the source of all magic.

"There's no more human medication that can save her,"
Three continues, his voice thick. "Late last night, I received
permission from Xander to borrow the sacred orb for a few
hours, so that I could expose her to its healing rays."

He hands me the crystal to examine. I hold it up, and for a
moment, the energy flares, sharp and vivid. The light reminds
me of the fire that's dancing in Mama's eyes.

"This crystal is what's making her better," Three says. "It's the only thing keeping her alive."

"And Xander just *gave* it to you?" I ask.

Three curls up his fangs. I think it's supposed to be a smile, but he only succeeds in looking like he's anticipating his next meal.

"You know Xander," Mama says wearily. "He doesn't do anything without taking something in return."

"What did he take from you?" I ask Three. It's obvious from the way he holds his body that the price was hefty. This isn't coconut water or even a tool for a set of windcuffs. This favor concerns the use of a crystal so sacred that it has to be guarded by a pit of crocodiles.

Three shakes his head like he doesn't want to answer.

And I don't want to take anything else from this man. He's already done so much for me and Mama, by bringing the orb to her, by healing her in a way I can't understand. But the betrayal by Bodin has taught me that I can't tell my friends from my foes. I need to know exactly who Three is.

"Tell me," I whisper. I said the very same words a few hours ago to a boy who crushed my trust without a second thought. I say the words now, expecting the worst but hoping for something positive.

Three sighs heavily. "Xander uses our humanity as a bargaining chip. A gift that we earn with our obedience. If we do exactly as he says, he allows us to endure on this island as half human, half crocodile, with some of our memories intact. But if we disobey or if we ask for a special concession, there's a cost."

With enormous effort, Three creaks over and sits on a stool beside the hospital bed.

"What's the cost?" I ask.

"Our memories," he rasps. "The very thing that makes us human. Take away enough of them, and I'll just be trapped in the body of a crocodile. I won't remember. I'll cease to be human. I'll cease to be…me. The closer I get to full crocodile, the more difficult it is for me to move in a human body."

"You traded in memories to bring me the tool to dismantle my windcuffs," I say as realization dawns. "For each lotus flower that you've brought Mama, for every drop of coconut water that you fed to her. And now…this." I extend my shaking hand at the IV bag dripping fluids into Mama, at the machines measuring her heartbeat. At the hospital bed that keeps her comfortable, at the clean sheets that make her feel like a semblance of her normal self.

And the last, and the heftiest, weight: the crystal itself.

Xander didn't provide these items out of the generosity of his stone heart. It was Three who siphoned off his memories, Three who sacrificed parts of his humanity. For us.

He nods. "Yes. I gave my memories for her, and for you."

"Why?" I ask. "Why would you do such a thing? You don't even know us."

He looks at me, and then he tenderly picks up Mama's hand. Because I am between them, their arms are joined over me.

And all of a sudden, I know. Because we've laid like this countless times before. The two of them holding hands, with me sandwiched in between. When I was a little girl and they soothed away my nightmares. And when we learned of Mama's terminal diagnosis a few months ago. All of my life, they have provided a united front, in sickness and in health, in human form and in crocodile.

"Hey, Three?" I ask breathlessly. "Why do colds make bad criminals?"

"Because they're so easy to catch." He, as always, supplies the punch line.

I launch myself into his arms. "Papa!"

CHAPTER THIRTY-NINE

I crash into Papa's chest, nearly knocking him off the stool. But he wraps his arms around me, righting his balance. Righting *me*.

His skin is rough and hard against my cheek. There are ridges along his back where muscle and flesh used to be. He smells like mud and moss and reptile. And yet, none of that matters. The feeling he creates inside me is the same. Papa's here, with us, once more.

"You're not dead," I say wonderingly. I pull back and touch his snout, the smooth underside of his jaw. "And you're very handsome, for a crocodile."

"Genetics." Papa bobs his head. "Where do you think you get your good looks, missy?"

"Hey!" I protest. "Are you saying I look like a reptile?"

"Just the eyes," he assures me. "The rest, you luckily got from your mother."

"I always did tell him to use lotion," Mama says, her eyes twinkling. "He never listened. And now look what happened."

Papa sighs dramatically and thrusts out his scaly hand.

"You win, woman. After twenty years, I finally admit that you're right on this subject. Happy?"

Mama giggles—and I freeze. How long has it been since I heard that girlish noise? Not since our trip began. Certainly not since her cancer diagnosis. I'd been trying to get Mama to smile 121 times in Koh Samui. I never even *dreamed* of a giggle.

Joy fills me, wild and fierce. I grip both my parents' hands, and they hug me from either side. I squeeze my eyes shut and savor the sensation. This moment. This time. I never thought I'd have it again. And it doesn't matter that Papa's blood runs cold. It doesn't matter that tubes are affixed to Mama's arms. We're here, transcending our physical bodies. Together. Family.

If I could crystallize this moment in time, I think I could be happy forever. But I can't. No matter how ferociously I live in the present, time passes. A second from now, two seconds, three seconds, what was once perfect is now a memory. Reality always encroaches. I only have to look at the speckled scales on Papa's face to see that.

"Why didn't you tell us sooner?" I ask.

"I wanted to." Papa bends his snout and nuzzles Mama's hand. "You have no idea how much I wanted to hold you both in my arms. It's not easy living inside this mind," he says softly. "It's so alien. Unfamiliar. I would've loved a reminder of the person that I used to be. But Xander forbade it. If I tried to claim any kind of identity, he said, he would take away *all* my memories, so that I had no identity left to claim."

"Did you know it was him, Mama?"

She smiles tenderly at Papa, her thumb stroking over his hand. "I'd like to say yes, that I knew immediately. Who doesn't want to believe that they would know their soulmate, no matter what form they took? But the truth is:

I only suspected. Some of his mannerisms were so familiar. It helped when I saw Mateo transform. That allowed me to wrap my mind around the fact that a mind and a soul could be the same, even though they occupied two different bodies. But I didn't know for sure until today."

I settle onto my half of Mama's pillow. I can't help but think about my own debacle of a romance, and the anger surges inside me all over again. But I will not let Bodin—or thoughts of him—ruin this moment. So I focus on the sensation of being a little girl again, lulled to sleep by my parents' bedtime stories. Except that our stories aren't gentle—and they're all too real.

"What happened to you?" I ask Papa. "When we left you on the yacht. Did the mother and her baby make it?"

"No." He ducks his head. "I was frantic. The explosions kept coming. Suzie and her baby lost too much blood, and I couldn't stem it in time." He pauses, his reptilian eyes reflecting true regret. "As a doctor, I know that I can't save everyone—and I learned long ago to accept that. But it still shook me. And, I don't know... I guess I was too close to the island and the sacred orb, or my emotions were too heightened, because their deaths—on top of not knowing when I would see the two of you again—did more than shake me. They *transformed* me. I watched as my own hands elongated and my arms shortened. My skin split and hardened. I touched my face, and in its place were sharp teeth and a snout.

"Xander's people whisked me off the yacht. When I woke again, I was in the crocodile pit with the others. That's when I began to learn the inner workings of this island.

"We all took a new name," he continues. "They called me Three because there are only three people in our family. I thought that might have clued you in to who I really was."

He lifts his snout as earnestly as a crocodile can. Mama and I look at each other and burst out laughing.

"Only Papa would think an obscure reference like that would mean anything to us," I tease.

"Not all of us do *The New York Times* crossword puzzle every day, my love," Mama says fondly.

Papa's shoulders shake—and I *think* he's laughing, too. It will take us a while to learn his new cues...if Xander allows us to be together that long.

All of a sudden, I feel crowded in by Papa's chest on the one side and Mama's shoulder on the other. "Is it stuffy in here?" I mutter, moving around in the bed.

"It shouldn't be." Mama creases her brow. "You can feel the breeze from the ocean."

I sit up, yank down my collar, and take a deep inhale of the salty air. That doesn't help. I clamber out of the bed, being careful not to dislodge any of Mama's tubes.

My parents turn to me with twin expressions of concern, which only adds to my unease.

"What's wrong, Alaia?" Papa asks.

"You know how when something feels too good to be true, it usually is?" I burst out.

Mama looks from me to Papa to the crystal orb on her nightstand, its glow never ceasing, its energy ever cycling. "Are you referring to us?"

"Well, yes. Mama's health has improved drastically. Papa's been returned to us. I *might* be the Lotus Flower Champion. What does Xander want me to believe? That there might be a happily ever after for me after all?"

"Wait a minute." Mama presses her hand to her chest, over the sensor. The beeping on the machine speeds up. "You might be *what*?"

That's right. In all the excitement of our reunion, my

parents don't know about the, er, *other* excitement. I fill them in as best I can, from discovering Rae's double-edged sword to stumbling onto the little boy's cryogenically frozen body to the dart breaking in midair.

"And then Xander told me to find my peace on the beach with Mama," I conclude. "'There are worse ways to live,' he said, 'than passing the rest of your days in paradise.'"

I move back to Mama's side, clasping her hands within mine. "I don't actually believe I'm the Lotus Flower Champion. That I can bring someone back from the dead. That kind of power…it's unfathomable. But if, on the miniscule chance that I *am*, then we wouldn't have to say goodbye." My voice shifts high, bordering on pleading. "Isn't that right, Mama? When you pass, I could bring you back to life, and we could be together forever."

Mama and Papa exchange a look. I used to think that they had developed their own silent language, through the speed of their blinks and the creases of their eyes.

"That's not what I would wish for," she says gently. "Everything comes to pass. Even life. Even me. That's the Buddhist way."

"But Mama—"

"When it is time for us to say goodbye, let me go in peace," she continues. "That's what I want. That's all that I desire."

I duck my head, hot tears flooding my vision. My heart breaks once more—although it shouldn't. Although I should've learned better by now. My goal this entire trip has been to give Mama a peaceful death. I could've predicted that this would be her reaction. I knew, deep down, that this was how she felt. And yet, I couldn't help but hope. Yearn. For an outcome different than this one. For a future where she and I could stay together.

I breathe deeply, reconstructing my fragmented heart.

It does me no good to mourn when I don't even know for sure if I'm the Lotus Flower Champion. When the scenario I've proposed is merely a distant possibility. For Mama, I'll refocus my energies where they're most productive: on understanding—and defeating—Xander.

I rise from the bed and pace the newly scrubbed tiles. If I force my body into action, then my thoughts will hopefully follow. "Xander doesn't act without reason. There's not a generous cell in his body. He's a scientist through and through. He treats us not as humans but as the subjects in his experiments. Why would he want me to live in relative peace, if he wants the rest of my abilities to manifest? Why would he want me happy and reunited with my parents once again?"

"I didn't think," Papa says, his snout swinging back and forth. "For the first time in my life, I didn't work through the permutations. I was in such a hurry to revive Mama. To tell both of you my identity. I didn't bother to wonder why Xander granted me permission to use the orb and reveal my identity, now of all times."

"There is no happiness without unhappiness," Mama says, her eyes finding Papa's once more. "No joy without pain. No love without loss. That's the yin and yang of our world, my love." She's talking to *me* this time, although she uses the endearment interchangeably. The only confusion that it creates is that Papa and I argue constantly about which one of us is actually her favorite.

"Xander knows that he cannot subject you to loss after loss, tragedy after tragedy, without you becoming numb to the pain," Mama continues. "You would come to expect devastation as a matter of course, and thus, his challenges would no longer yield the same impact. But…if he gives you a taste of happiness…" She moves her shoulders. "…only to yank it away…then he can plummet you to the lowest of lows once more."

I gape. "But that's just evil. And I don't want to be yanked away," I say in a small voice, edging closer to them. Whatever air I need, I need *them* even more. "I want to stay right here on this island with the two of you."

"I know, baby," Mama says. "But like it or not, Xander's got us in a bubble. We can only stop thinking about the rest of the world for so long. Our friends are imprisoned. A little boy lays on ice. And we all wait to see what abilities you'll develop."

"Don't think of Xander as evil," Papa adds. "He's cold. Calculating. He's trapped us on this island, and no matter what steps we take, we're always playing his game. You know what that means, don't you?"

No, actually. I don't. I grip the edge of the bedframe, the metal cold in my hot palms, and I've never been less sure of anything in my entire life. I don't know my next move. I don't know how not to be a pawn.

But Papa's looking at me, and it doesn't matter which eyes he uses—human, crocodile, or a combination of both. His steadfast belief in me—to be and do all the things— shines through.

And so, I take a deep breath. Because if he can phase in and out of reptilian form, losing more and more of his humanity each time, the least I can do is fight, no matter how insurmountable the odds.

"What's that, Papa?" I ask.

"You have to play your own game."

CHAPTER FORTY

Play my own game.

I wish I knew what that meant. I asked Papa to elaborate—but he said that part of playing my own game was figuring that out for myself.

We slept well that night—with Mama on the hospital bed, me on the couch, and Papa on a nest of blankets on the floor. It was just like the family slumber parties we used to have in the den, stealing one another's comforters and racing to see who would fall asleep first.

Except, you know, for the fact that Papa transformed into a full crocodile. Fun fact: crocodiles do *not* snore in their sleep, much to Mama's surprise. She teased that it was the most peaceful slumber she'd gotten in the last twenty years.

As much as I want to soak up every moment of my parents' attention, though, they deserve time together, just the two of them. And so, after Papa returns the crystal orb to its rightful location, back inside the crocodile pit, I leave my parents cuddling underneath the main villa and wander into the woods.

I'm not gunning for a destination this time. Not weaving in and out of the dark. I take a moment and just breathe in the sun slanting over the trees. The flowers unfurling their arms to the sky. The leaves dance to the melody of the wind, and it's actually...beautiful.

I forgot that there was a world bigger than Xander's game. That even on this island, there are places and moments not marred by his manipulation. That in the midst of this chaos, I'm still *me*.

Maybe that's what Papa meant by playing my own game.

I come upon a pond filled with rich golden liquid that sparkles wildly in the light. I suck in a breath. I've heard about this place before. But where? One of Mama's stories? The clearing certainly looks like a fairy tale. Dainty trees grow all around the pond's bank, their leaves silver and gold—just like Eduardo's sacred tree. A thin waterfall trickles over a large boulder, spraying up drops of water. Even the sunlight here feels diffused, as though it is filtered by the lacy filigree of magic.

I find a large, flat rock by the pond's edge and empty my backpack of its provisions so I can sit on it and listen to the water bubbling over the rocks. The pool might be golden, but it still has the characteristics of water. I...just...relax. For maybe the first time since my so-called vacation began.

And then, I'm pulled from my serenity by a rustling. More accurately, twigs break, leaves crackle, and branches snap. Someone—or something—is barreling through the woods, right toward these ponds.

Instinctively, I duck behind the rock as a figure crashes into the clearing. I blink. I thought I'd seen it all by this point, but this...this...human *tree* is quite unlike anything I've ever imagined.

This tall, tall tree is all limbs: thick trunks fused together to form legs, and long, willowy branches dotted with blooming pink flowers that function as arms. A face is carved into the trunk—two eyes, an elegant nose, and a mouth that's breathing hard. Do trees have lungs? This one does, apparently, as it flails about the clearing, snatching at thin air.

It takes another few blinks before I realize that this human tree is grabbing at the *leaves*—and failing spectacularly. Hesitantly, I creep back onto my rock, pluck a golden leaf, and hold it near the tree's branches, er, fingers.

The tree grabs the leaf, stuffs it into its mouth, and then collapses on the ground.

I peek between my fingers, afraid I'm going to see a stack of firewood. Instead, I see a naked human body curled into a fetal position.

And not just any human, either. Now that it's set back in the context of his face again, I recognize those finely shaped eyes, the proud nose—Bodin.

My heart should harden. I should stalk away and leave him on the ground, regardless of his welfare. But his face is twisted in agony, and he's letting out little whimpers. He may have betrayed me in the worst way, but he's obviously in pain, and I can't just abandon him.

I hover over him, not sure where—or if—to touch him. "Bodin? Can I help?"

"Give me a minute," he mutters.

"The transformation shouldn't be *this* painful," I say, remembering the ease with which Eduardo shifted from monkey to naga to pile of gold. "At least, it wasn't for Eduardo."

"It's not the transformation." He grunts as he tries to sit up.

Panicked, I look around for something to cover him, since he's, uh, *naked*. I almost find myself wishing he'd stayed a tree, because I'd rather deal with that than *this*.

There! Underneath the bushes—a set of neatly folded clothes, as well as a towel, thank goodness. So, the transformation was planned, then.

I toss him the athletic pants and avert my eyes while he drags them on. Only then does he seem to notice who's helping him.

"Alaia?" He gawks at me. "What are you doing here?"

"It's a small island," I say stiffly. "Since you and your dad have imprisoned me here, we're bound to run into each other once in a while."

"My dad's choice. Not mine."

"Same thing, isn't it?"

He snorts. "Hardly. You'd think I'd be here, like this, if it were up to *me*?"

I turn and look at him fully—and that's when I notice that he's cradling his left hand to his chest.

No, not his hand. Just an arm...and a cauterized stump where his hand used to be.

"What happened to you?"

He leans back against a tree trunk and grimaces, as though that slight movement caused him pain. "I begged him not to do it. But he was in a rampage last night, after seeing the dart break in the air inches before it hit you." His voice is resigned, rather than jubilant, at the prospect. "Xander's never been so close, and yet so far, from his dream, his one singular mission in life. He's waited so long to have his son back that I guess he couldn't fathom waiting even a few more days. So, last night, he made me transform once again."

"What do you mean?" I try to put on a brave front. Try—unsuccessfully—to keep my voice from pitching. Because whatever Xander made him do...it's got to be more awful for Bodin to endure than for me to listen to it.

"My ability is similar to Eduardo's," Bodin says solemnly.

"But instead of shifting into all sorts of nifty objects when I munch on a sacred leaf, I turn into one thing and one thing alone."

"A tree?" I take a wild guess. "I can see that. You're so solid, so strong. Solitary, too."

He lifts an eyebrow, and I flush, not sure why I'm complimenting him. *He* betrayed *me*, remember? I shouldn't have anything positive to say about him.

"Sometimes our ability seems to reflect our nature. And sometimes, it doesn't." He closes his eyes, as though exhausted by the whole conversation. "No one really knows. It's not like this island came with an instruction manual." His voice turns bitter. "Lucky me, I happen to possess the worst possible ability for someone whose father is inhumanly obsessed."

"Xander *did* this to you?"

"Oh, yes." Bodin's mouth twists. "As the folktale goes, if a boy turns into a tree—by way of a sacred leaf—and you pluck just the right amount of blossom, when he transforms back into human form, his pinkie finger will be missing. Dip that hand into a golden pool, and a gold finger will grow back in place of the missing digit. That finger, when pointed, will have the power to reverse death."

He bangs the back of his head lightly against the tree. "It hasn't worked yet, in the dozen times that Xander has tried. He sometimes plucks too little; most of the time, his greedy hands grasp too much. Not that it's ever stopped him from giving it one more go."

My mouth drops as the horror of his words sinks in. "You mean you've lost a hand before?"

"A hand, a foot. An ear or sometimes two. Any extremity is up for grabs. Once, I lost an entire leg. That was a long six months before that limb grew back."

"But it always grows back?"

"So far." He lumbers to his feet. "This is awkward, but I need to take a dip in the pool. Otherwise, my hand might not regenerate."

Oh. I'm blocking his way. "Of course." I move to the side, blushing.

He hooks his thumb into the waistband of his pants. "I'm going to strip again. You might want to look away."

Quickly, I drop my eyes. My cheeks flame even hotter when I hear the rustle of his clothes, and I see—in my peripheral vision—his bare feet step out of the pants.

The water splashes as he dives into the pond. Eleven seconds—that's what I'll give him. I could walk all the way to the other side of the pond in that duration. That should give him plenty of time to submerge himself.

I look up just as his head and chest pop out of the water. "Ahhh!" I scream.

He wipes his hand down his face. "Can't say I've ever had that reaction to my naked torso before."

"You scared me," I mutter. I sit on my backpack on top of the rock, carefully arranging my legs, so I don't have to look at him. One glance at the water sliding down his chest, and my cheeks are permanently red.

"Alaia, look at me. Please."

Reluctantly, I lift my head. His chest and shoulders are back underneath the water—but honestly? It's not any easier to see the droplets clinging to his eyelashes.

"I'm very sorry that I lied to you," he says. "I didn't want to trick you—or the others. I completely understand if you hate me. But I want you to know: my feelings for you are genuine. Every time we touched or kissed—it was all real. I never tried to manipulate you. I *like* you, Alaia. More than you could ever know. I only wish we had met in any other circumstance. I wish my father isn't who he is. I wish I...had any other life but this one."

"Oh, Bodin." I don't know if I can forgive him, but my heart aches for him. He's suffered, too. He's been a victim, too. It doesn't excuse what he did—and a lot of anger still simmers inside me—but I can't shut him out completely. "I'm sorry, too, that this is your life. But you can still do the right thing. You don't have to listen to Xander."

I lean forward. "I don't know how much of you is true, and how much is false. But I have to believe that I've glimpsed the real Bodin. And this Bodin that I see? He's good, at his core. No matter who his father is. No matter what circumstances he grew up in."

He ducks under the water, as though my words are a truth he doesn't want to face. This time, I keep my eyes on the concentric circles where he disappeared, on the air bubbles floating to the surface, until he emerges once more.

"I know that…he's a bad man," he blurts before I can say anything. "I've known that for a while, but it's taken some time for me to accept. I mean, he's my dad, you know? He hasn't always acted like a father to me. Hell, his paternal moments are few and far between. But he's the only family I have." He closes his eyes, breathing deeply as though that will keep his roiling emotions under control.

"A part of you buys into his dream, don't you?" I say suddenly. "You want your brother to come back to life, too."

"He's my brother," Bodin says, treading water, although I'm fairly sure the pond only comes up to his chest. "More than that, he's my twin. My other half. When he died, it's like I was sliced right down the middle. And without him, I know I'll never be whole again."

He falls silent. The only sounds are the gurgle of the water, the woosh of the wind. The intensity of his pause, filled with all the things he has yet to say. I get it. I, of all people, know how it feels to not be whole.

"But despite all of that, I want to stop this cycle of torture. I do," he says. "This time was different. Usually, Xander and I stay away from the castaways. There's no game, no challenges. The castaways believe that they're stranded on a remote island, without any answers. One or two of them usually manifest their abilities right away, but it would take weeks for all of the powers to surface. They would settle into their new life, form a community. Little by little, they would venture out, explore the island. And one by one, they would encounter the obstacles built into this island and slowly come into their powers."

"Why did you change it up this time?"

Bodin's hands splash up a little water. "Xander's patience is running thin. I don't know what the big hurry is, since he's already been searching for ten years. But for the first time, this island feels volatile. Like something's brewing and about to erupt. Xander didn't want to wait for weeks, so he made me join all of you as a fellow castaway so that I could hurry things along. He revealed himself and the truth of this island to you, maybe because your mom and Rae had already guessed, or maybe because he thought it would quicken the process."

Bodin swims closer to my rock. Not close enough to touch, not near enough that he risks exposing himself...but closer. "It changed me, being around all of the castaways, and especially you," he says softly. "It made tangible the hurt we were causing you. It cast Xander's quest as selfish and uncaring, rather than loving and noble. I...don't want to be this person anymore. But I'm not sure I can be the person you described, either."

"You can," I say firmly. Is this what Papa meant? Is this how I play my own game? Is this the way to finally beat Xander and save the people that I love? I take a deep breath. "And you can start by getting us off this island."

CHAPTER FORTY-ONE

It's not easy to convince Bodin. In fact, it takes another hour of talking, cajoling, and convincing before he's willing to admit that he can lift the keys to the helicopter. What's more, he actually knows how to pilot the chopper.

"Perfect!" I exclaim. "Our plan just got a whole lot simpler. You sneak me into the mountainous compound. We rescue our friends, pick up my parents, stuff everyone into the helicopter, and fly away. And then we all live happily ever after."

"When you put it that way…" Bodin drawls.

I frown. "Why? What's wrong with the plan?"

On the muddy banks of the pond, he plants his once severed hand, which has grown back to normal. Holy crap, that was fast. "Heads up," he warns. "I'm coming out."

I avert my eyes, but I can still see a blurry image of him in my peripheral vision. And when Bodin nonchalantly pushes himself out of the water, I blush. I can't *not* blush, even though I can't see anything in detail.

Bodin takes his time drying himself off, no doubt enjoying

my discomfort. When his clothes are finally in place, he sits next to me on the rock.

"I can't sneak you through the tunnels," he says. "Xander has sensors that can read thermal signatures. That's how he always knew where we were in the caves. But…" He stops and pushes the wet hair off his forehead.

"But what?" I prompt.

"There's a crevice in the mountain that you can pass through, just north of where you entered the cave," he says slowly. "You'll encounter an obstacle there—but it's nothing you can't handle. I'll meet you on the other side, and we'll enter the compound directly, bypassing the tunnels altogether. Easy, right?"

I swallow hard. His first instincts were right: it's much easier to simplify a mission to its core steps than it is to actually execute it.

A million things could go wrong. I could be detected at any turn. Xander might suspect that his son-in-name had a change of heart. The helicopter might be out of gas. The lot of us might not fit in said chopper. And oh, countless more missteps that I have yet to think of.

But it's a plan, a combination of mine and his. And more importantly? It's the only play I've got.

"So, what's the obstacle?" I ask.

Bodin gives me a long look, and then he dips his head and tells me.

I bury my face in my hands. "You've *got* to be joking."

Shortly after full dark, I leave my parents once more, under the guise of giving them more privacy. They don't question me. Papa's memories are growing fuzzier, and as much as we stick stubbornly to the present, I think we all feel the hands of the clock pressing down on us.

Only, this time, I don't have the luxury of lying on my side and counting the seconds.

I head into the woods in the same direction as the previous night, toward the northern end of the island, as Bodin instructed. My hands feel strangely empty with the absence of Rae's double-edged sword.

As much as Xander claimed that he wanted me to feel "comfortable," he confiscated my weapon—and didn't give it back. It's hard to blame him, I suppose. Last night, I made darts break in the air. There's no telling what I'll be able to do with a sword should I gain any other abilities.

I move through the woods swiftly but carefully. My senses have magnified even beyond their strength yesterday. I can now see as clearly in the night as I do during the day. The five-mile jog passes in less than one revolution around the clock, and when I reach the deep gouge in the island, formed by shifting tectonic plates, I'm not even winded.

Per Bodin's directions, I skirt around the small canyon and proceed up the side of the mountain, at nearly a forty-five-degree-angle. Here, I do get tired. The first drop of sweat appears when I'm a third of the way up, and by the time I reach the plateau, I'm gasping for breath.

Almost there. Bodin said I would see the crevice after a hundred yards. Ah, there it is: a black triangle cut into the rock, larger than—but strangely reminiscent of—the temple doors of the many wats I've visited. I duck through the opening—and freeze.

The ground ends abruptly, giving way to red-hot lava that bubbles and splashes. Bodin told me about the lava...but it's a shock to see the boiling floor nonetheless. I scan the cavernous space. The lava extends in a pool that splashes against the rounded walls of the cavern in brilliant shades of orange, yellow, and red. The walls rise sharply from the lava, smooth and unscalable. On the other side lies freedom: the back entrance to Xander's compound, where Bodin and a helicopter wait for me. But there is simply no way to get across, other than through the lava itself.

This is the obstacle Bodin told me about, the one that he was confident I could handle.

Then, as now, I don't know whether to laugh or cry. What kind of powers does he think I'll develop? The ability to fly?

No. My worries, doubts, and fears melt away, and my mind crystallizes on the hot liquid that is as menacing as it is mesmerizing. Xander is searching for a *lotus flower* champion, not a flying champion.

I've known this folktale since I was a child: the good queen walks barefoot across hot coals, unharmed, because lotus flowers bloom under each of her steps. I swallow hard. Lava lies before me, not coals, but the parallel is unmistakable. And something inside me tells me that I can do the impossible: I can walk across lava uninjured.

Am I being foolish right now? Probably. But what are my options, really? I can give up in the face of seemingly insurmountable barriers, as I've always done in the past. Or I can play my own game and believe in my own instincts, for once. Thinking too much has always been my downfall. Thinking allows space for worry and fear to enter. It gives room for doubt to grow. It stops us from taking a leap of faith, from rolling the dice on a move that might be unwise in the extreme—but that might save us all.

And so, it may be risky—it's definitely foolhardy—but I don't think. I take a step onto the lava. My canvas sneaker immediately sinks into the liquid, and a heat like I can't imagine surrounds my foot, piercing my skin like a thousand burning knives.

Yelping, I yank my foot out of the lava and back onto solid ground. Holy moly, what is wrong with me? This *not thinking* business is clearly not working out.

I plop onto the dirt and wrench off my shoe so that I can examine my foot. The skin there is red—and hot to the touch—but it's not bubbling or puffing up. In fact, despite that initial sensation, it doesn't hurt at all. Somehow, my skin seems immune to the lava, even though the sole of my sneaker has all but disintegrated.

So, what went wrong? If I *do* have some sort of ability with respect to the lava, how come a lotus flower—or a feather or a plate—didn't bloom under my bare foot?

Oh. I look at my foot, now resting gingerly on top of the ruined sneaker. My foot was covered, and that was a key part of the folktale: the queen walks *barefoot* across the burning-hot lava.

Damn it. Clearly, the queens in the old folktales didn't have OCD. Maybe they didn't even have shoes. They certainly hadn't gone the last five years without their bare feet touching the ground.

I look despairingly at the lava. I wear water shoes in the swimming pool. Slippers inside our house. Flip-flops in the shower. And my white canvas sneakers everywhere else.

There's about a zero percent chance that my feet are touching that lava.

At least that's what my OCD wants me to think. It rules in absolutes. Can'ts, nevers, and impossibles. It keeps a tight control over my language so that it can retain a tight control over my mind.

It's no big deal, I tell myself sternly. I've been sleeping in the sand (albeit on a sleeping bag). Getting mud in my hair. Dirt on every square inch of my body. Of all the surfaces on this island, my *shoes* probably have the most bacteria festering in them, since I never take them off.

These statements are all so very rational. So very logical.

And yet...and yet...I am rooted to the spot. I can no more take off my shoes than I can take flight in the air. The lava gurgles in front of me, each pulse echoing through the cavern.

You can't, you can't, you can't, the lava jeers at me. *Your shoes are the biggest protection you have. They're what's kept you safe all of this time. They've prevented germs from entering the cracks of your feet. They stopped the world from crashing down around you.*

I shake my head weakly. No. I try to argue; I try to protest. But my words are just noise, battling at the certainty inside of me.

This is what people don't understand. My OCD isn't a devil on my shoulder. It's not an alien entity enticing me to do harmful things. It's the voice of reason. The certainty in my gut. A knowledge that penetrates every cell of my being. A truth that fills every inch of my soul.

It works in disguises; it relies on tricks. It hides under my very own skin. At its most effective, there's no distinction between it...and me.

How do I fight back against so much certainty? How do I ignore what seems to be my gut? How do I trust myself... when that's the very last person that I should trust? I weep. At the unfairness of it all. At the maddening nature of my disorder. At the strangeness of my mind, which gives me the strength to walk on hot lava...but not to take off my shoes.

I don't trust myself. I don't trust Bodin, who's lied to me for the bulk of our relationship. I can't trust Papa, who's losing more and more memories with each passing day. Each passing hour.

So who do I trust?

The answer—although hard to remember, easy to forget—has always been clear.

Mama. Oh, not the fallible human being who walks on this Earth, but the person she is in connection to me.

I imagine her soft skin, her guileless smile, her clear eyes. She's not perfect. She doesn't belong on any pedestal. She loses her temper; she gets frustrated. She's *super* cranky when she's hungry. Sometimes, she says things that she doesn't mean. Sometimes, the things that she says *are* mean.

But there's one truth in this universe that I will never, ever question. She loves me, to the depth and breadth and height her soul can reach.

Maybe playing my game isn't about acting independently. Maybe it's not about following a trusted person's advice. Maybe, just maybe, playing my own game is a combination of the two: following the advice that I imagine someone I trust would give.

What do I do, Mama? What would you say I should do?

I take a deep breath, channeling Mama. And then, my fingers are attacking my laces. My breath speeds up as though I'm running a marathon. The voice tries to intrude, but I push back against it. I fight.

I kick off my shoes, and I jump from foot to foot. Even the brief contact my bare skin has with the ground floods my mind with images. The germs crawling up my feet, coating my feet like slime, sinking into whatever crack they can find.

I don't need to eliminate the feeling of distress entirely. I only need to accept my distress—and tolerate it.

I take my first bare step onto the lava. The hot liquid rushes under my soles, tickling but not injuring them. Something soft and silky sprouts under my foot. I peek down: a lotus flower. Delicate, pale pink petals that come together to make a powerful splash.

I take another step. Another flower, even more delicate and more powerful than the last.

The distress fades. So do my fears. Instead, effervescent joy fizzes out of me. It worked. The words that an imaginary Mama whispered to me worked. I'm not walking barefoot over the hot lava. I'm wearing shoes of lotus flowers.

It takes eleven steps in all for me to cross the lava. My magic number. But because I can, I take one more minuscule step, leading to one more minuscule flower, making the number twelve.

For better or for worse, my OCD is a part of me. It's never going away. But more and more, I hope I will continue to play my own game.

I touch down on the other side and raise my arms in triumph. Before I can truly celebrate, however, I hear a slow...and very deliberate...clap.

Xander.

I turn, and all of the peace drains out of my body when I see him standing next to Bodin.

CHAPTER FORTY-TWO

I can't breathe. It's like my lungs have collapsed and my three-dimensional heart is trying to beat in a flattened world. This…this can't be happening. Bodin couldn't have betrayed me…*twice*.

But the truth is standing right in front of me. There he is, cowering by his father's side. Not my friend but my enemy. Lying in wait for me in a trap that he carefully set up, his eyes trained on his shoes.

Glad *he's* protecting his feet, because *mine* are naked and vulnerable and planted squarely on the dirty ground.

It hurts even more that he turned on me while I'm not wearing shoes.

Xander's grin takes over his entire face. "Surprised to see me, my Lotus Flower Champion?"

Understatement of the century. How I'm still standing is anybody's guess.

"Thank you, by the way, for crossing the lava on your own initiative," he continues. "Somehow, I thought it would be more difficult than this. Hell, I thought we'd have to drag you, kicking and screaming, over the lava. But here you are, leaving a trail of lotus flowers in your wake."

He gestures at the hot lava, and I turn to see the flowers, as fresh as ever, floating on top of the hot, bubbling liquid.

"Amazing how the flower retains its structural integrity." Xander snaps his fingers and points at the lava. Obediently, Bodin walks to the lava's edge, drops to his knees, and leans over to fish out a flower.

I should push him right into that molten orange ooze. It would serve him right. But his reflexes are quick, while my knees are still magma. I'd be more likely than him to end up in the moving lake.

Bodin snatches up a flower, bouncing it from hand to hand, as though the traces of lava burn him. *Good*, I think meanly.

Soon enough, though, he passes the flower to Xander, who examines it with the scrutiny of a scientist, with the eyes of an awestruck child.

"Just amazing," he says, his tone hushed. "I've seen many wondrous things during my decade on this island. But this… this tops them all." He looks at me. "So, I thank you, Alaia. Your friends, I'm sure, thank you as well. You've saved me the trouble of torturing them."

"Torture?" I echo weakly.

"Why, yes." He smirks as though I've said something highly amusing. "How else did you think I was going to get you to cross? I would've started by dipping Lola's darling toes into the lake." In one swift movement, he crushes up the flower and tosses it back into the lava. "What a nice spectacle that would've been. Worms would've dropped from her mouth as she screamed out her curses. I can just see those segmented creatures frying to a crisp as they drop into the lava. After that? So many wonderful options to choose from."

He taps a finger against his cheek. "It would've been fun to rotate Mateo on a spit over a molten fire. Roasted crocodile is quite tasty, you know. Or I could've stuck a burning ember into Preston's pinhole mouth." He slaps his leg in hilarity. "Can you imagine the look on his face as he tries to spit out the ember—and can't?"

Xander sighs. "Ah, it would've been a good show. The memories of those tortures could've entertained us for months. But I suppose it would've been a lot of work. And I'm just like you. I hate to get my hands dirty."

He holds up his hand and wiggles his fingers. And Bodin—he just *stands* there, not doing anything. He doesn't even flinch at his father's tasteless joke at the expense of my OCD.

"You coward," I spit out at Bodin. "Aren't you going to say anything? Apologize? Offer one single sliver of remorse? You lied to me—again. It was my fault, I suppose, for trusting you. I let my sympathies get the better of me. But I was wrong. I thought you were a victim, too. What I didn't realize was that you *allow* yourself to be a victim. You participate in your own torture." I shake my head, disgusted. "My mistake." I put as much derision into those two words as possible.

Bodin doesn't respond. How could he? There's not a single thing that he could say or do that can justify his actions.

"Now, now," Xander says mildly, as though he's refereeing a disagreement between two children. "Leave the poor boy alone. For once in his life, he stepped up. He took the initiative, made a plan, and executed it. He may grow up to be a worthy man yet."

At this, Bodin hangs his head. Any lower and he'd be kissing the ground.

"Is this what this was about?" I continue to direct my words at Bodin. "Earning the approval of your dear old dad? Well, congrats," I say tightly. "You got it. Was it worth it?"

Bodin doesn't even bother to shrug. I need to rein in my anger. He's an easy target to direct my frustration at…but he's not the true enemy. He's not the one who holds my — and my parents' and my friends' — future in his hands.

"What are you going to do with me?" I ask Xander.

He blinks. "I thought that was clear. You are my Lotus Flower Champion. You are going to perform what the human mind believed to be impossible and bring my dead son back to life."

"And what if I *can't*?" I never truly believed Xander's wild theories. But I also never thought I'd walk across hot lava, either. "So what if lotus flowers sprout under my feet? So what if darts break in midair? What does any of that have to do with reversing death?"

"Ah, I'm glad you asked," Xander replies, his eyes bright. "I've spent most of my life studying this discipline, and my audience is woefully few. My son, who'd rather be plotting a way off this island." He side-eyes Bodin, who's studying the lava as though he expects a naga to leap out of it. "And a pit of reptiles who lose more of their human minds with each transformation."

He turns back to me. "My new theory is that the Lotus Flower Champion doesn't possess a bunch of disjointed abilities, each one separate from the last. Rather, the champion has *one* ability with different manifestations: the ability to bend the natural and unnatural world to keep themselves safe. That's why your energy was revived when your stores ran low. That's how you were able to navigate through the treacherous dark. These so-called abilities are simply ways that you protect yourself."

I shake my head, trying to wrap my mind around his words. "So what you're saying is…my ability is that I can make myself immune to danger?"

"Something like that."

I massage my temples. "That's wild."

"It's more than just wild," Xander says. "It's damn near miraculous. You have so much life force in you, so much will to survive. It's so strong that when you choose to share it, this life force will bring back the dead."

"But how?" I'm nearly pleading now. Xander has so much belief in this power. But I don't even understand it, much less know how to wield it.

"How?" Xander blinks at me as though the answer is obvious. "Why, any way you choose. The folktales can serve as a guide. They detail several methods of reversing death. It can be as simple as chewing on an herb and blowing it on a person you want to revive.

"Or, you might want to use a sacred object, such as a fan. Fluttered in one direction, the fan can kill; wave it in the other direction, and the fan will resurrect the dead.

"There are other, more complicated procedures. For example, one story tells of a boy whose heart is put inside a double-edged sword. When the sword is burned, the person to whom the heart belongs dies. And if you want to bring the boy back to life? You simply clean the sword once more."

Xander spreads his arms wide. "Take your pick, champion. You may use whichever method appeals to you." He jostles Bodin, catching him off guard and almost knocking him over. "Bodin here favors the double-edged sword, don't you, boy? He thinks it appeared in the sand on a moonlit night for a reason. As for me? I'm not choosy, so long as you bring my son back to life."

"How very kind of you," I say drily. "And how very generous of Bodin to share his infinite wisdom."

The sarcasm is lost on Xander, however. He's already backing away from me, from Bodin, exiting the warm glow emitting from the red-hot lava and ducking into the night. No doubt he will reenter his compound through the back entrance and resume running his evil empire.

"Bodin!" Xander's disembodied voice calls out, after his physical presence has blended with the shadows. "Please escort our champion to her cell. She needs to rest. Tomorrow is a big day. For me, for this island. For us all."

CHAPTER FORTY-THREE

I look at Bodin. He looks at me.

My mind whirls. It's just the two of us now. He outweighs me by a good fifty pounds. He has multiple inches on me, not to mention superior strength. Ordinarily, I'd never dream of taking him on. It's just not a fight I can win.

But now...I have the ability to bend the world to my will in order to protect myself from danger. That changes the equation. It evens up our skills. It might even tip the scales in my favor.

I crouch into a fighting position, my muscles bunching as I prepare to charge.

"Don't do anything foolish, Alaia," Bodin says, the first time that he's spoken tonight. "Let me explain—"

Too late. I rush at him at full speed, trusting that my abilities will kick in. I will the cave to rise up and slap rocky handcuffs on him. I summon the double-edged sword to fly into my hands from...wherever it is.

I crash into Bodin, and we both fall to the ground, our heads inches from the molten liquid. I hear it sizzle—and then the smell of burned hair fills the air. So much for my immunity.

Before I can check on my singed locks, however, Bodin flips me over so that he's trapping *me* against the hard rock.

"You—you shouldn't be able to do that," I stutter. "I'm supposed to be immune from danger."

He shifts onto his elbows so that he can hold his body weight off me. "That's because you aren't in any danger from me. Your ability knows that, even if your mind doesn't. Will you please listen?"

"I don't have much choice, do I?" I slide out from underneath him and retreat several feet away.

"I'm not escorting you to any cell," Bodin says, rolling to a sitting position. "I'm not going to lock you up. I didn't betray you, Alaia. I just didn't tell you the whole truth."

"Same thing," I mutter. I keep my eyes trained on his collarbone, the muscular curve of his shoulders, so that I can avoid looking at his face.

"No, it's *not* the same thing. At least I don't think so. Xander's got me so messed up that it's hard to figure out right from wrong." He hangs his head, which brings his forehead closer to my lips. "We needed to know if you were the Lotus Flower Champion. But I didn't want you to cross the lava Xander's way. You heard what he said. He was planning on this big torture show to persuade you across. He didn't mention your parents, but I know for a fact that he was keeping them in reserve. I wouldn't be surprised if he took them into custody as soon as you left camp. If all else failed, their torture would've broken you."

I blink. "My parents?"

"Yes. Xander gave you a glimpse of joy, just so he could rip it away. He granted you time with your parents so that it would hurt even more when you lost them for good."

So we were right. That was the true reason behind his "kindness."

I glance up at Bodin. My mistake. Because his eyes capture mine, and I'm unable to wrench my gaze away from his.

"I know you," he says softly. "I know you would walk over hot lava to save your parents. But I also know how much it would hurt you to see them suffer. I didn't want to put you through that, but at the same time, we had to know if you truly are the Lotus Flower Champion. Our next moves depend on it. I...compromised. I'm sorry that I tricked you. But it was the only way I knew how to get you across the lava while keeping your parents safe. If you knew it was one of Xander's challenges, I don't think you *would've* crossed of your own volition. Am I right?"

Yeah. I have such an aversion to playing Xander's game, to being under his control, that I probably would have flat-out refused. My OCD would never have allowed it...until I witnessed the torture of my friends, my parents. And Bodin's right again. That would've broken me. Bodin's way is gentler, kinder—even if it is deceitful. The story is a good one, the explanation solid...but only if it's true.

"Why should I believe you?" I ask. "Give me one good reason why I should trust anything that you say."

"I'll give you two." He stands, holding out his palms. "I am no threat to you. Your ability knows this. But I want your mind and your heart to know it as well. Check out that corner." He gestures to indicate the one he means, next to the yawning black space where Xander disappeared.

I catch a glimpse of something shiny and metal. A warm glow outside of the cave glints off the blade, and all of a sudden, I know what I'm looking at: the double-edged sword.

"I stand before you, vulnerable," Bodin continues. "You

held a blade to my neck before. Do it again. I won't stop you."

I walk to the sword. True to his word, Bodin doesn't react as I arm myself. He simply stands there, motionless. Watching me.

I stride over to him and hold the sword at his throat. "Let me get this straight." I press the blade against his Adam's apple. "I can do anything I want—even kill you—and you won't try to stop me?"

"No. I won't lift a finger." He looks directly into my eyes, trusting, calm. I can feel the peace in the slow, steady beating of his pulse. In contrast, my heart beats erratically. I don't know how this scenario will end…even as I settle on a course of action.

"Why?" I ask.

"I like you. I trust you," Bodin says immediately, as though he's been giving the matter some thought. "Your ability is a powerful one. So immense that I'd be very nervous if almost anyone else had control of it. But I'm not nervous, because it's you."

I raise my eyebrows. "You might change your mind after I do this."

And then, I lean over and kiss him.

He startles at first, but he recovers soon enough, his hands coming up to lightly graze my back. I shiver into his lips, and he groans as his mouth moves deeper. It might be the most intimate kiss we've ever had, since it holds so many emotions. Forgiveness. Fear. Trust. Hope.

I'm used to an amalgam of emotions coursing through me at all times—but they tend to be negative. Sticky, intrusive thoughts. Doomsday what-if scenarios. Self-reproachment over my past behavior.

But this…this is the calmest my mind has ever been. I wish I could keep kissing him…for more reasons than one.

But here is not the place, and now is certainly not the time.

I break the contact between our lips. "Um, Bodin? What's that glow right outside the cavern?"

He moves to the exit of the cavern, retrieving the crystal orb that lives in the crocodile pit, the same one that healed my mother and gave her life. It throws a sky's worth of sparkles onto the cave ceiling.

"Let's go," he says. "I'll explain on the way."

CHAPTER FORTY-FOUR

We don't have any time to waste. It will be ten minutes—twenty, if we're lucky—before Xander notices that I'm not in the cell. He'll call his army then—and power or no power, I don't like our chances against an island of armed croc-people and robotic monkeys.

Our destination, however, lies the way that I came. So, instead of entering the compound's back entrance, like Xander, Bodin and I dash back across the lava, using the lotus flowers as stepping pads. We weren't sure if Bodin would be able to cross the same way. Thank goodness my sturdy flowers held under his weight. I take the extra minute to locate my sneakers on the other side of the lava and put them back on, even if the sole of one of them is falling apart. And then, into the woods we go.

We scamper down the mountainside as quickly as possible as we head toward the clearing with the golden pond.

The moon's found its peak, and now that it's no longer competing with the luminescent lava, the crystal's internal glow emanates brightly from Bodin's duffel bag. Between the natural and magical light sources, as well as my newfound skills at night navigation, we move through the wooded slopes swiftly and easily.

The trees are still, even alert, as though they, too, are holding their breath in anticipation of our next move. Tonight, the branches are bendy, and the bramble makes itself scarce. It's like the entire forest is allowing us safe passage through its dense mass.

And knowing the extent of my power? It probably is.

And then, my foot lodges in a crevice in the rocks, and my ankle twists…but Bodin catches me before I fall. Interesting that my power didn't intervene. Or maybe it *did*—and simply acted through the conduit that is Bodin.

"Xander failed to mention one other method to reverse death," he says, tightening his hold on my hand as we traverse loose, crumbly ground. "It's one you already know about: the golden finger. What you don't know is that the Lotus Flower Champion can also access the golden finger. And it has a twofold power. Not only can it reverse death, but it will destroy any object at which it is deliberately aimed."

"Like a gun?" I ask.

"Exactly. Except it's many times more destructive, and the only trigger is your mind."

"How do you know?" It's amazing that I'm able to talk while sprinting, without so much as a pant. My new power, while scary, does have major pluses.

"After the first time my father plucked the blossom of my hand, I broke into his lab." Bodin takes a gigantic leap over a fallen log. I sail right after him. It's a testament to his athletic prowess that *he's* able to have this conversation. "I consumed all of his research notes. Studied every folktale there is concerning the golden finger. Whenever I got angry with him—which was ninety percent of the time—I'd daydream about bringing down his life's work and his entire empire."

We run ten whole strides before he speaks next. "You know the magic crystal orb that the crocodiles guard so closely?"

"You mean the one that's shooting rays of light out of your bag?" I tease.

"It's not subtle," he agrees. "But I guess it shouldn't be. This crystal is the magical source of the entire island. Without it, none of this would exist. Our powers. The creatures of our folktales, like the naga, who protects the perimeter of the island. Sacred objects, such as the weapons of lore and the trees with the gold and silver leaves. All of it is powered through the crystal."

He ceases running and turns me to face him. His dark hair and eyelashes swallow the moonbeams. And yet, I can see, as clear as ever, the solemn set of his lips. The determination in his eyes.

"We have to stop him, Alaia. The nightmare of this island doesn't end just because he's found his Lotus Flower Champion. He'll only want more power, get more greedy. He'll seek out even rarer abilities. All the while, we—and all of our friends—will remain trapped here. This island is his obsession. And the more you feed an obsession, the stronger it gets."

"Believe me, Bodin," I say. "You don't need to tell *me* that."

He drops his forehead so that it's pressing against mine. "I can't…live like this anymore," he says, his voice hollowed out with pain. "I can't actively participate—or even stand by—while innocent people get hurt, lose their freedom and their lives. All to feed the ego of a man who can't let go of his past. But I can't stop him without your help. The crystal orb is reinforced by its own magic. It cannot be destroyed with any brute human instrument. It requires the golden finger."

"You have my help," I say, cupping his cheek with my hand, "if I have yours."

"Always." He covers my hand, briefly.

And then we're running again.

Before I know it, we burst into the clearing. I might've thought that it would look less magical in the night, its vivid gold and silver colors cloaked by shadows. I would've been wrong.

The leaves, although not as brilliant in the night, gleam in the moonlight, taking on an ethereal, ghostly glow, while their trees rise majestically into the sky, reaching out with spindly fingers to grasp the stars. The golden surface of the pond turns into a mirror, reflecting the setting moon in the sky. For a moment, my senses are assaulted by two moons. Two Bodins. Two beams of light shining from two orbs.

"Wait a minute," I say as a panicked thought occurs to me. "Will I have to turn into a tree?"

"Nope," Bodin says. "The only reason I had to go through that transformation is because I don't have your power. If Xander's research is correct, all you have to do is dip your finger into the golden pond and will your finger to turn gold."

I frown at my reflection in the pond—and not just because this is the first time I've seen my sunburned cheeks and wild hair. "Will it work? My ability didn't listen when I tried to will the double-edged sword into my hand."

"You weren't in any danger from me," he reminds me gently. "In contrast, you are in very real danger from my father." He checks his watch, the creases in his forehead deepening. "Who probably sounded the alarm ten minutes ago. Guards are probably closing in on us as we speak."

I nod. And then, I put down my sword, focus on my unfortunate reflection in the water, and center my mind. I'm not being asked to do anything strenuous. Anything that will push me or flare up my OCD. Sure, I have to dip my finger in potentially unclean water. But I've already submerged my body in the murky waters inside the cave.

But this moment calls for ceremony. For solemnity and concentration. I'm not sure how else my ability will know to abide by my wishes.

Please, super special ability inside of me. Turn my finger gold. More than that, imbue that digit with all of the powers contained in the ancient folklore. The power to reverse death. The power to destroy the crystal. Any other cool, nifty powers you think I would like.

I take a deep breath, and then I plunge my pinkie into the water. I draw it up a moment later, holding my finger up to the sky.

Water trickles down its sides; my nail is in desperate need of an emery board...and that's it. No flashy gold color. No unearthly tingle, no unexplained warmth. Nothing to indicate any magic whatsoever has occurred.

"Did I do it wrong?" I venture.

"I'm not sure." Bodin stares at my finger, unblinking. He even takes the crystal orb out of the duffel bag and shines its light on my finger, as though the color *did* turn—and we just can't see it in the night.

But no. It's just a pinkie—no one would say it's long, but I still like to think of it as elegant.

"It's possible that your ability hasn't reached that level yet," Bodin says, frowning. "Remember, it's been showing up in stages. First, you were able to navigate through the dark. Then, the darts broke in midair. After that, the lotus flowers sprouted under your feet. Each phenomenon was preceded by an event that pushed you emotionally."

His voice speeds up as he warms to the theory. "Maybe

you haven't reached your emotional limit yet. Maybe there's something else that you need to do or endure before you can access this specific manifestation of your power."

"Like what?" I ask doubtfully. "Do you want me to throw myself into the sea and beg the naga to eat me?"

Before Bodin can respond, the woods come alive. Dozens of booted feet stomp on the ground. It's Xander's army, and they don't bother to hide their presence. In fact, they're probably emphasizing it in order to send a message. *Don't even bother running. We've got you surrounded.*

Two rows of croc-people march into the clearing, encircling us and the pond. Some wear misshapen masks over their faces, but most hold their crocodile heads high in the rapidly brightening sky.

Bringing up the rear is the big boss himself. The scientist who controls this entire island. The man whom I hate more than I've ever imagined possible.

Xander.

But he's not alone. He's dragging Mama behind him, locked up in glowing windcuffs.

CHAPTER FORTY-FIVE

Mama.

My knees buckle, and I nearly tumble to the ground. The only thing that stops me is the firm arm that winds around my waist. Bodin. Of course Bodin. Whether it's my ability that's convincing him to help me or he's acting of his own volition, I'm grateful.

But not grateful enough to forget the scene in front of me.

Xander crosses his arms smugly, and the rows of croc-people stand at attention. Mama's got red splotches on her forearms, no doubt from being yanked around, but her expression is defiant rather than scared.

And then, suddenly, my mind jumbles, and there's an overlay of images: Mama heaving over a toilet a month ago; Mama laughing as she teased Papa last night; Mama right now, a captive of Xander's.

I should've known. I should've expected her arrest. Bodin warned me, and yet shock still robs my airways, tightening the vise around my chest.

"My *son* thinks he's smarter than me." Xander emphasizes

the appellation with a sneer. "He thinks he can outwit me. When I'm the world's premiere expert on human behavior. I'm exquisitely aware of how people think. I can predict, with ninety-nine percent accuracy, what will push someone to their emotional limits. I've made this work my life's study. And Bodin wonders why I don't value him." Xander shakes his head disgustedly. "Maybe if he showed me and my work a little more respect, I would return the favor."

Bodin straightens to his full height, several inches taller than Xander. "Your life's work is torture. It's whisking people away from an idyllic vacation and imprisoning them here for the rest of their lives. All in pursuit of what? Scientific knowledge? A way to cheat death? You can paint it with as many pretty words as you want, but the truth is, your pursuits satisfy nothing but your own selfish needs. I wasn't able to see that for a long, long time. Now, I can never unlearn what an inhumane monster you are."

"You can stop talking now," Xander says dismissively. "I have but one son, and he lies inside a cryogenic chamber, waiting to be awoken from his deep sleep."

He turns to me, even as I find the sword in the grass and hold it firmly in front of me. The croc-people stand a little straighter. They grip their krabongs a little tighter. I'd guess there are about twenty of them, ten in each of the two rows. I'm protected, to a certain extent, by my immunity to danger. But I'm not sure what even my supernatural power can do if I'm rushed on all sides by an army of croc-people.

No matter the chances, I will not go down without a fight.

"Little girl," Xander begins. If he thinks *that* nickname will endear me to him, then he doesn't understand me at all. "You'd better think twice about what you and my former son were about to do. Because neither of you have thought through the ramifications of your actions."

"Really?" Bodin scoffs. "That's your strategy? Then you're even more clueless on human behavior than I thought. Alaia's not impressed that you've discovered a way to make the folktales come to life. She cares about people, not a bunch of scientific experiments. And she won't blink twice about turning this island back into what it originally was: an uninhabited plot of land, rising up from the sea, in the remotest part of the Gulf of Thailand."

"That's not all you'll turn back." Ignoring Bodin, Xander marches up to me, tugging Mama behind him. He releases Mama from her cuffs with a twist of a tool and then thrusts her toward me. She stumbles to me, and I grab her and hold on tight.

This is Mama, in the flesh, and she's by my side once more. I lower the sword and press my nose into her neck and just breathe. Jasmine. Mama's old scent, but one that she hasn't had since we've been marooned on this island. I don't understand it. Did Xander have Mama's favorite soap flown in, just for this occasion?

I don't dwell on it, because Mama's arms are around me, and they are just as adept as my ability in warding off danger. In making me feel safe.

Xander smirks, as though our reaction was exactly what he expected. And then he says, ever so casually, "If you destroy the crystal orb, then you'll also kill your mom."

I freeze. Icicles of fear crystallize along my spine. What?

Bodin shoves forward so that he's standing between Xander and us. "What are you talking about?" His voice is tight and savage. "Eradicating the crystal isn't going to hurt anybody. The people will just revert back to their former selves, memories restored, stripped only of their abilities—"

"Precisely," Xander says smugly. "What you haven't considered is that the good doctor here is dying. No amount of modern medicine can save her. The crystal restores her life force—through *magic*. Without the crystal, she'd be dead."

Pushing Bodin aside, Xander strides up to Mama and me. Maybe he's an expert on human behavior, after all, because he stops at the perfect distance. Not so close that he invades our personal space, but close enough to force my eyes to him—and only him.

"So, what will it be, champion?" he says, his tone even, unconcerned. Not at all perturbed, because the choice— to him—is obvious. "Stay here on the island with me, and your mama lives. We could do great things, you and I. Just think: if all the world's greatest minds had five more years, ten more years to live. What new discoveries could they make? What would their extra time on this earth mean for all of humankind? Why, with your ability, we could solve the world's biggest ailments. Country could live next to country in guaranteed peace. No child would ever go hungry." His voice drops. "We could cure cancer. You'd like that, wouldn't you? No teenage girl would ever have to lose her mother through that dreaded disease ever again."

"Lies!" Bodin bursts out. "You have never been interested in those outcomes. You've only ever cared about yourself, what *you* want, what would benefit *you*."

Xander steps forward, his eyes glittering. I couldn't break his gaze, even if I tried. "Or destroy the crystal. Lose the abilities that have been locked up inside us for so long. And…say goodbye to your mother. Forever. It's your choice, champion. And yours alone."

I sag, and even Mama's hold can't keep me on my feet. *So, that's why Mama smells like jasmine,* I think weakly. That manipulative jerk must've flown in the soap because he knew—damn it, he *knew*—that the scent of safety would make an impossible decision even more difficult.

Well, he's right. I can't make this decision. I *can't*. I'm not strong enough. I'm not…enough.

"Alaia. My dear Alaia." Mama gets on her knees beside me, cupping my cheeks with her hands.

Obediently, I lift my head, but already, her face is a blur. Already, tears have started clouding my vision. It doesn't help that the sun has begun its ascent into the sky, sending out rays that refract against my tears.

"You already know the right decision in your heart," she says quietly. "You have been prepping for this day ever since we found out that my cancer is terminal. You've been learning to detach from me. You've been learning to live… without me."

"No, Mama. I can't do it," I beg, like I've never begged for anything in my life. "Please, listen to me. I can't."

So many times, Mama or someone else has tried to persuade me to take an action that feels inconceivable. But this is not like getting on an airplane when my OCD tells me it's about to crash. It doesn't even compare to taking off my shoes so that I can walk across lava.

This is…Mama. My everything. All that I am, and everything that I could be, is because of her.

"I'm not ready yet," I plead. "I need more time."

Mama tucks a strand of hair behind my ear—and then does the same with the other side. It does little, I'm sure, to tame the wild bramble that I'm sporting. But I hold the gesture in my heart anyway.

"Time isn't going to help you here," Mama says. "All it will do is bring you more pain. It will make you second-guess yourself, a thousand times an hour, a hundred times a minute. Back and forth and back and forth. It's never-ending. You have to decide, and you have to do it now."

She moves her gentle hands to my face and swipes away

the tears. "I know that you love me, but I also know how strong you've become. Papa and I—we are so proud of you. For all the privacy you painstakingly gave us, these last two days, we spent half the time talking about you. Reminiscing about your early years, but more than that, just reveling in the astonishment that we somehow created a daughter this stupendous." She places her hands against my heart. "I believe in you, nam phung. I always have. And I always will."

As I look into her eyes—and see her unshakable confidence, feel her unflinching truth—I believe it, too.

I'm no longer the girl that I was at the beginning of this trip, when I begged Papa to abandon a woman in labor so that he could be with us. I no longer resent the time my parents spend away from me so that they can help other people.

I guess you could say...I'm my own person now. No longer attached to Mama. Not dependent on Papa. I love my parents. I always will. But I no longer need them.

Mama smiles as though she sees the final piece of the puzzle clicking into place in my soul. I don't know if it's the 121st time she's smiled. I've lost track of the number, with all the chaos that's racked our lives. But now I know that numbers aren't magic. They never have been. They may be a part of my life. But they don't have to rule me.

"That's a good girl," Mama whispers. "My time here is done. Let me go."

I kiss her softly on each cheek. "You're my mama," I say to her one final time.

"And you're my baby," she responds. "You will always be my baby. No matter what."

I straighten up. Fresh tears track down my cheeks, but I don't wipe them away. Instead, I face Bodin and address my next words to him.

"This is the hardest decision I will ever have to make," I

say. "This is the most painful experience of my life. Every other event pales in comparison."

Bodin nods, understanding my words. Acknowledging my intent.

I turn, and before the army of the croc-people can advance, I dip my finger into the golden pond. This time, the transformation is instant.

When I lift my pinkie in the air, it's a heavy gold, gleaming and glittering against the newly risen sun.

"Now!" I shout.

Without missing a beat, Bodin hurls the crystal orb into the sky. I very deliberately point my golden finger. In my mind, the orb shatters into a million pieces, raining down a confetti of sparkles onto the water. An instant later, real life imitates imagination, and the crystal breaks, sending down a shower of gold, glitter, glass…and magic. Can't forget that. It's one of the most beautiful sights I've ever seen.

But I can't appreciate it. Not now and maybe never.

Because Mama collapses to the ground, gracefully rolling onto her back. Her eyes are closed, and her smile is serene. But the life force has left her body, and my hand on her heart confirms that it's no longer beating.

May you rest in peace, my dear Mama. You deserve it.

CHAPTER FORTY-SIX

Two of the burliest guards, now human, descend on Xander. In moments, they have him cuffed and backed against a tree trunk. They stand over him, unmoving. Not a single ray of light emanates from the metal bracelets.

I hold Mama's hand as the world around me transforms. Every leaf on the sacred trees detaches from its branch and falls to the ground, the gold and silver essences flaking off and blowing away in the wind. The water in the golden pond turns clear, leached of all color, revealing instead the mud and rocks underneath. The double-edged sword is simply gone. Only an indentation remains in the grass where I dropped it.

The croc-people—or excuse me, just *people*—pick themselves off the ground, looking at one another and laughing in astonishment. Their snouts have shrunk, the scales have retreated inside their skin, and they're back in their human forms once more.

"Is that how you look, you old fart?" I hear one of them cry out. "You're even uglier than your crocodile face."

Familiar faces pop out among the newly human. Papa, of course, and Mateo, touching their faces to make sure the transformation is real. And the other guards, removing their oversize, misshapen hoods, are familiar as well. Lola, Rae, Kit, Khun Anita, Sylvie, Elizabeth, Eduardo. And even Preston, who is sticking his hands inside his mouth as though to measure its size.

All of my friends on this island are here, in this clearing. They've *been* here, all along, disguised as a part of Xander's army. But how?

"Looks like your dad's been hustling behind the scenes," Bodin says as he settles next to me, cross-legged. I realize for the first time that I am sitting on the ground, without a layer of protection between me and the grass. And although I know the dirt will continue to bother me in the future, at this moment, no intrusive thoughts rise.

"I hear he's become quite popular among his croc family," Bodin continues. "Once they took away your mom, he must've rallied a loyal few of them around our cause. They were probably the ones who broke out our friends, as well."

"Is that true?" I ask Papa as he approaches us. "Did you set our friends free?"

"I wanted you to have backup, in case you needed help," he says gravely. "Turns out, you didn't need it after all."

I blink, my eyes wet. "Papa, I'm sorry—"

"Shhh." He sits on my other side and winds an arm around my shoulders. "You did what you had to do. You should be proud of yourself."

I lean back against him, exhausted. But I can't be proud of myself yet. Not when Mama still lies before me, her skin rapidly cooling. Not when Xander still lurks, albeit cuffed—

I sit up straight. "Xander. The authorities—"

"On it." Bodin rises in one sleek motion, just as a woman

in a silver uniform approaches us, carrying a radio and speaking into a handheld transceiver.

"Yes, detective," she says. "We've been stranded on a remote island in the Gulf of Thailand. Yes... Hold on, please..."

She passes the transceiver to Bodin, who listens intently and then rattles off the coordinates of the island as he retreats to a quieter part of the clearing.

The woman turns and looks directly into my eyes. I've never seen her before — black hair, dark skin, in her twenties. But apparently, she knows me. "Thank you," she mouths and then walks away.

"She was one of the croc-people," Papa says. "Vanessa. She's been trapped on this island for three years. Her son was just a baby when she was kidnapped. She hopes...he remembers her still." He shifts forward so that he can look in my face. "She's one of the many, many people who have been set free today." His lips curve, in spite of the tears that gather in his eyes. "I know it doesn't feel like it, but for many others here, today is a good day."

I nod wordlessly. The feelings that gunk up my throat make it impossible to speak.

One by one, my friends surround me.

"Is it true?" Lola exclaims as she plops herself down across from me, a respectful distance from Mama's body. "Will I never have to experience a worm wriggling its way out of my mouth ever again?"

"Lola! Don't bother Alaia." Rae hurries up, shooting me an apologetic look. "Just say something negative and see what happens."

"But I can't!" Lola wails. "I'm so happy that it's finally over that I couldn't possibly say anything bad about anybody right now."

"There you go—no flowers, either." Rae shakes her head fondly. "I think you're safe, sissy."

"I will miss my flowers," Lola muses. "They were so pretty."

Behind them, Kit leaps from rock to rock as Khun Anita scolds him. "Get down from there. You're going to break your head."

"This is how I *felt* when I hopped from vessel to vessel," he explains. "I'm just trying to recreate that feeling in the physical world."

Before Khun Anita can respond, he jumps up, grabs a tree branch, and swings himself into the pond, whooping all the way.

Elizabeth and Sylvie come forward, arm in arm. They each bend down and kiss my cheek. "She was a good woman," Elizabeth says. "My life is richer because she was in it."

"I love you," Sylvie adds simply. "Whatever you need, I'm here."

In the distance, under a tree that once sported gold and silver leaves, Eduardo walks over to Bodin. Even though he's still speaking into the transceiver, Bodin embraces him with a fierce hug. Not to be left out, Preston joins them, wrapping them both between his arms and attempting to pick them up.

"Excuse me, detective," I hear Bodin say between the guffaws and laughter. "That was just some of my buddies showing you their appreciation."

And last but not least, Mateo hovers shyly in the distance, as though unsure how he'll be received, since he once spent time as a crocodile.

"Come over here, you," Lola calls to him. "I can't wait to kiss your human mouth silly."

I pat my eyes to dry off the lingering tears.

Mateo sits next to Lola, taking her hand, on the dirt ground that's growing increasingly more comfortable. "I'm so sorry, for both of your losses," he says in his heartfelt way, to both me and Papa. I realize that they must've bonded in the crocodile pit. This eases the anguish in my heart, just a little, knowing that they each made the other's time more bearable.

Soon, Bodin walks back to our group, finished with his conversation. "Help is coming," he tells the group of us, and my friends—and now family—erupt in a large cheer.

Bodin catches my eye and gives me a tiny smile. It's a small gesture, but that's all the reassurance I need to know that I'll get past this day. I'll forgive myself for this moment. I won't be tortured by my past, like Xander, and I won't live my days trying to reclaim it.

Instead, I'll simply live. For the present, in the moment. And I'll love with my whole heart, the way Mama taught me.

Out at sea, a loud noise trumpets. A cry that travels across the water and up the mountain for us to hear. But the sound isn't anguished. It's not tortured in any way. Instead, it sounds simply like goodbye.

In the distance, I can just glimpse a golden fin that I now know belongs to the naga. The mystical creature dives under the waves. I can't be sure if it disappears or swims away.

But I know that I'll never catch sight of its enormous body or untold power ever again.

EPILOGUE

I stretch out on a lounge chair, my face tilted to the twinkling stars. The mesh fabric is still damp from the late afternoon shower, the breeze warm and balmy against my skin.

Inside the villa, Papa putters in the kitchen, attempting to make nam prik kapi, a Thai dipping sauce made with shrimp paste, palm sugar, and limes. Mama's favorite—and her specialty. In the past two weeks, he's been working through her entire repertoire, pouring his grief into creating the food in which she took such joy.

Maybe it's helping us heal. Maybe it's not. But at least our stomachs are being filled with delicious food.

Xander is in jail, awaiting trial, where he will hopefully be locked up for a very long time. My friends are reunited with their families, scattered to their homes in the United States. Along with the rest of the magic on the island, the body of Bodin's twin brother disappeared. I guess he was sustained by more than just cryogenics, although perhaps we'll never understand how, barring Xander's confession.

And Bodin? He's lying next to me, taking up every inch of the lounge chair. His eyes are closed, his chest rising and falling in an even rhythm.

I like him like this. Carefree. Relaxed. As though the anchor weighing down his soul has finally been released.

He cracks open an eye, as though sensing that I'm watching him, and then rolls onto his side so that he's facing me. "Has anyone ever pointed out the seven stars shimmering in the night sky?" he asks sleepily. "We call them the mother hen and her six chicks."

"There was this boatswain once," I say. "Pretended to know a *lot* about constellations and omens. Folktales and myths. Painted quite the vivid picture of this mystical land." I lean closer. "But me, personally? I think he was just taking his best shot at impressing me."

"Was he now?" His lips quirk. "Poor guy had no idea what was coming. Well? Did it work?"

"Best pickup line I've ever heard." I fit my mouth to his lips and kiss him. Softly. Sweetly. There's no urgency to this kiss. No underlying thrum of anxiety. Our days aren't numbered, and no monsters lurk in the shadows.

I pull back, studying his face in the moonlit night. Each angle, each dip and curve of his features, has become so familiar to me.

"Bodin? Can I ask you something?" Ever since we boarded the gleaming white ship of the Royal Thai Navy, in order to be whisked over the choppy sea waves to safety, a thought has been niggling at me. Two weeks later, it's only grown more discomfiting.

"Only if you pay the question tax," he says.

I roll my eyes but lean over and give him a loud kiss on the cheek. "Happy?"

He gives me a goofy grin.

"We didn't tell the authorities about the magic," I say slowly. "Not a single one of us. By the time they arrived, fish had begun to swim into the waters surrounding the island again. The Buddha footprint sank back into the Earth, and the cave mouths closed. They might not have believed our stories—in fact, they probably *wouldn't* have. But shouldn't we have at least tried?"

He picks up my hand, threading his fingers through mine. "I think...certain stories are dangerous. In this case, we all instinctively felt like the knowledge was better off buried on the island."

"But I destroyed the crystal orb."

I wet my lips, twice, and then ask the question that's been haunting my nights. "Are there other ones?"

Bodin shrugs. "Xander certainly thought so. And Khun Anita's latent talent, which manifested way before she was even near the island, all but proves it."

"She still possesses her ability, you know," I tell him. "A fragrant lock of her hair arrived in the mail yesterday. It told me that she and Kit were settling back home. Kit's back in the gym, getting in a thousand shots a day. Had to make up for his 'rest' days on the island."

"That makes sense," Bodin muses. "Her ability presumably manifested because of a *different* crystal. So destroying this one should have no effect on her ability."

"So, you're saying there could be *other* islands, hidden away in remote crannies of the ocean, run by other evil Xanders?" Ice frosts over my skin, and I shiver, even in the humid, tropical air.

"Maybe. Maybe not." He rubs his hands along my arms, warming them. "It's useless to speculate."

He's right. I lay my head against his chest, right over his

steady, reassuring heartbeat. We're safe now. We'll never be Xander's captives, his pawns to control, ever again.

But whatever unspoken force compelled us to conceal the truth about the island was also correct. This tale needs to stay submerged in the crystal-blue seas, under the guard of our golden-finned naga, forever. We don't want any other power-hungry scientists combing the world for another crystal.

They might just find one.

AUTHOR'S NOTE

The twelve blind princesses. Golden flowers that drift from a kind maiden's lips. A queen who may walk across fire because lotus flowers bloom under her feet. Thai folktales such as these fueled my childhood imagination, and it is my and Love's great pleasure and honor to be able to bring these images to life in *The Lotus Flower Champion*.

It is important to note, however, that while the abilities showcased in this story are inspired by elements found in Thai folktales, it was never our intention to replicate the rich and complex stories themselves. Rather, we took the liberty of taking pieces from various tales and blending them together to create Xander's fictional island. Moreover, the overall concepts of the Lotus Flower Champion, a sacred crystal that powers the magic of an entire island, an invisible wall that surrounds the island, robotic monkeys, and the windcuffs are derived from our imaginations. (However, the circumstances and details surrounding these concepts—such as the crocodiles who do not need to eat or darts that fall midair—are inspired by various tales.)

If you would like to learn more about these wonderful folktales—and we strongly encourage that you do!—the following resources have been helpful to us as we wrote *The Lotus Flower Champion*:

The Rice Birds: Folktales from Thailand, edited and translated by Christian Velder and Katrin A. Velder, White

Lotus Press, 2003.

Thai Tales: Folktales of Thailand, retold by Supaporn Vathanaprida and edited by Margaret Read MacDonald, Libraries Unlimited, 1994.

Thai Children's Favorite Stories: Fables, Myths, Legends and Fairy Tales, by Marian D. Toth, Tuttle Publishing, 2019.

Fascinating Folktales of Thailand, retold and translated by Thanapol (Lamduan) Chadchaidee, Bangkok Books, 2011.

The Fascinating World of Thai Superstitions, by Amy N., 2016.

Happy reading!

ACKNOWLEDGMENTS

The Lotus Flower Champion is very special to us. Not only is this Love's first published novel, but it is also Pintip's first time co-authoring a book—and with her daughter, no less. Creating this story together is a gift beyond our wildest dreams.

Thank you, thank you, thank you to Alexander Te Pohe for reaching out to Pintip and seeing the potential in this idea and partnership. Molly Majumder, we are so grateful for your insights, which have made the story so much stronger and richer. Stacy Abrams, you are the ultimate wordsmith magician! Thanks to you—and to Liz Pelletier—for your support and enthusiasm for this project. The rest of the team at Entangled has been nothing short of spectacular, especially Elana Cohen, Brittany Zimmerman, Heather Riccio, Curtis Svehlak, Meredith Johnson, Hannah Lindsey, and Angela Melamud. We are so thrilled to be part of the Entangled family. Special shout-out to the unbelievably talented Elizabeth Stokes who created Lotus Flower's MAGICAL cover.

We have so much gratitude for Kate Schafer Testerman, our amazing literary agent. Thank you for your deft guidance and unflagging support.

Pintip:

I've said it before, and I'll say it again. I have the best family and friends on the planet! I don't know how I got so lucky to have your unconditional support in my life. I wouldn't be who I am without your love bolstering me. You know who you are, and I am eternally grateful to each and every one of you.

Of course, it's impossible not to mention my A's. Antoine, I love you to the depth and breadth and height my soul can reach. I said these words twenty years ago, and I mean them more than ever today. To Atikan and Adisai, my tall and baby basketball bears. I may mix up your names on a daily basis, but my love for each of you is singular.

To Love, my beautiful, brave bear. You came into this world with a light that shook my heart and stole my soul. And today, that light continues to burn, bigger with every obstacle you face, brighter with every challenge you conquer. You have within you the stuff to set the world aglow. I've got my front-row seat, and I can't wait to see the flames.

And last, but never least, to my readers. My stories would not be possible without your love and enthusiasm. Thank you, from the bottom of my heart, for allowing me to live my dream.

Love:

This is the very first book I have ever published and it has been an amazing experience. Ever since the fourth grade I have dreamed of the day I would be able to publish my own novel.

To my mother, Pintip. You represent everything that I want to be as an author. I have learned so much from you through this process, and I can't wait to hopefully do it again a million more times. When I was little, I looked up to you and the amazing books you have written, and the passion that you have for what you do. You have pushed me to reach for the stars and pursue my dreams, and nothing in my life could have been possible without you. I love you forever.

To my family, you have all been so supportive in this process, and I could have never done this without you by my side.

To my friends, you have encouraged me through the toughest of times and made this book possible.

And finally, to all the readers. I never imagined I could possibly write a book someone would want to read. So, thank you for taking the time out of your life to read this book—and then read the acknowledgments, because I usually skip them. So if you're still here, I'll let you in on a secret. I adore you guys more than you'll ever know.

A cursed girl can't be broken...

THE
MOONLIGHT
BLADE

TESSA BARBOSA

I promised my mother I would never come to Bato-Ko...and yet here I am.

Narra Jal is one of the cursed, cast aside her whole life, considered unlucky. But with her mother's life on the line, she will return to the city where she was born to face the trials: a grueling, bloodthirsty series of challenges designed to weed out the weak, the greedy, and the foolish. Trials to select the next ruler of Tigang.

Narra has nothing. No weapons. No training. No magic. No real chance of leaving with her life. Just her fierce grit and a refusal to accept the destiny she's been handed. Even the intense, dark-eyed Guardian she feels a strangely electric connection with cannot help her. Narra is on her own. But she'll show everyone what the unlucky can do.

Let the bloodbath begin.

Let's be friends!

 @EntangledTeen

 @EntangledTeen

 @EntangledTeen

 @EntangledTeen

 bit.ly/TeenNewsletter

entangled teen

an imprint of Entangled Publishing LLC